CW01630731

EDRUM

BASEMENT GAMES
1st edition
(First American edition)

Original title: Kellerspiele
1st edition
(First German edition)

REDRUM BOOKS, Berlin
Publisher: Michael Merhi
Translated by Simon Kossov
Editor: Monica J. O'Rourke
Proofreading: Jasmin Kraft
Cover design and concept:
MIMO GRAPHICS by using an
illustration by Shutterstock

ISBN: 978-3-95957-553-9

email: merhi@gmx.net
www.redrum-verlag.de

YouTube: Michael Merhi Books
Facebook page: REDRUM BOOKS
Facebook group:
REDRUM BOOKS—Nichts für Pussys!

SIMONE TROJAHN
BASEMENT GAMES

Hardcore Psycho-Thriller

About the Book

Karl is shocked when Toni kidnaps a young woman to keep her imprisoned in the basement of their house. His brother is a sadist. He's always been.

Karl is torn between pity, emotional dependence on his brother, and the need to satisfy his own urges on pretty Laura, who sees in him the only hope of rescue.

Will Karl do the right thing and help the girl escape, or will his dark side prevail?

About the Author

Simone Trojahn writes terrifying, realistic, profoundly ruthless fiction. Her stories are mercilessly authentic. This exceptional author has been in the social sector for many years and knows the dark sides of life. In a unique way, she shows what happens if we become the person we never wanted to be.

Contact

t.simone80@googlemail.com
facebook.com/simonetrojahn
'Simone Trojahn Fans' at Facebook

SIMONE TROJAHN
BASEMENT GAMES

The following story is purely fictional. Similarities with living or dead persons are unintentional and coincidental.

REDRUM BOOKS points out that Simone Trojahn's sometimes very drastic and extreme writing style may be unsuitable for sensitive people.

Read her books at your own risk.

Contents

LIFE IS AN ASSHOLE

Although the door was tightly locked, you could smell her out here in the hall.

It was the stench of something dead—a blend of rotten food and excrement, both animal and human. You could have said it fucking stank of shit and dirt—at least that was the vernacular.

As always, Karl approached the closed door with a feeling of disgust and fear. As always, he stopped in front of it for a few seconds and breathed through his mouth, although that didn't make it any better. And as always, he fought against the urge to run away immediately and never come back.

Which wasn't possible, of course.

No way! What would she do without him if he just left? She'd hardly survive … and who would take care of her then? Toni? Certainly not him.

And so he stayed. Of course.

Once again he swallowed his disgust and opened the door to wish his mother a good morning.

What Karl saw in the gloomy room was as familiar as it was terrifying. He suppressed a gag, pressing his fist against his mouth, and swallowed heavily. As always! The air was so warm and thick that he felt he was fighting his way through jelly to his mother's bed. Fat flies buzzed around his head. Something small and black scurried across the floor and disappeared in the shadows. Almost all the shadows here had eyes. It was his mother's cats. Half a dozen of them lived in this room with her. They ate and shit here—sometimes on the bed because there wasn't much space.

Dusty cardboard boxes and moldy books were piled up

on worn-out old shelves. The humidity made everything disintegrate over time. The curtains, which Karl pulled aside to let in a little daylight, were shredded by the cats.

The stench was almost tangible.

Karl swallowed again to suppress the retching. A round pale circle, surrounded by a yellowish wreath of tangled hair, peered out from under a huge mountain of tattered blankets and musty pillows. The face of his mother.

Frieda. Fifty-two years old and weighing more than 450 pounds. She hadn't left her bed in four years. Not her bed, not the room, not the house. Day in and day out she lay here in the dirt, surrounded by these damn cats. She shit, ate, and lived here, just like her stinking beasts.

Could that be called life under these circumstances?

Karl bravely fought against nausea. He gave his best, but his best was worth shit.

"Good morning, Mama. Slept well?"

She blinked and could hardly open her eyes. The huge double chin was covered with dense, fuzzy gray hair and dried-up food leftovers. Flies crawled on it. Frieda weakly raised a hand to scare them away. Her ugly yellow fingernails were way too long. Something brown stuck to her fat fingers, and Karl hoped it wasn't what it looked like. Hope always died last.

"Morning," she mumbled. She couldn't speak clearly since she'd recently lost a few teeth. "Did you make something to eat?"

Food. Of course! There were only two things left for Frieda now: cats and food … and food … and food.

"No, not yet. I just got up myself."

"Feed the cats, please!"

"We need to get those cats outta here, Mama. They shit everywhere!"

Jeez, how many times had he told her that? Would this

farce never end?

"You bought a litter box, right?"

Right, there stood the litter box—buried under a pile of shit and old litter. When was the last time he'd cleaned it?

"It's no good. They don't use it."

"Sure, 'cause you never empty it."

"Fuck, am I supposed to do everything around here?" he shouted, although he hadn't intended to. How many times had he had this intention?

Frieda flinched and started to cry. Now he felt bad. And she knew it. She always knew.

"I'm sorry. I'll get the cat food."

"Thanks, sweetheart. You know how much I love you, don't you?"

"Yes," he replied evasively.

"And then you make me something to eat, okay? Sausages would be nice."

Sausages. Sure! What else?

A new day in eternal hell had begun. Hallelujah!

***

Karl left to do his day's work. He took great care to securely lock her door. Not that the rest of the house looked any better.

At least there were no cats here, only a weak old St. Bernard named Lupo who only pooped outside.

But still, there was enough useless stuff that was slowly rotting away. Lots of old magazines, moldy brochures, and all sorts of crap that actually should be taken to the dump. Almost every day Karl planned to tidy up the house. But something always came up, so the chaos grew bigger each day. In some places the garbage was piled up

to the ceiling, and you had to make your way through a labyrinth, which was how Karl got from the hallway to the kitchen. Lots of flies swarmed here as well.

The window clattered. It usually remained open to better endure the stench. Everywhere stood dirty dishes on which vermin cavorted and some plates were covered in a thick layer of filth. Mold slowly but steadily crawled up the walls, and the mild September air couldn't blow away its peculiar stench.

Karl looked for a clean pan. He found none, so he grabbed a dirty one from the grimy stove. He turned on a burner and poured oil from a greasy bottle into the pan. That would somehow mix with the rest and … oh, who even cared? His mother wasn't sensitive. She had a stomach like a pig. That was necessary—for her and all of them.

He found a pack of sausages in the fridge. Only recently expired, so that was okay. The other groceries were in less good condition. Mold also thrived here.

Maybe he should finally tidy up everything.

Later.

Karl threw the sausages into the pan. Soon they sizzled and smelled really good. He even found a clean plate in one of the cupboards. He put the sausages on it and returned to his mother's room, carrying the plate, a carton of milk, and two cans of cat food.

***

Around eleven in the morning, Karl sat in the kitchen drinking orange juice—a little luxury he allowed himself. In the meantime he'd fed the cats, cleaned the litter box, and washed his mother. Afterward, he'd put a bowl under her ass and waited for her to do her business. Then he

wanted to wash her down there. That was hard work, which was why Karl avoided it most of the time. His mother didn't seem to care. At least she'd never complained before. Yet Karl was aware that he should have done more for her personal hygiene. He knew he'd have to wash her, change her clothes, and diaper her at least once a day because the bowl he brought her three times a day wasn't enough to hold everything she excreted. A lot of her urine seeped into the mattress. The worst thing was when she had diarrhea, which happened quite often.

All the care his mother needed was too much for Karl. On the one hand, even after all these years, he was still so disgusted by it that it haunted him in his dreams, and on the other hand, he kept forgetting something that might have been important. Theory was nothing compared to practice. Of course, he knew that there were institutions to turn to in such cases, but his brother would never have allowed him to hire a caregiver. His brother didn't tolerate strangers in the house. Karl doubted that the three of them would still live in this pigsty if a representative of senior care services had stopped by in past years. Frieda would certainly be in a nursing home, Karl in his own home, and Toni … God knows where.

Karl wasn't sure if that would have been such a bad solution. Toni said they could never send their mother to such a home, without her cats. That would be the worst thing for her. Her certain death sentence. But Karl often thought about whether she wouldn't fare better there—even without her cats. At least it would have been better for him. Maybe he would have found a job then. Or a girlfriend. Or—fanfare, please—even both.

Toni didn't care. He wasn't the one alone in the house with her all day or had to take care of everything. He wasn't the one who had to live on unemployment bene-

fits at the age of twenty-nine without a job or an education or any perspectives. And he wasn't the one who had to take care of his stinking, obese mother all by himself.

Karl was considered difficult to place. They'd already reduced his benefits three times because he'd been late or hadn't shown up at all for job interviews that had been arranged by the job center. Each time, his mother had been the reason—his mother and those goddamn cats! But nobody knew about that. Nobody had any idea how bad things were for Frieda Singer, who had been in early retirement for ten years and whose modest income made it possible for Karl to make ends meet when the employment office cut the money again. Not that he needed the money for himself in the first place. Most of it was used for Frieda's food. For all the sausages and fries and puddings and gallons of milk and cola.

His brother wasn't interested. He was literally a tyrant. Karl always danced to Toni's tune because he simply didn't know how to say no. Toni was stronger as a child, which wasn't solely due to the three-year difference in age. His superiority wasn't only physical but emotional. He was rude and mean and preferred to use his fists rather than words. Karl was helpless against it. Toni's opinion was the law. It had always been that way, and it would probably remain that way.

Toni worked during the day, while Karl took care of their mother. Toni didn't contribute a cent to the household budget and went to bars in the evening, while Karl … well, you know …

Toni had friends, he went to parties, and even went on vacation from time to time. Shit, last year he'd been to Mallorca, while Karl … exactly, you know …

And if Karl dared to contradict the great Toni, it usually ended painfully. His crooked nose (broken several

times during his childhood) and two knocked out incisors (he could not afford dental treatment) were mute witnesses of this unique brotherly love. Did Karl ever strike back? Yes, he'd actually dared … once. That was five years ago now. It had almost cost him his life.

But now wasn't the time to reminisce. Karl looked at the clock. Almost 11:30. Time for mother's bowl. And her cola. His stomach rebelled when he thought about it.

But he had no choice. It was his damn job.

***

That same evening, Karl stood in the kitchen again, waiting for a portion of ravioli to warm up in the microwave when Toni came home.

His brother entered the kitchen wordlessly and gave Lupo, who had approached him wagging his tail, a rough kick. Howling and with his tail pulled in, the animal retreated.

Karl didn't say anything.

Toni sat and put his feet on the kitchen table, which Karl had just cleared of the worst garbage. "I guess I'm just in time." He grinned.

Karl looked at him. He'd spent his last money to buy the ravioli this afternoon.

"I'm hungry like a wolf," Toni said.

Karl took a dirty plate from the sink and washed it off. Anger boiled in him. If only he'd made himself something to eat earlier! But Toni always came home at different times or not at all. Shit!

He dried the plate, took a fork out of the drawer, and put it on the table.

"And a nice cold beer."

Karl took a bottle out of the fridge.

Toni had bought the beer, and Karl would never have dared to help himself without asking. He placed the bottle in front of his brother.

"Open it! Please."

A volcano erupted inside Karl. Lava flooded his heart. On the outside he remained calm; only his jaw muscles worked frantically. He opened the bottle using a lighter, one of the few things he'd learned from his big brother.

Toni looked at him. For a second Karl returned his gaze. An outsider would hardly have thought the two men were brothers. Toni was tall and muscular, bald, and with hard features. Karl was quite a bit smaller, stocky, with blond, medium-length hair, and a soft, rounded face. The only thing they had in common was their radiant bright blue eyes. Heirlooms of a father they'd never really gotten to know.

"What's up?"

Karl lowered his gaze. At that moment the microwave beeped. He turned around jerkily, took out the steaming ravioli, and dropped them onto Toni's plate. The smell of the food caused his growling stomach to somersault, even if it was only cheap instant food. Better than nothing. But he'd go to bed hungry tonight because everything else he'd bought was for his mother, who could easily become nasty if she was hungry.

The ravioli smelled delicious. Maybe Toni would share it with him.?

"I asked you a question!" Toni took his feet down and was about to stand up.

"No," Karl said meekly. "Nothing. Enjoy your meal." He wanted to turn away, but Toni once again put a spoke in his wheel.

"You're hungry, right?"

You know it's my food, you fucking asshole! But you took it.

The way you always get everything from me, so what else do you want?

"No. It's okay."

"Have you actually looked around here? In this pigsty! I'd like to know what you do all day while other people work."

"I have to take care of Mama …"

"She just lies in her fucking bed and needs nothing more than a few caresses from time to time. That isn't hard work. But what about the kitchen and the bathroom? It's your job to keep this place clean, but it looks like you're sitting on your fat ass all day, picking your nose and eating."

He shoveled the steaming dumplings into his mouth. The delicious tomato sauce splashed from his lips as he yelled, "You start cleaning right now! I'll sit here and make sure you do it properly. Don't make a mistake, Karl, otherwise I swear I'll rip your ass open!"

Toni wiped leftovers from his mouth. "I hope you got the message! I've got nothing planned for today and can keep an eye on you all evening." He went on eating.

Hot tears burned Karl's eyes. He turned around in silence and started to clean while Toni enjoyed his dinner with loud smacking noises.

***

Karl worked for the next two hours, while Toni ate all the ravioli and drank one beer after another. He sat on the rickety kitchen chair like a king and had Karl bring him bottle after bottle. When night fell, Toni was considerably drunk and seemed to like his role as the domineering tyrant more and more.

The kitchen looked okay again. Karl had washed and

tidied the dishes, wiped out cupboards, scrubbed the stove, oven, and microwave. All he wanted now was to go to bed, away from Toni and his piercing gaze.

His brother burped loudly. "Very nice. That looks a lot better. Get me another beer!"

Karl did as he was told. It was the second to last beer in the fridge.

"You want one too?"

Of course he would have liked one! What a fucking question!

"Maybe I'm not as mean as you always think. Maybe you just have to ask me for it."

"All right, then. May I have a beer, please?"

"No! But nice of you to ask." Toni laughed spitefully, as he always did.

"Okay, that's enough for today. Your kitchen is clean. I'm going to bed."

"No, stay! Sit down and take your damn beer if it makes you happy."

Karl didn't think about it any further. It was always better to do what Toni said. Especially when he was drunk and tired. In this state, his mood could change quickly.

So Karl took a beer and sat at the kitchen table opposite his brother. Toni lit a self-rolled cigarette and pushed the pack of tobacco and the cigarette paper across the table.

"Help yourself."

"Thanks." Karl rolled a cigarette.

"I fucked up," Toni suddenly said.

"What happened?"

"At work. They'll fire me."

"Why?"

"I don't know, no big deal, actually. I just took some-

thing with me and got caught. Got snitched, to be more precise. By that asshole Maier."

Karl continued rolling his cigarette. His thoughts somersaulted. *God, if he loses his job, he's gonna be here all the time. Always! Every damn day. How will I stand that?*

"What did you steal?"

"I was supposed to deliver a package with a new PlayStation. I looked inside and there were two in it. So I thought, *Who needs two PlayStations? That must have been a mistake.* That's why I took one. And Maier saw it. The motherfucker laughed and said, 'Good idea. Nobody'll notice it. Maybe it was a wrong delivery.'"

He shrugged and took a good sip of his beer. "That's what he said, and then he went straight to our boss. I apologized and promised to give it back. I hadn't even unpacked it. But today I got a written warning …" He suddenly fell silent.

"Shit!"

"Yeah, shit! I know. Thanks."

"With a reason for termination like that, you won't get money from the unemployment office."

"Oh, great, Mr. Social Parasite knows all about that, of course."

Karl lit his cigarette. "Maybe we should get help for Mama after all. Then everything will be easier and I can finally go to work."

Toni hit the table with his fist. "You know damn well we can't do that. She's our mother! We can't just dump her."

"But we can't really take care of her either. She's got bedsores again … and I can't turn her properly alone … she—"

"Don't give me that shit, Karl! It's your job to take care of her. That's why you're here with her in the house, and

I expect you to do your job! Just try harder!"

"I do what I can!"

"You don't do shit! Anyone can see that! After all, we get the fucking money for caring for her at home. So don't act like the last fucker in God's wide world!"

It's you who takes the money, dear brother, not us, Karl thought, but he was smart enough to keep his thoughts to himself.

"She's in bad shape, and there's nothing we can do about it. It's too late."

Toni nodded. "It's not gonna get much better, yeah, okay, I get that. Nevertheless, she's happy here. This is her home. We're her family."

You should hear yourself talk, Toni. Family? Good joke! How long since you were with her? Days, weeks, months? he thought but remained silent.

Toni looked at him and shrugged. "If I really lose my job, we're gonna have to economize a little bit. You understand?"

You'll have to economize, dear brother, 'cause I've been doing it for years.

Karl kept that to himself too. He nodded silently and left the kitchen to look after his mother one last time for today.

***

The stench was miserable. Worse than usual, although that was hardly possible. Karl held his breath. He hesitantly entered the room.

"Mama?"

No answer. That wasn't really unusual. After all, it was already late, and she slept deeply.

Only this silence was strange. There was no sound.

Frieda snored when she was asleep. She sounded like a goddamn sawmill!

Karl was running out of breath. He opened his mouth, and the air tasted like black, rotten syrup.

"Mama?" He stared at her bed but could only see outlines in the darkness. The silhouette of his mother couldn't be overlooked.

Without turning his gaze away, he groped blindly for the light switch. It seemed to take him half an eternity to find it.

"Mama, is everything …?" The last word got stuck in his throat. His heart missed a beat or two before it frantically continued pounding. Karl felt it in his ears, in his throat and temples. Everywhere but in his chest. In the dirty yellow light he now recognized more than just outlines. More than he liked to see.

He stumbled backward. His back bumped against the wall next to the open door. He pressed his clenched fists in front of his dust-dry mouth. These eyes, which could only stare in disbelief, were the eyes of a child.

Mama! Oh my God, Mama!

Images appeared before his inner eye. He saw himself, maybe ten years old, with a chubby, always joking Frieda in her early thirties. Not much older than he was now. He sat at the kitchen table. A slim boy, too small for his age, with flaxen hair and bruised knees. He cried. Frieda squatted in front of him (at that time she could still kneel and could do everything else that wasn't possible for her later) and cleaned his wounds with a cool cloth. She spoke to him in a comforting voice. His Mama! She'd always been there for him. Why did he think of this long-gone sunny afternoon, when the world was still fine except for a pair of bruised knees? He hadn't thought of that day or of any other day of his childhood for years.

But now he thought of it because it was a memory. A memory not only of the child he'd once been but of the woman who was his mother and now lay here—no longer alive—in this terrible room. Alone! Alone except for her cats, all of which had hidden because they too could smell death. A stench that covered the room like a stinking black cloth. A shroud. Good God, she was really dead!

Karl's hands dangled limply. He had no strength left and couldn't move. Only his eyes still worked quite well. His eyes saw everything.

She lay in her bed, as always, like the last years. Her head rested on the pillow, tilted to the side, her gray hair spread out like a fan. The face had taken on an ugly bluish hue. The mouth was wide open, as were the eyes. Naked fear and pure horror lay in her gaze. The thick dirty fingers with the much-too-long nails (Karl should've cut them long ago) lay clenched like claws on her chest, very close to her neck, as if she'd strangled herself.

Of course, that hadn't happened. Karl knew better. His mother had suffocated—probably on her own tongue, perhaps during a cramping seizure—in this rotten room that had long since been a grave. Triggered by what? Dehydration? Infarction? Stroke? Had he given her enough to drink? Was it his fault?

She'd obviously tried to reach for her throat or mouth, but she hadn't succeeded. No one had helped her. Her sons, her beloved children, had been too busy arguing in the kitchen while she lost her last desperate fight here alone. Alone! Had she ever abandoned her sons when they were little and helpless? No, she hadn't. As long as she could, she'd always done everything to make her children happy and give them the best possible life, always putting her own needs aside.

She'd moved into this house with them and wanted to make it her inheritance ... but what had they made of the house? What had they made of their lives? What the hell had they done with their own mother?

"Oh God," Karl whispered in a hoarse voice. "Mama, oh my God!"

He ran to her and didn't notice the stench anymore. He fell on his knees in front of her bed and wrapped his arms around her voluminous upper body. She felt soft, just like before. She'd shit herself and the bed from top to bottom in her throes of death, but Karl didn't smell it. There was dried puke on her breast, but even when he clung to Frieda's dead body, crying, he didn't notice it either.

He remained in this position until someone suddenly grabbed him by the shoulders and brutally tore him back. It was like waking up from a nightmare, which immediately merged into the next. Karl landed on all fours. Before he could get up, Toni tore him violently to his feet and yelled at him. Karl didn't understand. The words echoed in his head without making any sense.

Toni slapped him in the face. Suddenly, Karl understood what his brother was screaming.

"What happened? What did you do to her? Is she dead? She's dead, damn it!"

Karl nodded. "Yeah, she's dead. It's my fault, Toni. It's my fault!" Finally the tears came. They felt like a revelation.

Toni ran both hands over his face and bald skull. He shook his head. Again and again. But he didn't look at her and didn't touch her. As far as Karl knew, he hadn't done that for years.

"What are we gonna do now?" Toni walked up and down the room like a madman.

Two gray tigers appeared under the closet. Their eyes were curious yet shy. They weren't used to people, at least not Toni.

Karl stared at the cats and then again at his brother, who frantically walked around in circles, rubbing his face and bald head. His skin had reddened.

Karl looked at his dead mother again. He pushed away the pictures from childhood days long gone that wanted to come to his mind again.

Not now! Maybe later, but not now!

"We ... we have to call 911 or something ..." he suggested timidly.

Toni stopped walking around and looked at him in disbelief. "Are you crazy? You don't really want any strangers here, do you? They could blame us. And maybe we're guilty! Look at this room! Look at this damn house! They won't let us live here, Karl. And what then? Mama wouldn't have wanted that. She wanted us to stay in the house forever. You know that."

"But she's dead now ... dead ... and she needs to be buried. She—"

"Do you know the cost of a funeral? I'm about to lose my job. You don't even have one. How are we supposed to pay that, Karl?"

"I ... I don't know. But we have to do something, right?"

Toni suddenly had a strange expression on his face that Karl didn't like at all.

He grabbed Karl's shoulders and looked him straight in the eye. "We mustn't rush things now, Karli! Do you understand?"

He hadn't called him Karli in years. "We're not gonna do anything. This room is fucked anyway. We can leave her here for a while, at least until tomorrow or so. Then

we talk again in peace. When I'm sober. I need to be sober for this. Tomorrow I'll try to get things straight at work and when I get home we'll sit down and discuss everything. What do you think of that, brother?"

"What do you want to discuss? I mean, she has to be taken somewhere, right? We can't just keep her here."

"It's only temporary. We need a plan, that's all."

"I don't know. Somehow I don't like that."

Without warning, Toni grabbed him by the ears. Karl flinched in pain. He tried to pull Toni's hands away but couldn't and finally gave up.

"This isn't really about your opinion, little brother! I just want you to do what I tell you to do, or it could be very unpleasant for you. Do you understand?" He grabbed Karl's ears even harder.

Karl screamed and sank to his knees. Toni squatted with him. He didn't let go.

"You do what I tell you. Is that clear?"

"Let go, please!" The pain drove tears to his eyes.

"Is it clear?"

"Okay, okay, I got it!"

"What exactly do you understand, little brother? I wanna hear it!"

"I do what you say. We won't call anybody."

Toni let go. Karl pressed both hands on his ears and lowered his head. He sobbed like a little child.

"You'll be alone here all day tomorrow. But you won't enter this room and you'll keep your fingers off the phone. And you won't leave the house. When I get home, we'll talk about everything. Got me?"

Karl nodded.

"Now get up and get your ass out of here! That's it for today!"

Toni didn't wait for his brother to react. Instead, he

grabbed Karl's upper arm, pulled him rudely to his feet, and dragged him out of the room. After switching off the light, he locked the door and made the key disappear into his pocket.

Karl watched in silence. What could he do?

***

When Karl woke the next morning, the first thing he thought about was preparing his mother's breakfast. Then the awareness hit him like an avalanche. He wouldn't have to go to his mother this morning. She didn't wait for her breakfast. Or for him. Her time for waiting was over.

Karl sat up. Tears shot into his eyes and he let them come, gave in to them completely. Like a little child, he held his hands in front of his face and cried while he rocked his upper body back and forth to the rhythm of his sobs.

Now he had no mama anymore. He was all alone in this desolate world. Alone with a crazy brother!

Karl thought about his childhood. Now he wanted nothing but that, to be a child again and not have to worry about anything. Because children had parents who took care of everything. At least that was the normal case. Of course, at some point they grew up and had to manage their own lives, but unfortunately, nobody had told him that this would happen so damn fast. At age twenty-nine, you're an adult, and if you weren't, you'd never be. Just like Karl, who felt like a little boy whose favorite toy had been taken away by some mean giant. And that's all he wanted to be. He needed someone to tell him what to do. He couldn't do it alone.

Dear God, he just didn't want to be alone!

***

With his arms crossed in front of his chest, Toni sat on an uncomfortable wooden chair in his boss's office. He didn't wear a work uniform, as he'd been ordered here before start of work. He slowly came to the conclusion that he wouldn't have to wear it today anyway. Not today and not tomorrow …

It was hot. Damn hot even. He had sweat on his forehead, and something wet slowly ran down his head and neck. The feeling was anything but pleasant, just like the situation. He moved nervously on his chair. He was nauseated. He wanted something to drink. What would he have given for a nice cool beer now? His soul at least, haha …

His boss, this goddamn asshole Mr. Schröder, had just put a white envelope on the table.

"Here you go," was all he said.

Toni stared at him as if his boss was the creature from the swamp. Schröder was a small slender man with ugly metal-rimmed glasses and a bald forehead that shined with sweat. He wore a short-sleeved white shirt and brown corduroy pants the color of shit. Wearing corduroy in this heat, my goodness!

For a moment, Toni saw himself jump up and reach over the table to grab Schröder with both hands. He saw himself driving the glasses into Schröder's watery eyes with just one punch. He even heard that pathetic motherfucker scream. In his head, this screaming sounded like the hysterical wailing of a little girl. Music to his ears.

But Toni did nothing like that. Toni had himself under control. Still!

"What's that?" he asked, and his voice sounded calm,

trembling only slightly.

"Your dismissal, Mr. Singer. There's no way I can keep you employed under these circumstances. You're lucky that we're not filing charges."

"Oh, how nice of you, really!" Toni's self-control slowly began to waver.

"I told you I wanted to give it back! I … it won't happen again. I've been working here for three years. You can't dismiss me because of this trifle!"

"Of course I can, Mr. Singer. I just did. Theft is completely unacceptable; you know that. Once is already too much. In the next few days you'll receive two weeks' salary, and that's all I can do for you." Schröder rose and pointed at the white envelope. "Take your dismissal and leave."

Toni snorted contemptibly. "That's all?" He snatched the envelope.

Schröder instinctively took a step back. Toni was almost two feet taller, and his anger oozed out of all his pores. He resembled a predator that had been cornered once too often.

"You're a fucking scumbag! You know I gotta take care of my sick mother, but you don't give a shit about that, right?"

"I'm very sorry about your mother," Schröder stammered. He knew nothing about Frieda Singer. "But you gotta blame yourself for the dismissal. I wish you all the best …"

"What's in it?" Toni hissed.

Schröder shrugged. He was probably wondering if there was anyone else besides them in the building who could hear him if he screamed for help.

"Mr. Singer, I'd like to ask you once again to leave now …"

Toni ripped open the envelope.

Schröder swallowed heavily. While Toni concentrated for a moment on his letter of dismissal, Schröder fumbled for his cell phone in his pants pocket. But before he could pull it out, Toni slammed the sheet of paper onto the cheap desk with full force. Schröder flinched. His authority was shaken.

"It says I was stealing! Are you out of your mind? How am I supposed to get a new job with this?"

"That's the normal procedure, Mr. Singer. I don't have any other choice. I have to mention the real reason."

"That's a joke, right? You're ruining me with this shit! You know that?"

"I must remind you again that you have to blame yourself for this, Mr. Singer. Theft is theft. However, you can still find a new job. A new employer doesn't need to know about this reason for dismissal. Only the employment office is interested, of course. You'll most likely be blocked for three months, so you'll have to make sure to find a new job as soon as possible."

"Yeah, just like that?" Toni's head was spinning. He saw himself jumping over the desk and grabbing this damn pussy by the throat. He'd kill that motherfucker if he had to, he'd—

"Mr. Singer, I'm very sorry, but that's all I can do for you. Find yourself a new job, and keep your hands off other people's stuff in the future."

Yeah, he'd kill him, no doubt!

Toni leaped over the table.

Schröder retreated to the wall. He held both hands protectively in front of his face. "You don't want to do this! Toni, please, think before you make another mistake!"

So, it's Toni *now, suddenly?*

"That'll only make it worse for you!"

"Shut up, you son of a bitch!" Toni yelled in his face. His saliva dotted Schröder's freshly polished glasses. They now stood so close that Toni could smell Schröder's fear. A great scent!

But he didn't touch his former boss. At least not yet.

"You're scared of me, right? You should be, you motherfucker! Maybe I'll come and kill you someday! It can happen any day now, so be careful!"

Toni turned away and was proud of his self-control. He left the dismissal on the desk. At the door, he turned around once more and pointed his finger at the trembling little man. "Be careful. Maybe I'll come by sometime to smash your skull!"

***

After getting up to get a drink, Karl looked out the window and saw Toni's dark green car turn in to the driveway. He looked at the clock: 10:20 a.m. Not a good sign.

He watched Toni get out of the car, slam the driver's door, and kick it several times. Every kick was accompanied by a loud "Fuck!" that was audible even through the closed window.

"Fuck!" Karl said. He wore nothing more than the same dirty boxers from two days ago. He hectically grabbed the T-shirt hanging over his desk chair and put it on. His jeans lay on the dirty linoleum floor. He slipped them on and rushed barefoot out of the room.

***

She stood in the bathroom and stared in the mirror.

There were tears in her blue-green eyes. Again she

raised her right hand and tried to apply mascara. Crying again, winking once, twice, three times … ugly black spots had formed under her eyes, which were already darkly edged. Everything smeared. Again. Shit!

"Fuck!"

Laura threw the mascara into the washbasin in front of which she had been standing for fifteen minutes in an attempt to make herself look more or less human. Black spots and stripes. Now everywhere. On her face. In the sink. In the mirror.

She stared into her eyes that were sore from crying. Ugly! Her face was an unhealthy pale. Eyelids were thickly swollen. Her nose was red and full of snot.

"Yuck!" Laura yelled at her own reflection and cried even more. There she stood, in her underwear, a sixteen-year-old girl, far too pale, far too lean, having to endure the shame of her young life.

She'd failed.

She'd have to repeat a grade.

Shit!

Not good enough for this stupid school.

Not good enough for this fucking world!

And today was the first day after the summer break. The first day of classes, only now she'd be the oldest, the one who had to repeat ninth grade. The one who hadn't been able to finish. Too stupid for English, math, and physics. Too stupid for this world!

And here she stood, skinny and trembling, a miserable picture of misery on the worst morning of her life, the worst day of her life. For the last six weeks she had thought of nothing but how terrible this day would be.

She'd cursed it. She'd longed for the end of the world. A plague or a flood, a goddamn mega-earthquake or a meteorite from space, terrorist attacks … anything, just

anything. Just not this one first crappy day, knowing she didn't make it and that she's a loser.

That shame was worse than anything. There was nothing her parents or anyone else in the world could have said to make it better. No one could understand what she'd been going through since that damn day when she got her report card. No one could understand her self-hate. She could not forgive herself for this failure. She would never be able to do that.

All the learning and practicing, the many private lessons, nothing had worked, zero, nada, niente …

Laura rubbed her tear-filled eyes until they hurt.

Never mind.

She wanted it to hurt.

Pain!

How could she even take one step into this school, let alone into this classroom, without dying?

No one would say anything, at least not in such a way that she could hear it, but the gazes would suffice. The secret glances and whispering. In the schoolyard and girls' room. In the classroom, during breaks, and during lessons. The teachers wouldn't notice. They never did.

How was she supposed to survive that? How could she go there without losing her mind?

Laura stared at the smeared makeup in her reflection. She looked like a mentally ill clown. Her face was a disaster, and her hair wasn't any better.

Definitely not pretty.

Furiously, Laura grabbed the brush and began to work her hair like a possessed woman.

Until it hurt.

It didn't feel that bad.

She looked defiantly at her reflection again, as if she wanted to provoke herself.

It worked.

She grew even angrier.

She grabbed a washcloth and scrubbed her face.

Rubbed until her skin bled.

Laura didn't care. She wanted to feel this pain. It seemed to be the only thing left to her after she'd lost her dignity and prestige.

"Laura?" She heard her mother's voice through the locked bathroom door.

There was a knock.

"Laura? Dear? You okay?"

Laura would have loved to laugh out loud. What a fucking stupid question! It could only come from her mother. Her dear, good-natured mother, who had never beaten her and who had only really yelled at her twice in her life.

What did she know how Laura was feeling? She had no idea.

Laura didn't believe her mother's lifelong dreams had ever gone beyond marrying and starting a family. And she'd married the first available man.

Laura loved her father and knew he was a good-hearted person, but she wouldn't have married this wimp for all the money in the world. He was the headmaster of a primary school, and even the first graders had him in their hands.

"I'm fine, Mama," she replied.

"You're late, sweetie."

Laura gritted her teeth. Her hands clung to the edge of the washbasin. "Just a minute!"

"Hurry up, please!"

"I do!"

"Okay. Papa's waiting for you in the kitchen. You have to leave in ten minutes."

Laura bit her tongue until it hurt. "All right!"

Since she didn't depend on the bus or other public transport, she could sleep longer than most of her classmates and had less stress in the morning. Today, however, she would have liked to do without this "convenience." If there was one thing she definitely couldn't stand today, it was her father's good-natured chitchat.

Damn!

But she had no choice. She had to hurry. If she was late on the first day, it would be even more embarrassing than it already was.

So she took a deep breath, styled her hair into a ponytail, washed her maltreated face, put on some lotion, and covered the red spots with powder. That worked reasonably well. She applied a little mascara. Voilà, that had to do for today.

Without risking another look in the mirror, she put on her jeans. Now the worst day of her life could begin.

***

They lay next to each other in bed, naked and sweaty.

Tanja turned on her side, her big soft breasts pressing against Toni's arm. She stroked his hairless chest. Her hand glided deeper, over his flat, muscular belly, pausing briefly over his navel and seconds later grabbing his flaccid penis.

His cock was still wet and sticky from her pussy juice. A moronic smile played around Tanja's lips as she worked on the limp penis, pulling and pinching it, circling and squeezing, massaging and pressing. When nothing happened, she took his testicles, which were thick and bulging, the way she liked it. She kneaded and squeezed, massaged, stroked.

Slowly, her efforts showed success.

"There you go," Tanja whispered.

She was startled when Toni suddenly shot up like an arrow and grabbed her wrists. Tanja could only make a frightened noise. She was already lying under him, small and helpless.

Toni pressed her into the mattress with all his weight.

"What …?" was the only thing she could say before his fist landed in her face.

A burning pain exploded in Tanja's head. She gasped and tried to free herself. Her nose was flattened; she couldn't breathe properly anymore. She struggled, wanting to push him away, but she had no chance. He effortlessly held her wrists with just one hand while spreading her legs with the other. His grip was absolutely firm.

Tanja wanted to scream or say something, but something warm ran into her mouth. Blood. Her blood! He'd smashed her nose and now she tasted her own blood while her boyfriend held her tight and forcibly penetrated her.

But Toni wasn't actually her boyfriend.

She'd only wished for that.

His penis was now rock hard again.

Tanja cramped.

Toni thrust with all his strength.

It hurt.

Tanja screamed, swallowed blood, coughed, screamed again.

Toni grinned as he brutally thrust into her.

"Stop it!" she yelled.

"Shut up, slut! I'll show you what a real good fuck is!"

"Get off of me, you bastard!"

Tanja had known Toni for about two weeks. She knew he wasn't squeamish in bed and didn't treat women with

kid gloves, and it was okay for her. Tanja thought most men were like that. He'd hurt her before, but always just a little. Always in a way that increased her lust, and she liked it.

Nothing could have prepared her for what was now happening. This had nothing to do with lust. Or love. This wasn't normal sex. This was rape! Not the first to happen to her since she'd been snared in the world of drugs, but more humiliating than ever.

She managed to free one hand from his grip and scratched him with her long fingernails.

Toni let her go and slapped her in the face.

Tanja screamed and fought back.

Toni struck again. And again.

And again.

He struck until there was no more resistance and she sobbed quietly.

There was blood now. Quite a lot.

Tanja couldn't see anything because her eyes were swollen.

She whimpered.

Toni kept thrusting into her.

"Please, Toni, please ..." Tanja moaned.

That just seemed to turn him on even more.

Toni pulled out his cock, grabbed the helpless woman by the shoulders, and turned her on her stomach. Now he had her big, soft white ass in front of him.

He licked his lips and grinned.

Tanja whimpered something into the pillow, but he couldn't understand her.

He hit her on the back of the head and then on the butt, leaving a red handprint behind. His hard cock pulsated.

"Lift your ass!"

Tanja didn't react.

Toni grabbed her by the neck and squeezed.

"I said lift your ass!"

Groaning, she leaned on her elbows and lifted her pelvis.

Saliva dripped out of his mouth. Shit, he'd never been so horny! He reached for Tanja's pretty ass and shoved a hand between her cheeks.

When she tried to press them together, he hit her on the back of the head again. Hard!

"Pull your ass cheeks apart!"

"No, please ..."

He hit her.

"Pull them apart! Now!"

Tanja lowered her head into the pillow and slowly fumbled backward with both hands. She grasped her ass and pulled the cheeks apart.

"Now stay like this!" Toni commanded.

He spat into the palms of his hands and thoroughly lubricated his penis. He repeated this process three times.

The sight of her little pink asshole drove him crazy. She had once mentioned that she didn't like being fucked in the ass very much.

Well, he didn't give a shit.

Toni shoved one finger into her anus, then two more.

Tanja whimpered into the pillow.

Toni pulled his fingers out. He moaned, grabbed his cock, and pushed it into the much-too-tight hole.

Now Tanja screamed, but she still held her ass cheeks apart.

Toni pushed as hard as he could. The tight feeling was unbelievably awesome!

He closed his eyes and moaned loudly as he thrust into her again and again, kneading her big butt with his hands.

Just before he came, he withdrew from her and squirted on the back of her head.

The climax was like fireworks.

It took Toni a few minutes to recover from the orgasm and to catch his breath again.

He sat on Tanja's back, and she sobbed quietly under him.

Slowly he climbed off her and lay next to her. Tanja didn't turn around.

"You go fetch a rag and clean me," Toni said. "After that, you can clean the bed."

Tanja slowly turned to him. Her face was smeared with blood and snot. "I'm in pain."

"I hope so."

***

She'd gone to the bathroom. Good girl.

Toni had forbidden her to clean herself or use the toilet because otherwise he would teach her another lesson. The feeling of having her in his hand like that was overwhelming. It drove him crazy and made his cock hard again.

Obediently, she returned a short time later with a wet washcloth and a small towel.

"And do it thoroughly, or you'll do it with your mouth. After all, it's your shit."

Tanja didn't say anything. Her face looked terrible. Later, he would allow her to take a painkiller. She probably would have had to see a doctor, but that was out of the question for little junkie brides anyway.

Toni sat up and swung his legs over the edge of the bed. The penetrating aroma of sweat, sex, and feces hung in the air. Stale, not at all erotic.

Tanja squatted before him. She moved very slowly and carefully. As she lowered her head, Toni saw the sperm in her hair. He'd squirted juice like he hadn't in a long time. There was nothing like a good fuck. It tickled pleasantly in his cock when the warm damp washcloth touched him. Tanja made a remarkable effort to please him.

Her luck!

When she was done, she looked up at him with a questioning gaze. Her face looked really bad. She was supposed to ice the bruises as soon as possible. He probably should have pitied her, but it actually turned him on to know she was so helpless.

"Good," he said, patting her swollen cheek. "You can go to the bathroom now and take care of yourself."

She nodded and rose ponderously.

Toni held her by the arm. Her big tits swung tantalizingly back and forth. "You forgot something!"

She looked at him questioningly.

"You haven't thanked me yet."

She stared at him.

"I could've put my dick in your mouth to get it clean. Would you have preferred that, sweetheart?"

A soft, indefinable sound came out of her throat. She swallowed. "Thank you."

Toni smiled. "You're welcome. Now get the fuck outta here!"

She turned around, and he slapped her hard on the ass. That must have hurt, but Tanja didn't show any reaction and disappeared into the bathroom.

Toni got out of the dirty bed (not that it would've been much cleaner anywhere else in Tanja's little hovel) and sat on the couch. He was still naked. With a satisfied sigh he grabbed the remote and zapped through the channels.

He'd never gone as far as today before. At least not

where the beating was concerned. He'd already raped many a slut, also from behind, and of course he'd humiliated them as well. He beat the women when he felt like it, but never before had one looked as bad as Tanja. He might perhaps have broken her cheekbone or nose—or both. The feeling of dominance was absolutely crazy.

Toni grabbed his cock and wanked while he remembered the events of the last half hour.

He'd gone further than ever before, and he knew he wanted to go even further—hurt them, make them submissive, humiliate them, become their one and all, their Lord and God—that's what he wanted. But he knew he was walking on thin ice. After all, he didn't want to end up in jail or get infected with some stupid disease. Like HIV, for example. The risk was high, as he'd so far sought his victims in relevant milieus: junkies, prostitutes, alcoholics, homeless women. They'd only tell the cops or go to the hospital in an absolute emergency, but he still had to deal with the risk of infection. On the other hand, these bitches were willing. They did anything for a shot or a warm bed. Most of the time he gave them some money when he said goodbye. After all, he wasn't a monster. And as for Tanja, she would somehow recover—even without medical treatment. She didn't have health insurance, and on top of that, she had a few skeletons in her closet.

Toni knew Tanja didn't like questions. He knew her past—robberies, theft and her brats were in a foster home because of maltreatment. No, Tanja was anything but a saint. She would neither run to the hospital nor the cops. That solved the first problem. The second, however …

Toni's fear of some nasty STD flared up again. In the heat of the moment, he hadn't thought of a condom.

Fucking was no fun at all while wearing a rubber. His dick had once again taken over the thinking for him, and cocks knew no gonorrhea. However, it wasn't unlikely to catch a little disgusting souvenir from the lousy, asocial women he picked up. That had been Toni's greatest concern for years, so he regularly had AIDS tests done and went to the urologist. He'd twice gotten genital warts and countless fungal infections. He ate antibiotics like others took aspirins. Nevertheless, he was always so stupid (cock-controlled) that he forgot the condom. The only solution was a normal, dear, decent, and clean girl, but with such a girl he couldn't possibly do all that without ending up in jail. He'd have had to kill her then, which was too risky on the one hand and not what he actually wanted on the other. It wasn't about killing, it was about torturing them. He wanted to control and dominate these little bitches. He wanted to own them because it was his right, and he wanted to fill each of their holes with his seed because this was the only reason for their existence.

***

He was still sitting naked on the couch after jerking off into a pink wool blanket.

Tanja came out of the bathroom and looked at him fearfully, which Toni liked very much. He liked Tanja's outfit less. She'd put on leggings and a big gray sweater. *She could put in a little more effort.*

"Make the bed. I want to lie down again!"

She nodded but didn't move. Her face was no longer bloody, but it was deformed. Her lower lip had an ugly cut, and her nose was crooked. She looked like a monster, so even the sloppy sweater didn't matter anymore.

"Don't stare at me so stupidly, you ugly piece of crap! I

certainly won't fuck you!"

She took the dirty laundry off the bed. Her wet, freshly washed hair fell into her eyes.

Toni watched her contentedly. She was scared shitless. And he was the reason. That felt great.

When the bed was ready, Toni turned off the TV and rose from the couch.

"If you want, you can shoot up now. I'll take a nap."

Something like gratitude flashed in Tanja's eyes.

"You forgot something …"

"Thank you."

He nodded contentedly. "Fine. You were a good girl."

It flashed again in Tanja's eyes, but this time it were tears. "Thanks," she whispered once more. Then she went to the living room table, where her equipment for shooting up was waiting. There was no better medicine for her.

Toni granted it to her. This time.

***

When Toni woke, it was dark. He was lying alone in Tanja's bed. The television was on, and on the couch he saw a figure in a dim, shadowy, half-sitting, half-lying position. Tanja. She was still high, it seemed. *CSI: New York* was on TV. Old episodes that Toni already knew. Nevertheless, he watched briefly before he rose with a moan.

His clothes were scattered. Toni searched for his boxer shorts in the semidarkness but couldn't find them. He turned on the bedside lamp, bent over, and looked under the bed. There they were. He grabbed them and dressed.

It had gotten cold. After he finished, he went to Tanja and looked at her motionless body. Her eyes were closed, and she was completely spaced out, her face a disaster. In

her left arm, which she'd tied with a leather strap just above her elbow, several punctures were visible, surrounded by bluish-green swellings.

Matching her face, Toni thought with satisfaction.

The used syringe lay on the living room table beside a spoon and an empty cellophane bag. Next to it stood an overflowing ashtray. Dozens of empty beer bottles completed the picture. These were on his account. An almost-empty bottle of vodka lay on the floor. Toni picked it up and unscrewed the lid. The alcohol caressed his palate and his dry throat. Way too quickly the bottle was empty. Toni sighed. He licked his lips. He wanted and needed more. But he knew this was the last of the alcohol in this dump.

Time to go home.

Toni took one last look at the unconscious woman. For a junkie bride of about thirty, she actually still looked quite good and wasn't as emaciated as most others; she had some pretty curves in the right places.

Toni felt something move in his pants as he watched the helpless Tanja. He could have done anything with her now. She was completely at his mercy. But the pounding in his head and the sighing of his dry throat told him something else, and those voices were louder than those in his pants. For now. He desperately needed something to drink.

And fast.

Toni turned away from the sight of the motionless woman.

He left the cheap one-room apartment without looking back.

***

Karl was grateful every time he had the house to himself. Now that no more obligations were waiting for him, he'd slept long and then spent most of his time in front of the old television in the living room. He only dared to do that when Toni was away. Where was his brother? He hadn't been home for three days. Food supplies were running low, and Toni had left him no money. That was the only drop of bitterness.

Karl drank from the tap and ate what he could find, like the bag of chips in the living room closet that had only recently expired. For this feast he indulged in one of the DVDs from his brother's collection. It was a pretty brutal horror flick. A woman was raped by several men and took revenge afterward. Karl considered the movie cruel but somehow fascinating. Toni only had films of this kind. Worst of all were the hardcore porn movies in which women were tortured. Even if Karl hadn't watched them, the cover pictures were enough for him. Toni had always had a tendency toward extreme violence and sadism. Who should know better than Karl? He'd grown up under his brother's brutal hand.

***

On the way home, Toni stopped at a supermarket outside the city and bought two cases of beer and several frozen meals, as well as potato chips, cookies, and some milk. After he stowed everything in the trunk, it was almost eight p. m. and pitch-dark. The air smelled of autumn. Summer had definitely said goodbye.

Toni lit a cigarette and took a beer. He sat behind the wheel and emptied the bottle in one go. As always, the alcohol had an enlivening, even stimulating effect on him. A pleasant warmth spread in his stomach. He sighed with

satisfaction and threw the empty bottle onto the passenger seat. His hands were no longer shaky, and his heart no longer fluttered like a frightened bird. The world had calmed down. Toni Singer as well.

He stuck the cigarette between his moist lips and started the car.

The house where Karl and he lived was located in a remote forest near Lake Starnberg. An unpaved access road led there, accessible only for residents and people with special permission.

While Toni was driving along that road—through the dark forest, past lonely clearings and a few isolated haystacks—he realized for the first time how lonely it was out here. They could actually do whatever they wanted. There was nobody here who could have been interested. Nobody, except Karl.

When the weather was nice on weekends and public holidays, walkers would sometimes get lost in the area, and of course the ranger would pass by the house from time to time, but otherwise, even the mailman didn't drive all the way to the house but put the few letters and advertising mails in a mailbox which their mother had placed across the road decades ago exactly for this purpose, along with a note saying that parcels should also be left there. It was okay for the deliverers, as it spared them the trip up to the house. This arrangement had been fine with Frieda Singer, since she didn't necessarily like surprise visitors very much.

Toni didn't mind that his mother was rotting behind the bedroom door for almost a month now. He wondered what the cats had done to the dead body in the meantime. All the cats in this little room with this huge dead woman? No, Toni didn't want to think about this room, these cats, and this dead woman.

Actually, it barely smelled. Just a little, if you walked right past the door. You could quickly hold your breath, and you didn't have to think about it. The door was locked, the key gone and forgotten.

Since he'd lost his job, he'd hardly been home. However, he couldn't afford his trips to Munich forever. What could he do? Should he look for women around here? No, that was almost impossible. The area was too small; too many people knew each other, and there were by far not as many lost souls as in the big city. The risk was simply too high, unless …

Toni didn't finish the thought. Not now. He'd just parked the car behind the derelict barn. From outside, the house made a poor impression. Well, actually, not only from outside. The property was desolate. Garbage and rubble were piled everywhere. The small windows were filthy and were blocked with all kinds of junk, so you could hardly look inside. Which was perhaps better.

But Toni saw a light in the living room and the TV flickering. The little shit was probably watching one of his movies again.

Toni lifted a case of beer from the trunk and stomped to the back door. It wasn't locked. That was typical! He opened the door with his elbow and stepped into the hallway. Here too it was anything but tidy. Shoes and clothes lay everywhere. What was this little motherfucker doing all day?

Toni felt his anger boil. Karl often triggered these emotions in him. It had been like that since their earliest childhood.

"Hey, asshole!" he yelled through the open living room door. He heard the TV, which was turned up quite loudly. Sounded like *I Spit on Your Grave.* At least it wasn't one of his pornos. The little freak would have gotten a bloody

nose for that. Maybe more!

"Move your fat ass over here! Now!"

It didn't take ten seconds for Karl to stand in front of him. His blond hair was too long, unwashed, and stringy. He wore a dirty white T-shirt and sloppy sweatpants. His feet were stuck in slippers.

Toni looked at him disdainfully "What's wrong with you? When was the last time you took a shower? You're disgusting."

Karl avoided his gaze. He remained silent. Crumbs of chips stuck to his T-shirt.

"Can you do anything other than eat?" Toni slapped him in the face.

Karl's head was thrown to the side. His cheek turned red.

"Look at you! You are getting fatter and fatter."

Karl was silent. He stared at the floor. Just to be on the safe side!

"I've got stuff in the car," Toni said harshly and handed him the car key. "Bring everything in and fucking lock the front door. Put two pizzas in the oven right away. But don't think you're getting anything. You've eaten enough."

Karl took the key without a word.

Their eyes met.

"Everything else okay?" Toni asked. He thought of the locked bedroom door and what was behind it.

Karl nodded. He didn't think of anything. He'd learned at least that by now.

***

While Karl carried the groceries into the house and put the pizzas into the oven, Toni sat in front of the TV. He

switched off the DVD player and watched one of the hundreds of American crime series instead. This one had an interesting plot, so he stared spellbound at the screen. A mentally ill guy had set up some kind of torture chamber in the basement. He brought women there, humiliated them, raped them, and tortured them until they were dead. Although one didn't see so many details in this type of series, of course, Toni had an erection because his imagination did the rest. The memory of Tanja and her sweet little asshole was still fresh. Toni wanked as he watched a pretty blonde woman hanging naked from the ceiling in the madman's torture chamber waiting for her certain death. He came quickly and intensely. Panting, he squirted into his boxer shorts.

The episode was over, and he hadn't even seen the end. Now his head was busy with a new idea, a thought that was new, exciting, and fucking evil. A film, directed by him. Only a few props were missing and (very important) the lead actress, his goddamn star!

***

The smell of the hot pizza made Karl's empty stomach turn somersaults. He tried to ignore the feeling as he put the food for his brother on two plates.

Toni sat in front of the TV and apparently had just wanked. His flaccid penis was still hanging out of his pants. He didn't make any effort to hide it when Karl came in.

Karl put the plates on the coffee table. Grunting, Toni reached for the first pizza. Karl handed him cutlery. Toni ignored it.

"Bring in the beer and put it next to the couch."

Karl obeyed. He always did everything his brother told

him to do. Just to be on the safe side.

When he came back, Toni stuffed a greasy piece of pizza into his mouth. His penis was still hanging out of the sperm-stained shorts. Karl didn't care. The only thing that interested him was the smell of the food. His stomach growled angrily. He hadn't eaten properly for days.

"Can I have a slice, please?" he asked carefully.

Toni stared at him. "I told you you're not getting anything. You're way too fat. Just like Mama. You get your cleaning stuff now and clean up here. The workout will do you good. And next time the house is such a pigsty, I'll beat the shit out of you. Do you understand?"

Karl nodded.

"Good. Get going, then!"

***

Karl spent the next hour scrubbing the living room floor while Toni gave instructions. He enjoyed eating his pizza and drinking several bottles of beer. Not really a new situation. Toni had always enjoyed humiliating his younger brother. It gave him enormous satisfaction, and every now and then it even gave him a hard-on. But today he imagined for the first time how much hornier this situation could be, if—instead of his stupid fat brother—a naked woman would be on her knees in front of him. And after she'd done everything to his satisfaction, he would fuck her thoroughly. He could do that every night. Or every morning. Every goddamn day. Whenever he felt like it. That would be awesome!

He needed something like the guy in the series had. A place where he could enjoy himself undisturbed without anyone knowing. A place where he had a woman all to himself … then he could do with her whatever he wanted

… he'd be her God then …

***

Perverted bastard! Karl thought. While he had to clean the floor on all fours, his brother sat there with a greasy chin and had a boner. And now he even jerked off! Karl wouldn't look. He stared at the floor and concentrated on the humiliating task of scrubbing the old floorboards with a small brush. He ignored Toni as good as he could.

Unfortunately, Toni had no intention of ignoring him. He squirted with a loud moan. Then he took off his boxer shorts and threw them over to Karl.

"Take these with you and do the laundry now."

Karl picked up the shorts carefully with his thumb and index finger and stood up. His knees hurt.

"And bring me some fresh clothes!"

Karl nodded. As always.

***

He put the dirty laundry in the washing machine and then went to Toni's bedroom to get fresh clothes. It was the only tidy room in the whole house. Toni never left anything lying around. All his clothes hung neatly in the closet. The bed was made. On the desk lay open letters on two piles, presumably sorted by relevance. Karl opened a drawer and took out fresh boxer shorts. He hurried. Toni didn't like to wait.

The way back led past Mama's room. Just a moment ago he'd managed not to pay attention to the smell. Now he couldn't. Karl stopped in front of the locked door. His heart pounded up to his throat as he pressed one ear against the gray wood and … listened …

He heard something. A soft … scraping … something scraped across the floor. Karl closed his eyes. He now felt his heartbeat all the way to his temples. What he heard couldn't be exactly defined, yet he now had a picture in his mind that was all too clear.

He saw Mama's cats. All the cats … how many could there be by now? Five? Six? Ten? In his mind's eye he saw them sitting on his dead mother, their claws tearing moist, half-rotten pieces of flesh out of her bloated body, licking their paws. Karl got sick at the idea. His growling stomach contracted painfully, but he couldn't stop thinking of how those damn cats were eating his mother. They had no other choice. Toni had locked them in there. In order not to starve, they had to eat their dead mistress. And it was an especially big portion of mistress. Karl had no idea how long it would take before … were cats scavengers? Karl didn't know, but he suspected that some of them mutated into scavengers when it came to life and death. But he couldn't imagine how long it would take for Mama's little friends to eat her completely. He also had no idea how long a cat could live without food or how long it would take for the corpse of a woman weighing 450 pounds to decompose. Would the cats leave anything at all?

Whatever. Sooner or later nothing would be left to eat in this terrible room. What would the cats do then? Attack each other until only the strongest remained? How long would this process take in total until nothing and nobody was left in this room—except perhaps the insects, the flies, the maggots, and the woodlice? A month? Two? Longer? Karl wasn't a forensic scientist or a biologist. So how would he know? He only knew that he would never open this door again in his life. No matter whether he had the key or not.

The room upstairs had two windows that were almost completely covered with ivy. Thank God! Even without the ivy it would hardly have been possible to look inside. There was no balcony. Not anymore. The dilapidated thing had simply crashed about ten years ago.

Karl forced himself to avoid unpleasant thoughts. It made no sense to burden himself with them. He couldn't change the situation. None of this could be reversed. His mother wouldn't come back to life, no matter whether her corpse was eaten by cats and maggots in this room or if it rotted in some cold grave. The facts remained, and he had to try to come to terms with them. Toni made it so hard for him, and sometimes he asked himself why he didn't run away or put an end to the misery in some other way. But he lacked the courage to do so—as he lacked the courage to do anything else.

Karl quickly walked away from the door and hurried downstairs.

***

Meanwhile, Toni had drunk more than ten bottles of beer and felt pleasantly sleepy. Karl finally brought him fresh boxers. What was the little fucker doing for so long?

"You finish the floor and then the kitchen. I'll go to bed. If everything isn't clean tomorrow morning, you're in real trouble." He looked at Karl from head to toe and wrinkled his nose. "And take a shower. You stink."

"Okay," Karl replied meekly, got back on his knees and took the brush. A night of hard work lay ahead of him.

***

Laura had somehow survived the first day of school, and

it hadn't been as bad as she'd imagined. Her new classmates had looked at her stupidly but weren't interested in her. Fortunately! Laura had always been a moderately popular student—without friends but also without real enemies. In the new school year this would probably not be any different. Of course she had less contact with the girls from her old class now, but she'd never had a real girlfriend anyway.

In her new class was a blonde, somewhat shy, and not very pretty girl who sat in the back row and seemed likable to her. Her name was Annika, and she might become a friend in the next few weeks. Laura was content so far. It was certainly annoying to repeat last year's subjects, but she also had to admit that it wasn't necessarily bad for her in English and math. So it was a good thing to repeat the classes, and she was neither more or less popular than before.

Soon, she met Annika regularly at the weekends. Laura had indeed found something like a soul mate in this girl. The two became more and more intimate and soon shared their secrets, of which there were plenty at age sixteen.

It was also convenient that Annika had a moped driver's license because Laura lived in a small village quite off the beaten track and with poor bus service, picturesquely situated between meadows and woods, only a few miles from Lake Starnberg, but somewhere in the middle of nowhere. Since childhood Laura had hoped that the bus service would improve at some point, but this hadn't happened yet and it probably never would. Her parents loved it. They'd bought the house because of this seclusion. The perfect place for children. Well, maybe small children. There was little traffic and plenty of room to play and romp, but as you grew older and wanted to meet

up with friends in town from time to time, you realized how annoying it was to constantly depend on your parents. It was the boondocks here. She couldn't even go shopping alone. Her parents didn't want to pay her moped license because her mother was afraid something might happen to her. Laura had a different opinion, of course. For example, she was sure she'd already have a boyfriend if her parents allowed her to go to parties and clubs more often. She was sixteen and no longer a child. Unlike the girls her age, she had to stay at home. As a virgin!

That's exactly why it was advantageous in many ways for Laura to be friends with Annika. She lived in Wolfratshausen, a small town that wasn't really exciting but was still more exciting than this Hicksville. She came every weekend to see Laura or to pick her up. They went shopping or to the movies. And sometimes Laura was even allowed to spend the night with Annika. Not that Laura's mother allowed it too often, but freedom was no longer an abstract term.

So how do you get to meet people? Where could she meet a boyfriend? How would she lose her virginity?

Laura hadn't been able to answer these questions for months. Since she had improved so much at school that her failure was no longer hanging over her head like a sword of Damocles, the fact of her involuntary virginity had come to the fore again. Of course she'd talked about it with Annika, who was also a virgin, but she was ten months younger than Laura, which for Laura was a significant difference.

Together they enjoyed watching romantic movies and then imagined being in the place of the protagonist. Some of their favorite films were the Vampire-series, based on the books by Stephanie Meyer. Both were very fond of

Robert Pattinson and would have loved to take the place of Kristen Stewart, whom they deeply admired. When Laura's parents had once again forbidden her to do anything else, the two girls often sat for hours in Laura's little basement flat on weekends and languished, while they watched their favorite films for the hundredth time, consuming tons of tissues and chocolate.

Until Laura became increasingly worried about her figure. She'd always been very slim, rather petite, similar to Kristen Stewart. Lately, however, she'd noticed some growing bulges on her stomach and thighs. Annika always assured her that she was super slim, even slimmer than Kristen Stewart, but Annika herself was a bit chubby and therefore not necessarily the right person to judge. For her, of course, everyone was slender.

"It's actually perfect here," she told Annika, while lounging on the couch with a bar of chocolate and watching *Good Times—Bad Times*, their favorite daily soap.

"Perfect for what?" Annika asked with a full mouth.

"Perfect for jogging," Laura replied. "With the forest and everything. Do you actually know how huge this forest area is? There are many paths that hardly anyone uses. So no annoying spectators like in the gym."

"Uhm, what are you talking about? Do you want to go jogging or what? "

"Exactly. It's time for me to get the chocolate off my hips. You in?"

"And what if you get lost in the woods? You know it's huge!"

"Bullshit. There's a main road. It's just a forest road, so it's not paved, but that doesn't matter. There's hardly anything going on during the week. At the weekend you might meet some cyclists or people with dogs, but otherwise it's really quiet."

"Kind of creepy, though, right?" Annika said. "If it's so lonely there …"

"I don't care"

"I don't know …" Annika took another bite from her chocolate bar.

"If you join me, it's not lonely anymore. So, what about it? We can jog together, that'll be great," Laura suggested.

Annika shrugged. "I'm not that sporty."

I can see that, Laura thought and then said, "Too bad. But I'll definitely do it. At least every third day. I'm sure it's good for me."

"If you say so. As long as the evil wolf won't eat you—like *Little Red Riding Hood*," Annika said with a grin.

***

Being unemployed and blocked for three months was a growing problem for Toni, especially regarding his trips to Munich. He didn't notice it right away, but after the first four weeks, the money gradually grew short. Despite the lower gas prices, he couldn't fill his car as much as he liked. But he depended on the car and had no other way to get anywhere. The money his brother got from the office was ridiculously little, and the care money for their (dead) mother was only a drop in the bucket. Toni knew he had to get a job as soon as possible. But he seldom managed to pull himself together to browse newspaper ads or the Internet. He knew that being dismissed because of theft would hardly give him a chance on the job market anyway.

His reports and evaluations were never the best, but so far he'd somehow managed to get by. He could be charming when he wanted to be, and that often benefited

him—with the bosses and the women.

But now his luck seemed to have run out. He couldn't do much more than wait for the three-month deadline and then go to the office to at least get unemployment benefits. But that wouldn't be until December. Until then he had to economize.

At the end of October, Toni imposed a "Munich ban" on himself. During the next weeks he only wanted to leave the house if there was no other way. Karl had to give him all his money, which he (of course) did willingly. He'd trained the little motherfucker well, that much was certain.

Once a week he drove to the nearest discount store and bought the essentials. Beer. Frozen dishes. Chips. Milk. Cornflakes. Coffee. Tobacco. From time to time he allowed himself a bottle of cheap booze. Most of the time, the beer had to be enough. He kept Karl on as short a leash as possible. He got some food and could drink from the tap, otherwise he didn't need anything. He never needed anything.

Unlike Toni. There were so many things that he needed and missed more and more. He missed them so much that it drove him to the brink of madness. He tried to satisfy his desire with hardcore porn from the Internet. While watching such a movie he sometimes jerked off up to four times. But it wasn't the same.

He painfully remembered Tanja, the last bitch he'd put through the wringer. He wondered if there was any way he could take her home but knew she wouldn't play along. She was a junkie. She needed her drugs. She would never come with him to this abandoned place.

At least not voluntarily. *Voluntarily.*

Maybe this voluntariness could somehow be circumvented somehow …

But what would he do with a junkie like Tanja in the house? Soon the withdrawal symptoms would become so severe that she'd be of no use. And he didn't have the money to supply her regularly with drugs. So that wasn't an option. Unfortunately!

Okay. If not Tanja, maybe another bitch. Did he know one who would be suitable for his purposes …? No. All the women Toni had sex with were junkies and hookers. He could neither finance their addiction nor did he want to mess with their pimps. That wasn't worth it. Did he want to take these risks for some dirty sluts who would perhaps give him gonorrhea or worse? On the other hand, how long could he last without a real woman to satisfy his needs? Damn!

So, what could he do? The movies were a nice little distraction, but they weren't enough because they weren't real. He'd already wanked his cock sore, but it wasn't the same. He wanted to do something and shove his dick into the orifices of some slut. No matter how old or pretty. If he was done with her, she wouldn't win a beauty contest anyway. It would be in his hand what she looked like in the end. He could let the fat ones starve or fatten the skinny ones. Either way, he'd be God. Yes, God!

You gotta find one! You gotta catch one! This idea came to his mind one night after he'd just watched one of his beloved SM pornos, where a woman was locked in a cage and fixated in such a way that she could be fucked comfortably in the mouth, pussy, and ass. Several naked men with huge cocks did this job extensively. At the end she was raped with a metal pipe and died in agony.

Toni rubbed his penis until it hurt. He moaned loudly and drooled as he came. Four times! While his sperm only glued his naked thighs, the men in the film shot theirs right in the face, on the ass, and on the horny tits of the

immobilized bitch. Shit!

He needed a woman, as soon as possible. Of course all this had to be considered thoroughly. He'd have to make some preparations even before he could even begin to think about how he'd approach the woman.

Toni surfed the internet looking for the right equipment he would need to hold a woman captive in his house. He found far more than he'd thought possible. In fact, there seemed to be quite a few people who furnished torture rooms all by themselves. With cages, fucking machines, and all that. Everything the perverted heart desired could be found online, but not for free. Like everything in life, it was a question of money or extreme craftsmanship. Toni didn't have either. To his relief, however, he found that with a few hundred euros he could already come quite close to his goal. He still had 500 in savings. For bad times. Well, these times had probably come now …

Toni had handcuffs but decided they were just toys—for sluts who participated almost voluntarily. He needed something massive for his project. So he ordered hand and foot chains made of real steel, with real locks. To make a woman submissive, he had to be able to fixate her so that she had no chance to free herself. And not only for hours, but days or even weeks.

Months?

The idea alone excited him. He continued browsing through the virtual paradise for sadists. He was particularly fascinated by the neck cuffs. And although they cost almost another hundred euros, Toni ordered them. This item had a small steel ring at the front, where you could attach a dog leash, for example. He'd take Lupo's. The dog didn't need it anyway because nobody walked it.

The idea of leashing and leading a woman around in

this way excited Toni even more. He'd done this a few times before with women who wanted it. But how hot would it be to force someone who didn't want to do it at all, but who in the end had to submit because Toni was the stronger one and because he was her master? Her God!

For this purpose, Toni ordered an electric cattle prod. This shit surely hurt a lot. He loved it when the women screamed and begged.

After sending the order and reducing his savings by almost 400 euros, he decided to take a look at the basement. The largest room down there was about sixty-five square feet, was concreted, cold, damp … and stuffed to the ceiling with all kinds of shit.

"Fuck!" Toni cursed, while he inspected the chaos. He should've known. Neither Karl nor his mother were tidy people.

But he hadn't thought it was so bad. Boxes, newspapers, and old shit that nobody needed anymore was piled up everywhere. There was everything from old toys to broken kitchen devices. Toni took a few steps into the room illuminated by a naked light bulb. He picked up a few things and dropped them again with a sigh. It would take at least two days to tidy this room up. Only then would he be able to start insulating the walls. He would have to do some research, but Toni was sure he'd find some instructions on YouTube.

He examined the only window in the room, a tiny hole covered with spiderwebs through which not much would get outside anyway. And even if it did, who would hear it in this godforsaken area? Not even the mailman would get close enough to the house to notice anything suspicious. The only path was more than two hundred feet away. The occasional walkers, joggers, and cyclists

wouldn't be a problem. Basically everything was perfect … except for this bulk garbage, but Toni would find a solution for that too.

***

"And why should I do that?" Karl asked meekly when they stood in the basement. "What you wanna do down here?"

Toni slapped him in the back of the head. Karl twitched.

"It's none of your fucking business. I told you the room has to be empty and you're doing it *now*!. Period."

"This will take forever." Karl sighed, but Toni had already grabbed him and pushed his face into a box of old Lego bricks while he pressed his knee into his back.

"Did I ask for your opinion?"

Karl moaned but said nothing.

"Did I?"

"No, you didn't," Karl finally replied. He noticed his lip had chapped.

Toni loosened his grip so Karl could lift his head. A Lego stuck to his forehead for a moment before it fell back into the box and blood ran down his chin, but his brother wasn't finished yet.

"I need this room, and soon enough you'll find out why. If you want something to eat tonight, you'd better start working. I've checked the room opposite. Everything should fit in there if you stack it properly. You can dump the rest behind the house for now. The main thing is that everything in here is empty. Understand?"

"There shouldn't be anything left in here?"

"Yes, you genius! Absolutely nothing."

"Okay."

Toni took away his knee and helped his brother to his feet. Karl's lip was bleeding. Toni gave him a tissue. Karl took it and held it to his bleeding lower lip.

"So, everything all right? I'll come back later to see how you're doing."

Karl nodded. He had tears in his eyes, but they only came from the pain. He'd long since stopped weeping out of shame. He had no fucking choice.

Unfortunately, nobody had taught him that you always had a choice.

***

While he was working, Karl thought about how much his situation had worsened since Toni was unemployed. He used to have the house to himself all day and for many nights. When Toni came home, there was always trouble, and Karl often received blows and humiliating words, but as long as he didn't have to endure it every day, it was all right with him. But since September (and that was almost two months now), Toni was always here. He probably couldn't afford his trips anymore.

Karl had his own ideas about what Toni had done in Munich, but he'd never been brave enough to ask. So he now got beaten almost every day, was abased by Toni and had to do humiliating work. Every day Toni seemed to come up with new punishments for him. *For what?* The basement was now his latest prank. Karl was pretty sure he only let him work here because he enjoyed seeing him suffer. He couldn't imagine why Toni needed this room. After all, he had a house at his disposal. The cellar had never been interesting for him.

When they were children, Mama used to store food here, but that was a very long time ago. The few supplies

they still had were in the kitchen and the pantry. So why the cellar?

Don't think about it. You can't change it anyway. Just keep going and stop thinking.

Karl gritted his teeth and did exactly that.

***

Three hours later, Toni returned with water and beer.

"Looks pretty good already," he stated and appreciatively patted the perspiring Karl on the shoulder, who had just dragged another box into the opposite room and placed it on a pile that was steadily growing.

Toni handed him water. Karl thanked him and drank greedily.

Toni sipped his beer with a grin. "You deserve it, kiddo." He took a contented look around the now half-empty room.

"You can do the rest tomorrow. Now you may shower and make food."

Karl nodded humbly. His entire body hurt. When Toni patted him on the shoulder again, it didn't make things any better. Toni smelled of alcohol. Karl would have become a drinker himself long ago if Toni had let him.

Maybe he'd be lucky tonight and his brother would be gracious enough to give him a bottle.

Hope died last.

***

An hour later they were sitting together on the couch in the living room. A rare sight.

Karl had taken a shower and put on clean clothes, which hadn't happened for some time. Wet hair hung in

his eyes while he ate the salami pizza that he had been allowed to prepare for Toni and himself. After the hard work and the past days without real food, the cheap frozen pizza tasted delicious. Divine, to be honest. Karl enjoyed the salty taste of the hot salami. He also enjoyed this moment of almost heavenly harmony.

They really sat together on the couch eating pizza, watching TV, and drinking beer! Toni had even given him a second bottle. Karl almost felt like he was in heaven. This was one of the rare moments in his life when he was happy and at peace with himself and the world. He even felt something like … he didn't know what to call it, but maybe it was actually something like love. At least for a short time Karl felt a strong affection for this person who had treated him like shit all his life.

Karl took what he could get. In this unique moment he felt somehow safe, somehow secure, and somehow at home. *Somehow.*

The moment passed just like all special moments. What remained was the memory. No need to complain.

"Do you wanna know why I need the basement room?" Toni asked after eating his pizza and wiping his greasy fingers on his pants.

Karl gave him a scrutinizing sidelong glance. He'd also finished eating and was balancing his empty plate on his knees. He greedily took a sip of his beer before Toni could perhaps change his mind.

"Yes," he said slowly, not quite sure if that was the right answer.

Toni stared at the TV screen. Some documentary …

"I have a plan … or rather an idea … it's not really a plan yet."

"Okay …"

"I want to kidnap someone."

Karl choked on his beer. He coughed and retched a few times, then gasped for air and stared at his brother in disbelief. "What? Who?"

Toni shrugged. "I'm not sure yet. Some woman."

"And you want to lock her up down there?"

"Bingo!"

"But … why?"

"Why not? Because she belongs to me then. I want one for myself. One who does anything I want and whenever I want it. No one does that voluntarily, so I'll have to force her to do it."

Karl's mouth was wide open and he blinked in disbelief. "But you'd go to jail."

"I don't intend to get caught."

"The woman will report you."

"She'll never get the chance, genius."

"That means you wanna kidnap a woman and never let her go again?"

Toni nodded. "That's the plan."

Karl was silent for a moment but then shook his head. "You can't do that, Toni. That … that …" He struggled for words but couldn't find any.

"Only we'll know, Karl. Both of us and the woman, of course. But she won't be the problem. I'll take good care of her. I've already ordered a few aids online. And I want to install a new door with a more stable lock. And now it's about you."

"Me?"

"Yeah, you. Because I can't do this without your help, Karl. You'll have to take care of her if I'm not here or if I don't have time. And you'll have to keep your mouth shut. But of course you may use her. I'm not a monster." He grinned.

"What does that mean? I can use her? You think I'd

rape a woman? Never, Toni! I'd never do that!"

"Well, Karl, that's your business. You can stay a virgin forever."

"I'm not a virgin!" That was true. Karl had had sex twice in his life, with his first and last girlfriend, Stefanie. At the time he'd been eighteen. But whatever!

In any case, he wasn't into hurting or humiliating a woman. That was his brother's job. But so far he hadn't suspected Toni being so insane. He could have guessed, of course. Those disgusting pornos! Good God!

"Whatever," Toni finally said. "The main thing is that you shut up and help me when I need you."

"But I won't help you hurt or rape anybody. You can't expect me to do that, Toni!"

"Wait and see what I can do."

Toni looked at him with a cold gaze. Cold as ice!

Karl's heart was beating up to his throat. "I don't want you to do something like that! Please don't!"

"The question *if* I'll do it no longer arises, Karl. The only question is *when*. And you don't have to worry whether you want to help me, dear brother. Because you will. I just leave you no choice."

Karl gritted his teeth. The pizza suddenly lay heavy in his stomach, making him want to puke. There it was again, the problem of not having any choice. At least not in this life.

"Where do you even want to get a woman from?" he asked. At least there was still some hope that Toni wouldn't be able to kidnap someone. There was still a lot that could go wrong. Right?

Toni shrugged. "We'll see. First of all, the basement has to be ready. Then I'll look around. If necessary, I'll just try it online. There are some websites where willing women offer to come to strangers' homes so they can get

a good fuck. There are so many desperate sluts out there." He grinned crookedly. "It'll work somehow; don't worry."

"But you can't be sure no one knows anything when you meet a woman online. She could tell a friend before she comes to you. Or they could check her computer and her chat history after she's disappeared. Then they'll have you by the balls."

Toni sighed. His stupid little brother's objection made him think.

"Well, maybe. Never mind. It's just one of many options."

"I really hope you'll get this idea out of your head. You'll get us in a hell of a mess."

Toni laughed dryly. "Brother, we've been there for a long time."

***

Two days later, Toni attached a massive iron ring to the floor of the now-empty basement room. Later, he planned to attach the chain for the ankle cuffs to it. He'd found an old moth-eaten mattress between all the useless stuff. Toni placed it in a corner of the room, next to the iron ring. The floor was dirty. Dead beetles and spiders lay in the corners. From time to time you could also see living insects scurrying across the floor and the damp walls. The most disgusting were the centipedes. Toni hated them. But you had to live with them down here.

Luckily, he didn't plan on staying here too long. That was just his dungeon and the prison for his future slave. She wouldn't need any luxury.

He'd make that clear for her as soon as possible. He was looking forward to it like a little child on Christmas

Eve.

So, there—she has a bed.

Toni looked at the dirty mattress and pondered. What else did a person need?

A pillow? Too much luxury.

A blanket? She would have to earn it first.

Toilet? That would be necessary. He couldn't just have her shit and pee on the floor. Not that he really cared. Only, the stench would quickly get pretty bad. And it would also attract vermin. No, he'd have to give her something for her need. After all, he didn't want to take her upstairs each time. So what then?

Toni thought. The solution was more than simple. He took a dented metal bucket from the former laundry room and placed it next to the mattress. Well, that would do it. Karl or the slut would have to empty it regularly. And of course he wouldn't be the one to do it. No! He was the master, not a servant.

What else could she need?

Toni thought while he looked around the barren room.

She'll also have to wash herself sometimes.

Okay, that was clear. Otherwise she'd soon stink badly. And get ugly hair everywhere. Disgusting teeth and bad breath. That wasn't very sexy. Toni wasn't overly picky when it came to personal hygiene, but he didn't want to fuck a stinking woman either. His own sense of well-being obliged him to give her regular washing facilities. For showering and brushing her teeth, he'd simply take her upstairs, as it didn't have to be every day.

He could hose her off down here.

Toni grinned at the idea and immediately got a boner. He rubbed his crotch while he pictured a naked trembling woman crouching in the corner, shivering in the ice-cold jet of the garden hose.

Great idea!

Maybe he'd do it sometime.

Otherwise Karl could bring her the water in a bucket. The little asshole would surely enjoy it.

Anything else? He had no idea. She could lie down and use the bucket while she was chained. That was enough. It was cold and damp, of course. Especially now in autumn, and it would get worse in winter. He could give her an electric radiator so she wouldn't freeze. But it was the same as the blanket—she'd have to be a very good girl to earn such privileges.

Clothes, pillows, blankets, heating, even food and beverages would not be a matter of course for his prisoner. She'd have to learn to say goodbye to the comforts of everyday life and to work hard for every privilege, no matter how small. According to his rules. How awesome was that? Toni could hardly wait.

The erection pounded in his pants as he wondered what it would be like to be the master and God of such a helpless, hungry, anxious, freezing bundle of a human being. She'd only sleep, eat, and shit if he allowed it. She'd be just as thick or thin as he wanted her to be. She'd be as clean or dirty as he liked. She'd be naked whenever he wanted her naked. Each of her orifices would only exist to take in his mighty cock. To receive it gratefully. Just awesome!

And if he told her to eat his jizz for breakfast, she would. If he said she had to quench her thirst with his piss, she would. And if he said she had to crouch naked on a leash in front of him on the floor like a damn dog while he watched TV, she'd do that too. She'd lick his feet clean whenever he wanted and suck his dick for as long as he wanted. Everything, just everything in this woman's life would only happen the way he wanted it.

She'd only exist to satisfy him. She'd be a worthless something, crawling around in front of him and doing whatever came to his mind!

Toni pulled his penis out of his pants and rubbed it brutally and violently. He came with a soft scream of satisfaction, thinking of things no normal person could have endured.

***

Karl had barely been able to sleep since he had to live with the terrible certainty that the body of his dead mother was eaten by her own pets just a few feet away.

The situation became even worse after Toni told him what he intended to do with the basement room. Karl hadn't been down there since he'd cleared it out, but he noticed Toni going into the cellar several times a day—sometimes with an empty bucket, sometimes with tools, and finally with several large foam mats.

Today he'd heard him hammering for about an hour before Toni showed up sweaty in the kitchen to get a beer.

"I'm going to the hardware store again," he explained to Karl, who stood in front of the sink and, following Toni's orders, washed the dishes of the past few days.

"What are you doing?" Karl asked without turning around.

"I just told you. Hardware store. Need more foam."

"Why? What are you doing down there?"

"Ever heard of soundproofing, dude? That's what I'm doing down there. Everything has to be perfect when my sweetheart moves in."

"So you think she'll scream?" Karl asked stupidly.

"Of course she'll scream," Toni replied without hesita-

tion. "What do you think? She'll scream like a pig. At least in the beginning. I guess she'll stop as soon as she realizes it's pointless."

"I still can't believe you really want to do this." Karl turned around, but Toni only grinned maliciously.

"Just be happy that I won't do all this with you, man."

Karl, who was really happy about it, remained silent.

***

One week after Toni had placed the order, the drover, the hand and foot chains and the iron neck cuff arrived in an inconspicuous parcel, which was, however, incredibly heavy.

Toni immediately carried it down to the basement.

The steel chains seemed very stable at first glance. As promised in the description, there was also a long chain that could be attached to the hand or foot cuffs to connect them to each other or somewhere else. Toni tried it and pulled the chain through the iron ring in the floor. His heart beat faster. The sight of the chains alone caused excitement in him. He licked his lips.

Then he ran upstairs to get his stupid little brother. He needed a test subject.

***

"Now take off your shoes and socks and sit on the mattress," Toni ordered in a hard voice.

Karl looked at him doubtfully. "But I don't want to."

"I don't give a shit! Now do it!"

Hesitantly, Karl bent down and finally took off his dirty sneakers.

"That's good. And now the socks. Come on!" Toni

sounded rushed and excited. He kept licking his lips and stepping from one foot to the other.

Karl took off his socks, which had also seen better days. The floor under his bare feet felt unpleasantly cold and damp. He shuddered.

"Sit on the mattress."

Karl obeyed and slowly squatted, although it disgusted him insanely to touch the rotten mattress. An unpleasant moisture spread under him, and it stank of mold.

Toni came to him, the new chains in his hand. He bent down and put the ankle cuffs on Karl. They fit well, but the bitch for whom all this was meant wouldn't have such strong joints.

After the ankle cuffs closed with a click, he attached the chain that was already connected to the iron ring. The length was perfect. So his prisoner had enough room to move, to lie down or stand up and walk the few steps to the metal bucket that served as a toilet. However, there wasn't enough room to get near the door or the only window.

Toni nodded contentedly as he looked down at his chained brother, who was anything but happy. "Looks good," he said.

Karl nodded. "Okay. And now you free me, right?"

"Not so fast, my dear brother. After all, I need to know whether all that stuff can really withstand anything." He tossed the key in the air and caught it again.

"I'll go now. For an hour. And you scream here and try to free yourself. But you should really try hard, understand? As if it were a matter of life and death for you. Try to free yourself somehow. I'll see if you've exerted yourself."

"Do I have to? I can try it and see if it works."

"No. I'll give you an hour. And scream your throat out.

I wanna know how much I can hear up in the house and outside now that I have insulated all the walls and window."

"I wish you wouldn't do that to me," Karl said.

"Be glad it's only for an hour," Toni said calmly, as if it was nothing but a television ban.

Then he left the room and closed the new door with a loud bang.

***

Karl was now alone—in almost complete darkness. Toni hadn't even left the light on for him! Alone with the disgusting insects. Alone with the cold and the humidity. Alone with himself and the fear.

His feet were already as cold as icicles. His pants were disgustingly damp. The shackles were so tight that they cut into his flesh. He tried to open them with his fingers. He pulled and tore and turned them. No chance. They were bombproof.

So he stood up and shuffled with tiny little steps over to the iron ring that Toni had anchored in the floor. If anything, it would be the only way to free himself. Karl knelt in front of the ring and pulled on it. Nothing. He shook it, pulled it again, turned it until his fingers hurt. Nothing happened. Toni had done a great job. Congrats!

You gotta scream! Karl remembered. *Or he'll be damn pissed.*

Karl hesitated, feeling stupid at the thought of yelling like a madman. But then suddenly something crawled over his foot. That was enough. Karl threw his head back, closed his eyes, and screamed.

***

Fifty minutes later the door opened with a loud clank and the light went on.

Toni was back.

Karl sat on the mattress and blinked into the suddenly much-too-bright light. The shackles were still where they should be. The iron ring as well.

"So?" Toni asked. His voice echoed in the almost empty room.

Karl sniffed and rubbed his aching ankles. "These shackles are really strong."

Toni nodded. He squatted in front of Karl, already holding the key in his hand. "Did you scream?"

Karl cleared his throat. "Yes. Until I was hoarse. I almost panicked. Didn't you hear me?"

Toni shrugged. "Hardly worth mentioning. Upstairs in the kitchen and in the living room I heard you once, but outside not at all."

"Good. Now, will you free me?"

"Have you really given your best?"

"Check it out."

Toni unlocked the shackles and removed them from Karl's ankles. Red weals became visible, and the skin was chafed and raw.

Toni grinned contentedly and patted his brother's shoulder approvingly. "Very nice. Thank you."

He reached out his hand and helped Karl stand up. Karl picked up his shoes and socks but didn't put them on. His ankles hurt. He just wanted to get away from here, from this stinking place, this terrible prison. At that thought he shuddered. He already felt sorry for the woman who would have to endure this terrible fate. Especially because being imprisoned would perhaps be the most "pleasant" part about it. He didn't even want to know

what Toni had in mind. He knew some of his hardcore pornos …

The fears he was confronted with were worse than any horror movie.

***

In mid-November, a few days after his "trial visit" to Toni's torture chamber, Karl had to go to the employment office again. As a rule, he had to show up at the office every three months, but this was only a formality. Since they knew he cared for his bedridden mother, he got his money each month without any problems. They only wanted to know again and again whether anything had changed about Frieda Singer's condition. There had been a change—and Karl would rather not think about how exactly this state had changed in the meantime—but of course he'd leave it unmentioned. Otherwise Toni would have probably killed him.

The office was located in Bad Tölz, about thirty minutes away. Toni had agreed to drive Karl there and wait in the car until he was finished. Karl could've driven on his own, but Toni didn't want to give him the car.

So the two brothers left the house together. It was a mild Wednesday morning and far too early.

Karl's appointment in Bad Tölz was at nine. Both hadn't slept enough and were tired and grouchy as they trotted side by side to Toni's car. Karl was about to open the passenger door when he saw the girl.

Toni froze.

Both looked down the driveway to the narrow path that led past the property.

They stared at the blonde jogger with the seesawing ponytail, black leggings, long gray sweatshirt, and pink

running shoes. She had small white headphones in her ears. Her anything but small breasts moved visibly under the thin fabric of her sweatshirt. She looked over at them, just for a moment, and then turned her gaze forward again and continued running.

Karl and Toni gawked at her until she disappeared behind the next bend in the road.

Both thought the same thing, but neither said a word.

Finally they got into the car.

"Have you ever seen her before?" Toni asked as he started the car.

Karl nodded. "Once or twice. But always only in the evening."

Toni mumbled something incomprehensible. They drove along the path for a moment. Then she suddenly reappeared, running on the edge of the path to let the car pass.

Toni reduced the speed. He stared out the window as they slowly drove past her. The blonde ponytail bounced up and down—just like her little ass and those gorgeous tits Toni was now looking at in the rearview mirror. She had not only a great shape but also an acceptable face. Not a beauty from a Playboy mag but okay. Definitely prettier than most of the other girls Toni knew.

"How old do you think she is?"

Karl shrugged. He looked sick. Probably peeing his pants in fear. Such a loser!

Toni, on the other hand, enjoyed the mental images that triggered a mighty hard-on.

"Not older than eighteen, right?" he asked, drooling as he spoke. He suppressed a moan and wiped his mouth.

"Uhm." Karl seemed desperate.

"She's perfect," Toni said excitedly. "It should be her! That has to be destiny, man. The perfect girl runs right

past our house. Shit, dude! Incredible, isn't it? Now all I gotta do is find out if she runs at certain times and—"

"I don't think she jogs at certain times," Karl shouted.

"What? You just said she usually runs past our house every evening. Which would be great because there's nobody around at this time."

"But I only saw her once or twice."

"You said twice at least."

"I … I think, I was wrong and today was only the second time. You never know if and when she'll be here next time."

"Okay, we'll find out."

Karl turned away in silence. Toni frowned. Was it really possible that the little motherfucker didn't even move when he saw this horny slut? Toni's penis throbbed in his pants as he imagined her naked. Chained up in his cellar. Helpless. His very personal piece of fuck meat. Available at any time. No real man could resist!

But his little brother didn't show any reaction. What a loser!

***

Two guys came out of the old farmhouse while she jogged by. They stared at her as if she were some rare animal. She felt a strange tingling sensation in her belly and quickly continued running. Somehow she didn't like them. Just like the house. Laura had never seen anyone there before, but she'd noticed the dilapidated building and always wondered who lived in this ugly place. It looked deserted, but it wasn't, because a car (an old rusty Golf) was often parked out front, and because she'd seen light in one of the windows.

In her opinion, normal people couldn't live here be-

cause the house looked terrible. The plaster fell from the dirty gray façade, only a few sad remains were left of the balcony, and the paint crumbled from the crooked shutters. The garden was overgrown with weeds and completely run down. Garbage piled up everywhere. The former stable in the back area, above which the threshing floor was located, had already more or less collapsed. It'd be life-threatening to go in there. According to what could be seen from a distance, the house made a completely ramshackle and pitiful impression. Not a good place, Laura presumed. Or perhaps a good one, but certainly not a happy one. She imagined a sad old woman, abandoned by God and the world, on her own and no longer able to pay for the repairs to her house, that she probably didn't want to sell because her heart was so attached to it.

Laura imagined it like this every time she walked past this creepy house. She was all the more surprised that Wednesday morning when she saw the two young men coming out of the house. Her first two classes had been canceled, so she jogged that morning. There was also a math test on the agenda that day and she hoped the morning detour to the woods would clear her head.

When Laura saw the two weird guys in front of the scary house, she was suddenly in a hurry to get home, even though she was well in time. She fell out of step as she ran, her breathing speeding up … and then she got a side stitch at the moment when the car with the two guys drove past her.

She ran as far to the edge as she could but maintained her speed. The car slowed down. It passed her at an unbearable snail's pace, and the two guys stared greedily at her. It was a nasty feeling, as if they were undressing her with their eyes. Not beautiful at all. Laura now breathed

hectically, her meanwhile well-trained condition gone, the stitch becoming so bad that she had to press one hand to her side. But she gritted her teeth and kept running, didn't want to show any fear as long as the guys gawked at her.

It seemed to take an eternity until the car was finally out of sight. Laura stopped and breathed a sigh of relief. She pulled the plugs out of her ears and bent far forward to ease the stitch.

Shit, what kind of freaks were they?

Laura shuddered at the idea that these two guys lived together in the old hut. Strange! She'd believed old people lived there.

And how they had stared at her! That wasn't normal. Of course men looked at girls, but those looks—especially from the bald one on the driver's seat—were somehow different. Not the way a man looks after a woman because he thinks she's cute. Something was threatening about the way the bald guy stared at her. So greedy. Yes, that was the right word. As if she was a piece of meat, like a juicy steak. Not a nice feeling, and it didn't get any better with time. She even screwed up the math test because of her queasy thoughts about this bald guy, his cold eyes, and this creepy house.

***

After this encounter, Laura seriously considered whether she should change her running route. You might call it a presentiment. She couldn't get the men out of her head. And although Laura was a person who listened to her gut feeling, she felt childish and even a bit hysterical. She considered talking to Annika about it but finally gave up the idea because she didn't want to look like a stupid little

girl in the eyes of her friend.

It was bad enough that even Annika now had a boyfriend with whom she was planning her first time, while Laura could still only dream about it. But instead of imagining Robert Pattinson kissing her passionately, she got some weird ideas about antisocial guys who lived out in the woods trying to get their fingers into her panties. Not a surprise with all the puberty hormones, but still pathetic. She should finally face reality and get a date herself. Preferably with Basti, a boy from high school, whom she felt attracted to—without him knowing about it.

So instead of discussing crazy panic attacks in the woods, Laura told her about Basti, who had recently looked so cute with his new hairstyle. And Annika reported in detail about her date with Tom. They'd been to the movies, sat in the back row, and wildly made out. Laura listened with interest, nodded, giggled, and played the dear friend while she was almost bursting with envy. Annika was in love and full of joy. She was on the verge of her damn deflowering—something that Laura would probably never experience. Life was just unfair!

Nobody wanted her. And the fact that the two hillbillies had gawked at her ass had certainly been just imagination. Maybe she only had a booger on her face or just looked ridiculous with her pink headband and sloppy shirt. Sexy was different. She'd remain a virgin because she was fat and ugly. So Laura finally rejected the idea of finding a new route for her jogging. Besides, she liked the lonely track through the forest—without other joggers, cyclists, or grannies with dogs. Would she let those two idiots ruin it for her? Absolutely not! She'd had a funny feeling, of course; the two guys weren't quite normal, but that was no reason for panic.

It was ridiculous to act so stupidly. She wasn't Little

Red Riding Hood, and the two guys weren't the bad wolf. She was too old for fairy tales now, and it was time that she behaved appropriately if she didn't want to die as an old maid. No more dreams and fantasies. She was ready for the real life!

Laura had no idea that she'd actually lose her innocence.

Very soon, in every possible way.

***

About every second day around five in the afternoon, Karl saw the girl jogging past the driveway. She always wore the same pink running shoes and—since the days became cooler—a white, softshell jacket. Her ponytail bobbed teasingly back and forth. Just like her breasts. She always wore earplugs. She was always alone.

Why couldn't she just go jogging somewhere else? Karl hoped there would soon be the first snow, preferably a lot, so that jogging on unpaved forest paths would be out of the question. He also hoped every damn day that Toni would be drunk by early evening and forget to look for the girl. Of course that didn't happen. Despite his progressive alcohol addiction, Toni had himself under control.

***

"She always comes this way on Wednesdays—have you noticed that?" Toni's voice sounded behind Karl as he stood at the kitchen window, from where he had a good view of the path. The girl had just run past.

Karl swallowed. Yes, he'd noticed that.

"The other days vary, but it's always the same time on

Wednesdays," Toni said and put a hand on Karl's shoulder, who tried not to flinch.

He struggled for composure. Not so easy. While he kept staring out of the window and watching the girl—just a colorful blob in the barren landscape, soon not to be seen again—his gaze fell on Lupo, their old St. Bernard. The animal lay in the driveway and seemed terribly emaciated. The sight stung Karl's heart.

When was the last time we fed him? He turned to Toni to ask him. But his brother stared out the window with glazed eyes, a hand in his pants, and gasped. "Next Wednesday I'll grab her!"

THE GAME BEGINS

A week before Christmas, Laura sat at dinner with her parents. Her mother had made spaghetti bolognese, Laura's favorite dish, but today she had no appetite and just listlessly poked around in it. She got two bad grades yesterday—an F in both English and math. Damn it! It could hardly be any worse.

She'd already repeated the grade, so another lap of honor wouldn't be possible. If she screwed up now, she'd have to leave school and go back to the idiots of middle school, some of whom she still knew from her grade school days.

At that time she'd been the one who felt cool because she'd achieved the average grades for high school so easily. Today they would gossip viciously about her failure. Although, on second thought, even the idiots she knew from the old days would have their degrees by then. Only she had failed. Shit!

But until the autumn break it looked as if she could make it. Then it had rapidly gone downhill. Only because her head was filled with Basti in particular and boys in general. How could she think clearly when she was always busy with asking herself how she could finally lose her virginity before her seventeenth birthday? Damn shit! It was especially bad since Annika and Tom were together. Two weeks ago she'd slept with him for the first time. She'd had sex, while for Laura a tongue kiss was still the ultimate feeling—and it had only happened twice, at parties. With some idiots who meant nothing to her. Drunk and stoned. Not at all romantic. Not like Annika and her Tom. She stayed with him almost every weekend and had no time for Laura anymore. She was in love, of course.

Who blamed her? Laura wouldn't have behaved differently in her place. If she were with Basti, she wouldn't voluntarily spend a minute without him. That was first love—which apparently wasn't granted to her.

When she lay alone on the couch watching movies at the weekend, she always had to think about how Annika was with her Tom right now. How they lay together on the couch, arm in arm, a heart and a soul, the goddamn perfection in person! And this content, smug grin that Annika now showed almost all the time. Awful! She'd told Laura about her first time in every detail. It had been "incredibly phenomenal." She'd never experienced anything comparable before … blah, blah, blah. Sometimes Laura just couldn't stand this chitchat any more.

Yes, Annika deserved being happy, no problem, but it just wasn't fair that now everything had to go wrong in Laura's life. School sucked. Her friendship with Annika sucked. Basti sucked because he still didn't notice her, not even for a second. Life was really a complete asshole.

Now she sat here with her boring bourgeois parents in front of a steaming plate of pasta and would have liked to vomit when she thought how bad it all was. Simply unfair. Yes, it was fucking unfair!

The only thing that comforted her was the fact that she'd actually lost some weight since she started jogging and paying more attention to her nutrition. She'd already lost fifteen pounds. Not bad! Jogging was the only activity at the moment where she could forget her crappy life for a while. Whenever she jogged, she was at peace with herself and the world. She was proud of the performance of her body, and her self-confidence got a boost every time she stood on the scales. Running, it seemed, was the only thing she was really good at. She saw the success in her figure and felt it in her new body feeling. Any guy

who didn't appreciate that should fuck off! Also Basti. Especially Basti, that asshole.

Annika could also fuck off. Annika preferred to coo with her guy instead of worrying about her best friend. Actually, she was a backstabber, like all the other friends who had come and gone with time. Laura hadn't been able to count on any of them when the going got tough. In the end, everyone was for themselves. One should never forget that.

All these thoughts went through Laura's head as she sat over a plate of spaghetti bolognese on the last evening of her "normal" life. Only a few days later she'd kill for the spaghetti. But now she was annoyed by her parents and friends. She'd soon scream for them in her lonely cold nights until her lungs burned.

None of us can foresee the future, and nobody knows what fate might have in store for us behind the next turn.

Laura Hermann would have ripped her carotid right here and now with the fork in her hand if she'd known what kind of nightmare awaited her.

By this time tomorrow, her life as Laura Hermann would be over.

This Laura Hermann would no longer exist.

For what awaited her was nothing more or less than the involuntary lead role in the perfidious play of a mentally ill sadist.

***

Toni's heart pounded like crazy as he walked around the kitchen with the knife in his hand. It was shortly after four. Time to get ready. The anticipation almost took his breath away. What if she wouldn't come today? He swallowed dryly, but the lump in his throat remained.

Lupo lay on the dirty floor and wheezed. Toni kicked him as he walked by. Just to vent. The animal howled but remained lying. This stupid old dog wouldn't live very much longer. Fuck it! Toni didn't care. One less hungry mouth to feed. He positioned himself again at the window and stared down at the path.

Nothing and nobody to see. It was windy and raining. Maybe she'd rather stay at home. Had she been deterred by the weather so far? He wasn't sure, couldn't remember with the best will in the world whether she'd run past here in the rain. When was the last time it had rained? It seemed an eternity ago.

Toni stared at the blade. It was a sharp knife, made to cut meat. It hadn't been used for a long time.

He walked into the hallway. His parka hung on the coat rack. He put the knife on the floor and put on the parka and hood. He was already wearing his heavy brown work boots. Tightly tied. He pulled the zipper of the parka up as far as it would go and grabbed the knife. He paused, pondered … opened the zipper again, put the knife carefully in the inner pocket. He left the zipper open so it was at hand. Fuck the cold! Again there was such a lump in his throat which he couldn't swallow. Toni ignored it and went to the front door. His cock was a hard throbbing something—squeezed into his pants. When was the last time he was this horny?

***

Karl was upstairs in his room. Toni didn't want the little motherfucker to come with him. He'd mess everything up with that damn face he pulled. Toni would need him later, but for now it was better to do it alone.

He left the house and left the door unlocked.

Once he'd caught the girl, there would be no time to rummage for the key.

***

A pleasant calmness overcame Laura's head while she jogged in the cool drizzle through the forest. The scents of moss, pine needles, and fresh earth filled her nose. Wonderful smells. She felt good. As good as it hadn't been in a long time. For some reason she thought of Christmas and for the first time this year felt the warm breath of anticipation. Christmas meant no school, no stress with grades, no stupid classmates, no Basti, no Annika. She'd sleep late, watch movies, perhaps read a book … go jogging in the afternoon, and then drink hot tea and nibble some cookies. And who knows, maybe she'd even have a date during the holidays …

Hope died last.

There was this friend of Tom's who Annika had recently introduced to her and who had sent her a friend request on Facebook today. He was actually quite cool; he was handsome and seemed to be smart. Anyway, you could have a good conversation with him. Why had she been so obsessed with this stupid Basti? That was over now! She had to be open to something new again. After all, she was only sixteen, and life still lay ahead of her …

All these thoughts went through Laura's head as she jogged along the dark forest path. She had her hood on and her iPod earbuds in her ears. She just passed the last bend in the road before the long straight stretch that passed below the rundown farmhouse. Her thoughts were everywhere, except for the *here and now*, and she almost collided with the man in the brown parka, who appeared out of nowhere at that very moment.

She stopped, startled. Her heart made a little leap. She pulled the plugs out of her ears and now stood panting in front of the man who'd crossed her path in such a clumsy way.

"Whoa, you scared me!" she gasped.

The man in the brown parka grinned. He'd pulled up the hood, his eyes hidden in the shadow. An ugly three-day beard grew on his cheeks and around his pale lips. He seemed scary. Laura didn't know him but suspected he was one of the men who'd been staring at her the other day.

"I'm sorry," he said. His voice was deep and somehow toneless. The rain pelted down on his hood and dripped on his shoulders, which seemed quite wide in the thick parka. He stood very close to Laura. She could have touched him if she'd stretched out her arm.

Or he could have touched her.

The thought pierced her coldly and mercilessly.

"I'm looking for my dog," said the guy with the toneless voice.

"Did you see one back there?" He stretched out his arm now, but without touching her. He pointed the direction she'd come from. "A St. Bernard. Pretty big. He ran away earlier. An old dog that's slowly going mad. I'm afraid he might attack someone."

His words made Laura shiver. Big St. Bernard. Old and crazy. Could attack someone. She involuntarily thought of Stephen King's *Cujo*. Goosebumps crept over her back.

"No, I didn't see anything," she said truthfully.

"That's strange," he replied. "Because he ran exactly in that direction." He pointed again with his arm.

"Uhm, well, I dunno, maybe …" Laura said.

Right at that moment, the guy lifted his arm. The hood

slipped off his head and exposed his bald skull. His piercing blue eyes narrowed.

"Oh shit," he shouted, and the saliva sprayed from his lips.

Laura felt the disgusting wetness on her forehead.

"What's he doing?" He sounded completely panicky. And that's how he looked. His eyes were fixed on something behind Laura's back. Whatever there was to see.

And Laura did what anyone would have done in that situation. It was a reflex she couldn't control, yet she'd later hate herself for it. She'd never be able to forgive herself for falling for Toni Singer's diversionary maneuver so easily, even though she wouldn't have had a chance anyway.

Now she made it very easy for him by turning around to see what had apparently upset him so much.

Then everything happened in a fraction of a second.

While Laura turned around, expecting to see a mangy, possibly rabid monster of a dog, she was brutally grabbed from behind. She felt something soft and at the same time hard around her neck, and she realized seconds later that it was the man's arm. The pressure on her larynx was hard and relentless. She couldn't breathe, couldn't even think of screaming, couldn't swallow. Something pointed drilled into her back. At first Laura thought of the teeth of the St. Bernard, but a crazy dog would probably have been the least evil.

"What you're feeling is a knife," said the man—now very close to her ear. His stubble tickled her cheek.

Laura froze. She felt something inside her giving in, and only much later would she'd notice that she'd peed her pants at that moment. Her knees became soft, as did her intestines, not to mention the region between her legs. Everything was soft and light and somehow moist

and warm and yet cold again—ice cold!

A noise came out of her throat without her realizing it. The grip around her neck became looser; she could gasp for air. Just for a moment. The tip of the knife drilled painfully into her flesh. Laura had no idea if he'd already hurt her. Was she bleeding?

"I'll stab you, girl, I don't care! I'll kill you as soon as you make even one wrong move! And don't you dare to scream. You'd regret it, believe me."

Laura couldn't answer. She couldn't move. Her body felt light and heavy at the same time. Paralyzed! She could only wait and see what came next.

"We're going for a little walk now," the man whispered in her ear. And she still felt his cheek on hers. It scratched and tickled.

"We're going up to the house. I think you know which one I mean. You do what I tell you and don't make a sound or I'll cut your spine! You understand that, girl?"

Yes, she did. She understood perfectly! Laura wouldn't make a sound. She'd do anything this man wanted, so that he wouldn't hurt her. He'd probably rape her. She was pretty sure it would happen. But she'd somehow be able to stand it. She had no choice. She'd obey him. Only then she might have a chance of getting out of this alive.

Alive? a mean little voice whispered in her head. *You really think he'll let you live? You know exactly where he lives and who he is. You really think he plans to let you go after he fucks you? Oh girl, how naive are you? This guy will kill you. He'll rape you and then stab you. You know the stories, don't you? You know exactly what'll happen: raped, stabbed, buried in the forest.*

Even the location was perfect, not to mention the old rotten house. A perfect place to die, plus a perfect forest to hide the body.

She kicked herself for running around out there. How

stupid, especially after finding everything about the house and those guys so scary.

How often did he watch her? she wondered. For how long? How long before he came up with this idea? How often did you let him stare at your ass out here in the woods? You could have sent him an invitation right away. Oh Laura, how could you be so stupid? Every little kid knows what creepy men in lonely woods do to little girls, right? We all know that! Oh Laura, it's all over now. Now you'll pay for being so stupid! And he will do bad things to you! You can see it in his face. He will hurt you terribly before he slits you open at the end. You'll probably even beg for your death, yes, you will! And who is to blame besides you? You stupid, stupid girl.

All these thoughts roared in Laura's head as she slowly walked along the muddy path, through the rain, toward the house. At first she thought her legs would just give way and she wouldn't be able to take a step, but then it somehow worked out, although now she couldn't feel anything from the belly down. Everything down there had somehow floated away.

The man was so close behind her that she felt his heat. His arm was still around her neck, but he'd loosened the grip a bit. With every step the knife drilled into her back. She felt him bumping against her again and again as they walked, she heard his hectic breath, tasted the bitter aroma of panic in her mouth that wasn't able to scream for help. Did she have a chance? If somebody would suddenly appear—another jogger, a walker, the ranger—Laura would be saved and her kidnapper would be fucked. That was his risk and Laura's last glimmer of hope.

Someone will show up soon! Then this guy will let me go and he'll run away as fast as he can.

Everything will be fine. Yes, in the end everything will be fine be-

cause something like this can't happen to me. Impossible!

Laura got so involved with this idea that for a moment she actually believed she saw someone. Right over there! A man with his dog! Or was it a woman in a jogging suit? An old lady with an umbrella? A young man with a stroller?

***

It was almost five and already dark on this rainy afternoon in December. Toni had taken a more or less calculable risk. Sure, it could've gone wrong. He could've been discovered and then he'd have needed some good advice. No excuse in the world would have saved him from this situation. They probably would have arrested him for attempted kidnapping. Tough luck! No risk, no fun.

But in the end, Laura was the unlucky one, which had been the more likely option from the start. They reached the Singer house without being seen. It had only taken four minutes. Four minutes that decided Laura Hermann's future.

She wanted to scream when they finally stood in front of the door. It would be her last chance to be heard before the devil's house swallowed her up. She took a deep breath.

The man seemed to read her mind because suddenly the knife was at her throat. Laura swallowed the scream with a thick lump of fear. Tears shot into her eyes.

"Open the door!" Toni commanded. There was no mercy in his voice.

Laura stretched out a trembling hand and put it on the rusty door handle. "Please … pleasepleaseplease," she whimpered.

"Open the door!"

She pushed the handle down and the door opened as if it were the gate to hell.

Laura looked into a dark hallway. The blackness seemed to swallow everything. The man pushed her inside and slammed the door behind them. Laura sobbed. From the corner of her eye she saw shoes, boxes, piles of newspapers, and even more boxes. She saw ancient wooden planks. Shadows crawled everywhere. It was so dark.

Toni pushed her forward to a staircase. It was one of those old wooden spiral staircases, like they had in very old farmhouses. It wound its way up into complete darkness. Her kidnapper gave her a push. "Go up there!"

He let go of her. Finally!

The arm had disappeared and so had the knife. Laura turned around carefully, one hand already on the worn wooden railing. It smelled musty in here. Old and damp somehow.

And there was something else she couldn't define at the moment. A penetrating, somehow sweetish smell. She looked at her kidnapper. His eyes flashed. The bald head glistened with wetness.

"Please let me go," she implored.

He smiled and put a big heavy hand on her shoulder. Heavy and big, like himself. Laura estimated him to be at least six feet two, probably two hundred pounds, broad and muscular. She had no chance against him. Not physically!

"Please … I … I'll do anything you want if you let me go … I won't tell anybody—I promise!"

He was still smiling. His hand pressed her shoulder. Almost gently. "You'll actually do anything I want, sweetheart, but I won't let you go."

Laura stared at him. Tears ran down her face. She

shook her head. "Please. Please!"

Her kidnapper also shook his head as he slowly but vigorously pushed her forward. "Forget it. You'll still need your energy today."

With these words he directed her up the old creaking staircase.

And hours later it would be the same stairs and the same day, but not the same girl who ascended this staircase now.

***

He took her to a dark room that must have been his bedroom. A large double bed stood in front of a small window, a low, old-fashioned wooden cupboard in the corner. The cracked floorboards were covered with a large, colorful patchwork carpet that actually looked quite pretty. Laura's gaze scurried upward. The ceiling was made of wood. Dark. Low. The guy had to duck his head. He seemed used to it. He pressed a light switch next to the door, and an ugly old-fashioned lamp next to the bed threw its dirty yellow light into the room. The world outside the window was dark.

"Stay there!" he ordered, as Laura stood right in the middle of the patchwork rug. Her sneakers had left traces of mud. Just like the man's shoes.

He went to the bed, knelt on it, and closed the curtains. They were brown and as ugly as everything in this terrible house.

Now he took off his jacket and sat on the edge of the bed. He wore a simple black T-shirt. His shoulders were indeed very wide. His arms were muscular, pale, and covered with countless tattoos.

Laura stood on the carpet about three feet away and

stared at him. He stared back. He licked his lips. His eyes were shining. Then he reached back and pulled the T-shirt over his bald head.

Laura couldn't stop staring. His upper body was pale, his chest almost hairless, his navel a bit more. Laura swallowed. Suddenly she realized her underpants were wet. She'd pissed herself. She blushed.

He looked at her from head to toe. "Your turn!"

Laura hesitated. She didn't move and barely dared breathe.

"Come on," he growled at her. "Undress!"

Laura took a hectic look at his knife lying next to him on the bed. The bedding was blue with white stripes. Jacket and knife didn't really fit there. Laura risked another, even more hectic look over her shoulder … to the door. It was closed, but she was sure he hadn't locked it. She could try to escape, could run away, now or never, but he'd catch her easily. She had no chance, probably wouldn't even make it to the door before he grabbed her. And then what? Surely he'd hurt her. Much worse than he certainly intended to do now. So it was better to cooperate. Right?

Slowly she raised her hands, unzipped her anorak, and took it off. She wore a gray sweatshirt underneath.

He watched and waited.

Laura took off her sneakers.

"Keep going!"

She put the iPod aside and pulled the sweater over her head.

Now she stood there in a white top and her sweatpants. The sports bra. Panties. Socks.

He leaned back a bit. He seemed to be sweating, although Laura found it bitterly cold. She could see a bulge in his crotch that was (*maybe … no, please no, please no, dear*

God) his penis.

I've never undressed in front of a man and I've never seen one naked in front of me. Don't let him be the first one! Please, dear God, do something so this guy won't be the first guy I have to do these things with! Oh please! Oh please, please don't!

"Everything!"

Laura was weeping and pleading. "Please don't … please …"

"Stop that begging, girl! You do what I tell you! Shut your mouth! If you have to open it again, I'll let you know!" He grinned angrily. Something flickered in his eyes.

Laura suppressed a sob. She took off her top. He stared at her breasts. She bent down trembling and pulled the socks off her feet. It was so cold! Now she stood there only in underwear and felt horribly exposed. The carpet was strangely rough and bumpy against the soles of her feet. Her trembling became stronger. It crawled through her body like an evil virus.

Now he rose, came closer. *God, he's so big!* Laura whimpered, could no longer control the trembling.

"Take your clothes off, or I'll help you," he shouted at her.

Laura obeyed. She took off her bra and tried to cover her breasts with one hand while pulling down her wet panties with the other. Then she straightened up again, looking at the floor. Her cheeks glowed. Her breasts weighed heavily, and she was aware of every little movement. She pressed one hand in front of them as well as she could, and behind the other hand she hid her sex.

Her kidnapper was now so close that he could have touched her. He didn't. Not yet! His breath went fast, wheezing. The bulge in his pants was huge.

"Put your arms down."

Laura forced herself to comply. Tears and snot dripped from her nose and ran into her mouth. She tasted the salt and the fear.

Now he touched her. He stretched out both hands. They glided from her bare shoulders over her collarbone and finally reached her breasts. He pinched her nipples, gently at first, and then harder. Laura flinched, suppressing a scream. She pressed her lips together and stared at the carpet, studying every fiber, every knot …

He kneaded her breasts. His hands were warm, rough, and callused. He scratched, pinched, kneaded, and squeezed as his breath grew faster and faster while he pressed himself closer and closer against her. Laura's nipples became hard and erect, but this was only due to the pain and cold. It seemed to make her tormentor even hornier. He worked Laura's nipples until they began to bleed. She managed to stand still, counting the knots in the carpet and gritting her teeth. At some point he'd have to stop. He couldn't go on forever. She only had to endure it a little longer, and then it would pass. Like at the dentist.

He lowered his head, and now she felt his stubble on her bare skin. She smelled him—his sweat, and something like garlic on his breath. He brutally grabbed her right breast and pushed the nipple into his mouth, sucking on it first and then pulling it between his teeth and biting it. Laura moaned. That hurt!

She raised her arms, grabbed him by the shoulders, and tried to push him away. He let go of her, but only to punch her right in the face with his fist. Laura staggered. Everything turned to black before her eyes. She stumbled backward and hit her back against something hard. Her legs gave way, and she sank to the ground.

He was over her and kicked her belly with the heavy

work boots. Laura writhed. He kicked again. This time with the tip of his shoe between her thighs. The pain was unspeakable. An explosion in her intestines. Now Laura screamed. He grabbed her by the hair and brutally pulled her back to her feet.

"Look at me, girl!"

Laura wavered. She tried to stand straight and raise her gaze, but the pain brought her to her knees again. He immediately grabbed her by the hair again, pulled her up.

"Stand still and look at me!"

Laura forced herself to obey. Blood ran from her nose and dripped from her chin on her breasts. Again he lowered his head and started sucking, nibbling, biting them. This time she pulled herself together and let him. It seemed to take an eternity for him to finish. The pain was terrible—all over her body, but especially in her breasts. Her nipples were bleeding.

"And now get on your knees!"

She sank to her knees, and he stepped in front of her until her face was right in front of his crotch. "Open it!"

With trembling fingers she fumbled with his zipper. Finally she managed to open it.

He pulled his pants down himself. Laura saw checkered boxer shorts … and then this huge penis. Never before had she had a man in front of her. She knew all about it, of course. But only from biology classes and the few pornos she'd watched on the Internet with Annika. And of course from the teen mag BRAVO. But not so … so close, so huge! She stared at that thing and just couldn't believe she had to get acquainted in this terrible way with something she'd longed for so long.

"Come on. Take it in your mouth! It won't get any bigger!"

Laura hesitated. She couldn't do that. Now she not on-

ly saw the thing right in front of her but smelled it. Sour nausea rose in her throat. She swallowed several times to suppress it.

"I … I've never done anything like this before," she whispered.

He laughed. "I'll teach you, girl! Don't worry!" He touched himself and pulled the foreskin back a bit. With the other hand he grabbed Laura's head. Her lips collided with his disgustingly wet glans.

"Open your mouth. Now!"

The wet tip of his penis rubbed against her lips. Laura closed her eyes and opened her mouth, and the penis disappeared almost completely in it. She choked and had to cough, but now he wouldn't let her go. He held her head firmly and rammed it violently back and forth. Laura's mouth was completely filled with this huge thing. She breathed frantically through bloated nostrils as she tasted salty slime that made her choke again.

Her tormentor didn't care. He just rammed his thing deeper and deeper into her throat and gave her orders like: "Go! suck it!" or "I wanna feel your tongue!"

She had no idea how long it took. At some point his motions became faster, jerkier. He gasped and groaned. Seconds later he came into her mouth.

Laura was horrified. She choked and swallowed, choked again, and could finally breathe freely again. Her throat burned. She tasted him. Everything in her mouth now tasted like him. She choked again but somehow managed not to vomit.

"All right, girl, that was your dinner." He laughed. "And hole number one, that's all mine now. With this it is solemnly inaugurated."

She was still kneeling in front of him and staring at the floor, counting again the knots of the carpet. There was a

strange emptiness in her head. *It ain't over yet!*

He pulled up his pants and walked past her to the closet. Laura heard him rummaging around. She didn't look. She felt like she was wrapped in cotton wool—dull and miles away.

"Hands behind your back!"

He was back, grabbing her wrists. Something cool and metallic closed around them. Handcuffs! These handcuffs sealed her helplessness. *It ain't over yet!*

She knelt stark naked on a colorful patchwork carpet and had her hands shackled behind her back. She felt dull pain all over her body where he'd scratched, pinched, bitten, and kicked her. Her mouth was filled with the stale, salty taste of his sperm. She felt so incredibly dirty! Could it get any worse?

Laura lowered her head and waited. What else could she do?

He sat on the edge of the bed again and watched her … like a wild animal watched its prey.

His lips formed a victorious smile. He'd made it. He had her exactly where he wanted her. His plan had worked out.

"You've got fucking awesome tits," he said approvingly. He sounded satisfied, completely at peace with himself. "Sexy, big solid boobs, just the way I like them. They belong to me now. You belong to me now. Everything on and in you. Each of your orifices is only there to serve me as a fuckhole. You understand? The sooner you realize that, the better for you. I won't treat you well, but I'll treat you even worse the more you fight back. So let it be! Just accept it. You have no choice anyway."

She heard yet didn't hear him. What he said came to

her ears but somehow not her brain. He took the knife, rose, stood in front of her. Through a veil of tears Laura saw his shoes now touching her knees.

"Look at me!"

She raised her head, blinked, his face blurred before her eyes.

"I'm taking your stuff with me to burn it. From now on you'll wear nothing but the chains I put on you."

What did he say? She heard it but didn't understand a word!

Silently, she watched as he picked up her clothes and the iPod and then left the room. This time she heard the sound of the key as he locked the door.

Laura Hermann curled up on the carpet and made herself as small as possible.

From her throat came a painful whimper that hardly sounded human.

***

Toni stood in the kitchen smoking and with a beer in his hand. He felt great.

The thought that she was now lying up there in his bedroom, naked and handcuffed, completely at his mercy, made his cock immediately hard.

He'd just had the orgasm of his life. Not because the little one could suck cock so well (she definitely couldn't) but because he'd forced her to!

He'd rammed his cock into her mouth until she almost puked and then squirted explosively in her throat, and she had to swallow every single drop of his juice. Because he wanted it! She was his little fuck-toy—from now and forever.

It had actually worked out. Everything had been exact-

ly the way he'd imagined it in his dreams.

Now she was finally here and belonged to him.

The idea made him dizzy. At this minute he could go to her and simply do everything imaginable (and above everything unthinkable) with her. Awesome! He greedily gulped down his beer, burped, took a second bottle from the fridge, and lit another cigarette. He thought of his sweet little fuck-toy and the way it had looked, seen from above, on her knees, with his cock in its mouth.

How it had whined … and moaned … begged and pleaded … how these incredibly hot tits had felt when he made the tender warts bleed. They were hard, yes they were. So his fuck-toy had had fun!

Good God, nothing in life had ever been so great! He'd never come close to this feeling with any of his former bitches.

Toni licked his lips. His dick was throbbing. Fuckin' hell! Was that supposed to be a permanent condition now? He grinned. He had no objections. He closed his eyes, saw his little naked fuck-toy crouching on the floor in front of him, and rubbed his crotch with pleasure. Everything inside him was in an uproar. He was running on full blast. It was about time! Yes, after this little refreshment, it was time to finally fuck her properly.

Toni emptied the second bottle of beer and put out his cigarette in a hopelessly overfilled ashtray. He burped once more and then went for a piss before going upstairs.

***

It cried. Of course! His little fuck-toy lay on the carpet and wept. The nose was covered with blood. The tits had slipped to the side and somehow seemed too big compared to the slim body. Yes, his fuck-toy was small and

slim. Thin. Very thin. You could see almost all the bones. Toni generally preferred curves, but with his new toy, he liked exactly the way she was. Somehow it seemed even more helpless. It wouldn't get much to eat. Just enough that the tits remained nicely plump.

He squatted, pushed the sticky hair from the swollen, blood-stained face. She rolled her eyes, didn't want to look at him. Toni pulled her hair until she screamed softly.

"Look at me!"

She rolled her eyes once again, closed them briefly, and finally looked at him. Toni didn't think her face was particularly pretty, but it didn't matter.

"I'll fuck you now."

She stared at him, but said nothing. Apparently she began to understand.

Toni stood up and pulled her hair until she stood on her feet, whimpering. She trembled like an aspen leaf. And cried. Of course! Why did women always have to cry? Why couldn't anybody tell them that this whining was ugly and damn unsexy?

Sighing, he took a look between her legs. Was the little bitch still a virgin? Her pussy was shaved like with most of the sluts he'd seen before. Who did they do that for, if not for a guy?

Toni stretched out his hand and drilled a finger between the soft labia, touched the clitoris, rubbed it … but apart from tears and trembling, his fuck-toy showed no reaction. He pushed one finger into her hole, then a second one. With the third it became difficult. She moaned in pain. She was really damn tight and dry down there. But that would change soon.

"You've got a great fuckhole there! We'll just have to stretch it a bit!" He grinned, pulled out his fingers, and

smelled them.

"Hm, pretty tasty."

She was silent.

Toni laughed and undressed. This time he took off all his clothes, except for the socks. His boner throbbed hard and demanding.

He directed his toy to the bed and let it lie on its belly over the edge, its face on a pillow, its feet on the floor, its hands on its back, in its expensive handcuffs. The investment had already paid off. His little fuck-toy looked gorgeous. How horny would it make him to see it hang helplessly from the ceiling in the basement? The throbbing in his cock became more demanding.

"Spread your legs!"

She obeyed. Now he could look directly into the little hole. Once again he tried with his fingers … two, three … but then his lust gained the upper hand. He gently pressed his glans against the orifice, plunged in, found pleasure in the tightness … and rammed his cock into it.

She screamed. Of course! He thrust again, brutally, deeply, felt moisture as the hymen tore. She screamed louder. He put one hand on the back of her head, pressed her face into the pillow. Better, much better! And then he fucked her and felt like God.

Toni fucked his new bitch hard and long. Hole number two was officially declared open. And while he was fucking her like no other before, he stuck his thumb into hole number three. Stretched it, smeared it with his seed that shot out of him like hot magma, and finally buried his still-hard cock in her ass. He pushed her head further into the pillow, gave her just a second to catch her breath, and fucked her asshole until he got tired and limp.

Then he released the back of her head. She reared up, opened her mouth, and inhaled greedily. That was very

convenient for Toni. He held his half-slackened penis in front of her face. Blood, sperm, and excrement stuck to it.

"You've made it all dirty ... you'll have to clean it." He pushed his cock between her lips.

"Lick it clean—it's your dirt after all."

And Laura Hermann had to lick for a long time until her tormentor was satisfied.

***

When Toni was finally done, he took her downstairs.

To the basement.

Laura noticed it only vaguely. She couldn't think straight anymore. Her head was empty, and the pain raged in her body. A pain that was much stronger than any thought could have been. There was no place in her brain for brilliant flashes of genius anymore. Maybe it was better that way. The pain down there was unimaginable. It pounded and burned as if everything was shredded.

Laura didn't know what hurt more, her ass or her pussy. Both seemed to have turned into a single feverishly throbbing, furiously raging mass. She didn't think it would ever stop. She didn't think she'd ever be able to sit or use the toilet again. Would she ever feel anything other than that abnormal pain down there?

It went up to the abdomen, which had become painfully cramped like with a gastrointestinal infection. Her restrained arms also hurt, as did her face, mouth, pelvis, and legs, which had been spread beyond the threshold of pain.

But this pain was a ridiculous nothing compared to the torments that raged in the middle of her body. Besides, there was this terrible taste in her mouth. A mixture of

his body fluids and her feces, which she'd licked from his cock. Laura didn't want to think about it, but she did. In the end, she'd do anything he told her to do, if only he'd leave her alone, as soon as he'd let off steam on and in her. She'd hopefully become boring for him then. Hopefully!

She hobbled down the stairs to the basement and felt the cold concrete floor under her bare feet. Her tormentor walked close behind her and held her upper arms in the iron grip of his big hands. She didn't even know his name.

He doesn't know yours either, Laura Hermann. He didn't ask because he doesn't want to know, because you're his damn fuckhole, no more and no less. Fuckholes have no names, no minds, and no feelings … fuckholes are simply there for you to stick things into them and make them bleed. That's how it is, Laura, you now have a job, a destiny! You're no longer Laura Hermann, not even Laura, but just a fuckhole … Welcome to your new life!

He'd dressed again in the meantime, while Laura was still stark naked and freezing pitifully. As she descended the stairs, something warm and sticky ran over the inside of her thighs. Probably blood, but it could have been anything. She didn't have time to check, and she didn't want to.

They came to a massive iron door that Toni had installed. He let her go so he could rummage in his pockets for the key. He found it quickly and opened the door. He pushed Laura into a room that couldn't have been more desolate, colder, and more horrible. There was hardly any light, just a cobweb-covered naked light bulb on the low ceiling. Everything was made of gray concrete, only the walls seemed to have been covered with something that looked like foam. In one corner lay a mattress that was stiff with dirt. No sheets. No pillow. No blanket.

There were two buckets next to it. That was all.

As she came closer, Laura saw that one bucket was empty, while the other was filled with (probably? hopefully!) water.

There was an iron ring in the floor, a massive chain was attached to it, which in turn was attached to a pair of handcuffs.

"Sit down there!" He gave her a rough push and Laura landed astride on the mattress, half sitting, half lying. She remained in this position.

"Look at me!"

She forced herself to raise her gaze. He stood with his legs apart above her and looked at her with a pejorative smile. Laura no longer cared that she was completely naked and that he could look directly between her legs and at her breasts. After everything he'd just done to her, it didn't really matter anymore. There was nothing about her he hadn't seen before. And not only that …

"From now on, you're mine. I don't expect you to understand that immediately. So pay attention! Here's the rules: You'll live down here. Okay? You can shit and piss in the bucket over there and drink from the other one, which you'll also use for washing. You'll eat from a bowl or from the floor like a dog, without using your hands. To make sure you learn this immediately, I'll leave your handcuffs on for now. Maybe we can talk about it later, if you perform well. We can also talk about a blanket then. You won't get one at first, so you'll learn what it means to suffer like a dog. You gotta learn what it means to respect your master and do everything to his satisfaction. As soon as this has worked out for a few days, we'll see. Then maybe you can come back upstairs to the house from time to time. Of course this is as it should be for a dirty bitch—on all fours and on a leash."

He laughed. "You'll see how well you'll obey me soon."

He bent over and stroked her head. Laura sharply sucked in the air. She'd have preferred to flinch, but she forced herself to stay calm.

He'll leave soon, she thought, full of hope. *He'll be gone in a moment.*

Tears ran down her face.

Grinning, he took his hand away and bent over the shackles, which she had initially taken for handcuffs, and put them around her ankles.

"Be my good little fuckhole and my bitch in heat, and then I'll take good care of you."

He stroked her again. It hurt so much!

Then he turned around to leave. He left the light on.

Laura waited until he had closed the door and the sound of his heavy footsteps on the stairs had stopped before she curled up like a fetus on the damp mattress and thought of nothing but pain.

***

Karl lay on his bed and covered his ears when his brother next door raped the girl. It didn't help much. He could still hear them—her crying and sobbing, and his groaning.

But it wasn't as loud as he'd thought it would be. It was relatively quiet, and Karl wondered if Toni had gagged the girl while she endured torments he didn't want to think about. He didn't know exactly what Toni did to her, but he knew the videos his brother loved to watch. You didn't really need to know more.

Karl had watched through the window as his brother had caught the girl and brought her to the house. She

hadn't stood a chance. Although Karl had hoped fate would be merciful and let someone come along at the last moment—a walker, a jogger, a ranger, the Lord Jesus himself, just someone who would have prevented the inevitable. Someone who wouldn't let his insane brother grab this poor, innocent girl to make her the plaything of his perverse fantasies. But no one had come. Nobody was there. Except for Karl.

He'd watched Toni enter the house with the girl and then had eavesdropped. The sound of footsteps on the stairs. The occasional sobbing and whimpering of the girl, a few screams in between—God alone knew how much he pitied the poor thing.

Karl had been surprised when his brother didn't take her straight to the basement. It was probably too cold and dirty for him there. At some point, however, he'd heard them coming out of the room and walking down the stairs. And he'd heard the girl crying. Toni gave instructions and his voice trembled with excitement. He'd probably just had the time of his life. Karl shuddered.

He'd waited until there was nothing more to hear and closed his eyes. He just wanted to sleep and forget everything. He wanted to forget what he'd seen and heard. Was that asking too much?

There was no light on in the room, and the darkness had spread like a musty black cloth. Karl kept his eyes closed and tried not to think of anything. He wanted to sleep. Just sleep. No more thoughts of the wailing girl who had his brother's cock in her mouth like a disgusting lollipop. No more thoughts of his mother rotting only two rooms away, eaten by her cats. It was so easy to forget everything when you could finally sleep.

Karl really tried, but he had no luck. So he finally got up and went down to the kitchen to get a glass of water.

***

Toni sat in front of the TV drinking beer. He wore boxer shorts and slippers. His face was red.

He looked up and grinned as he noticed Karl standing stiff as a stick in the door staring at him.

"Shit, man, that was the hottest fuck ever!" Toni rubbed his crotch.

Karl was silent but felt something working inside him. His temples pounded painfully. He clenched his teeth.

"She's downstairs now. In her room." Toni laughed. "If you're a good boy, maybe I'll let you have some fun with her sometime."

Karl gasped for air like a fish on dry land. His lungs burned. "Never in my life would I do such a thing. You are such a … bastard!"

Toni continued to scratch his crotch. He was totally unimpressed. "And what are you going to do about it now, my dear brother?"

"I could do many things."

"Oh yes? Tell me! I'm really curious."

"What if I call the police? Right now. They'll arrest you, man!"

Toni disparagingly swayed his head. "Uhm, okay … that's what you wanna do? But you know who they'll find besides the little cunt, right? I hope that won't be a problem for you, Karl. Especially when I tell them how you should take care of Mama, how you even took money for it, but you actually let our poor mother die like an animal! I can tell them, right? And how you left her lying there in that room so no one would ever know and the damn cats would be able to eat her before they tear each other apart. Surely I'm allowed to tell all that. Right, Karli? You only

did it because you wanted to continue cashing in the money and the pension, because you're too lazy to drag your fat ass to work! That's right, Karli, do we agree on that?"

Karl slowly shook his head. His expression was full of horror as he pictured his mother in front of him again. Probably only a skeleton with some rotten flesh was left of her.

"You … you won't do that. You know it was your idea to leave her in there. You … you made me do it, Toni! And it's you and not me who's taking all the money!"

"It's all registered in your name, baby!" Toni taunted.

"But you know I didn't want any of this … with Mama!"

"Yeah, I know that, Karl. But they won't know, and I'll make sure they won't find out. You'll be the one who's responsible. You and nobody else. With a bit of luck, I'll even make you responsible for what happened to the girl!"

"You can't. All the evidence speaks against you. And she can tell them who it was."

Toni shrugged. "If she still can talk by then, sure."

"What does that mean?"

"Just stay calm and take care of your own shit and everything will be fine. Don't start threatening me with cops or shit, or I'll kill you. I mean that, Karl! I'll beat you up so badly that you don't even remember your name, my dear brother. Just don't forget where your place is, and everything will be fine. But if you stab me in the back, you'll regret it bitterly."

Karl didn't say anything. The thoughts somersaulted in his head. Above all, he thought of his mother and what she might look like by now. What was left of her? He prayed to God that he'd never have to find out.

"Now come here and have a beer with me. This was a very successful day, and I wanna celebrate that!"

Karl obeyed. He simply didn't know any better.

***

Karl was allowed to drink exactly one beer and watch half of an action movie, of which he didn't understand much of the sparse plot. They sat silently next to each other on the couch. Karl tried to ignore the penetrating smells of his brother. It was a mixture of old and new sweat and other body fluids. Karl called it a 'sex smell'. Human genitals smelled like that when stimulated. He smelled that way when masturbating. Even (God forbid!) Mama's vagina had sometimes smelled like that when he washed her.

It was an aroma you couldn't really describe. Partly disgusting and partly pleasant, depending on who you noticed it on and in what kind of situation.

So while sitting next to his brother and drinking beer, Karl formulated a thought that couldn't be more logical and cruel: After raping someone, you don't smell any different than after normal sex.

He secretly watched Toni, who looked like always. The skin on his face and upper body seemed flawless. No scratches or bruises. That meant she hadn't fought back. He hadn't given her a chance.

He'd probably tied her up before he abused her. Was she still shackled? Had he left her naked and tied up down there in the cold?

Karl knew it might be a mistake to ask him, but he couldn't help it. "Did you give her a blanket?"

Toni obviously didn't want to be disturbed while watching the film. Reluctantly he looked at Karl. His eyes

were small and bloodshot. He'd already drunk a lot. "What?"

"Did you give the girl a blanket? It's freezing cold down there."

Toni grinned. "What do you think, huh? She's in the learning phase. It's like properly training a dog. First she has to learn who's her boss. She gets nothing from me the first night. She's naked and tied up. The next few hours won't be nice for her. But tomorrow she'll make all the more effort to please me so that I might be a bit nicer to her."

He laughed and patted Karl on the thigh. "You've got no idea, kiddo!"

Karl clenched his fingers around his beer bottle until they hurt. "And if … if she gets sick?"

"She can take it, don't worry. You'll probably be amazed at what a person can endure, little brother."

And Toni should be right.

***

In the beginning she concentrated on the pain in her body, which was really everywhere and took her breath away in the truest sense of the word. There was her nose, of course, which had almost broken under his punch. Laura still tasted the blood, mixed with the sticky and salty aroma of his sperm and the disgusting taste of her feces.

It felt like it was all still somehow stuck between her teeth and on her tongue. It stuck to her throat, and every time she swallowed, she had a disgusting-tasting lump in her throat. Thick spit had formed in the corners of her mouth, and Laura feared she'd never get rid of the rank taste.

And then there was the pain in her abdomen, her vagina, and her butt. Fluid still seeped out of her. She would have liked to have touched herself there, gently palpating everything, but her hands were cuffed behind her back. She could only move her fingers a little. But she felt them less and less, and her arms were numb. Laura almost welcomed this numbness. She longed for this dull feeling to take possession of her body. Then she'd no longer feel pain or anything.

She lay on her side and pulled up her knees as high as her shackles would allow. In this position the pain in her abdomen was more bearable. And so was the cold.

All this was so overwhelming that Laura didn't notice the cold until much later. How long had she been down here?

She'd just closed her eyes for the first time and perhaps slept for a fraction of a second. Or longer?

The cold now spread to her limbs like an evil animal. She trembled. Her teeth chattered uncontrollably. Her legs felt like icicles. Not only her legs. The pain receded into the background. Was that possible? The cold was now the most powerful component of all suffering.

Laura whimpered. She tried to curl up, but since she couldn't wrap her arms around herself, she was helplessly at the mercy of the bitter cold. She was the helpless victim of that evil man who had brought her here and hurt her so terribly.

Laura wondered what time it was now and whether her family was already worried. How long would it take until they'd start searching for her? And where would they search? Would they even come up with the idea of looking for her on this path, in this forest? Did her parents even know that she jogged here? She couldn't remember ever having talked to them about it. She'd mentioned jog-

ging, but she didn't know if she'd discussed her route.

Only Annika might know. She'd once talked to her about this forest. Right? Maybe even about the lonely house and the two strange men? No, she'd considered telling Annika about the men, but then she hadn't. Dear God, why hadn't she told her friend? And why had she continued jogging this stretch at all, even though the house had been so creepy—just like the two guys?

Two guys … *two*! Yes, there had been two who had come out of the house and then sat in the car. Where was the second guy? Did he know she was here? Were they accomplices? Would the other guy also come to hurt her? When? Maybe tonight? Or did he not live here at all and had only been a visitor? That would be possible. Everything was possible! Maybe tomorrow morning they'd come in twos to take turns raping her. Or at the same time!

Maybe they'll kill me!

But that wasn't his intention, right? Laura remembered the man's last words before he'd left her alone down here. She'd be his good little fuckhole, then he'd take good care of her. Give her a blanket or take her upstairs into the house. On all fours. Like a dog. That's what he'd said, and that's what he seemed to have in mind. He didn't want to kill her but to keep her here like an animal. Even worse! He wanted to rape her. Again and again. That's what he'd hinted at. That's what was in store for her. Whether he'd do it alone or together with someone else didn't really matter. Silent tears ran down Laura's now bluish face. That should be her life now, if nobody found her here? She'd vegetate like a caged animal and be abused every day by this sick swine? Or by his buddy, or both?

"Oh please, please, get me out of here! Please, Mama,

find me and get me out of here! Oh God, please!"

Laura whimpered with her blood-smeared mouth into the dirty mattress, but nobody heard her.

Nobody?

***

Toni wanted him to clean up the kitchen. Karl spent about half an hour scraping leftovers from pots and pans, and he was more or less successful. Then he sneaked to the door, which was only half-closed, and secretly looked into the living room. Toni had collapsed on the couch. His chin was on his chest, his eyes were closed, and he snored quietly. Some empty beer bottles lay at his feet. More bottles stood on the coffee table. He'd had enough. For today.

Karl breathed a sigh of relief. Toni didn't usually wake up too fast once he was drunk enough. He probably wouldn't move before ten tomorrow morning.

Karl hung the stained towel over a chair and quietly left the kitchen.

The hallway was dark. It smelled bad. Karl turned on the light. The shadows withdrew into the corners. On the wardrobe lay a plastic bag that hadn't been there this morning. Karl looked inside. He pulled out a white iPod and put it on the floor. Inside was a white anorak with a hood, a gray sweatshirt (it smelled really good, of perfume), a white top with thin straps, gray jogging pants in size S, a white bra (not so sexy, rather athletic), pink Adidas sneakers (size seven), and white sports socks (also Adidas). Karl put everything on the scratched floor. Now there was only one crumpled little thing left in the bag. Karl grabbed it, his heart jumped. It was a panty. So small. All white. He held it up and pulled the thin fabric

apart, wanted to smell it but didn't. A tremor went through his body. He swallowed, held his breath, smelled it now. He couldn't help it. It had been too long since he'd last smelled a girl. Damn long ago!

He held the panties under his nose and took a deep breath. It smelled sweet, mmm, delicious. Of girls. Of a woman. Of pussy. Karl pressed the cloth to his nose and inhaled the smell of this strange girl, of which his brother had made extensive use in the last hours. Tears came to his eyes, but he hardly noticed. He breathed in … and out … in … out …

God, that was so good!

At that moment he thought for the first time consciously that there was a naked, tied up girl in the basement who couldn't defend herself and with whom he could do whatever he wanted.

The thought frightened him deeply. He stuffed the panties and the other things back into the bag. Then he pushed the bag into the furthest corner of the closet, behind an old pair of his mother's rubber boots, which had been standing there for years. He jumped to his feet and shook his head, patting the mighty boner in his pants.

I'm not like him! Absolutely not! Never! I'd never do such a thing! And it doesn't excite me! It doesn't excite me at all!

The only thing that had excited him was the smell of the panties. It was normal for a man his age who hadn't had sex in years. At least not real sex. With another person. That wasn't the point either. It wasn't about his own unsatisfied needs, but only about the madness of his brother, which Toni shouldn't get away with. No, he wasn't allowed to do that. Actually!

***

He walked sluggishly as he descended the basement stairs. His movements were those of an old man. He stopped in front of the massive iron door and looked at this steel bulwark. His brother had done an amazingly precise job for someone who wasn't particularly talented in craftsmanship. His madness had driven him to give his best.

Karl bent forward and pressed one ear to the cool iron. He held his breath and listened.

He actually heard something. A weeping. A whimper. Stifled sobbing. Exactly what he'd expected, to be honest. At least she could still make sounds. Karl, who knew his brother quite well, wouldn't have taken that for granted. He was glad she could at least still weep. He felt sorry for her, and the thought of her helpless, hopeless situation no longer triggered any excitement in him, only sadness and pure despair. His erection was gone. Thank God! For a moment Karl remained in this position and listened to the girl's soft wailing on the other side of the door. Then he turned away and went up to his room. It was already after midnight and time to go to bed.

As he lay under his warm blanket ten minutes later, he stared with wide open eyes into the darkness and prayed to God that the girl wouldn't suffer too much from the cold.

His prayers weren't answered this time either.

***

Every time she was about to drift into the desired sleep, something cramped inside her. She flinched, the pain suddenly coming back, and Laura was wide awake. She still had no idea what time it was. Down here it was impossible to tell the difference between day and night. The

constant light of the light bulb was always the same and made it even harder for her to fall asleep. Laura tried to turn around a little and shift her weight somehow, to give her aching limbs at least a little relief, but that didn't work. With her hands cuffed, it was almost impossible to find a comfortable position.

And it was so cold.

Terribly cold.

She was grateful that the feeling of numbness had spread to her arms and shoulders. She didn't think about whether she'd ever be able to move her limbs again. For the moment, she was only interested in the painlessness. Laura closed her teary eyes. She wanted to sleep, to pass out, no matter what, as long as she didn't feel anything, didn't think anything. But she wasn't able to escape into a nirvana outside this hell.

She became more and more aware of the disgusting taste in her mouth, which simply didn't want to vanish. And there was this almost unbearable dryness in her throat. It hurt when she swallowed. Now, a little water would certainly drive away the taste … and the thirst.

There was a bucket of water. At least she hoped there was water in it. It stood right next to a second empty bucket that she was to use as a toilet. Was that right? If she confused something, he'd surely punish her! All she had to do was get on her knees and slide a few feet to the right to reach the bucket. It wouldn't be pleasant, but it was doable. She had to put her head in the bucket and drink from it like a horse. She could drink if she wanted. It would certainly hurt to move and it would hurt even more to crawl over there, but she probably had enough time. She could do it and then she'd feel better.

As soon as she didn't have to taste *him* anymore, she'd definitely be better. Maybe she'd even be able to sleep.

Just a little bit. Until the pain subsided and she could think clearly again. Only until the exhaustion was defeated.

She clenched her teeth and got on her knees. Something wet ran down her legs. Laura cried softly as she slipped off the mattress. The chain between her ankles clanked with every movement. But it wouldn't be a problem because it allowed her enough room to move. Not that it would have helped her much.

It took ages for Laura to reach the bucket. And it hurt. The pain in her raged with every movement. But she made it, put her head in the bucket, and sniffed it like a dog! It smelled quite normal. Just like water. So, actually, of nothing at all. That was good.

There could be poison or drugs in it, she suddenly thought. And only one second later: *Fuck it! That stuff would at least stun or kill me …*

She bent down even further. The bucket was about three-quarters full. Laura's disheveled hair first reached the surface before her lips did. She closed her eyes and opened her mouth. The cool liquid flowed in. Laura groaned, relieved. Not only did it taste normal and good, it tasted delicious. Never in her life had she drunk anything so good. All the pores of her mouth and throat seemed to open to absorb the water. The disgust got washed away. And with it the thirst. She drank and drank. And she was grateful. As grateful as never before.

She was grateful to *him* for leaving the water there. She was happy that *he* had done that for her.

For a few minutes Laura actually forgot everything else he'd done.

The water was there, and only the water was important.

She drank until she felt as if her stomach was going to burst. Then she dragged herself back to the mattress and

dropped.

Sleep came quickly.

It would be short and dreamless.

***

She awoke in the early hours of the morning with no idea what time it was. But Laura knew immediately where she was and with whom. She hadn't woken from a sweet dream to find herself in hell. No. Severe cramps in her abdomen had woken her from her sleep and reminded her far too quickly of what she was now: a fuckhole. A raging pain tormented her intestines in ever shorter intervals. Laura pressed her legs together and held her breath. Goosebumps crept over her body, so intense that it hurt. The cramps left her hardly any time to breathe.

"Fuck!" Laura cursed between clenched teeth. What had she done to deserve this shit? In the truest sense of the word. Because the cramps in her stomach were unfortunately no diffuse pain this time, but made it completely clear: she had to empty her bowels. Now! Quickly! It felt like a goddamn giant load of liquid manure!

The thought of having to go to the toilet now almost made her lose her mind. There was only the bucket. No toilet. No flushing. No toilet paper—which wouldn't have been of much use with tied hands anyway. It would stink. She'd get dirty. He'd see it—and smell it!

Laura pressed her face in the musty mattress and gasped. More cramps blazed through her intestines. She had to reach the bucket. Now! Otherwise she'd shit right here on the mattress. Although it was dirty and old, it would probably be her home for an unforeseeable period of time, which had to be kept as clean as possible. She now had to crawl to this bucket and somehow manage to

sit on it. She had to! Otherwise *he* would punish her. For sure!

But it's his fault! It all happens because of him! He put his cock in my ass and now I get diarrhea! It's not my fault! Only his!

These thoughts were of no use to Laura. Not now! The question of guilt was a minor matter. The only thing that mattered now was to get on that bucket in time and relieve herself and escape *his* punishment.

Laura forced herself to crawl to the two buckets again. She sobbed unrestrainedly without being aware of it. She struggled to get to her feet and stared at the empty bucket. It seemed to grin at her. *Well, come on, girl, sit down. Fill me up. This is going to be a party. Dare to!*

The next spasm shot through her tummy. Not only the question of guilt was forgotten but any sense of shame. In a flash, she squatted down on the bucket, suppressed the pain, and breathed a sigh of relief … until she felt the burning … as if her anus was bathed in acid.

Laura had to sit on the bucket for a long time. The tissue that had been shredded by the penetration pulsed. Every time she had a spasm and something splashed out of her into the bucket, her rectum burned like fire. The narrow rim of the bucket cut painfully into her thighs, but this pain was nothing compared to what was raging in her abdomen.

When her bowel finally calmed down and the cramps subsided, she'd have preferred to remain seated despite the pain. She couldn't clean herself, which meant she had to get back on the mattress as she was.

Laura Hermann finally made a decision—the first, but by far not the last one in this stinking hole.

***

In contrast to Laura, Toni experienced a moment of disorientation on this Thursday morning.

He woke up on the couch in a half-sitting position. The TV was running. Empty beer bottles surrounded him. He stood up, moaning. His back hurt, and it was cold as shit. He only wore boxer shorts, and the oven had gone out overnight. Where was his useless brother?

There was a disgustingly dry taste in his mouth. His throat hurt. He'd have liked to get the next beer, but he was much too tired for that. Grunting quietly, he reached for an old blanket lying next to him on the couch and wrapped himself in it. Then he stretched out and closed his eyes. He had a headache. His eyes were burning. He was thirsty. And he felt sick. A terrific morning!

His balls itched. Toni scratched them thoughtlessly. He noticed that his pubic hair was sticky. Suddenly everything came back to his mind.

She's here! She's still here! And she belongs to me now!

Unbelievable, but true! He forgot the headaches, the thirst, the cold. He had his own personal sex slave. In his cellar. He'd captured her! He'd done everything right! And now she belonged to him. He could do whatever he wanted with her.

I could go downstairs right now and fuck her shot through his head in a flash.

But he felt too shitty at the moment, probably wouldn't even get an erection.

How do you think she feels?

Toni quickly pushed this new thought aside. He didn't feel the need to take care of the mental state of this little bitch. She'd been introduced to her new destiny yesterday. She'd serve him. Nothing else. Maybe he'd even be nice to her from time to time. Depending on how she behaved. It was only up to her. Her decision. Period.

Blinking, he opened his eyes. The *Morning Show* was on TV. It was 7:22. Fucking hell! Much too early to get up! Maybe he should go upstairs to his bed and sleep some more. The bitch was in good hands. She couldn't run away.

Or should he look in on her?

Toni rubbed his aching temples as he thought about it. Gray light fell through the small windows into the gloomy room. The weather seemed to be as lousy as yesterday.

A perfect day to stay at home and have a good time.

But there was a real danger that there wasn't any beer left in the house.

Toni took a cigarette out of a dented pack on the dirty coffee table. "Smoking causes cancer" was written on the pack. Well, if they say so. Toni lit the cigarette and inhaled deeply. That was better.

He closed his eyes again and tried to think.

Finally, something like an idea came to his mind. So he got up and dragged himself into the kitchen.

***

Lupo was lying in front of the corner seat, sleeping.

Toni didn't give him a look. He headed for the fridge, opened it … and gave a sigh of relief. There were still six bottles of Augustiner. Thank God!

He grabbed one and greedily gulped it down while constantly scratching his balls.

He felt instantly alive again. A feeling that was better than sex. Almost!

Toni grinned as he put the empty bottle down.

Now he wasn't cold either. Everything was fine again …

He went to a ten-pound sack of dog food standing in the corner under the window. Cheap stuff. Lupo spurned it a lot lately. If anyone even thought of feeding him. Next to the sack was a bowl sticky with leftover food. Toni took it and filled it halfway with dry food. Then he went to the sink and added some warm water. The food stank like decay. All the better. He grinned again as he went to the cellar with the bowl in his hand.

***

The key was hanging on a little hook above the door. Toni had thought it would be wiser to leave it here than to carry the stupid thing with him all the time. As he knew, it wouldn't have taken him long to misplace it. His self-evaluation was quite good.

While opening the door with one hand and holding the bowl with the other, he realized that he was still wearing only boxers and it was freezing cold down here.

Never mind. It wouldn't take long. He wanted to fuck her later anyway.

Toni's heart somersaulted when the key clicked in the lock. He could hardly wait to see her. Naked and tied up. Even his dick came back to life.

What would it be like to see her again this morning, after everything he'd done with her yesterday and after her first night in her new home, which she certainly hadn't enjoyed?

Toni was as nervous as before a first date.

He pushed the door open—and froze.

What was that smell? So sharp and penetrating!

Toni covered his nose and mouth with his hand. He retched.

And while he was still trying to deal with the smell, this

noticed it. She just stared at him with that empty and pleading look as she swallowed her own snot.

Toni didn't really know what to do. He'd have liked to throw her to the ground to fuck her right here and now, but he didn't want to stay a second longer in that stinking hole.

"Okay," he finally said, just to say something. He stood up. Suddenly he was uncomfortably aware of his own nudity. It was cold here. Icy cold! How had she endured that?

"I'll be back in minute," he said to the sobbing girl. Then he turned abruptly and left.

He closed the door but didn't lock it, leaving the key in place. Then he quickly went upstairs, slipped into jeans, a sweatshirt, and slippers. He finally stopped in front of his brother's room. It didn't smell much better up here than down in the basement. It was clear where that smell came from, but Toni, like Karl, had meanwhile stopped consciously perceiving the smell of decay. He stood there and wanted to open the door when something else occurred to him. The key for the hand and foot chains—where did he actually put it?

Should be in my pocket, Toni thought and instinctively reached for it, but there was nothing but a lighter and some jingling coins. Sure, the wrong pants. And yesterday's were still downstairs in the living room. So he'd get the keys later. First it was Karl's turn.

Toni pushed the door open. Stuffy darkness surrounded him. The curtains were closed. Good-for-nothing Karl was lying in bed.

Toni turned on the light. No reaction. Only Karl's head was visible. The blond hair was stringy and greasy as ever. The rest of him was hidden under a light blue blanket.

With an angry snort Toni tore it away.

Groaning, Karl tried to grab it again, but Toni had thrown it to the floor. Karl sat up with a jerk and rubbed his eyes. Questioningly he blinked at Toni. He looked miserable. His T-shirt and boxer shorts were covered with grease stains.

"What's up?" he asked with a husky voice, cleared his throat, and rubbed his fat face, on which ugly stubble sprouted.

Karl could have been an attractive young man, but he wasn't aware of that, so he let himself go. Under the T-shirt, which was far too tight and yellowed, a stately belly appeared. This wasn't the first time Toni wondered how his little brother could be so fat when he got so little to eat.

But that wasn't his problem, and it was the last thing Toni worried about.

"Get dressed," he ordered harshly.

Karl didn't move.

Toni roughly punched his fist into his soft upper arm.

"I'll see you down in the basement in five minutes! Hurry up!"

He left Karl's room and slammed the door. He knew his brother would obey. There was nothing more reliable than a well-trained shithead who knew exactly what to expect if he didn't do as he was told.

***

Karl actually showed up exactly five minutes later. He wore gray sweatpants and still the same T-shirt.

Toni was waiting for him.

"What's up?" Karl asked, running a hand through his too-long hair. He seemed nervous. "Something wrong

with the girl?"

Toni grinned. "You can say that, man."

Karl's eyes widened. "She is … she's not … please, Toni, don't tell me she's dead."

Now Toni actually had to laugh. "Why do you think that? I love the little one, man. I'm not going to kill her. I want some fun with her, genius. However, that's not possible right now. That's why I need your help."

Karl looked at him without understanding. "My help? Why?"

"You gotta do something you've practiced." With these words, Toni opened the door.

***

The first thing Karl noticed was the smell. It was thick and penetrating. To be precise, it stank of feces in here.

Then he saw the girl. She sat in the middle of the barren room on one of the buckets.

Karl knew, of course, that it was the same girl that his brother had brought here last night, but he hardly recognized her. Her beautiful light-blonde hair was matted and stuck to her face, which was black and blue—like the rest of her slender body. The pale skin was covered with dirt, blood, and feces. The beautiful big breasts were pressed flat on her thighs. She let her head hang and stared at her chained feet. Her arms were not visible, her hands seemed to be tied to her back.

Some liquid (tears? snot? both?) dripped slowly from her face onto the concrete floor and her bare feet.

It was a horrible, pitiful sight. A beautiful, proud person who had turned into this broken heap of misery within hours. Karl couldn't understand how you could feel anything other than compassion at such a sight. But of

course he didn't understand how it was possible to put another person in such a state and feel joy at the same time.

Karl turned to Toni, who stood close behind him, as if he wanted to make it impossible for him to escape.

"What have you done to her?" he whispered, almost in tears.

"Well, what do you think? Did you think I wanted to cook something tasty with her and play gin rummy? What you see here is exactly what the whole thing is about, little brother. It's about bizarre sex, submission, and humiliation. Maybe the info will help you." He laughed dryly.

In the meantime, the girl had noticed them and lifted her head. Her face looked really bad. Swollen, unnaturally discolored, her nose encrusted with blood.

Karl swallowed heavily. He'd almost forgotten the stench.

"You can imagine what you have to do, right?" Toni muttered, pressing one hand to his mouth and nose.

Karl shrugged.

"Oh, man, how can one person be so stupid?" Toni slammed his fist into his brother's back. Karl staggered.

"You goddamn weakling, go upstairs now and get something to wash her. And then you make sure she does it properly. If I fuck her later, I want her to smell like a damn violet!"

He grinned maliciously and then covered his nose again. "Is that clear so far?"

Karl nodded.

"But first you bring the shit out and make sure that everything is clean again. Understand?"

Karl nodded again.

"The key for the handcuffs is in my pants in the living room. You can take them off her as soon as you empty

the fucking bucket. But not before, understand? And the foot chains stay on. After she's washed herself, cuff her hands again, but this time in front of her belly. Clear?"

Karl nodded again.

"After that, lock the door, hang the cellar key over the door, and bring the other one back to me."

"Okay."

"Did you really understand everything?"

"Yes."

"Don't get the key for the handcuffs until you're done with the fucking bucket! All right?"

"Yeah, I get it."

Toni patted him on the shoulder. Karl twitched.

"Are you afraid of me? That's good! All right. I rely on you. Don't mess up, otherwise I might lock you up with her. Understand?"

"Yes, I'll do it like you said."

"One more thing, Karl: I don't want you to talk to her, all right? Not a single word! When she starts begging, you tell her to shut up. Okay?"

"Yeah, okay."

"Fine. You've been practicing these things, right?" Toni laughed. "Care-specialist Karl! Better than nothing, right? And somebody has to do the dirty work!"

Toni laughed at his joke, which wasn't funny. He almost bent until the stench caught up with him again and made him choke.

"I'll go upstairs to take a nap," he said before he left the room.

***

Karl's heart pounded in his neck as he approached the girl. He'd already forgotten the stench. He felt so sorry

for her. He'd have loved to have just taken her in his arms. But his fear of Toni was bigger than his pity.

"H-hey," he stammered as he finally stood in front of her, probably more ashamed than she was.

The girl raised her head as far as she could and looked at him. Her gaze couldn't be interpreted. At least not for him.

"I'll help you stand up. Okay?"

Toni had told him not to talk to her, but that was impossible. Karl wouldn't have known how to avoid that, and he didn't care. Toni wasn't here.

She said nothing, but a whimpering noise came from her throat. Karl didn't understand immediately. That sound. That look. But then the scales fell from his eyes: she was afraid! Afraid of him!

"Listen, I'm … I'm not gonna hurt you. I'm not like him. I just want to help you, really."

When she spoke, he got goosebumps. Her voice sounded so helpless and sad that he felt a pain in his heart.

"You won't hurt me?"

"No, never."

"W-who are you?"

Karl looked hectically over his shoulder. Toni had told him not to talk to her. *Do not react to her questions.* But the door was closed. Toni was upstairs, so he couldn't possibly hear them. It was probably time to resist. At least a little bit.

"My name is Karl. And yours?"

Fresh tears ran down her cheeks. "Laura. My name is Laura."

"Hi, Laura. I-I'm so sorry that we have to get to know each other under these circumstances. Believe me …"

"Are you …?"

"I'm his brother."

"But why are you here? Why are you doing this? You can help me, right? Can you get me outta here?"

Karl put a finger on her lips, which felt unpleasantly rough and chapped. "Shh! Not so loud! Stay calm! I can't explain it all to you, but I promise I'll help you as best I can. First of all, I'm going to help you get off this bucket. Okay?"

"Okay. But please be careful. I'm in pain all over."

Karl nodded. He carefully put his hands around her upper arms and was surprised at how thin they were. He could completely enclose them with only one hand.

He looked her in the face. "Ready? I'll help you stand up now."

"Okay."

Karl pulled her up. Laura moaned with clenched teeth. Her face turned all red. She must have been in terrible pain. Karl didn't want to know any details. Finally she stood swaying next to the bucket. Her skin was ice-cold.

The contents of the bucket and the source of the stench were now visible, but neither Laura nor Karl looked.

"I can't stand," she complained. "I gotta sit down. Can you take off my handcuffs?"

Karl shook his head. "Not yet. I'm sorry. I gotta get the key first. I'll take you to the mattress, okay? You can lie down there."

"But I don't wanna … make it dirty."

Karl looked over at the old mattress, which was one big piece of dirt. But he knew what she meant.

"Lie on your stomach. I'll help you."

He put an arm around her narrow hips and supported her. He ignored the fact that she was naked and completely frozen, injured, and smeared with blood and feces.

He wasn't disgusted, and her shameful situation didn't excite him. He simply took care of her, just as he'd taken care of his mother. Toni was probably right. He was good enough to do the dirty work.

When they reached the mattress, Karl helped her lie on her stomach. Her naked dirty butt looked like a silent accusation to him. He also saw the dry blood between her buttocks and thighs. He could imagine where that came from. He thought of the disgusting porn movies but then chased away the memory like an ugly insect.

She doesn't even have a blanket.

When he noticed that, he felt a stinging pain in his heart.

"Get some rest, Laura. I'll be right back." Karl took the bucket and left.

***

Karl emptied the contents of the bucket in the guest toilet. He had to flush several times until everything was gone.

Then he cleaned the bucket with the garden hose in front of the house. He barely noticed the cold on his naked arms. He didn't notice anything else, either. He only thought of Laura all the time. How she'd looked at him. How she'd spoken to him. As if he was her God. As if whatever would happen to her would only depend on him. As if he was really important! Yet he was nothing more than an ordinary henchman. The devil's henchman.

When the bucket was clean, Karl went back into the house. On his way there he discovered the small tub in which they had bathed as children outside in the garden when the weather was warm. The memory gave him another sting. How beautiful the time was when Toni and

he were still children. Well, maybe not. Since he could remember, Toni had always been mean, had pushed him around and used him for his own purposes. Karl had never learned to defend himself against it. Mama had always said that Karl shouldn't tolerate everything. But what else should he have done? Toni had been older and stronger. All attempts to fight back had ended in painful regrets.

When he was thirteen, Toni had beaten him up so badly that he had to go to the emergency room. His nose was broken. His upper lip had to be sewn with four stitches. The scar was still visible today. Mama hadn't said much about it. She scolded Toni, but he was sixteen at the time and could no longer be controlled. Actually, she was afraid of him. With this beating, Toni taught him a lesson that was called "I'm the boss." And Karl had learned his lesson.

The reason for the beating had been the fact that Karl had refused to steal something for his brother from an electronics store. Toni had told him to put several computer games and DVDs in his backpack. Karl had refused. So loudly that an employee noticed them and finally threw them out of the store. At first Toni hadn't said much about the matter. They'd gone home together. Once there, Toni lured him into the shed with a pretext and beaten him with a wrench. The first three blows went right into his face, smashing Karl's nose and lip, closing his right eye. When he was already lying on the floor, whimpering and covered in blood, Toni continued to thrash him. Karl cried, screamed, and begged him to stop.

But Toni only stopped when he thought it was enough. Then he knelt next to his little brother in the dust and stroked his sweaty hair almost lovingly. "Next time I tell you to do something for me, you won't refuse, little

brother, right?"

No, he wouldn't. No matter what. He'd do anything. That was his tearful answer. And Toni had told Mama to take the little wimp to the hospital. Karl and she were supposed to claim that some strange boys had beat him up like that and to file charges against unknown persons. That's what they did.

From that day on Karl regularly went stealing with his brother. Toni simply said what he wanted and Karl pocketed it. He was caught a few times and was even previously convicted. But he didn't dare to give even one more objection. He'd learned his lesson. Until today.

All these thoughts and memories went through Karl's head as he filled the old tub in the kitchen with warm water. Once again he did things his brother demanded of him, although everything in him resisted. He did it because he was afraid, because Toni was the only person in his little lonely world since Mama's death. Yes, Toni was mean and treated him like shit, but on the other hand, he took care of him. Karl couldn't imagine living on his own. He was twenty-nine and had no idea about the world out there. After school, which he'd had to leave after several miserable attempts without graduation (he was just stupid and good for nothing, just like Toni always said), he'd worked as a dishwasher in a kitchen for a while. He'd liked the job a lot, but then Mama became ill and was dependent on his help. Since then he hadn't worked and had hardly been among people. Mama! He missed her.

Just like he'd miss Toni. Actually, he should hate him, but he didn't. He loved his brother. Somehow. And he needed him. Somehow. He needed the emotional support that Toni gave him. This last bit of continuity in his life. Toni was at least someone who even talked to him, who

was interested in him. Somehow. And sometimes he treated him quite well. He watched TV with him, drank beer with him, and asked him (now and then) for his opinion.

Therefore Karl was proud that his brother was now dependent on his help and couldn't handle the situation all alone. It was good to know Toni needed him. Just as Mama had needed him. And this girl. That made him feel important. Somehow. Of course Karl would never have admitted that. After all, it was absolutely terrible what Toni did to this girl. There was no apology for that, of course. Yet it made him feel good to know Toni couldn't do it without him. Without him, he'd have failed on something as simple as a shit-filled bucket.

And what about Laura, without his help?

Karl feared the worst. He thought it was quite possible that Toni would have killed the girl if there had been no one to deal with the mess. Yes, he was important. And from this point of view, Karl had perhaps even saved her life.

The thought made him feel warm inside, so he returned to the cellar in a much better mood.

***

The young man named Karl came back. Laura found him rather strange, but compared to the other guy, he seemed like an incarnate angel.

She felt his closeness and his warm body as he bent over her and loosened the shackles from her sore wrists. Finally! Laura could move her arms, but it didn't bring her the desired relief. Instead, there was an almost unbearable tingle. She carefully sat up and moved her arms as gently as possible. She would have loved to scream

because it hurt so much. She longed for the numbness she'd felt before.

"Does it hurt much?" Karl asked.

She nodded and groaned. She was vaguely aware of the fact that he could now gawk right between her legs, but in a bizarre way that was irrelevant. She'd never have thought that she could lose any feeling of shame so quickly.

Never say never, she thought bitterly, as she waited for the blood to return to her arms.

Slowly the pain subsided.

Laura moved her fingers, which now felt less numb, and rubbed her wrists, where dark red and partly bloody pressure marks were visible. But she endured the pain, which was by far not the worst.

She sat up.

"Is it getting better?" he asked. He'd waited patiently without looking at her in a way that would have made her feel uncomfortable.

"Yes, slowly. But every part of my body hurts. Do you think you can … try to talk to your brother so that he … lets me go?"

Karl sighed. "If it were that simple, I would have done it long ago, believe me. You have to be patient. First I'll try to make your life here a little more comfortable. Maybe I'll be able to bring you a blanket today. And something to eat."

While he said that, he looked at the filled dog bowl. He didn't know if she'd noticed it yet.

"I'll never do him the favor of eating that!" Laura hissed.

Karl nodded thoughtfully. "But I fear that he'll make you do him many favors. You just have to try to play his game as well as possible. Making him angry won't do you

any good. I know him, believe me."

"Then why are you still here?"

Good question.

Karl shrugged. "It's about time. Come, we'll wash you now."

He pointed to the little orange tub he'd brought with him. It reminded Laura of a baby bath.

"Otherwise the water will get cold," Karl said and tried to smile.

Laura laboriously got to her feet. This time she did it without any help.

Karl had also brought her a washcloth, shower gel, and a large bath towel. Laura would have liked to wrap herself in it right away. It was so cold down here.

"So now I'm supposed to wash myself so he wants to rape me again later?"

Karl shrugged again. "If you want to look at it that way. But the water will do you good. You'll see."

Laura took the washcloth, dipped it into the wonderfully warm water, and squeezed some shower gel on it. "For Men" was written on the bottle. The smell was pleasant.

She began to wash herself. First the face (very carefully because the swellings hurt badly), then neck and upper body. Finally the legs and thighs. Only at the end did she clean her genital area. Although she was very careful, Laura moaned in pain several times. But Karl was right. When she was finished, she actually felt better. The water in the tub had turned brown.

Karl handed her the towel, and Laura gratefully wrapped herself in it. She was happy to finally be able to hide her nakedness. Only now did she realize how strongly she trembled.

"Dry yourself well. Then I'll have to shackle you again,

unfortunately."

"M-may I keep the towel?" she asked hopefully.

Karl seemed to think about it, but then he shook his head. "I can't leave it here. I'm sorry. But I promise to talk to Toni later so that you can have a blanket. Just do everything he demands of you. You don't have a choice anyway."

Toni, Laura thought. *That's the bastard's name. Toni. Like some normal guy. Just Toni.*

Somehow she couldn't believe it, even though she wasn't sure which name would have been more fitting for a son of a bitch like that. She dried herself carefully and would have loved to cry when she had to return the towel.

"Now your hands, please."

She reached out and Karl handcuffed her. Compared to his brother, he was quite clumsy. His fingers trembled, and a sharp smell of sweat came from him. Laura didn't believe that he'd washed himself today. Or yesterday. He seemed unkempt. In her normal life, Laura would never have talked to such a guy. She'd have called him antisocial. But here and now it was different. Here and now he was her only ray of hope, and she didn't want to let him go at all. She would have loved to hold him and stop time so the other guy wouldn't come back to hurt her. Of course, it was a pure utopia.

"Sit down. I'll be right back with the bucket."

Laura was about to say that she didn't want the disgusting bucket anymore when she realized she had no choice. Sooner or later she'd have to pee and shit again, and she wouldn't do herself any favor by doing that somewhere in the corner. The stench was so bad anyway. Luckily, it wasn't so strong anymore. She smelled the fresh shower gel on her skin and was grateful for it.

She went back to the mattress and sat down. Now she could at least put her arms around her knees to warm herself a little. She watched as Karl dragged the washing things and the tub out of the room. He closed the door behind him but didn't lock it. Not that it made any difference. Her chains made any escape impossible.

***

After he'd returned the toilet bucket to her, Karl left the cellar without a word and didn't engage in another conversation when Laura tried to talk to him. He already had a bad feeling about it. Not only did he know her name now, but she knew his. And Toni's, if he remembered correctly. Now all she had to do was say their names, and Toni would find out that they'd spoken to each other. He'd be damn angry, and Karl wasn't sure who he was going to take his anger out on, her or him.

However, it made little sense to worry about it now.

Karl decided instead to lie down again after cleaning the tub.

Sleep came surprisingly soon this time.

***

Despite the constant pain and the unpleasant cold, Laura dozed off after Karl left. She fell into a light, dreamless sleep, which at least temporarily gave her some rest.

The awakening turned out all the more harshly. When Laura opened her eyes, she saw a pair of brown shoes. Heavy work boots with dirt stuck to them. He'd worn the same boots yesterday …

Laura's heart jumped, and she was immediately wide awake. Her gaze wandered from the boots up, over blue jeans and a gray sweatshirt to the unshaven face of the

baldheaded man, who looked down at her with an eerie sparkle in his eyes.

He grinned when their gazes met. Laura looked away. Now she was all too aware of her nudity again.

"I hope you slept well," he mocked. Then he squatted next to the mattress.

Only now did Laura notice that he was holding something in his hand. Her brain, however, was incapable of making a connection at first. What he held in his hand was a collar (made of brown leather and already quite worn) and a leash. The collar was quite thick. For a big dog, Laura suspected. But she still didn't understand what he wanted with it. After all, there was no dog here.

Then she automatically looked over at the bowl. It was also big and looked used. The strong smell of the soaked dogfood floated in the air.

Laura looked back at the leash in Toni's hand and then at his grinning face. Finally, her tortured brain made the logical connection.

He'd already told her yesterday that he wanted to keep her like a dog. This morning he'd brought her the bowl. Now the leash. His plan was as simple as it was dreadful. He wanted to make her his dog, and everything he needed was here.

Laura swallowed hard. Her throat was sore and aching. She'd have liked a sip of water now, even from the bucket. But she didn't dare ask.

She lay there very still, staring at the leash and listening to the throbbing of her heart.

Toni reached out and grabbed between her legs. "Legs apart!"

Laura spread her legs. She didn't move when he pushed first one, then two, finally three fingers into her. It hurt because she was so sore, but she didn't whine. No

sound came over her lips.

Toni pulled his fingers out again and smelled them. He nodded approvingly. "Everything fresh again, huh?"

Laura was silent. She didn't know what to answer.

Toni stuck his fingers in his mouth and sucked on them. He didn't take his eyes off her for a second. Finally, he pulled them out again and rubbed his sticky saliva on Laura's lips and chin.

She fought the disgust that rose in her and forced herself to stay calm.

"Get off the mattress! On all fours!"

Laura struggled to straighten up. It wasn't easy with her hands tied. She crawled from the mattress to the cold floor. On all fours, looking down to the floor.

Toni planted himself in front of her. Now she had only his boots before her eyes ... and the leash, which he let dangle beside them.

"Raise your head!"

Laura obeyed.

He put the dog collar on her and locked the buckle so tight that it choked her, but Laura didn't let on. He then fastened the leash to the collar, pulled hard once, and Laura's head was torn forward. She moaned and coughed.

"Let's go for a dog walk, baby!" Laura started moving. For the next fifteen minutes he let her crawl in circles on all fours until her knees were chafed. He kept pulling on the leash when she became too slow.

If he wanted her to change direction, he kicked her bare butt with his heavy boots.

That worked miracles. Laura learned really fast.

***

Although this game gave him a great boner in the beginning, it became boring after a while to watch her crawl, to pull the leash until she choked, and to kick her naked butt, which was dirty again. The only thing Toni still liked to cum to was her big tits hanging down and dangling sexily while she crawled.

He was in the mood to pinch her a little bit. So he finally ordered her to stop. He pulled the leash until she screamed softly and started coughing again.

"Kneel!"

She groaned and straightened up. Toni pulled on the leash until her neck was stretched. He saw her larynx moving frantically. There were tears in her eyes.

Toni held her neck stretched with one hand and pinched her breasts with the other. His erection began to throb painfully. He licked his lips with a grin as he pinched her nipples, one after the other. They were still red and sore from the last time, and he bet it hurt like hell. This time, however, she remained surprisingly calm. Was she already so blunted? After only one day?

Toni couldn't really believe it. On the other hand, he had no real experience with such things. He only knew situations like this one from the cheap S&M porn he regularly jerked off to. They usually had a running time of ten to thirty minutes, and the women in these movies were of course as trained as expected. He didn't know how long this would take in real life. He'd never thought about it until now. Maybe it was just a question of training. If you stayed firm and strict from the beginning and you didn't let them get away with anything, you could certainly reach your goal faster.

Toni seemed to be good at teaching little bitches to obey. Almost as if he'd finally found his destiny.

He loosened the leash and grabbed the girl by her hair

instead, pressing her face against the concrete.

"Come on! Taste the dirt! Tongue out! Lick the floor clean, you cunt!"

Her tongue timidly peeked out between her lips and she carefully licked the dusty concrete.

"I think I've got something better!"

Toni stretched out one foot and held his boot in front of her nose.

"Let's go! Lick it clean! I don't want to see any more dirt!"

That was a great idea because his boots were really damn dirty after he'd walked around in the mud yesterday. Fat chunks of ground had dried on them.

The girl stared at the boots. She hesitated.

Toni kicked her in the stomach.

She screamed and gasped in pain.

"Lick them, baby! I don't have all day."

Panting, she bent over his shoe and let her wet tongue glide over it.

And Toni made sure she did it right.

On both boots.

***

His boots weren't quite clean yet, but Toni couldn't stand it any longer. He'd cum in his damn pants at any moment if it didn't go fast now. So he pulled down his pants, threw the girl on her back, and raped her on the spot. She was silent and lay there quietly while she stared at the ceiling with big eyes and an open mouth with some dirt still stuck to it.

Not a word! Laura thought again and again as he thrust his cock into her. *This time I won't give the slightest peep.*

It was quickly over. Just before the ejaculation, Toni

pushed his penis into her mouth, and Laura swallowed it all.

Without the slightest peep.

IT S YOUR TURN

While only a few miles away her daughter was swallowing the sperm of her tormentor for the second time, Karin Hermann sat at the kitchen table with her shoulders hanging. She stared into a cup of cold black coffee. Her tearless eyes were red and burning. She hadn't cried as much in her life as she had in the last twenty-four hours. Her husband, Peter, sat on the couch in the living room, staring at the television with a similarly empty look. For a while they had cried together, but now there was nothing they could share. One could have thought they would comfort each other, but neither had any comfort left to give.

The most important thing they had in common was no longer here.

Laura had disappeared.

She was no longer there.

No one knew why.

No one knew where she'd gone.

Whether voluntarily or forced.

There was no trace and no clue.

Her sneakers, which she wore for jogging, were gone. Her iPod was gone. And her anorak.

Laura wasn't a little child anymore, so her mother didn't know what other clothes were missing. Karin also didn't know what Laura had worn (apart from the sneakers and the white anorak) when she left the house. She had last seen Laura yesterday morning. On the way to school she'd worn blue jeans and a checkered blouse. Karin had later found jeans and a blouse in the bathroom, where they hung over the edge of the bathtub. Laura had put them there when she'd changed for jogging.

So Karin could only assume that her daughter had left yesterday afternoon to run, as she'd done regularly for some time.

She'd also told the police all that. They'd asked if she was sure her daughter had left the house to go jogging. Karin had said no, but she'd explained that all the circumstantial evidence was in favor of it. Laura's cell phone was lying on her desk in her room. She would have taken it with her if she'd gone somewhere else. Just like her wallet and handbag. Everything was still here. Except for the iPod. And she always took it with her jogging.

Her little girl had gone jogging in the afternoon—despite the bad weather and the fact that it would soon be dark. And her daughter hadn't come back.

Those were the facts.

The police wanted to know what route she usually took. Karin could only guess. She didn't know, had never talked to Laura about it. In fact, they hadn't talked a lot lately. Why? Laura had become withdrawn, seemed dissatisfied, even sad. Karin had attributed this primarily to puberty and Laura's problems at school. Perhaps a change of school would've been better? But Karin and Peter were too stubborn to consider it. They had insisted that Laura stay in high school and graduate in the classic way, although it wasn't easy for her to keep up with the pace. Why? As if there was only one way to lead a good life. Crazy! In retrospect it was so damn crazy. And stupid. They had wasted so much precious time that they should have spent with their daughter, instead of putting her under pressure and constantly making her feel guilty about the stupid school. Laura had been unhappy. Very unhappy.

Karin had suddenly realized all this. Too late! And she'd been naive enough to tell all that to the cops. For

them it was unfortunately just what they'd been waiting for because now they assumed Laura had probably run away. For the police, Laura's disappearance was routine.

Karin had objected that her daughter would never run away without her wallet and cell phone. But the officers insisted on their experience. Things like this happened all the time. People disappeared without a trace and without taking the things from their old lives with them. For some, that was exactly what they wanted, they told Karin. These people wanted to leave everything behind and start anew somewhere.

Karin thought it was nonsense. She couldn't believe someone would deliberately run away without even taking a bit of money with them. No one with a sane mind would do that. And certainly not a sixteen-year-old girl with an (repeatedly tested) above-average IQ like Laura. So there was no other possibility than that something had happened to her. Karin knew her daughter, at least she believed so. Something must have happened. There were enough possibilities. She often saw it on TV.

Where had Laura been jogging?

She could have run around in the village.

Into the forest.

And where to then?

There were several options. Countless gravel roads led through the big forest area. Some of them ended in the middle of nowhere, others led to Lake Starnberg.

So she'd explained this to the cops and had cried, begged, threatened. Again and again. Until the officer in charge finally gave the order to comb the forest area and finally search for her Laura.

They were still searching. For hours! No result so far.

Karin imagined that someone had dragged Laura into a car and then God knows where he took her. This scenar-

io seemed most likely to her. What else should have happened? If Laura was still out there somewhere, she'd have been found by now. Right?

The highway wasn't far from here, and there was at least one parking lot within the forest area, which meant the perpetrator could have come by foot. It was a lonely place. Especially at the time when Laura had been jogging. It got dark early these days.

Surely she'd screamed and fought back. But who would have heard it? Nobody lived there. The highway was loud. And who went for a walk in the woods at this time of day and in such bad weather? No. Very unlikely.

So how could you find them? Where would she be by now? Was she still alive? Was she in pain? Was she afraid? Was she desperately begging for her life?

All these thoughts circulated in Karin's head in an endless spiral. On the one hand, she didn't believe the police would be successful with their search. She even hoped so! On the other hand, she kept imagining the doorbell ringing and a pale policeman telling her that her daughter had been found. Maltreated and buried. In some shrubbery.

Dead.

Karin hid her face in her hands and began to sob unrestrainedly.

Dead.

Now she was weeping again.

Dead.

Her sobs were so violent that they strangled her throat.

Dead!

Peter Hermann rose from the couch and sneaked into the kitchen like a ghost. He knelt in front of his sobbing wife, put both arms around her waist, and did the only right thing: he cried with her.

***

This time it took him a long time to fall asleep. It was already after midnight. But Karl had stayed awake. He'd drunk coffee and water and had sneaked down about every thirty minutes to have a look into the living room, where Toni, as always at this time of the day, was sitting on the couch, watching TV and getting drunk. Earlier that evening he'd been shopping. Alcohol and cigarettes. Something to eat. But not really much. For Karl he'd only brought a bag of cheese chips this evening (as so often).

But he told himself there were worse things, while he thought of the dirty dog bowl that Laura hadn't eaten from. Not yet! Karl knew it would only be a matter of time before Toni made her do it. Of course he could have forced her directly, but that didn't seem to be his plan. He probably wanted to wait until she did it on her own. Karl understood on a deeply cruel level that this would make things even worse for Laura. By humiliating herself almost voluntarily, she gave Toni even more power.

That was exactly what his brother wanted. It was about breaking her will. And her pride. He wanted to take away her last bit of dignity and humanity. Physical violence alone wasn't enough. She had to be broken from within, and only then would she really be destroyed, even if the external injuries healed at some point. If they got a chance to do so.

Karl wasn't nearly as stupid as his brother thought. He knew exactly what Toni had in mind. That was exactly why he waited until Toni had fallen asleep on the couch in front of the TV.

When he finally heard his brother snoring, Karl sneaked up on tiptoe. He had to be sure. Toni's eyes were

closed, his mouth slightly open. He stank like a distillery. There was saliva in the corners of his mouth. The lips looked dry and were chapped. He wore boxer shorts only, with unmistakable stains in his crotch.

While Karl was looking at his brother, he suddenly realized that Toni was completely helpless right now.

He could have done anything with him. Now, at this moment. Spit on him. Hit him and kick him. He could have tied him up …

Or kill him! a voice in his head whispered. It sounded like his own, only a little lower, somehow more masculine.

Get a hammer and smash his skull!

Karl held his breath. The voice was so loud! It scared him.

A knife! Ram it into his throat! Or stab it in his chest! No matter! If he's not dead immediately, you stab him again. And again! And again! Over and over again! Until he no longer moves! No matter how! Just do it! Do it now and do it fast! Save her! Save yourself!

Karl licked his lips. He stared at his sleeping brother and felt the blood freeze in his veins. Both hands clenched to fists, and he stood there and couldn't move an inch.

Go get the knife! demanded the raging voice in his head. *Do it, Karl! Now! Save yourself! Save her! Save the world from this pig!*

But he couldn't do it! This was his brother! The only person he still had in this world. What should he have done? How should he live without him! He didn't know anyone out there! Where would he go? And what would happen to Mama then? And the house? And him? And this girl? Would Laura testify in his favor? Or would she hate him? Because he'd also been there. From the begin-

ning. And because he'd known everything. Because he'd watched. Without doing anything.

Too much had already happened. The kidnapping. The rapes. All the cruelties. He'd known about it. From the beginning. They would ask him why he hadn't done something before. And they would ask him why he hadn't called the police instead of brutally murdering his brother. He'd go to prison for that. For a long time. For many years. Until he was old and broken.

Then don't kill him! It's enough if you call the cops! They'll be there in half an hour at the latest and everything will be fine!

But was that true? Would everything really be all right? What would they find here besides his drunken brother in the living room, a maltreated minor in the basement and …

… and a corpse eaten by cats in the bedroom …

How would he explain that?

Would they think they killed their mother?

To get the care money.

Then what? What would Toni say? He'd do anything to involve Karl in the trouble.

There was no doubt about that at all.

And he couldn't count on Laura's testimony. She was completely unhinged and in shock.

Maybe she'd even mention that he'd helped her wash, but would that make anything better? He'd tied her up and locked her up. So much for the facts. There was no way out for him. He was just as much involved as Toni. Sure, he hadn't touched her. Neither sexually nor otherwise. That would at least give him extenuating circumstances. Perhaps. And then? Fifteen years in prison instead of twenty?

That wasn't enough, damn it! The price was too high. He couldn't help her, as much as he'd have liked to. At

least not in this way. He could help her a little. And he'd feel better then. He'd feel like a little hero because he'd be a hero for her. In this little cosmos that was now Laura's life, he might even be her God! It didn't take much. Just a little patience and a watchful eye.

With these thoughts, Karl finally broke away from the sight of his sleeping brother and went into the kitchen. There lay an old wool blanket on the corner bench in which Frieda had often wrapped herself before she couldn't leave her bed anymore.

Their mother had often been freezing because her boys had once again forgotten to stoke the stove. Nowadays nobody complained when it was too cold. Toni and Karl were not that sensitive. At least that's one thing they had in common.

Karl knew, however, who was freezing miserably in these minutes. And he also knew how grateful this person's gaze would be if he handed her this old musty blanket as if it were the most precious thing in the world.

Karl was looking forward to this gaze.

It would be grateful. Submissive. Obedient.

***

It was so cold!

So terribly cold!

Laura had rolled herself up on the filthy mattress. She would have loved to sleep. But it was so cold! She'd been lying here for ages. Naked. Her body had seized, cramped up, and every muscle hurt. She had no strength left yet she trembled. Couldn't fight it. Her body led a life of its own—in a desperate attempt to squeeze out a little bit of warmth somewhere. Why couldn't she at least pass out? All thoughts of her family and her fate had given way to

this terrible cold. Even the fear of Toni seemed insignificant and void compared to it.

When Karl came in, Laura didn't even notice him. He was already standing right in front of her and had said something when she finally became aware of his presence. Laura blinked at him without understanding. He kneeled and handed her something. Laura wanted to grab it but couldn't get out of the icy rigidity.

Karl seemed to know that. Without a word he spread the blanket over her body and rubbed her back with both hands.

Laura felt the warmth and welcomed it as a gift. She groaned in relief, grabbed the blanket, and pulled it even tighter around her. Karl rubbed her back, arms, bottom, and legs. That was good. So good. Gradually the warmth spread, relaxing her aching muscles. The feeling was incredible. Had she ever felt anything so fantastic? Karl rubbed her like a father rubbed his child. Laura let it happen because it felt so damn good!

"Thanks," she whispered. Her voice trembled, and tears ran down her swollen face.

Karl smiled. Now he stroked her back. In the past, Laura would never have let a guy like him touch her. But today wasn't the past. Now she was grateful that he touched her and that he was here.

"Thanks, Karl," she repeated.

"It's okay. He's sleeping now. He drank a lot. Do you know? He does that every night. He won't wake up before ten in the morning and will certainly not show up here either. You can keep the blanket. I'll come tomorrow morning and get it back. Okay?"

She nodded gratefully—even if it was anything but okay.

Karl rubbed her back one last time. Then he yawned

and rose. "I'll now go back upstairs and get some sleep. I'm very tired. You know?"

"Okay," Laura whispered. She also wanted to sleep, dream, and forget everything.

"Good night," Karl said.

"Good night," Laura replied and snuggled into the musty blanket.

***

Laura woke when he knelt next to her on the mattress. He wore gray sweatpants and a once-white T-shirt with several moth holes. An unattractive three-day beard grew on his face. He wasn't the kind of man who seemed cool and daring. He just looked fucked up—and smelled like that. The stale aroma of old sweat and bad breath made Laura flinch inside. Still, a dull feeling of gratitude crept up in her again. He held a cup in his hand. A steaming cup. Something to drink. Something warm.

Laura sat up clumsily and held on to the blanket. Her treasure! Carefully he handed her the cup. It was hot. A pleasant shiver ran down Laura's back. Slowly she led the cup to her lips. Since her hands were still in handcuffs, it required a certain amount of concentration that almost exceeded her capabilities at the moment. Finally, she managed to suppress the trembling and took a sip. It was hot. It was good. Tea. Chamomile. Very sweet. She would have liked to gulp it down, but she didn't want to scald her throat. Her stomach began to growl quietly and reminded her that it was now her third day without food. There was the stinking dog bowl, of course, but she didn't want to think about it.

Karl watched her drink while emanating his unpleasant stench. A shower and a toothbrush would have worked

miracles. How much she longed for it.

Personal hygiene didn't seem to play a major role in Karl's life. In this respect, his psychopathic brother was clearly ahead.

Be happy, Laura. After all, it's Toni's cock you have to suck.

The thought was so bitter and disgusting that it made her sick. She quickly drank another sip and then put the cup down to look at Karl.

"Thank you."

"You're welcome. You know I have to take the blanket with me now?"

She wanted to scream and cry, and she wanted to hold on to the blanket with all her might. Her treasure! But she only nodded weakly. Of course she knew.

"Do you … do you think it's possible to bring me something to eat? Not much. Just a little something?" She looked at him pleadingly.

Karl didn't answer.

"Karl?"

"Drink your tea. I gotta go in a minute and take the cup with me. He mustn't see it down here."

"Yeah, but don't you think it's possible with the food? Just a piece of toast or a candy bar?"

He sighed. "You know what you're supposed to eat."

"You mean what *he* wants me to eat?"

Karl nodded.

"Yes, but I won't eat that! No way! That disgusting stuff from that dirty thing there … that … I'll never touch that! I'd rather starve!" Laura noticed that she was crying. She'd become loud and almost spilled the tea. Her gaze wandered to the dog bowl. She could smell the stench.

Karl put a finger on his lips. "Shh. Not so loud, girl. He could hear you."

Laura clenched her teeth so she wouldn't scream. There were tears in her eyes.

"That's exactly why I can't give you anything to eat, as much as I'd like to," he said calmly.

"Why?" she asked without understanding.

"Because you'd never touch the dog food then."

"What do you mean?"

"He keeps you hungry because he wants you to eat the dog food. Voluntarily. He knows that sooner or later you'll do that in order not to starve."

Laura shook her head.

"Yeah," Karl replied. "You will, believe me. Your survival instinct will make you do it. People have already eaten other things in order to survive. Toni knows that. I know it. And you certainly will. If you get something to eat from me, your hunger will never be big enough to go to the bowl. Then he'll notice something's wrong."

"That's bullshit!" Laura objected. "He doesn't have to know that!" Now she'd spilled some of the tea over the blanket.

Karl took her cup. "You should drink that," he said in a fatherly tone. "Toni would notice if I gave you something to eat. I know that for sure. I'm sorry, but I can't help you. You'll have to give him this satisfaction. Maybe he'll give you something else afterward. You'll have to overcome it yourself. As long as you don't do that, you'll have to starve, unfortunately."

Laura cried. The trembling became stronger again. She reached for his free hand and clasped it. "Why are you so sure about that?"

"For various reasons. For example, you'd still have bowel movements if I gave you something. Toni's not stupid. Trust me! He's sick and a drunkard, but he's not stupid. I try to trick him as best I can. But when we get

blown, he'll get both of us. And I don't even know for which one of us it will be worse. That's why I don't take that risk. Eat the dog food! It certainly doesn't taste that bad. Besides, it's not poisonous. On the contrary, it contains important nutrients."

Laura shook her head and let go of his hand again. "How can you say that? How can you ask me to do that?"

"I'm not asking you to do it. I'm just giving you some good advice. In your situation, it's no use to be stubborn. He has the upper hand, you know? Give him what he wants and your life will be easier, believe me."

"So you're saying I should play his good little puppy just so he feels good? For the rest of my life? Is that what you're telling me?"

Karl stood up. "I don't say anything. I'm just trying to help you and stay realistic. That's all."

"Can I at least finish the tea?"

"Too late. I'm sorry. Next time you talk less and drink faster. That's more good advice. And now please give me the blanket!"

Laura pulled it closer.

Karl stretched out a hand.

Laura didn't react. She didn't know if her behavior was smart, but at that moment she didn't care at all. She was much too angry!

"Laura, please give me the blanket. You're not doing yourself a favor."

"And if I don't give it to you? What will you do then?"

"Then I'll take it and never bring it back."

Laura looked at him for a few seconds. She seemed to weigh her chances. Finally she let go and lowered her head. "Then take it, asshole!"

Karl grabbed it.

Laura was naked again and felt more helpless than ev-

er.

She didn't try to hide her nakedness from him. She felt his glances on her breasts and crotch. Slowly she raised her head, and their eyes met.

"You're really beautiful," Karl said. Then he turned around and left the room without looking back.

Laura remained alone with her nakedness, the cold, the dog bowl, and all her confused thoughts.

***

He'd just arrived in the kitchen and filled food for Lupo into a plastic bowl (now that the dog food bowl had found another use) when the doorbell rang.

Karl froze. His heart stopped at least one beat and then raced all the faster. He put the bowl on the floor and remained in a stooped position. It rang a second time, then a third.

His knees trembled.

"Karl?"

Toni's voice. From the living room.

"Karl!"

It rang again.

"Y-yes?"

"There's someone at the door! Go look, dammit!"

"But what if …" *it's the cops?*

"Hurry up, man! And if it's the cops, you know what to do!"

Did he know that? Really? Did he even have the slightest idea?

Without thinking any further, Karl walked through the dark hallway. The front door was windowless. It rang again. Who could that be?

Karl gasped for air as he grabbed the handle with a

trembling hand. He opened the door jerkily. Two policemen stood in front of him. In uniform. Quite classic. Not the usual detectives in plainclothes, as he knew from all the crime series on television. These were only two ordinary Bavarian patrolmen with their ridiculous caps on their heads. They had neither weapons nor handcuffs ready. The one on the right was tall and slim, in his forties, with an old-fashioned mustache and piercing blue eyes. The left one wasn't even thirty. Smoothly shaved, sharp-edged face, somewhat smaller than his colleague, but with wider shoulders.

"Good day!" the older one said.

The other one nodded.

"H-Hello," Karl stammered. His voice sounded strange in his own ears.

"Mr. Singer?"

Karl nodded. "Yes, Karl Singer."

"Uh, Maier and Hoppe from the Wolfratshausen police station. We're here to interview witnesses in a missing person case. Perhaps you've already heard about it in the media."

Karl shook his head.

"It's a sixteen-year-old girl," the younger one joined in. "She's been missing since Wednesday evening. It's suspected that she might have jogged through this forest area and disappeared during this time or shortly afterward. Now we're asking residents of the surrounding area whether they might have seen something suspicious. The forest path that the girl might have jogged along more or less leads past your house."

"Do you live all alone out here?" asked the older one. "It's pretty lonely."

"My brother and my … my mother live here too," Karl said quietly. "I … I'm mostly at home because I care for

my mother. She is very … seriously ill. But I didn't see anyone. Not here and not out there. No, I'm sorry."

Suddenly the younger policeman pulled something out of the pocket of his uniform jacket. Karl held his breath. It was a photo of Laura. She wasn't smiling. Nevertheless, she looked pretty. Very pretty. Quite different from now.

"Laura Hermann. The missing girl. Have you ever seen her before?"

Karl stared at the photo without really looking, then he shook his head. "No. I don't know her."

"Didn't you ever notice a young jogger out here?"

Karl shrugged. "No. Not that I know of. But I don't pay much attention to such things. I'm rarely outside, and the way can only be seen from our kitchen window, where I stay the least. I have no idea who's passing by here."

"Is your brother at home?"

What should he do now? Should he lie or tell the truth? Karl's thoughts overturned. But what if they had already heard their voices through the door? If he lied now, he'd make himself damn suspicious.

"Yes, he's home. But he was still asleep when you rang the bell. I would first have to look …"

"No problem," said the senior police officer.

"And your mother?" the younger one interjected. "Old people are often very attentive to what's going on around their house."

Karl shook his head energetically. "Not my mother. She's bedridden. She never gets up, and her room is in the back of the house, overlooking the garden."

"I see. But would you be so friendly to wake up your brother?"

"Yeah, sure, I'll go get him."

On trembling legs, Karl went back into the house.

***

"They wanna talk to you!"

Toni hectically dressed in his jeans and the sweatshirt he wore the day before. "Shit! What did you say?"

"Nothing. That I didn't see anything and nobody."

"Good. Okay. We'll handle that. They don't suspect anything, right? They're just doing a routine interview."

"Yeah, looks like it."

Toni patted him on the shoulder. "Good. Great. I'll take care of it. No problem at all."

Karl nodded. He stayed in the living room while his brother went to the door.

***

A few minutes later Toni was back again. The relief was visible in his face. He even grinned. "All's well, brother."

Karl looked at him questioningly, but Toni rubbed his hands and laughed. "Man, I almost shit my pants. Awesome! But everything's fine, they have no suspicion against us. They just ring the bell at every door in the area and talk to the people. Just routine. Everything easy!"

He rubbed his bald head and walked up and down the room shaking his head. "Man, you looked at me as if you were puking in my face every moment! Unbelievable! There's no reason at all, you weirdo. The cops are searching the forest, they said. With dog squadrons. The volunteer fire department is also participating. Imagine that, man! Even a helicopter with a thermal imaging camera was there. It's amazing what they do because of a single slut. Really gross!"

"I'm sure her parents are totally worried," Karl said

quietly.

Toni looked at him. "So what? Why should I care? They should have taken better care of her. Now she belongs to me! Her name is Laura. Did they tell you that too? Laura Hermann. And she's sixteen. But I thought so already. She's older in tits, but I deflowered her. Did you know that? My cock was the first … and the last one. How cool is that? Man, all the excitement has made me really horny now! I'm going to the basement and fuck her a little while these idiots with their dogs and thermal cameras are running around out there looking for the needle in the haystack! That is such a horny feeling! Awesome, dude!"

Karl could see the hard-on in Toni's pants. Disgusted, he turned away.

"See you later, brother. I'll now visit my personal fucktoy. Oh, the little bitch will be happy!"

Toni disappeared into the cellar.

Karl stayed behind. He imagined what would happen to Laura and felt compassion, disgust, sadness, and envy (but only a little)—because there was another person in this house who would have liked to have sex with this girl. A second person who now had an erection, but he had to deal with it alone and secretly.

***

That's how the third day after Laura's capture began. And so would the following days.

As soon as Toni had enough alcohol in the evening to fall into his typical coma-like sleep, Karl went down to the basement and brought Laura the blanket and sometimes something to drink. Mostly tea. From time to time cola or juice. He gave her nothing to eat, no matter how

much she begged.

But she knew she shouldn't force her luck too much, so she was mostly quiet when Karl asked her to be. Even if she wasn't content, she was honestly grateful that this strange guy did something for her and took a certain risk. Just the fact that he brought her the blanket was an incredible relief. This gave her at least a few hours of sleep, peace, and warmth, without which she might have died long ago. The hunger was torture. The initial slight growling of the stomach had turned into painful cramps, and only Karl's chamomile tea was able to give her some temporary relief. Nausea and dizziness followed, presumably because her circulation was gradually breaking down. Of course!

Nevertheless, Laura remained steadfast as far as the meanwhile miserably stinking food in the dog bowl was concerned. She knew Toni was just waiting, but she wouldn't do him that favor. She wanted to retain at least her last bit of dignity.

So she swore it to herself until the sixth day.

Toni led her like a dog on a leash on all fours up the stairs into the house. He took her to a gloomy, terribly filthy bathroom. There she had to use the moldy shower while he sat on the toilet seat and watched. She wasn't allowed to take off the chains. Toni gave her a shower gel and a simple wet razor. He wanted her to shave not only her armpits and legs but her genitals. Despite the feeling of shame, Laura enjoyed showering again and feeling the (warm!) water on her skin. She washed her hair with a men's shampoo. Normally she used a conditioner, but even now she felt something like gratitude to at least be allowed to take care of herself a bit.

When she was finished, Toni handed her a large towel. Not quite clean, but she long overlooked such trivial mat-

ters. She was grateful for every little piece of normality.

She was especially grateful for the luxury of being allowed to leave this terrible cellar for a while. Nevertheless, she couldn't forget her hunger. It was now omnipresent, and not a second passed without her thinking about something to eat.

She took a look in the mirror above the washbasin and to her horror she hardly recognized herself. She looked ugly. Pale and emaciated. Thick brown rings under the eyes, deep in the sockets. The clavicle and ribs stood out all too clearly. Blackened spots and bruises at various stages of development covered most of her body. Her nose was unnaturally crooked and flattened in the middle. An ugly red scratch blemished her forehead. Her lips were dry and chapped. Worst of all, however, were her nipples, which he maltreated every day with fingers and teeth. Bloody and sore, the remaining skin green, blue, and purple, swollen. Laura could do nothing but turn away in shock. Was that still her? She looked like a corpse—and actually, she was long dead. Tears came to her eyes.

"You like what you see?" He grinned right in her face.

Laura lowered her gaze in silence. She'd learned by now that she wasn't allowed to look at him directly.

"Here. Take that! You have some very bad breath!" He offered her a toothbrush that had seen better times. Probably his own.

Laura took it. A crushed tube of toothpaste lay on the edge of the sink. She squeezed it and brushed her furry teeth without risking another look in the mirror.

***

After brushing her teeth, he forced her back down to her

knees. She had to crouch next to the toilet on all fours while he peed standing, and several splashes of urine landed on her face.

When he finished, Toni closed his pants but didn't flush.

"Quite dirty, this toilet," he said. And then: "Lick it clean!"

It was crazy that Laura first thought about telling him that she'd just brushed her teeth to get rid of bad breath and that this would probably ruin the effect, but she bit her tongue. Just in time. She swallowed all the words. If he ordered her to lick the toilet clean, she would have to do it. He'd force her anyway, whether she resisted or not. Laura had understood by now that it was much better for her to do what he demanded.

So she bowed her head over the toilet bowl. Pretty dirty, how true. Apart from the fact that there were splashes of his fresh urine everywhere, this toilet was a total shithole. Calcified to the top, excrement and urine stains everywhere. Laura looked to the left, where an old toilet brush was collecting the feces of years. In recent times, it had probably not been used very often.

She couldn't suppress the gag reflex that rose in her throat. Toni seemed little impressed. He just laughed.

"Go ahead, girl! Once around the rim. And I don't want to see any more stains of piss and shit, otherwise I'll beat the shit out of *you*. Understand?"

Laura nodded. Then she closed her eyes, stuck out her tongue, and started.

***

After the toilet had been cleaned to Toni's satisfaction (Laura had managed without vomiting, which she proba-

bly owed to her empty stomach), he took her into his bedroom. And although Laura knew what came next (the erection that had already formed in his pants during the "toilet cleaning" was hard to ignore), she was relieved that he didn't take her back down to the basement. Up here it was at least warm and relatively clean.

Even though it seemed incomprehensible, sex had almost become routine in the meantime.

Toni always took her first from the front and then from behind. At the end she had to lick his cock clean, and he usually came in her mouth. Laura was horrified to find out that she swallowed his sperm almost greedily by now. Her aching stomach reared up to fill at least a little of its yawning void with Toni's salty, sticky ejaculate. Laura hardly felt any real disgust anymore. It was frightening how quickly a human could become inured to such horrors. The only really unpleasant thing was the way he treated her breasts before and after. He bit, scratched, and pinched, always making the already sore and aching parts bleed. Laura feared that an inflammation had developed in the meantime, but she didn't dare ask him to stop for a while so the wounds could heal.

She didn't dare because part of her knew that her request would only lead to more pain. She wasn't here to let Toni listen to what she had to say. She was here to let him do with her whatever he wanted. If he wanted to hurt her breasts, he'd do that. As long as he thought it was right. Her feelings didn't play the slightest role. Maybe he'd give her a break if the wounds began to fester so badly that he felt disgusted. That was the only chance she had.

No particularly rosy prospects, but Laura was just getting used to it.

***

It was on the sixteenth day that Laura struggled her way out from under the blanket, which Karl still reliably brought every evening and took away every morning without Toni suspecting anything. Toni probably didn't think his brother was capable of such a degree of disobedience.

Laura had just woken from a confused dream, in which she'd sat with her parents at Christmas dinner and ate masses of sausages with potato salad—the usual Christmas dinner of her family. But not this year. In fact, today was December 26, and Christmas was over. Her birthday was in two days. Not that that played any role for the new Laura. Her only meal yesterday as well as the days before had been a tangy portion of semen, and her gifts had been a dirty blanket and a cup of lukewarm peppermint tea with sugar. She rarely thought of her family or anyone "out there." Her new life was here, and there wasn't much except for pain, humiliation, and in the evening, gratitude toward the brother of her tormentor. She didn't want to think of much more because it would have hurt too much. She forced herself to always stay with her thoughts in the here and now and to live from moment to moment. The little bit of life she still had was primarily about the relief the nights and mornings brought before Karl came to get the blanket and (especially) before Toni showed up.

But now she'd been dreaming of home. Not for the first time, yet unusually intense. She still had the taste of sausages on her tongue. And her mother's voice echoed in her head. Her mother. How she'd laughed. How she'd looked at Laura. Her hands, so warm and familiar. How her mother had covered her up and stroked her. Back

then. So much comfort came from these thoughts. Her mother's hands. Her mother's voice. The smell of her father. The light in the dining room. Warm. Bright. The Christmas tree. With the red Christmas balls and golden tinsel. Candlelight. The scent of cookies. Her grandmother, who stayed overnight on holidays and always drank a glass of eggnog in the evening. Only one. To fall asleep. The soothing blue flickering of the television when they all sat in front of it and watched Christmas comedies. The clinking of the wine glasses. The smell of the roast on Christmas Day. Afternoon walks through the forest.

The forest.

There she was now. Not far away from home. She could've walked home. To her mother. Her father. To the candlelight. The scent of cookies. To the Christmas roast. She'd be there in less than twenty minutes. Absurd! So close and yet light years away. If her parents only knew where she was. Her father would have come and got her out of here. Her mother would have broken the neck of that damn Toni. And her grandma. What did they all do now? Without Laura? Did they think of her? Were they still searching for her? Did they cry? What would they do if she was never found? Forget her? Bury her? Sit and watch *Aktenzeichen XY (*Translator's comment: A German broadcast, quite similar to *America's Most Wanted*)? What happened if people disappeared and never showed up again? Had she ever thought about it before? No, not really. Why should she? If she died down here, Toni would probably throw her body into the forest. Then they would find her and understand what had happened to her.

Was that what she wanted? Yes, it would be better than that uncertainty. Her parents would be able to bury her. Then she'd be home again. Somehow. So death wasn't

the worst thing that was waiting for her down here. Maybe it was even her salvation. Toni would soon get tired of her anyway. Then he'd kill her. Hopefully! The thought soothed Laura in an eerie way. She wanted that to happen. It would put an end to all this.

But for now, she wasn't dead yet. She was thirsty. But she was even hungrier. Crying, Laura crawled to the water bucket that stood next to the toilet bucket. She greedily drank the stale tap water. At least she hoped it was tap water, but Karl mostly brought it to her, and she trusted him so far. He was also the one who emptied her "toilet" every two days. Toni didn't get his hands dirty with it. A few times he'd insisted Laura do it herself while he watched. Every time she'd dumped the contents into the toilet, she had to lick the rim before she could flush. He loved to humiliate her that way. Once it had even turned him on so much that he raped her on the spot.

Laura looked at the dog bowl, which had been standing untouched in the same place for two weeks now. Thanks to the cold the food hadn't started to mold yet, but it looked really repulsive and smelled the same. Laura suddenly wished he hadn't soaked it with water because then it would have remained hard but much more appetizing. Instead, it had turned into an unsightly, gluey, dried mass. For a moment, Laura played with the idea of asking Toni for fresh food tomorrow. Then she would eat it. To hell with her dignity! She'd flushed it down the toilet anyway. She also knew he wouldn't give her fresh food. She could eat this or nothing at all. He'd certainly punish her for the outrageous question. Maybe she'd have to drink his urine again. He'd pissed directly into her mouth once before and meticulously made sure she swallowed everything. That had been bad. Really bad. Much more disgusting than the sperm thing she'd become accustomed to.

"If you vomit, you'll lick it all up," he'd threatened. And somehow Laura had managed not to puke. Thank God!

Maybe next time it'll be something a lot worse than just piss. He hasn't done everything possible to you yet. And in the meantime, you've even come up with some ideas he might have, right? We don't want to say it, but we know exactly what this is about. That's why we don't want to provoke him at all. No, we'll never provoke him. The idea of what he'd do if he knew about the blanket and the drinks is enough. Right? Karl thinks that in this case he'd be the one to get the most severe punishment, but we're not so sure about that. Isn't that right, Laura? We know that the punishment of little Laura could be extremely unpleasant in this case. So keep your feet still, girl! Don't fall from grace unnecessarily!

No, there was no way she'd risk that.

And her hunger was so big, so infinite …

Thanks to Karl's sweet beverages she'd probably endure a little longer, but at some point there was a limit. How long could a human survive without food? She didn't know.

But you'd probably be willing to eat shit before it all ended. As Karl had said, the human survival instinct is strong. Starving people have already eaten other things than old dog food. And was it all about the damn food? Of course she was disgusted by it, but in the last two weeks she'd already swallowed much worse than a handful of dog food.

First and foremost, this was more about the principle. The food was the only thing she'd successfully refused him so far. It was about her last bit of dignity, the last bit of "old" Laura that was still in her. A part of her knew (just like Toni) that she'd give herself up for good if she ate from that bowl. He could have forced her long ago, just as he'd forced her to do all these unspeakable things.

But he didn't. Why? He left it to her to make a final decision about giving herself up. Her alone. She could choose starvation to escape her martyrdom. Toni gave her the choice. He let her do it consciously because he wanted her to surrender to him voluntarily. He wanted her to choose on her own free will: death … or a life with him. The last own choice she had.

And the new Laura, who would never be Laura Hermann again, crawled to the dog bowl on all fours to make the perhaps last free decision of her life.

***

When Karl came into the basement that morning, as always with a cup of steaming contents in his hand, Laura had long been awake. She sat crouched on the mattress and buried herself up to her chin in the blanket, which didn't belong to her. The thought that he now had to take it away from her immediately triggered various emotions in Karl. Compassion was one of them, the most bitter satisfaction was another.

He approached Laura and his gaze fell automatically at the dog bowl.

It was empty.

Dirty and sticky, but empty.

So she'd done it.

Finally.

Karl felt relief. She'd already looked very bad. Emaciated. Thin. More dead than alive. Even her breasts seemed ever smaller to him in the last few days. Which could well be the case. Famished women were rarely busty, unless a surgeon helped with silicone.

Without showing any emotion, Karl handed her the warm cup. This time it contained coffee. With some milk

and lots of sugar. Laura drank greedily.

Karl sat next to her. "How are you?" he asked after some time.

Laura didn't answer. Their eyes met, and at that moment they both knew what the other was thinking. If one could have opened the skullcap and looked into their heads, there would have been an empty bowl in both of them. But some things were better left unsaid.

"Better," Laura finally replied.

Karl nodded. The bowl in his head was still there.

"It was the right decision," he said.

Laura gave a trembling sigh. "I'm not sure."

***

Later that day, Toni showed up in the basement.

Laura sat on the mattress with her knees pulled up. In the last few hours she'd already had to use the toilet bucket three times to pee. Probably because of the coffee. Now, an unpleasant, biting smell of urine hung in the air.

Toni wrinkled his nose. He wore jeans, a blue T-shirt, and his work boots, which Laura had just licked clean yesterday.

He held the leash that matched the collar that Laura had to wear since he first put it on her.

With heavy steps he came toward her, probably just about to say something.

Then he saw the bowl.

A grin came to his face.

"The mutt has finally eaten," he said with satisfaction.

Laura was silent. She was only allowed to speak when he directly told her to. She'd learned that in the meantime. That and much more.

Toni patted his thigh. "Come here!"

Laura crawled down from the mattress and stayed right in front of his feet with her head lowered.

"Look at me!"

She raised her head. Toni attached the leash to the collar.

"Turn around and show me your asshole!"

Laura did as she was told. She lifted her ass as far as she could.

She already felt Toni's fingers—one, two, three—and finally his whole fist in her anus. Apparently he'd greased it with something. It still hurt damn bad, but she bit her teeth together. The fist was turned a few times, pulled out and rammed in again. To Laura it felt as if her guts were being torn out. She held her breath until the pain subsided and he gave her the order to turn around.

His fist was right in front of her face. It was covered with feces. Her feces. The digested remains of dog food.

"Look at that mess," he yelled and punched her in the face with his fist.

Laura was thrown to the side. She tasted her own excrement as she licked her bleeding lip.

"Clean that up, you fucking cunt!"

She hadn't seen him that aggressive in a long time.

Laura immediately started to lick his fist. She didn't even think about it. Toni rammed it so deep into her mouth that she had to choke. But she kept licking until he ordered her to stop. He hit her on the injured lip again, which swelled like a rubber dinghy and became numb at the same time. Again she had to turn around so that he could rape her from behind. First vaginal, then anal. As usual, he wanted to come in her mouth, which Laura could hardly open because of the swollen lip. But Toni pushed until it bled. In the end, the floor, Laura, and he were completely sullied.

Breathless, with blood on his penis and thighs, he stood in front of her and pointed to the floor. "That'll be clean before I come back, you dirty cunt! You lick it all up, otherwise I'll beat the last bit of shit out of you!"

With these words he left, and Laura stayed behind, sobbing and bleeding in all the mess.

***

She used the water from her drinking bucket to rinse away the blood. She was meticulously careful to save enough water to make ends meet, if necessary, for the next few days.

His aggressive behavior forced her to be cautious. What had suddenly gotten into him?

She'd assumed Toni would be gentler when he saw that he'd finally broken her will. But she must have been wrong. Quite the opposite. He'd behaved more brutally and insanely than ever before. For a moment she'd actually been afraid he'd kill her. He was surely capable of doing it. The furious pain in her mouth and abdomen spoke for itself. He'd attacked her like a rabid animal.

Now she lay on the dirty mattress. Naked and bloody. The taste of copper and salt in her mouth. Blood and sperm. It almost seemed to her that from now on it was her wine and bread. Donated by a sadistic deity.

Laura lay there, keeping her eyes closed and her hands in front of her mouth, trembling with cold and praying to one good god that the evil one would not come back so soon.

***

At the same time, Karl painfully learned in the upper part

of the house why Toni was now in such a bad mood

He was sitting at the kitchen table, drinking a cup of coffee when Toni came in. Karl immediately saw that something was wrong. His brother's eyes sparkled. His cheeks were reddened. There was blood on his clothes. Just like on his hands.

He stomped wordlessly toward Karl and slapped the cup out of his hand onto his lap. The coffee was fresh and accordingly hot. Karl jumped up as if stabbed by a tarantula. His chair fell over. The cup landed on the floor and broke into pieces. Its contents had landed almost entirely in Karl's crotch and on his thighs.

That hurt damn bad.

"Shit!" Karl cursed and immediately regretted it.

"Hey—" Karl swallowed every word when Toni grabbed him by the neck. He instinctively stepped back and stumbled over the fallen chair and the broken cup.

Both men fell to the floor, only Toni managed the softer landing on Karl's belly. He was still holding his brother's neck, and he squeezed until Karl wriggled his legs and the first veins burst in his eyes. Perhaps the sight frightened Toni. He let him go. Karl coughed and choked. Toni sat on his brother's stomach, watching him struggle for air as fine droplets of saliva flew through the air.

He waited. Finally he said, "Have you looked around here? You're going to clean up this mess! Understand? You'll clean this damn kitchen like you're fucking Mister Clean! Is that now in your Mickey Mouse brain?"

Karl coughed, nodded, coughed, nodded.

"Things will be different around here soon, I tell you."

Karl coughed. "Why? What's going on?"

"From January on I have a new job."

Karl stared at him, still coughing.

"I don't like it right now, but there's no way to change it. I got the job offer from a buddy and can't refuse it because we're up to our necks in shit, as you might have noticed. We're almost broke."

Karl coughed. "What kind of job is it?"

"A great one," Toni mocked. "Garbage collection." He spat the word out like an annoying lump of slime. "I know it's shit, but it pays quite well. We need the money."

Karl nodded, coughed.

"That means, of course, that from now on you'll be alone most of the day. Here. With her."

Karl remained silent. Coughed.

"So it's fucking important that you're aware of that responsibility. You mustn't fuck up, dear brother, otherwise we'll all regret it. Always remember, you're just as involved in this as I am. You're an accomplice. You can't get out of this, baby. Is that clear?"

Karl nodded.

"I wanna hear it! From your mouth!"

Karl coughed, cleared his throat. "Yes."

"Yes *what*?"

Karl cleared his throat again. "Yes, it's clear."

Toni suddenly looked thoughtful. "Maybe not clear enough, what do you think?"

Karl looked at him without understanding.

"Have you ever hurt her?" Toni asked.

Karl shook his head truthfully.

"Did you fuck her?"

Another shake of the head.

"So you haven't touched her yet, in any way?"

"No, I didn't."

Toni showed his teeth with a nasty grin. "Then it's about time, man!"

***

Laura stopped breathing when the cellar door opened. This time there were two of them!

Karl had bloodshot eyes and was white as a sheet. He moved awkwardly and almost in slow motion. The corners of his mouth twitched, and it looked as if he'd start crying at any moment. Or vomiting. Maybe both.

Toni, on the other hand, seemed more alive than ever. His eyes flashed. His face was of healthy color. A scornful grin played around his lips.

Shoulder to shoulder they stood in front of her.

More or less. Karl was smaller than Toni.

The unwashed, dirty blond hair stuck in greasy strands to his forehead. He stank of sweat. Toni, on the other hand, had showered and changed. He smelled of aftershave. His freshly shaved bald head shined as if polished.

"Hello, Laura," Toni said.

She didn't answer. It would have been hard for her anyway because her lips were still swollen and hurt like hell.

"May I introduce to you my cute little brother?" Toni continued.

He gave Karl a rough slap on the arm.

"Say hello, Karl!"

"Hello," Karl said.

Laura stared at him. *What the hell is going on? Does he know anything? Is it the end now? What is he up to?*

"Answer him!" Toni roared.

"Hello," Laura muttered with her head lowered.

"Karl's here to fuck you," Toni explained. "Now spread your legs so he can see your hole."

Karl now cried indeed, but he didn't move.

"Come on!" Toni kicked her in the shin.

Laura spread her legs as wide as the shackles would allow.

"There it is, our little fuckhole! It's perhaps a little worn out by now, but it'll do for you, Karli!" Toni roared with laughter.

Karl still sobbed and tried not to look at her. Toni slapped him in the face. "Look, you fucking loser! Here's your hole and you'll fuck it now until you're both sore! Get it?"

Karl didn't answer. But now his gaze wandered over Laura's body to her displayed sex. He said nothing, but his face spoke volumes. He put his hands in his pants pockets. Tears ran down his cheeks.

"What's up?" Toni nagged. "Are you gonna start, or can't you get a boner?"

Karl turned to his brother but still didn't say a word.

Laura remained in position.

"Fucking shit! Can't you do anything without my help? Not even fuck?" Toni slapped his brother in the face. An ugly red print remained on his cheek. Karl didn't move.

"Now go ahead, you stupid asshole!"

Toni hit him again. Now on the other cheek.

Karl staggered one step back.

"Do it!"

Karl pulled his T-shirt over his head. A pale, hairless upper body with some fat on his chest and hips came to light. The belly hung over the pants to such an extent that one could hardly see the waistband.

Toni acknowledged this sight with a dirty laugh. "Look at him, girl! Isn't he a feast for the eyes? Oh God! The damn chips really went straight to your hips, right?"

Karl dropped the T-shirt on the floor and stood there, lowering his gaze to his feet.

"Continue!" Toni commanded.

Karl fumbled around at a place under his imposing belly, where he probably suspected the pants button was. It took him an eternity to finally find it. He pulled the pants down and his belly and breasts wobbled vigorously, making Toni laugh again.

"Laura, I'm really sorry that I can't offer you anything better than this fat dumpling here! But don't worry, I'll compensate you for what the idiot is screwing up now."

Karl now stood barefoot in boxers.

Laura could see several stains on the worn fabric. *Please God, just let it be normal sex! Please don't let him put in my mouth! Please, please, please!*

But she was down here in the basement of the Singer family. And there was no God down here. At least not a good one.

"Come on now," Toni shouted cheerfully. "Show us your pathetic thingie and let's move on!"

Karl took off his boxer shorts. His penis was of average size, surrounded by dark blond pubic hair, and probably hadn't seen any water for at least a week *(Dear God, don't let it be true, don't let it happen!)*.

"Shit, girl, I really wouldn't want to be in your skin right now," Toni said amusedly. "What a stench!" He roared with laughter. "Now crawl over there and give him a fucking blowjob! I finally want to see some action, guys!"

Laura hesitated a second at most and then crawled over to Karl. The smell of his unwashed body penetrated her nose as she knelt in front of him. She would have loved to hold her breath, but that was impossible.

She looked up, and for a moment their gazes met. Karl seemed absolutely desperate, and although she was the one in the worse position here, she felt pity for him.

"Come on, now! Open your mouth and let it in." Toni

sounded like the director in a cheap porno. "Back with the foreskin! I want you to lick it absolutely clean!"

Laura took Karl's flaccid penis in her hand and pushed the foreskin back. Almost instantly it woke up to throbbing life. For a moment she could still see the thick whitish smegma that had formed there due to lack of hygiene. She closed her eyes and reduced her senses to zero as she took Karl's penis into her mouth and began to lick it clean as thoroughly as Toni expected her to.

***

The pain in Laura's maltreated lips struggled for the upper hand with the disgust in her throat as she sucked and licked Karl's unwashed penis. She forced herself not to consciously pay attention to the taste that flooded her mouth. Just lick and swallow. Don't think. She'd learned that in the meantime.

The worst thing she had to endure was that disgusting taste. A mixture of rancid cheese and old fish. Not pretty, not at all. Until recently, that alone would have brought her to the brink of madness and to the limits of what was bearable. But in the meantime, she'd really learned a lot. Toni had shown her what she could really endure and what unspeakable things people could do to each other without perishing. At least in a physical way. What it looked like inside her was another question she didn't want to think about. She was scared shitless to look into this abyss. Because we all know that the abysses of our souls can become dangerous once we start to deal with them. We look into them and they look back. They look into us. Deep. Long.

And God knows what they see.

Laura swallowed spasmodically in order to get the taste

out of her mouth as quickly as possible, but her saliva became thicker, until at some point she couldn't swallow it anymore.

Karl's penis, however, had swollen to a relatively considerable size in her mouth. Laura already felt the first salty sperm on her tongue (a real pleasure compared to Karl's smegma) when Toni grabbed her by the hair from behind and brutally tore her back. She fell on her back, panting but grateful to have escaped the disgusting taste. Grateful!

Karl stood motionless in front of her. He looked at his hard-on, then at her naked body, and finally at Toni. He breathed heavily.

"Do it! Fuck the little cunt! Show her who's boss," Toni chanted.

Karl slowly approached Laura. She spread her legs and he lay between them. His soft belly pressed against her emaciated abdomen, his face very close to hers. And again she smelled him. Rancid sweat, mixed with fresh sweat, which was now pouring from all his pores.

He moaned as he slowly penetrated her.

It didn't really hurt, it was just a little uncomfortable because of all the sore spots she had to thank Toni for. Karl thrust carefully. But with the excitement, his ruthlessness grew, and his movements became faster and harder.

Toni's voice continued to cheer him on.

It didn't take long. Karl's orgasm was as short as it was violent. He emptied himself into Laura and then remained lying on her, wheezing and sweating. She almost felt crushed by his weight and stench.

Laura closed her eyes in relief as he finally stood up while Toni applauded in the background. She just lay there and felt Karl's semen sluggishly flow out of her.

It was the first time a man had come inside her. Toni had always made sure that this happened in her mouth (or somewhere else).

'Cause you can't get pregnant from that, shot through Laura's head.

Pregnant.

She didn't want to think about that. So Laura quickly pushed this thought into the furthest corner of her mind, where it could share the space with various other unwanted flashes of wit.

***

Karl didn't waste any time collecting his clothes. He just wanted to leave. Away from Toni's roar.

Away from Laura. From Laura's nudity. From Laura's helplessness. From Laura's beauty …

Away from this sex odor, which was as beguiling as it was cruel.

Away from this feeling.

Away from this feeling that was somehow good and somehow terrible.

He couldn't think clearly anymore. He didn't want that either. Not at that moment.

He just wanted to get out of this situation. Away from Toni, who was to blame for everything. Away from Laura, who (somehow) was also guilty. She'd finally driven him to do it—with her damn lips and her diabolical tongue. Couldn't she have refused?

Toni couldn't have forced her to do that to him.

Or had he?

Had he not also forced him?

No, Karl, you did it all by yourself. Toni just stood there. You both did it all by yourselves! Why didn't you say no? Why didn't

you leave? Why did you even have a boner, damn it?

Wasn't it what he'd wanted all the time?

Didn't he find her attractive?

Hadn't he thought of her when he jerked off in bed in the evening?

What had he thought of?

Her nudity? Her helplessness?

That she was at his mercy?

About what she'd possibly do just to get a blanket and a cup of tea from him?

And what she'd do for him when he brought her a candy bar?

Or gum after Toni's been with her for hours?

This list could continue endlessly.

The question was, had he thought of it? Of one of those things? Or all of them? And much more? Had he asked himself what she'd do? And how it would feel?

There were answers to all these questions that were hidden deep inside him. Karl knew these answers, but he'd repressed them. All the time. Until today. Until just now. But now they wanted to come to the surface. The questions and the answers. They sloshed up and down in the ocean of his consciousness and he stretched out both hands to push them back into the depths of oblivion. He was indeed a master of repression. But the feeling in his still-throbbing penis couldn't be suppressed. Not anymore.

Karl hectically collected his clothes from the floor and went naked upstairs to his room.

He locked the door and fell to his knees in tears. He held his hands in front of his face. They smelled of her. His penis stuck wet and limp to the inside of his greasy thighs. The moisture was hers. He'd felt her, had been inside her, very deep. And he hated himself for it, hated

himself with all his heart and with all his fervor, but he just couldn't deny how much he'd liked it.

And how much he longed to do it again.

***

After Karl left the basement in such a hurry, Laura had no time to think about what had just happened because Toni was far from finished with her.

While Karl's semen dried on her thighs, she had to play the dog again for Toni and crawl through the room for a quarter of an hour. He pissed in her drinking bucket and she had to drink it all. He pulled her by the hair and kicked her in the stomach. She had to lick the soles of his shoes until they shined.

Then he left her alone for a moment and returned with an iron rod.

Since he didn't want to fuck her after his stupid little brother had poked around in her (that's how he put it), he used this new toy on her and let Laura lick it clean as a whistle after anal penetration.

Then it was finally over and he left.

That night Laura waited in vain for the blanket, just as she waited in vain for tea the next morning.

The last spark of hope in all this insanity seemed to have gone, and she wept the most bitter tears of her life. So far!

***

Karl sat at the kitchen table looking out the window while sipping his coffee. It had snowed. Winter had come. Today was New Year's Eve.

Lupo lay at his feet and snored quietly. Karl let his arm

hang down and stroked the dog absentmindedly. He just sat there staring outside. For two hours. He tried not to think of anything, but he couldn't avoid thinking.

About his mother.

About Laura.

About Toni.

Of what had happened recently in the basement and what was going on there in those minutes.

Toni had gone to the basement about an hour ago. With an iron bar, a rope, and a folding chair. Karl didn't think about what his brother would do with the iron bar.

He didn't think about the chair or the rope either.

Or about the last time he was down there himself.

No blanket for Laura. No warm beverage. Maybe even nothing to drink at all. How many days already?

Karl wasn't sure whether Toni cared about such matters of his prisoner. Probably not.

The toilet bucket hadn't been emptied either, and there hadn't been any water for washing since then. Toni hadn't told him to take care of these things, and Karl was happy about it. He knew he wasn't doing Laura any favors, but he was doing himself one and that was more important at the moment.

She must have suffered terribly. Without water. Without a blanket. With Toni, who came to her every day and had this iron bar, rope, and the folding chair with him.

Now you're thinking about it again, Karl admonished himself. He rubbed his forehead and then his eyes. He knew what he was doing to Laura by no longer going into the cellar. But Toni didn't seem to need his services at the moment, Karl thought. He was unable to go to the basement. He didn't want to see her. He didn't want to talk to her. He couldn't and didn't want to endure this feeling. He'd raped her; that couldn't be denied. It didn't matter

whether Toni had forced him or not. It had been his damn cock. His cock alone. Toni had been there but hadn't done anything, so who was to blame for the misery now?

But even worse than his self-pity was the fact that every night since then he dreamed of doing it again. The urge to jerk off became so overwhelming that Karl searched the Internet for pornos to distract him from the images in his head. But no matter which women were in the movies, he always had Laura's face in front of him. Her gaze. Compassionate and accusing at the same time. She knew it exactly. She knew he was a pig. A perverted little bum she wouldn't have given a second glance in real life. Now she was nice to him and pretended to like him because he was her only support in this nightmare. She probably still hoped that one day he'd get her out of there.

Her savior? Ridiculous!

After that, she'd give a shit about him. He would have died for her. She'd laugh at him. And he'd never fuck her again.

He knew he disgusted her. He understood that. He *was* disgusting. What would a gorgeous girl like Laura ever have done with a guy like him?

Does that still matter now? She's here and so are you and you can help her. That is all that matters, don't you think?

Karl wasn't so sure. Of course he wanted to help Laura. A bit. Until she felt better and was grateful to him. But freeing her had never really been a matter of debate for him. Not only because he was afraid of Toni, but also because …

… because you won't let her go. Right, Karl? The truth is you're just like Toni. You want her to stay here forever and you wanna have her in your hand. You want her to belong to you and be dependent on you. You're not the good one here, Karl, but just another

sick bastard who seizes the opportunity to make this girl submissive. You do it differently than Toni, but your goal is the same.

Karl rubbed his eyes and forehead as if he could wipe away all the harmful thoughts. He just didn't want to believe that in the end he might actually be like his brother: a lousy dirtbag. And that's why he didn't go to the basement anymore. He wanted to prove to himself that he didn't need the feeling of power that Laura's dependency gave him. No, he'd resist the temptation.

Instead, he took his smartphone and looked for more movies that would distract and satisfy him at the same time.

Unfortunately, he wasn't successful. Only ten minutes later he jerked off to an incredibly amateurish hardcore porn in which a petite Asian woman was raped by a giant baldheaded guy in a public toilet. Among other things, an iron rod was used. That was exactly the kind of trash Toni was into. Only Toni himself now played the leading role in a disgusting porn.

After Karl had cum and cleaned himself with some paper towels, he hid his face in his hands and cried like a little child. He cried over his own weakness and this damn inability to fight his inner swine.

He didn't want to be someone like that!

But for a long time, Karl Singer had been exactly what he never wanted to be. The insight hit him hard.

And with it, the year 2014 slowly came to an end.

***

He'd tied her hands and feet behind her back with a rope. She lay there for half an hour already. The iron bar was stuck in her asshole. The pain had subsided to a dull throbbing. Apart from that, Laura didn't feel much. Not

even the cold. No hunger or thirst. Of course he'd given her enough to drink in the last few days. He'd often peed into the bucket.

At the beginning of her ordeal, Laura couldn't have imagined that things could get any worse. In the meantime, she knew she'd been wrong. It could always get worse!

Now there was nothing but pain, anguish, and humiliation. Not even a warm blanket in the night or the feeling that there was someone there from time to time who did something good for her.

But Laura didn't want to think about it anymore. She felt herself getting weaker from day to day. Due to permanent hypothermia and dehydration, her physical condition deteriorated noticeably. Toni mistreated her to his heart's content, but sometimes she didn't even notice it anymore, drifting into a grateful unconsciousness again and again, for which she longed more and more. She also thought only rarely of her family, or the time before she was brought to this basement. It almost seemed as if this life hadn't existed at all. She clung to it less and less from day to day. As if she'd always been down here. Alone with Toni and the pain.

She stank too much for him now, so he only penetrated her with the bar or let her give him a blowjob. Laura didn't know why she wasn't allowed to wash. Maybe it was too troublesome for him to take her up with him. Maybe he just didn't care because he preferred to do it with the iron bar anyway.

Karl could have brought her washing things and emptied the stinking toilet bucket, but he never showed up. Laura knew, of course, that this had something to do with the sex they had had at Toni's behest. For her it hadn't been a big deal, compared to everything else she'd

been through. For Karl, however, it seemed to be much harder. He probably had a guilty conscience and felt ashamed somehow. Laura would have liked to take all those bad feelings away from him, but he didn't give her the opportunity. So she'd lost her only anchor and was now drifting completely alone and helpless in the ocean of torment that Toni thought up for her.

Right now he was sitting on the chair he'd brought with him a few days ago, watching her.

He was smoking and was naked from the waist down.

The result of his last ejaculation stuck to his thighs and the chair. He'd already jerked off twice during the last thirty minutes.

"Are you hungry?" he asked suddenly.

Laura forced herself to open her eyes and look at him. She nodded barely noticeably.

"Will you eat well-behaved if I fill the bowl for you?"

She nodded again.

"Do you know what day it is today?" he continued.

Laura shook her head truthfully.

"It's New Year's Eve," Toni explained. "Most people celebrate that evening. They drink. They eat something good."

He rose, sighing, and slowly approached her. "We didn't celebrate Christmas this year. Not for the first time, but what the hell? I thought we should at least celebrate New Year's Eve a little. I bought something."

He laughed. "For you, some premium dog food. For Karl and me, some meat and sauces for fondue. If you are a very, very good girl, you might get some. What do you think?"

Laura was silent. She wasn't even sure if she could believe him.

"Karl doesn't know anything about it yet, but I've al-

ready planned everything. Will be one of my last quiet evenings, you know? Then I gotta go back to work and won't have so much time for pleasure anymore. That's why I want to party today!"

He threw his cigarette butt carelessly to the floor and bent over her to pull out the bar. That hurt, but Laura didn't show it. Next was the rope. Toni removed it, and Laura could finally stretch her limbs out again. They pricked and tingled terribly as the blood flowed back into her hands and feet, and this time she moaned.

Toni grinned. He also took off her handcuffs. Tears of relief burned in Laura's eyes.

"Thank you," she whispered.

He nodded. "You'd better stay grateful, girl."

She returned his nod.

"I'll put you on a leash and you stay on your knees, but you can come upstairs with me. And if all goes well today, I might be willing to give you a blanket from now on—and a pillow. Well, what do you think of that?"

Laura looked at him hopefully. "I'll do anything you want."

"That's good! Very good indeed, my girl!" He ran his fingers through her greasy hair. "That's all I want!"

***

"I'm supposed to *what*?" Karl asked, surprised. Actually, he'd already understood his brother the first time, but he couldn't quite believe what he'd just said.

"Are you deaf, man? You're supposed to set the table for two and put on the fondue pot. Look in the kitchen cupboard. I bought everything necessary. It's New Year's Eve. We're celebrating today!"

Karl looked at him doubtfully. "We?"

Toni nodded with a grin. "Yeah, the three of us."

"The three of us? I-I thought I was only supposed to set the table for two?"

"You got that right, brother. Our guest gets the seat of honor." He headed for a plastic bag next to the fridge and dug out a can of dog food.

"You may serve that for our guest. Under the table, of course."

Karl stared at his brother.

"Everything clear so far?"

"I don't know if it's such a good idea, Toni."

"I think it's one of the best I've ever had. I'm sure we'll have fun, believe me." Toni pat Karl on the back.

"So don't worry, just do your job. In the meantime, I'll make our guest socially acceptable." He wanted to turn away but then hesitated. "Oh, and a shower wouldn't hurt you either, by the way. You can use the bathroom after us."

***

He took off her shackles and only put on the dog leash. Then he led her to the bathroom. Laura's knees hurt as she crawled, but she remained very still, eagerly awaiting the shower she was about to get. How long had it been since she was allowed to wash?

In the bathroom, Toni took the leash off the collar.

Laura crouched in front of him, her gaze lowered. It was cold in here, but she didn't want to complain.

"You can now stand up and get into the tub. Wash yourself properly. Also the hair! You can use everything here."

Laura nodded.

"I can't hear you!"

"Thank you." She raised her head and looked at him. "Thank you, Toni."

He nodded contentedly. "That's all right. Start now!" He sat on the toilet lid, where he had a good view of the bathtub.

Laura rose sluggishly and climbed into the dirty tub. She trembled and turned the water as hot as she could stand it. Then she started to shower. The feeling that flooded her as soon as the warm water hit her skin was indescribable. A delightful shiver ran through her, and she almost forgot that Toni was here watching her. At the moment she didn't give a shit. Laura enjoyed her shower. As much as she'd never enjoyed a shower before.

There were always good moments in life.

Even in hell. And that was a new insight.

***

He handed her a towel and allowed her to dry herself. But Toni didn't allow her to wrap herself in it, as Laura had hoped at first. As soon as she'd gotten out of the tub, he forced her to her knees again and put her on the leash.

Laura felt cold and her hair was still wet. And still she felt better than … when? Never mind. Time didn't matter anymore. Now only the moment counted.

Toni led her down the creaking wooden stairs. In the hallway she noticed the strange smell she'd noticed before. A smell of something dead that rotted in a corner.

Probably leftover food. It was obvious that the two brothers hadn't cleaned the house for a long time.

Toni first led her down the stairs and then through the gloomy hallway into a room Laura didn't know yet.

The kitchen.

It was bright in here and warmer than in the rest of the

house. Even the rough wooden planks she had to crawl on felt pleasant. Apart from that it was as dirty and littered with garbage as the rest of the house. A corner bench with a large dining table stood in front of the only window. A crucifix hung on the wall. Beneath it stood a finely carved figure of Mary with the Child Jesus in her arms, surrounded by a sea of flowers. Next to it lay a rosary. Laura found these symbols so out of place in a house of madness that she almost would have laughed out loud.

Her gaze wandered to the window. It was almost dark outside, and you could hardly see anything. Just enough to noticed that it snowed a lot the last days. Toni saw her gaze. He quickly went to the window and closed the curtains.

In the middle of the table stood a pot on a coaster, under which a small flame burned. Those sick motherfuckers had prepared a fondue to celebrate the day! Laura didn't know whether to cry or laugh. The smell of the warm fat made her mouth water. She desperately licked her lips when she realized the table was only set for two people. Plates with fondue skewers and wine glasses were set. There were napkins and small bowls filled with olives, pickled gherkins, and baby corn.

Sliced white bread lay in a breadbasket.

Laura's heart grew heavy at the sight and smell of all these delicacies. At home they always made fondue on New Year's Eve. It looked very similar to this one. And it smelled like it too. Her homesickness hit her harder than Toni's blows. It strangled her throat. An unimaginable weight lay in the middle of her body. Her empty stomach cramped up painfully.

Somewhere in the background a song was playing on the radio and reminded her of her old life. When she last

heard this song, everything had been fine. Back then (it seemed ages ago) her only problems were school and her virginity. Had that really been her life?

Laura couldn't hold it back any longer. She began to sob unrestrainedly as all these impressions flowed into her tortured senses.

All these things here weren't meant for her.

A dog bowl stood on the floor under the table.

Laura crawled there and remained seated in front of it.

The tears were running, but by now she knew where her place was.

Toni nodded contentedly and stroked her damp hair. "Such a good girl."

Laura held her head down. If she looked up without being asked, she was beaten, she also knew that by now.

She was a good girl and had learned a lot.

"If you keep being so well-behaved, you might get a treat later!" Toni patted her head.

Then he sat in the corner seat and pulled Laura a little further under the table. He wrapped the leash around his wrist. There was a bottle of wine on the table, and he filled his glass.

"Here's to you, my girl," he said solemnly and raised his glass. "And to all the fun you'll give me!" While he was drinking, his free hand kept patting Laura's head.

***

A short time later, Karl came into the kitchen, followed by a large, ponderous St. Bernard, who was probably very old.

"Take the dog to the living room," Toni ordered.

Karl grabbed the dog by the collar and led him to the door. He disappeared and returned alone shortly after-

ward. He didn't look at Laura crouching on the floor.

"You can get the food now," Toni said.

Karl nodded. There was a can of dog food on the worktop that was filled with all sorts of stuff. Karl opened the can and squatted next to Laura and the empty bowl.

"Fill the bowl," explained Toni.

Karl poured the entire contents of the can into the bowl, which had not really been cleaned before. The food was mushy and interspersed with shiny jelly.

Laura stared at the bowl. She held her breath. Karl left with the empty can.

Toni pulled on the leash so that her head was torn back a bit. "Eat!"

Laura hesitated. She slowly lowered her head. The smell of the food got into her nose and she choked dry. At the same time, her empty stomach made some excited somersaults.

Karl came back to the table and sat on a chair opposite Toni, who jerked on the leash again.

"Hurry!"

Laura stuck her face up to the tip of her nose in the soft dog food. She started eating without using her hands. Just like a dog. She knew Toni wanted it that way.

The taste was disgusting, but she tried to ignore it. Just as she'd learned. Just as he'd taught her.

She was hungry enough.

While she ate (chew and swallow, swallow and chew, just don't think ...), she felt Toni and Karl's gaze on her. But she managed to successfully ignore that. Somehow.

And she ate everything. Somehow.

Toni stroked her head when the bowl was finally empty—after less than five minutes.

"Good girl. So, now we can eat too. Karl, get the

meat!"

Karl got up and went to the fridge. From her position under the table, Laura could only see his legs. He came back, probably with the meat. Seconds later they put the first skewers into the pot with the hot fat.

It was bubbling. Laura smelled clarified butter and frying fat. She heard every sound the two men made while eating. All she saw was their feet and pant legs, between which she squatted on all fours. They both wore jeans. Toni's were bright, Karl's dark. And Toni was wearing his work boots. Karl wore Adidas sneakers that had seen better times.

For the next two hours it went on like this. Laura crouched under the table while the men above her ate and drank to their heart's content. The radio played along. Another hour until midnight.

The two barely talked. Most of what Laura heard were eating and drinking noises and the clinking of cutlery. She noticed that Karl got up several times to get something. At least once it was a new bottle of wine.

Then there was beer.

And later schnapps.

Laura was terribly thirsty, but she knew that she wasn't in the position to ask for anything. Only Toni decided if and what she drank.

Her knees hurt awfully, but she didn't dare make even the slightest movement as long as Toni didn't tell her to.

She constantly kept in mind that despite all the pain and humiliation she could now at least be in a warm room.

And she could listen to the radio.

And she could smell real food.

She was grateful for it, even though it made her feel strange.

She was grateful not to have to lie alone in the cold cellar.

Grateful for company.

Grateful for her full stomach—although it was only dog food.

Grateful to simply be allowed to crouch down here on the ground, in the warmth, without being maltreated.

At Toni's behest, Karl later filled her bowl with water.

And again Laura was grateful.

Good Lord, she almost felt like she was in seventh heaven!

***

Shortly before midnight, the meal was finished. While Karl was cleaning up, Toni took Laura with him into the living room. He turned on the TV and sat on the couch. Laura had to crouch so he could put his legs on her back. He left his shoes on. It was a very painful position in which Laura hopefully wouldn't have to stay too long. Toni's massive work boots lay heavy on her back, the heels pressing uncomfortably into her ribs. She looked at the television, where the big New Year's party at the Brandenburg Gate was shown. So many happy and carefree people. How could they celebrate in this very moment while Laura sat naked on the dirty carpet and had to play doormat for a psychopath?

The countdown for the turn of the year began. Karl came from the kitchen and had two glasses of sparkling wine with him. He sat next to Toni on the couch.

Toni took his glass and lifted it up.

Then the time came. Midnight!

Welcome, 2015!

The nightmare went into the next round!

Laura heard the sounds of the big party in Berlin. Cheering and screaming, these damn assholes greeted the New Year and apparently had no idea what kind of madness was going on in the living rooms of some people.

The two men toasted.

After he drank, Toni tipped the rest of his wine over her head.

Laura stared down as the champagne dripped from her hair and ran into her neck.

"Happy new year, baby! You may lick up anything that lands on the floor!" He giggled. "And a happy new year to you too, my dear brother! Here's to further successful cooperation!"

Karl said nothing.

The champagne from Laura's hair slowly dripped to the floor. She conscientiously licked up every drop. She knew Toni's words hadn't been a suggestion but an instruction.

He deliberately pressed his shoes firmly into her back.

Laura moaned but remained in this uncomfortable position. She was a good girl.

"Get some more drinks!"

Karl went to the kitchen again and returned shortly afterward with a bottle of wine. He swayed while walking and was already quite drunk. He probably couldn't keep up with Toni's drinking.

Now they drank from the bottle, while the party on TV was in full swing and fireworks lit up the screen.

The Singers' house, on the other hand, was in the dark. Nothing was to be heard, except for the party on television and the two men, who now burped alternately. No rockets. No firecrackers. No music. No people. They were much too secluded, here at the edge of the forest. Out here in the sticks.

Nothing happened in the next few hours. The men sat on the couch, watched TV, drank, and talked from time to time. Laura crouched at their feet and had to endure Toni's weight on her narrow back until it was barely possible anymore. She froze pathetically, had the aroma of cheap champagne in her nose, and soon didn't know which part of her body hurt the most.

Was it her back? Or her knees? Arms? Neck?

She wished for nothing more than to finally get rid of this weight and be allowed to lie down. Only his few visits to the toilet brought her some short relief. In those moments she was alone with Karl, but he only drank more wine, kept silent, and didn't seem to notice her at all.

"Are you up for fucking?" Toni asked when he came back.

Laura flinched inside.

"No, I'm much too drunk," was Karl's reply.

"Really? Well, you don't mind if I let off a little pressure, huh?" Toni chuckled.

Laura couldn't understand Karl's muttered answer. Toni grabbed her by the hair and pulled her up. Then he brutally pushed her forward. She landed on the coffee table on her stomach. A half-full bottle of wine tipped over. Laura was in the middle of a mess of spilled wine, cigarette stubs, and empty beer bottles. Something was drilling into her belly.

Toni pulled down his pants and got on his knees behind her. He spat in his hands and rubbed the saliva on his cock. Seconds later he penetrated her anally and tore open old and fresh wounds. Laura gritted her teeth to avoid screaming. Karl sat on the couch as if frozen. Their eyes met. This time he didn't look away.

Laura was brutally torn back and forth while Toni

fucked her.

Her imploring gaze drilled into Karl's eyes.

***

Watching Toni fuck the girl in her little ass while her tits were being flattened on the coffee table triggered a variety of emotions in Karl. He couldn't move because the gruesome spectacle right in front of his eyes captivated him so much. He smelled the champagne in her hair and the spilled wine. Everything turned in his head, and that didn't just come from alcohol.

Almost without noticing, Karl grabbed his crotch with one hand and slowly started massaging his penis. He didn't take his eyes from Laura's face for a second.

Her pain was visible, and he felt infinitely sorry for her.

Karl opened his pants and reached in.

Laura's lips trembled. Her facial expressions showed pain and horror.

Karl didn't even want to imagine how she felt.

What it felt like for his brother would have interested him more.

With a jerk, he pulled his erect penis out of his pants and took it in his hand.

This time the two brothers came almost at the same time.

And there was even a repeat for Karl, when Laura had to lick Toni's penis clean, which was covered with slime, blood, and excrement.

The first real fireworks of 2015.

And it wouldn't be the last.

***

When it was over, she had to crouch in front of the couch again and play the footrest for Toni. Laura struggled with the gag reflex she thought she'd long since lost. Her body was one big battlefield of screaming pain. She didn't know how long she'd last before her trembling knees finally gave way. She tried to distract herself from all the pain by looking at the TV, focusing on the sounds. The party wasn't over yet. Some pop singer stood on stage. The music was shitty, but the audience was still in almost unbelievable ecstasy.

Laura slowly turned her gaze away from the TV screen and over to the two men on the couch. At some point she'd heard that most men fell asleep after sex, disappointing their cuddly wives. What happened to *drunk* men after sex?

Not that you could really talk about sex in Karl's case. She still hadn't fully understood what had just happened. Had it excited Karl to watch a rape? *Her* rape, to be more precise. Was that really possible? After everything he'd done for her? After all the sweet words and actions that had given her so much strength?

In a way that Laura couldn't really understand or explain, Karl's reaction to what Toni had done to her was much worse for her than the rape. Not only had he accepted it, but he'd jerked himself off!

Twice!

Unbelievable! As if he'd been waiting for it all the time. He wasn't a savior or Samaritan! In the end, he'd only screwed her over to make things worse.

Probably he'd conspired with Toni from the beginning and everything else had been just a nasty little game they were playing with her.

Was that really possible?

Laura could imagine it.

But back to the topic …

Alcohol plus sex plus men … what was the result of that equation?

Very slowly Laura's gaze wandered upward. She turned her head hardly noticeably. She pushed her tongue out and licked her dry lower lip. She was thirsty. Dear God, such a fucking big thirst!

Her gaze first fell on Karl, who sat there with his legs stretched out and his head in his neck. His mouth was open, just like his pants. Laura couldn't see his eyes from her position, but she was sure he was asleep. The quiet snoring suggested it.

There was also snoring on the other side of the couch.

Laura carefully turned her head a little further. Her champagne-glued hair slipped into her eyes. That annoyed her, but she ignored it. She couldn't risk any unnecessary motion. Toni had tilted a bit to the side and collapsed over the armrest. Laura could see that his eyes were closed. He hadn't put his jeans on again. Only the boxers. Laura imagined her tearing them down to take his damn cock in her mouth for one last time. She wouldn't suck and lick. No, she'd just bite … and bite … and bite …

Her heart pounded wildly in her chest at the thought of it.

But she really had no time at all to indulge in such thoughts.

Because she wasn't locked up *down* in the basement.

And she was *not* tied up either—only the dog collar was still around her neck.

She was in the living room and could (theoretically) move freely.

There were windows. And a door. At least one. Through which she'd entered the house once.

She knew she had to go out into the hallway to get to that door. A few feet! Those were really only a few feet!

Laura swallowed. The thirst had disappeared. She didn't feel the cold, either. Crazy, frantic pictures shot through her head. She saw herself running away. Naked. Into the night. Into the forest. Into the snow. Naked. But it didn't matter because she'd be free. She'd be out of here! Escaped! Saved!

Laura's breath went faster and faster.

Stay calm, she admonished herself. *You gotta stay calm!*

She looked at Toni. Then at Karl. Then at Toni again.

They were sleeping! Really! Both of them!

Sex and alcohol! That was the damn secret recipe!

Now there was only one problem left …

The feet! His fucking feet on her back! How could she get rid of them without him waking up?

Laura held her breath for a moment. She thought about it but had no idea how deeply Toni was actually sleeping. Would he notice if she crawled away under him? His feet would then fall down and slam on the floor.

He had to notice that!

Or not?

How was she supposed to find out?

I guess the only way is to try it, kiddo.

True!

Laura exhaled noisily, only to suck in air greedily again.

Then she held her breath again … and slowly made herself smaller … she ducked as low as she could. Until she lay almost on the floor. And with her back Toni's legs also lowered, which didn't seem to affect him so far.

Nice and slow. Just nice and slow … it might work.

Laura cautiously ducked further and further and pushed herself away from Toni and his legs at the same time. They finally slipped down from her and landed on

the floor. There was hardly any noise, only the quiet snoring.

Then Laura was suddenly free. Her tormentors still slept like babies. It took her a moment to grasp this happiness, and then she crawled off toward the corridor.

When she arrived there, she realized there was no reason to crawl anymore. She had two legs and could walk.

Laura stood up, trembling, and did exactly that.

***

She immediately ran to the front door, the sight of which she particularly remembered. It was the last thing she'd seen before her life had taken this drastic turn.

The key was in the lock.

Laura held her breath and froze for a moment.

She couldn't believe it! Was it possible to be so lucky?

Or was it just in the end only a dream?

It felt like that.

She slowly moved again. She didn't notice anything around her. She walked past the closet, jackets and shoes, without having the idea to get dressed. After all, there were subzero temperatures out there. But Laura didn't care. The only thing she was interested in now was this door and the key.

She reached for it with a trembling hand that didn't really seem to belong to her.

She turned the key and her stomach cramped, but everything was fine. It was quite simple. The door was now unlocked. Laura clasped the handle … and pushed it down. The door opened. Ice cold air blew toward her and let her breath freeze. Instantly, snow was blown into the house. Also over her bare feet. Unimportant. The only important thing now was—

"Hey! Stop!"

The words cut through the cold air like a knife.

Laura froze. No! *Oh no*! That can't be true! Not now! Please no!

Urine ran down her legs. She didn't notice it.

Fragments of thoughts shot through her mind like arrows. He was behind her!

Karl.

The fat dumpling.

How fast could he run?

He'd been drinking.

He was drowsy.

He was overweight.

He was a goddamn pussy!

She could make it! As long as Toni didn't come, everything was fine.

Laura inhaled the ice-cold night air, tasted snow, fought down some sudden (now completely unimportant) childhood memory (something about New Year's Eve on a snow-covered mountain hut and her father, who had perhaps drunk too much for the first time in his life), and ran off.

***

"Shit!" Karl stumbled across the hallway and tried to put one and one together while his body was still fighting dizziness, nausea, and leaden tiredness.

The front door was wide open. Snow blew in. It was cold. Cold as hell! She'd run outside. Completely naked. She had pissed on the doorstep. He'd seen it all, but somehow he hadn't quite understood it. Laura had escaped. She was gone. And Toni would kill him if he didn't bring her back.

He glanced briefly at his shoes as he walked past the closet but didn't stop to put them on. There was no time for that now. She was barefoot out there. And stark naked. He'd follow her in socks. He had no choice if he wanted to catch up with her. If that was even possible! Karl was definitely not one of the fastest runners. Only two weeks ago he wouldn't have had a chance against Laura. But today was today, and Toni had put the girl through the wringer. She was half dead and couldn't last five minutes out there, let alone run through the forest. Through the snow. Naked!

Karl ran through the puddle of urine Laura had left behind and followed the girl out into the night.

The hunt had begun.

***

He saw her running along the snow-covered path. Her wet hair whirled around her head in the bitter-cold wind. Her pale little ass was almost invisible, perfectly camouflaged in this dazzling white, cold winter landscape. It wouldn't be long before snow and darkness completely swallowed her up. But Karl could still see her in the diffuse light that came from the house.

He ran after her as if he was out of his mind.

After a few seconds he couldn't feel his feet anymore. It was slippery, especially without shoes. And he knew exactly that it would be over if he fell. He wouldn't be able to catch up with her then. Not to mention finding her again in this darkness.

It was a starry night, so the moon had to be somewhere (unless there was a new moon, which Karl doubted). Not that it helped him in any way. The trees were simply too dense. High fir trees blocked the view. And at

the places, where a piece of sky was to be seen, there were indeed dozens of stars, but not a bit of moon.

It was dark as a whore's asshole. He'd lose sight of the girl as soon as she'd leave the cone of light that came from the house. Which would happen at any moment if he didn't catch up with her right now!

***

Laura ran. She didn't dare to look around and had no idea where she was heading. Away from the house. Away from Toni. Away from Karl. Into the snow. Into the darkness. Into the deep dark forest. She didn't care.

Even if she got lost. That didn't matter. Even if she froze to death. Never mind. Nothing mattered as long as she managed to get away from here. This madness had to end. Never again should this bastard touch her. Never again should he shove his disgusting cock into her. Never again did she want to believe Karl was the good one, although he was just a nasty self-righteous asshole who had watched too many S&M porn movies. Never again did she want to be locked up in this cold, damp cellar. Never eat dog food from a bowl again. She never wanted to be looked at again the way Toni always did before he took his damn gross penis out of his pants. Or before he used the pole. Never again did she want to think that this swine had robbed her of her innocence. Never again did she want to have to endure this pain, never again to endure this shame, never again play the good little dog, which was there only for fucking. Never again … never again … never again …

That's all Laura thought of as she ran through the snow. She didn't feel any cold. She didn't worry about the condition of the path. She only had eyes for the fir trees

at the end of the forest road. She headed for them. There she could hide and he wouldn't find her. He was a fat dumpling, just like his brother had said. He was out of shape. He couldn't catch her. Never. He was weak and stupid … a stupid, lying motherfucker, and he'd never get her …

Laura had to stop thinking because suddenly her feet were no longer where they should be. Somehow they no longer touched the ground. She'd slipped and twisted her right foot. Now she was lying on the ground while her legs were still twitching helplessly—in a desperate attempt to keep running because her brain hadn't understood that it was too late. Laura lay in the cold snow and fidgeted like a fish on dry land. She lifted herself up with all her might, wanted to get up again, but her feet no longer carried her. She'd sprained her right ankle or maybe even broken it. She couldn't walk anymore. But Laura was far from giving up. If she could no longer walk, she'd just crawl. That's what she'd learned. Moaning, she started to move. The cold penetrated her body and drove away some of the adrenaline. Laura clenched her teeth, crawled on. She was used to pain. And cold.

She still wanted to crawl away when she was grabbed by hands that were as cold as she was. Karl let himself fall half on and half beside her. He gasped like a broken boiler. The clouds of his breath were everywhere. He'd dropped himself on Laura's legs from behind and held her body with both arms.

Laura screamed with all her might and gasped her own clouds of breath into the crystal-clear air. She screamed partly out of resignation and partly out of pain because Karl lay on her injured foot.

He remained in his position, apparently totally exhausted. He held her in an iron grip, wheezing and coughing

like a lung cancer patient in his terminal stage. Laura could smell him. It was a mixture of sweat and alcohol.

"Let me go," she whimpered.

Karl grabbed her even harder. He coughed too hard to be able to reply.

Laura tried to free herself from his grip, but she didn't have a chance against his weight. Finally she gave up. Sobbing and shivering with cold.

In the meantime, Karl had regained his breath. He got on his knees and pulled Laura closer so that she sat half on his lap while he wrapped both arms around her. His hands grabbed her breasts, but Laura held still because she got a little of his body heat that way and she desperately needed that right now.

"Let me go," she said again. Her voice was little more than a whisper.

"I can't do that! You know I can't!"

"Please, Karl … please … I'll do anything you want. Just let me go!" While she was saying it, Laura realized how pointless it was. She'd actually do what Karl wanted. Just as she'd continue to do everything his perverted brother wanted. She had no choice because she'd still be their prisoner.

And was he kneading her breasts?

"We'll get up now and go back to the house," Karl said calmly. He pinched her nipple.

Laura flinched. Now she felt something hard on her butt. He actually had an erection. Here! Now! She couldn't (or wouldn't) believe it.

"I … I sprained my ankle!" she whined.

Karl massaged her breasts. "I'll help you."

He stood up clumsily and pulled her more or less gently upward with him. For now, Laura was just happy that he no longer had his hand on her breasts and that she no

longer had to feel his penis.

She put an arm around Karl's shoulders, and he supported her with his arm around her hips. They made it back to the door together, without Laura having to strain her injured ankle.

All the way back to the basement she forced herself to think of nothing but the next step.

For a short time it even worked.

***

As soon as she sat on the mattress again, Karl put her in chains.

Laura asked him to spare her injured ankle, but he didn't respond. He tied her hands behind her back, which even Toni rarely did.

"Why don't you at least leave me my hands?"

Karl slapped her in the face, which didn't hurt much, but it came so suddenly and surprisingly that Laura screamed.

"You got a lot of nerve, girl!" he yelled at her. His cheeks were red, probably from the cold. His lips, on the other hand, had taken on a light blue color.

Laura didn't want to know what her own looked like. She was still bitterly cold, and the damp cellar didn't make it any better.

Karl trembled all over, although, unlike Laura, he was at least dressed.

"Do you have any idea what Toni would have done to me if you'd really gotten away?" he yelled.

Laura felt his saliva like warm rain on her face.

"He would have totally freaked out! He probably would have killed me!"

"Why you?" Laura countered sobbing. "It wouldn't

have been your fault!"

"Do you think that would have interested him? He'd have let his anger run wild on the first person around. And who do you think that is?"

"I … I just don't understand what's wrong with you! I thought you wanted to help me!"

Karl shook his head in rage. "That's over now. I can't help you anymore, Laura. I'm sorry."

She stared at him with tears in her eyes.

"Why are you saying that now, Karl? You can't really blame me because I ran away! You would have done the same if you were in my place!"

He looked at her for a long time and seemed to ponder. He sat with her on the mattress. His gaze wandered to her breasts.

"Karl?"

He reached out one hand and stroked her left breast and then the right one. Laura tried to look him in the face, tried to catch his gaze, but she didn't succeed. Karl seemed to only have eyes for her breasts and the center of her body, and with her hands tied behind her, she didn't have the slightest chance of covering herself.

"Karl?" she tried again.

No reaction.

He stroked her further. So gently that it almost felt good.

Almost.

While his left hand continued to play with her nipple, the right hand moved down. Between her legs. Laura didn't try to stiffen. It would have been of no use. She simply let him do it. His hands slowly got warm again, at least warmer than she was, and it didn't feel bad to be touched like that. Under normal circumstances Laura would have imagined this as tenderness between a man

and woman. Back then. At another time. Only there was seldom anyone kept in chains.

While Karl explored the region between her legs with one hand and gently massaged her clitoris, he pushed her with the other until she lay on her back on the mattress.

That was okay. It didn't hurt. She couldn't even feel her ankle now. And suddenly (it was completely crazy) Laura almost wished he'd finally lie down on her. He'd be warm and soft. Almost like a blanket. She wouldn't have to freeze anymore. It was actually quite all right.

Laura opened her thighs a bit more so Karl's fingers could penetrate her even deeper. That didn't feel bad. Somehow tingly. And so very different from everything she'd experienced with Toni. Now he actually lay on her. Laura took a deep breath. He didn't smell good, but he was warm. That was more important.

She turned her head so that she could look at him. This time he returned her gaze.

"Be my friend, Karl. And stay my friend. I beg you."

He put a finger on her lips.

"I'm begging you," Laura whispered. "Be my friend." She spread her legs even wider, as far as her shackles allowed.

Karl's face came closer to hers. His lips found her mouth. Laura closed her eyes and opened her lips. Karl's tongue slipped in. It felt big and slick. She pushed her own against it and the feeling subsided. She tasted alcohol. That wasn't bad. She had only kissed two other boys so far. At parties. They had tasted like him.

While they were kissing, Karl pushed himself even closer to her. He was heavy, but that was bearable. The warmth was so much more important. He rubbed against her, and Laura felt his hard penis through the fabric of his pants.

He was fiddling with his belt while he continued to kiss her. Then he paused and took off his pants. Both pants.

Laura spread her legs to take him in. Karl kissed her again. At the same time he penetrated her. That was beautiful. Somehow. Laura felt a warm tingling sensation in her abdomen.

"Be my friend," she whispered in his open mouth.

"I promise," he replied. He moved slowly inside her.

Laura sighed. "Don't tell Toni."

"Never."

And then he silenced her with another kiss.

They kissed until Karl reached orgasm …

After that he stayed with her for a long time and gave her his warmth.

Laura had fled today to save her life.

Karl had captured her and brought her back to the place where she'd already lost this life.

Then he'd tied her up and raped her.

But Laura felt gratitude.

What she'd already lost wasn't only her life. It was everything.

KILLJOY

Toni learned nothing of the events of this New Year's Eve.

When he finally got up in the late afternoon of the first of January to take a shower and eat something, Karl had long since removed all traces.

He'd brought Laura down to the cellar again and tied her up after Toni had fallen asleep. That was the story he told his brother during a sparse dinner in front of the TV. They ate the leftovers from last night: cold meat with sauce and a few remaining olives and pickled gherkins.

Toni nodded. He seemed satisfied with this explanation.

Shortly afterward he went into the cellar, but five minutes later he came back to the living room and nodded to Karl (who had just had his heart beating up to his throat). It was as if last night had somehow sealed their union as accomplices. It probably wouldn't have bothered Toni to hear that Karl had fucked her. He seemed to have the right to do so now.

Just like that.

Nevertheless, Karl didn't mention it (of course).

Toni didn't feel like talking this snowy New Year's Day. Tomorrow was his first day as a garbage collector. Karl could understand his mood. That wasn't necessarily a dream job. Apart from the change of the accustomed unemployed existence to the rhythm of the time clock, it was certainly not a delight to empty stinking trash cans eight hours a day and stand on a truck, where it stank like in a sewer. Karl wouldn't have wanted to swap places with him. But a job was a job, and Toni was right. He wasn't in a position to choose, and they needed the mon-

ey.

Damn urgently, actually.

So Karl was glad that it had come to this. And not only because of that.

He was looking forward to having the house to himself all day again from now on. It had been damn exhausting with Toni, who constantly looked over his shoulder and reproached him for every fucking reason. Now he'd finally be able to start the day relaxed again and only had to worry about Toni's moods in the evening.

But it wasn't just about Toni's whims.

Karl would now be alone with Laura all day long. When he thought of it, he got wet hands and palpitations. He'd be able to go to her whenever he wanted. That was even in Toni's interest, because who, if not Karl, would continue to take care of the girl?

She needed fresh water regularly, the toilet had to be cleaned, and she had to wash herself so that she wouldn't smell when Toni went to her after work.

In fact, Karl was given precise instructions later that evening as to how to deal with their prisoner. Toni expected her to be freshly washed every evening and to have a clean toilet ready. She should get fresh drinking water every third day, which was perfectly sufficient in Toni's opinion. However, Karl wasn't allowed to feed her. Toni wanted to watch her when she ate from the bowl in the evening. That always made him so damn horny, he explained to Karl. The way she lifted her skinny little ass up and how her tits hung down and dangled while she ate turned him on immensely.

Karl also noticed that something was moving in his pants during these descriptions, and he asked Toni for permission to be there when she was fed.

Toni grinned and patted him on the shoulder. "Of

course!" He winked at him. "But only if you're a good boy. And you can even fuck her if you're up for it. But please make sure that she washes herself afterward. I don't want your cum on my cock!" He roared with laughter, and Karl joined in.

So everything was fine so far. The two hadn't been in such agreement for a long time. Maybe even never before.

***

Three weeks after Laura Hermann's disappearance, the police still had no information about her whereabouts. In the meantime, however, they doubted a crime had actually been committed.

Laura's best friend, Annika, had told the police that the girl was very unhappy and dissatisfied with her life situation for a long time. When asked if she'd dare her girlfriend to just run away, Annika shrugged. She didn't really believe it, but she wasn't quite sure. She said Laura had problems at school. She already repeated the class, but still had bad grades, which had led to fierce arguments with her parents.

And how was—in Annika's opinion—the relationship between Laura and her parents? they asked her.

Rather bad, was the answer.

The Hermanns denied this, but they couldn't deny that it was *sometimes difficult with Laura*. She didn't take school as seriously as she should. She spent too much time hanging out with friends and studying too little.

She didn't have many friends, Annika explained, and the relationship with her had also become a little complicated since Annika had a boyfriend. Laura would have liked to have a boyfriend too. *More than anything*, Annika

told the police officers. But love just didn't really work out for her. That' s why she often had been unhappy and frustrated.

All this was evidence that Laura had decided to leave her old life behind and start anew somewhere. The objection was that apparently she hadn't taken any personal belongings or money with her. The officials insisted that something like this happened often. Besides, Laura was almost seventeen, not seven. This reduced the likelihood of her becoming a victim of a crime. Seven-year-olds seldom ran away. Seventeen-year-olds, on the other hand, did this as a hobby. One would have to distinguish. The statistics and so on …

The Hermanns couldn't believe it. Laura would never have just run away like that.

But the policemen had experienced it more than once. And the parents were always the ones who couldn't believe it. Of course. It had to be like that. They were parents.

Nevertheless, a crime couldn't be ruled out, but as long as there was no indication, the investigative work would be stopped for the time being.

Even Mrs. Hermann's hysterical fit didn't change anything. Two days later she was sent to a psychiatric hospital because of a nervous breakdown. Mr. Hermann remained alone in the large, empty house. He could no longer work and was on sick leave until further notice.

During the day he took long walks in the forest to clear his head, but he never succeeded. He often walked past the house where his daughter suffered terrible pain in the cellar.

But he had no idea.

How could he know?

Male intuition?

He didn't have second sight.

He also walked past the house in the forest on this sunny day in April, before he finally took his own life in the basement of his own house.

He couldn't hear his daughter's screams, even though he thought of her all the time.

He died without ever knowing what had happened to her.

A blessing? Perhaps.

***

Days, weeks, and finally months passed in the Singers' basement. Laura barely thought of her old life in order to bear the new one a little better. She'd become the plaything of two very sick guys without even being aware of it.

Karl came to her during the day. He brought her washing things and fresh water and emptied her "toilet".

When she was freezing, he gave her a blanket, which he later took away again—Toni still didn't allow her to cover herself, even when she was alone.

Sometimes he'd bring her a bit of chocolate or some gummy bears. These were highlights for which she thanked him on her knees. Apart from that, he didn't give her anything to eat. Toni would have noticed if she hadn't been properly starved. Every third day he filled her bowl with soaked dry dog food. He always watched her eat. Most of the time he was naked and masturbated. The ejaculate landed in her bowl as "icing on the cake." Laura was used to all this. She didn't even feel disgust anymore.

Toni usually showered before he came to her after work. Laura was happy, because if he didn't shower, he stank terribly of garbage, decay, and rotten stuff. That

was worse than the smell of sweat or an unwashed body. As with Karl.

Depending on his mood, he played a little with her. He let her crawl around on a leash, made her lick his shoes clean, or things like that. Sometimes he just fucked her quickly and finally came in her mouth. From time to time he shot his sperm in her ass but never in her vagina.

Laura knew by now that she was pregnant. She'd had her last period at the beginning of February, although she'd hardly felt anything due to malnutrition. Now there was no period anymore. Her breasts had become more sensitive. In addition, there was morning sickness that seemed almost ridiculously clichéd to her. A few times she'd puked in the toilet bucket. After everything that she'd swallowed, the two men had apparently not suspected anything so far.

Laura was afraid of what would happen if Toni found out about her pregnancy. So she tried to repress it, which she did most of the time—after all, it wasn't the only thing she had to repress in her new life. When she thought about it from time to time, she hoped to have a miscarriage before her belly grew visible. That she didn't get her period anymore didn't seem to have occurred to the men so far. Nobody paid attention to such details here. Perhaps they had simply assumed that it was a malnutrition-induced hormone disorder. That was what Laura herself had thought at first. What she'd forced herself to think. Her mind just didn't allow the fact that her half-starved body was capable of getting pregnant.

But her body seemed (unfortunately) to function so well after all. A life grew inside her. A little innocent life, for which she could—if at all—only feel hate, because it made everything more complicated. Laura didn't believe Toni would let it live if he found out about it. She didn't

even know if she'd let it live herself.

Who would want a child from a sadist and a horrible rapist?

And anyway … what kind of future could a child have down here?

It was crazy to even think about it.

That made Laura dizzy in the head and terribly sick in the stomach.

That's why she tried not to do it. She'd learned to wipe away thoughts that did her no good. Like all thoughts and memories of her former life as Laura Hermann.

Toni raped her every time he came to her. Sometimes even twice in a row.

Karl didn't always do it.

It also felt less like rape with him—even though Laura knew in her deepest core that it wasn't anything else.

When he came to her, they sometimes just talked. Or he'd sit with her and just be there.

Laura liked that.

Of course she knew he was keeping her prisoner, too. That he didn't help her, although he could have. That he took advantage of her situation in his own way just as shamelessly as his brother. That she'd never let him touch her voluntarily in her former life. She'd have been disgusted by him. She'd have been afraid of him. He'd have been about the last person to ever spend time with. He was nothing but scum in her eyes. She would have gossiped with Annika about someone like him—about this godawful asocial guy, whom no woman would want to touch even with a pair of tweezers …

She knew all that.

But this wasn't her former life as Laura Hermann.

This life was over.

In her new life, she was the girl in the basement who

had to serve as a sex slave for a psychopathic rapist. And for Karl, for whom she probably also served as a sex slave on some level, but who at least didn't treat her like one.

She'd gotten used to the fact that he smelled bad and was overweight. She even found it pleasant to feel his heavy, wobbly body on top of her. Because he was warm. And tender. He never hurt her. Only sometimes—when she was still quite sore from Toni—she felt pain when he penetrated her. She then told him and he tried to be as careful as possible.

Or he didn't fuck her at all if it hurt her too much, and Laura gave him a blowjob instead.

That was okay with her.

At least he was there and he even stayed if she asked him to, sometimes the whole morning or afternoon. Only never longer than five in the afternoon, because Toni came home punctually at five thirty.

They were talking or he was holding her. She was allowed to wrap herself in a blanket or in one of his sweatshirts—most of them smelled bad, but that didn't bother her.

He was her boyfriend.

The only one she had.

And she was his girlfriend.

The only one he'd ever had.

He'd kept his promise.

And she was grateful for it.

The fact that Karl raped her almost every day and had impregnated her didn't matter to Laura.

It was completely insignificant compared to everything else she had to endure in this new life.

***

For some weeks Laura didn't have to wear handcuffs anymore when Karl was with her. She stroked and caressed him, and he enjoyed it. Every minute. Every touch.

In fact, his life had become so much more precious and worth living since Laura was here. Sometimes he even thought about thanking Toni for the kidnapping because it had given him more happiness and satisfaction than he ever thought possible.

He felt stronger and more balanced since he had regular sex with a real girl. And she wasn't just any girl but a great one. Really pretty with fantastic tits and a cute little butt. What more could you ask for? Unfortunately, she was a bit too skinny, because Toni wanted it that way, and she only got to eat every three days, but otherwise she was almost perfect.

Karl would never have dared to dream of leading such a fulfilled sex life. Toni's action had made this possible, and his initial hatred as well as his disgust and anger had vanished.

Toni had done him the favor of his life by allowing him to use Laura just as he did himself. And when they didn't have sex, they talked.

Like real friends.

Sex and conversation? Wasn't that almost like a relationship? At least it was close to it. Closer than Karl had ever been to a relationship. He believed that maybe he'd fallen a little bit in love with Laura.

Really in love.

Not as if she were a prisoner who was only here because she couldn't leave, but as if she were his girlfriend who was here voluntarily. At least that was how he imagined it. He sometimes dreamed of it—in his sleep, but also when he was awake. He completely ignored Toni's

role. As if there was no Toni at all who went into the cellar every evening to abuse his girl.

As long as Karl could convince himself that there was no Toni, he also managed to feel good. Every single day. Like in a real relationship. Almost. Okay, they didn't go out for dinner … or to the movies … or for a walk, but they had good conversations and fantastic sex.

Karl was definitely happy.

And when winter finally gave way to spring, the first flowers blossoming in front of the house and the buds sprouting on bushes and trees, it was also spring in Karl's heart. It made a real jump when he saw the first butterfly of the year dancing across the meadow next to the house. He thought of Laura, who was waiting for him to come and hold her in her arms.

That was a nice thought and a great idea. Never before had a girl longed for his embrace. But Laura always smiled when she saw him. As if the sun would rise in her heart at the sight of him. An unbelievable feeling that was only possible if you really loved each other.

Karl returned to the house that morning in April (the day after Laura's father had died) in such a lively way and was just thinking whether he should bring Laura a small pack of gummy bears when his gaze fell on Lupo, who was lying in a corner of the kitchen and … was he sleeping?

No. The dog didn't look like he was sleeping. He'd stretched out all fours and lay in a strange angle that couldn't be comfortable at all. Karl forgot all the butterflies for a moment and fell on his knees next to the big animal.

The St. Bernard's tongue hung out. His eyes were slits. He didn't seem to be breathing. Karl touched him. He felt cold … and stiff. Karl shook him. Lupo didn't move.

His body was already hard. Rigor mortis had set in.

Karl stared at the lifeless body and couldn't believe it. Sure, Lupo had been old and not really healthy … and they'd never been to the vet because Toni didn't want to spend the money. Nevertheless, Lupo had walked around only yesterday evening (more or less lively). It was unbelievable and totally wrong that he should be dead now!

Tears ran down Karl's face. He bent over the dead dog and put his cheek to his fur.

"Oh Lupo! Lupo, no!" The moment he said Lupo's name, a huge lump formed in his throat that could not be swallowed. Karl cried his eyes out as he hid his face in Lupo's thick fur.

He thought of times when Lupo had been young and vivacious. In addition, there was the memory of his mother, who had been younger at that time, albeit no longer really spirited.

It occurred to him that she too had long since died.

To be more precise: her corpse, eaten by cats, was lying in her bedroom at this moment, on this beautiful spring day, only a few yards away, attracting flies. If there was enough left of her to attract anything …

Maybe I should go and have a look?

This thought was so new and just as plausible as it was shocking that it sent cold shivers down Karl's spine.

When was the last time he even thought of his mother?

Not since he first fucked Laura, right?

What would Mama have said about them keeping a girl down in the basement like an animal and taking turns raping her?

But Toni hurts her! I'm good to her! I'm her friend!

Could he really be her friend?

Karl let go of Lupo and hid his face in his hands. He shook his head.

None of this was right or even normal.

Upstairs in the bedroom lay his mother's corpse, locked up with dozens of cats who were probably also dead by now …

And now Lupo! He'd just died. During the night. As if it were the most natural thing in the world. Wasn't it?

Shouldn't Toni have seen him this morning?

That was the next question.

A good one.

Toni had definitely seen the dog, there was no doubt. He always went to the kitchen in the morning to drink his coffee.

His cup even stood right here on the table.

And there lay a dead dog. Next to the table.

He imagined Toni sitting here slurping his coffee. Lupo lay next to him. Dead! Hadn't he seen that? Or had he not been interested?

Maybe Lupo was still alive this morning?

Karl knew it was impossible. He didn't know much about rigor mortis, but enough to know that it would have been less distinct if Lupo had been alive two hours ago.

So, yes. Toni just didn't give a shit. He'd left Lupo lying there so Karl would take care of it later.

Because he always had to do the dirty work.

That was normal for Toni. It was part of his everyday life, like his morning cup of coffee and the afterward shitting.

His digestion was as reliable as clockwork. Karl had always envied him. He couldn't go to the toilet for days or sat on the bowl for an eternity.

His mother had called it "irritable bowel syndrome".

Right now there was a lot of rumbling in his intestines. Probably from the excitement and shock of Lupo's sud-

den death, combined with the realization that the dog wasn't the only dead thing in this house.

Not by a long shot.

Suddenly he couldn't hold it any longer. A cramp twitched through Karl's intestines. He ran to the toilet but couldn't avoid a brown stain in his underwear.

***

Karl sat on the toilet for almost an hour before he dared leave the bathroom again.

The cramps finally subsided.

Without thinking much about it, Karl walked past the kitchen. He didn't look inside but marched on into the cellar.

He needed a friend now.

***

Laura immediately saw that something was wrong with him. He'd been crying, and his face was strikingly pale.

Before he sat with her, he took off his hooded jacket and handed it to her. Laura accepted it gratefully and put it on. The warmth of spring hadn't reached down here yet. In no way.

She waited to see if he'd say anything. But Karl just sat there in his holey T-shirt, his hands in front of his face.

She broke the silence. "What's going on?"

He took his hands down and looked at her.

Laura timidly touched his arm. "Did something happen?"

He suppressed a sob.

"Karl?"

"Lupo is dead."

"Lupo?"

"Our dog."

"Oh … I'm sorry. Was he … what was wrong with him?"

Karl shrugged. "I don't know. He just died. He was quite old, but … but Toni just left him lying there. You understand? He didn't give a shit. He left him so I would find him."

Laura, who had expected nothing else from Toni, nodded. "And what do you want to do now?"

"What do you mean?"

"You want to bury him? Outside in the garden or something?" She licked her lips "I used to do this every time a pet died."

Karl looked at her doubtfully. "Lupo is a St. Bernard, not a hamster or anything."

"I can help you," Laura replied. She was eager to leave the cellar and get out into the air. She hadn't been outside since her attempted escape on New Year's Eve.

Not even upstairs in the house. Toni had found that it was too risky, so she wasn't allowed to leave the basement anymore. Karl had meticulously followed these instructions. Until now. Now he was hurt and weak. Her chance. Possibly.

"What do you think?" she asked.

"I can't do that. You can't get out of here."

"But it's still early, isn't it? Toni won't be back for a long time."

"Nevertheless, Laura. It doesn't work. Somebody could see you. Toni would kill me."

Laura tried not to let her disappointment show.

"What do you want to do then?"

"I'll bury him alone. Behind the house. Later."

"Okay. As you like."

He nodded and stared at her. His gaze had changed. The despair had given way to something else.

Greed.

"But first, I want to feel better. I want you to help me."

Laura nodded. She struggled to smile. "Of course. Anything you want." She knew what was coming now. His eyes told her all too clearly. And she wanted to be a good girl and do anything he demanded. Maybe then he'd change his mind and take her outside with him. Later.

So Laura stretched out her hands and opened his pants. Karl's breath immediately became faster. He slipped closer to her. Laura put one hand in his pants and began to stroke his penis, which stiffened immediately.

She bent over and kissed him on the mouth. He hadn't brushed his teeth yet, but neither had she, which made it more bearable. She helped Karl out of his pants while they kept kissing.

When he took off his boxer shorts, an unpleasant smell went up her nose. Laura hesitated for a moment. It smelled of feces. She opened her eyes as she helped Karl out of his shorts and saw that they were smeared with excrement.

He noticed her look. "Sorry, I hadn't thought of that at all."

Laura put the boxer shorts aside with pointed fingers. She suppressed all disgust (which wasn't easy considering the intensity of the smell) and spread her arms. Karl took off his T-shirt and then let himself fall into them.

This time the now-familiar stench of sweat was covered by the smell of feces. The act lasted almost ten minutes, and Laura fought bravely against nausea. She almost made it, but finally, after Karl had already come and slumped contentedly next to her, she had to vomit into the bucket. It was the sparse remains of yesterday

evening's dog food.

"I'm sorry," Karl said. "That was my fault. I'll clean it up later."

Laura was silent. Even with the best will in the world, she wouldn't have known what to say about it.

***

After Karl had cleaned the bucket and (hopefully) himself, he returned to the basement. He put the bucket in its usual place and then turned to Laura with a questioning look. "May I sit with you again?"

Considering all the facts, Laura found the question ridiculous, but she nodded.

Karl sat down so that they wouldn't touch each other. He wore the same jeans as before, but a fresh T-shirt—and hopefully fresh underwear.

"Our dog died today," he said quietly. His tone was dull and difficult to interpret. It gave Laura goosebumps.

She suddenly prayed that he'd stop speaking. She didn't really want to hear anything that would come out of his mouth at any moment. She'd have rather spread her legs and let herself get raped again. At least she had some practice with that, and there were no more surprises. At least not when Karl was involved.

But Karl didn't want to fuck her. Not now. He wanted to pour his heart out to her. And who would stop him?

"Our mother died about half a year ago," Karl continued. His voice cut painfully into Laura's tense nerves.

"I'm very sorry about that, Karl. I didn't know," she said. How could she have known? Half a year ago she'd been Laura Hermann with the life of a normal sixteen-year-old.

"Toni didn't give a shit back then, either. He didn't

even cry. Not even once." Karl looked directly at her. He had tears in his eyes. "Can you imagine that? He didn't cry."

Laura was silent. She could actually imagine it.

"He just left our mother lying, too. Just like Lupo." Tears and snot dripped on his blue T-shirt and covered it with new stains.

"What do you mean?" Laura asked, although she suspected that the answer wouldn't be very good.

It took a while until Karl had calmed down enough to continue speaking. Laura put one hand on his massive shoulder. A gesture of consolation for which she had to overcome herself more than she ever thought.

"She died in her bedroom," Karl finally said. He sniffed and wiped his unshaven face.

"In her bed. She'd been lying there for a long time, you know? She was sick. She couldn't get up anymore." He sighed. "I took care of her," he added almost defiantly.

Laura nodded. "Of course you did."

"Yes, but it was pointless!" He spat out the last word like a poisonous lump. "In the end, she died and I couldn't help her. Toni … Toni said that nobody should know. Because of the welfare money and her pension. You understand?" He stared at her desperately.

Laura, who indeed understood, nodded slowly.

"But I didn't want that. I didn't give a shit about the money. But Toni … he forced me to just leave her there. In her bed. With her cats. She loved her cats, you know. So we probably even did her a favor. But it still wasn't right! I know it wasn't right. And I'm so sorry!"

Laura, who could have spontaneously named a few more points that weren't right here, nodded again. She'd just remembered the strange smell she'd noticed in the stairwell at the very beginning of her "stay".

She thought of the dead woman in her bed and swallowed heavily. "That means she's still lying there?"

"Yes." He let his head hang and stared at his hands folded in his lap. "I know what you think of me now! But it was Toni! He forced me to do it! Like now, here, with you! All this is not me! It's all Toni!"

"But maybe it's time for you to be yourself, Karl," Laura interjected.

Karl stared at her as if she'd just given him the revelation of his life.

"You know I can't do that, Laura. He's already made sure it's no longer possible. He made me his accomplice."

"But that wasn't Toni. That was you, Karl. You're an individual. You gotta decide for yourself what's right and what's wrong."

"What if I can't?" He stared at her. His face was that of a man, but he had the eyes of a child. And Laura, who had aged by years in these past months and had lost all innocence, took this face in her hands and looked into those young, desperate eyes for a long time.

"I can help you if you want. We can help each other," she whispered. The gentle kiss she pressed on Karl's dry lips made her shiver herself. "You should face reality, Karl. Toni is crazy … and dangerous. Sooner or later I'll lie here dead, just like your mother and your dog. And he won't care about that either. But you do, don't you?"

Karl nodded. "Of course! I wouldn't let it come to that!"

"Oh yes, you will," Laura contradicted him. "If you continue as before, then you'll allow it in any case. And do you know what?"

Karl shook his head. "What?"

"Someday you'll also be dead, and he still won't give a shit! That's why you gotta do something about it now. As

long as you still can."

"But what should I do?"

"You know that, Karl."

"You're talking about letting you go?"

"I'm talking about calling the police to stop this madness! Your brother is destroying me. He probably also destroyed your mother! And he'll destroy you too! How long shall it go on like this?"

Karl suddenly broke away from her and jumped up.

Shit, Laura thought desperately. *That was too fast! I expected too much of him at once! I should have taken it slower! Dammit!*

"Karl?"

He shook his head wildly. "I gotta go! I have to think!"

"Wait! Let's talk again in peace …"

He just kept shaking his head. "I gotta go now … I'm sorry …"

He left the cellar. And he didn't come back so soon.

***

After chugging three bottles of Augustiner in the living room, Karl finally felt able to go into the kitchen. Lupo still lay there. He knelt next to the dead animal and tickled it behind the ear. Lupo had always liked that very much and mostly had answered by wagging his tail and tilting his head. The memory put a little smile on Karl's face.

The beer had made his head pleasantly light and spread the cloak of deceptive calm over his senses. Not even the fact that he'd drunk Toni's last beer affected him at the moment. He lingered next to his old comrade for some time. Then he got up ponderously and looked around the kitchen thoughtfully. Finally he took a roll of

big garbage bags from one of the drawers next to the stove. The bags weren't big enough for Lupo, so he took two.

He pulled one over the dog's head to about the middle of his body. The other one was pulled up over the tail and hind legs as far as possible. Only a narrow strip of light brown fur was visible where the two bags met. Karl bent down and grabbed Lupo by the forelegs. In death, the dog seemed to have become much heavier. Was that possible? Karl couldn't manage to lift him, so he dragged the carcass over the floor. The rear garbage bag got stuck at the first door. Karl gave a frustrated sigh but moved on and left the bag behind. He dragged Lupo on until he'd made it to the meadow behind the house. He was bathed in sweat, sick and dizzy. He also had to piss like a racehorse.

Karl laid Lupo in the yellowed grass next to a densely growing hazel bush. He wiped the sweat off his face as he looked around. The back wall of the house was mostly overgrown with bushes and weeds. Bulk trash and other garbage also piled up here: an ancient refrigerator that had belonged to his grandparents, rusty and without a door. The broken guest toilet, which he himself had torn out a few years ago and (temporarily) put here. An old children's bicycle that had first belonged to Toni and later to him. Various garbage bags with questionable contents. Some rubble from the never-finished renovation of the upper floor. More rubble from Toni's renovation of the cellar. A rotten clothesline. Half rotten car tires. Trash and scrap, and lots of it. So it could probably be summarized.

Karl finally took his eyes off it and risked another look up to the dilapidated remains of the former balcony, which was almost completely overgrown with ivy. Behind

it was Mama's bedroom window. It was dusty, dull, and gloomy and didn't really differ from the other windows of the house. For a moment Karl tried to imagine what it might look like behind it. How much was left of her? And of the cats? How did it smell?

He shuddered at the mere idea and forced himself to quickly look away again. He'd need a spade. He'd fetch it now, so that he could dig.

But first Karl peed into the hazel bush right next to his old bike. He probably didn't know whether this was symbolic.

***

The ground was hard and interspersed with roots. It took Karl almost two hours to make the hole appear deep and wide enough. He was at the end of his rope. The spring sun was surprisingly strong and burned relentlessly on his neck, so he'd get a proper sunburn. Karl wasn't used to physical work, and drinking alcohol early in the day wasn't exactly good for his condition. Nevertheless, it was a pity that there was no beer left. Toni would be anything but delighted, but Karl didn't want to think about it. Quite the opposite. He'd just thought of the bottle of Obstler that stood on the shelf in the living room.

Karl went to get it. And then he drank to his faithful old friend Lupo after he'd dragged him into the hole. It wasn't deep, but he fit in well, and Karl hoped that nothing (and nobody) would try to dig him up again. He drank straight from the bottle before finally starting to fill in the hole again. That was easier than the digging.

The sun slowly disappeared behind the house, and Karl was grateful for the cooling. Then he drank another one from the bottle. And another one to take a short break.

And two more when he was finished.

Time passed. Hour after hour. In the meantime, it gradually got dark, and the bottle was almost empty. Karl drank the last sip, because it didn't matter anymore anyway. Then he pissed on Lupo's grave.

"Here's to you, old boy. Rest in peace or whatever they say."

He raised his head to look at his mother's window. In the dark it looked like the black eye socket of a zombie. "And to you, Mama." He grabbed his cock again and burped. "May you also rest in peace. You deserve it. You both deserve it."

He thought about taking the spade back with him and tidying up here, but decided against it. Back here it really didn't matter. That's why he also left the bottle there.

Slowly and with his shoulders bent, he staggered back into the house. He was too drunk to close the door. In the living room he dropped onto the couch and wanted to watch TV, but he was too drunk to pick up the remote. Finally, he just fell into a deep and dreamless sleep.

Until Toni came home.

***

He woke because his head hurt. It hurt badly. That was a hell of a hangover.

Karl forced himself to open his eyes. The world was dazzlingly bright, and he blinked desperately. He couldn't see much. Just someone who hit him with fists of steel.

Karl lifted his arms to protect his face. They were beaten away, and again he felt the pain on his head and forehead. But he was still much too dizzy to fight back properly.

"Ouch! Stop it! Ouch! Please!"

The punches actually stopped. Instead, he was brutally grabbed by the neck and dragged off the couch. Karl's legs couldn't carry his weight, so he sank to his knees. Toni held him by the collar of his T-shirt, which was already torn open.

"Are you crazy, you drunk motherfucker?"

Karl felt hot nausea explode in his stomach. He'd vomit right away, that much was certain. No chance to avoid it.

"Toni, I … I gotta …"

Toni shook him like a naughty little girl shook an unloved doll.

"You don't have to do shit! You drank away everything that was there! Who gave you permission to take my booze? You pathetic freak!" He hit him in the face and shook him again.

"I gotta vomit!" Karl gasped, but it was already too late. With the last word a mighty (and well shaken) gush of vomit poured over Toni's bare legs and feet—he wore only boxer shorts.

The element of surprise was on Karl's side, because Toni let him go immediately and took a step back. Karl looked up at him with watery eyes. The next moment he started choking again, and the next load landed on his own clothes and the floor.

Toni looked at him with big eyes. "That can't be true! You pig! You damn pig!" He took another step toward him and stepped right into the vomit, which didn't seem to bother him.

The stench brought tears to Karl's eyes. And he was still not sure if anything would follow. He felt terribly sick and his head almost exploded. He did what he always did in a hopeless situation: he whined.

"Please don't hit me anymore! I'm sorry! I'll clean it up!

I'll clean it immediately!"

Toni came very close to him. He put one hand on the back of Karl's head, a gesture that seemed almost comforting, but then the second hand came along and he pushed Karl down, face down, directly into his own vomit.

"Now lick it up, you pig! Eat it like a dog!"

He pushed so hard that Karl's nose and lip began to bleed. Karl opened his mouth to beg his brother, but only blood bubbled out of it while his vomit got into his mouth, so that he swallowed and suddenly had the feeling of suffocating.

"Eat it, you pig! Eat it!" Toni screamed as he pushed even harder.

Karl desperately tried to lift himself up with his arms, but he had no strength. His legs twitched helplessly across the bare wooden planks, and he made a series of choking sounds. Only when his legs barely moved did Toni let go of his head.

Karl remained lying. He didn't move.

***

"Shit!" Toni hissed. He grabbed his brother by the shoulders and turned him around.

Now the pig was lying with the hair in the vomit, but was still spaced out. His face was a mask of blood and puke.

Toni patted both cheeks. Only slightly. Then harder. In the end, he slapped Karl. And finally the little motherfucker opened his eyes and frantically took a breath. He coughed and choked, but he was conscious again. Thank God! Toni still needed the little shit!

"Karl? Can you hear me, man?"

Karl's eyelids fluttered. He raised a trembling hand in front of his face.

"I won't hurt you, asshole!"

Karl hesitantly let his hand sink again.

"Man, I thought you were going to bite the dust!"

Karl had a mighty coughing fit, and Toni waited until it was over. His anger had now subsided. For the time being.

"I'm sorry," Karl stammered. "I … I buried Lupo. And that was somehow so bad and sad and I felt so alone, that … that I probably wanted to give myself liquid courage."

Toni helped him sit up. Everything was full of blood and vomit. A truly devilish mess. But he'd let him clean it up. Tonight. Half dead or not.

Toni didn't go into the matter about Lupo. Karl had to get tougher when it came to these things. After all, he needed him as a sidekick for a while, and he didn't know how long he'd keep the girl. At some point Karl would have to bury her out there, that much was certain. And who knew if she'd be the last one? God alone knew. Or the devil. Probably both.

"I'm gonna go take a shower and wash off this shit!"

Karl nodded.

"Afterwards I'll drive to the gas station and get myself something to drink. You'll clean up here in the meantime, Karl. Understand?"

Karl nodded.

"And I know you're feeling shitty, but you're gonna do it anyway. You got that?"

Karl nodded again. "I'll clean everything. I promise."

Blood ran out of his nose, and he wiped it away with the back of his hand. "May I go to the bathroom first?"

"No! You take a tea towel for your nose and then you

start cleaning!"

"Okay." Karl stood up in agony. It looked as if he'd puke again, but that didn't happen. He dragged himself into the kitchen to stop the blood flow.

Toni was already gone when he came back into the living room, armed with a bucket of soapy water and a cleaning rag.

Karl started to work. Nevertheless.

***

The next day, Karl had a mighty hangover. Without exaggeration it was probably the worst hangover of his life.

He woke from a dreamless sleep shortly after eight in the morning. He had a terrible headache. He'd have liked to just lie there longer. But he had to pee damn badly … and he was really thirsty. So he struggled to get out of bed. He noticed that he was completely naked but couldn't remember undressing. He still knew he'd vomited all over the place down there, including on his brother. After that, he had to clean. He remembered this vaguely. He had felt sick. And dizzy. Nevertheless, he'd scrubbed and wiped everything as if his life was at stake.

Toni had come back sometime—with two six-packs and cheap vodka. He'd contentedly inspected the floor and then released Karl, who had immediately gone to bed.

Karl had taken off his blood- and vomit-soaked clothes before he lay down.

Apparently.

Here they were, right next to his bed. Blood and vomit had dried in the meantime, but that was no less disgusting.

Karl stepped over it. As soon as he'd walked a few

steps, the pressure shifted from his head to the middle of his body. His stomach was somersaulting.

This time he made it to the toilet just in time. He puked until he had tears in his eyes. Then he peed and drank cold water from the tap. It tasted better than anything he'd ever drunk.

After he'd had enough, he staggered back to his room and lay down again. The sheet was pleasantly cool on his sweaty skin. Karl closed his eyes and slept.

He didn't get up again that day.

***

In the basement, a desperate girl waited in vain for his visit. It's easy to imagine who came instead.

Toni had the iron bar with him, and she really needed a friend when he was finally done with her and she was lying on the mattress trembling and bleeding. Someone to hold and stroke her and whisper in her ear that everything would be fine.

But that someone didn't come, and Laura started to believe he'd never really existed.

***

Three days after Lupo's funeral and his hangover, Karl went back to the cellar.

Spring was taking a break, and outside it was pouring rain, so badly that Karl had already wondered if this deluge would wash Lupo's carcass out of the sodden ground.

Unlikely. But if you lay alone in bed at night, only a few yards from your mother's cat-eaten corpse, and listened to the wind sneaking around the old house and the rain

constantly pelting against the dark window panes (even against the panes in Mama's room), even unlikely things suddenly seem damn real.

But now it was daytime. With bright daylight. Eleven in the morning. Toni was at work. Lupo was buried under a few pounds of soil, where he belonged. Frieda lay in her bed, where she belonged. With or without cats. That was the way it was. And why did he keep thinking about those goddamn creatures all the time?

Laura was down in the basement.

She didn't really belong there. Not in the real world. But Karl knew very little about such a world. Most of what he knew was so wrong that any halfway normal person would have felt bad.

The clanging of the key seemed unnaturally loud to him. Karl held his breath before he entered. He was a little afraid of what to expect. Toni had been down here with the iron bar the last few days, and that meant she wouldn't be well. He wouldn't even be able to have sex with her. After the torture with the bar, she was always so torn open that even the slightest touch caused her hellish pain. Toni didn't care the least. But Karl wasn't Toni. He could never have hurt her.

The first thing he noticed was the empty mattress.

Laura wasn't lying there. She was sitting on a chair instead.

She'd turned her back to Karl. The chair stood in a dark corner of the cellar, far away from the dirty window that the rain pelted down on. There she sat, like a naughty, repenting child. Her arms were tied to the backrest with a rope that looked very taut. She wore handcuffs and foot chains. She was naked as usual. Her head hung flaccidly. Her hair was stringy and greasy.

When Karl came closer, a strong smell stung his nose.

Excrement.

No surprise.

She hadn't had the chance to use the toilet bucket.

Karl tried to breathe only through his mouth. He walked around the chair. Laura's head hung so low that he couldn't see her face. But he saw her breasts. They were full of weals and blood, and gaping bite wounds were all over her upper body.

It's getting worse, Karl thought. *How much longer will she last? He'll kill her. Sooner or later. That's what he's after.*

"Laura?" He squatted in front of her and pushed back her dirty hair. Her face was bloody and swollen.

She moaned softly and opened her mouth. Saliva ran out and stuck to her chin. Her eyes were so swollen that she could hardly open them.

"Oh, Laura!" He put his hands on her thighs and stroked them. "I'm so sorry! What did he do to you?"

She moaned again and said something that sounded like "atta."

It took Karl a moment to understand. Then he knew what she wanted.

The water bucket was empty. He filled it and came back with fresh cool water, a glass, a straw (he couldn't imagine how else she'd drink), and a washcloth.

First, he let her drink until she had enough. Then he cooled her eyes and face with the wet cloth. She still couldn't look at him, but she was able to speak again.

"Where have you been?"

"I'm sorry, Laura. I … I didn't feel well … I needed to rest." He stroked her thighs again because her face didn't look like it could stand a touch.

"He'll kill me, Karl. Very soon. Because in the meantime, he's done everything with me that comes to his mind, and the only thing that's still missing is my mur-

der."

"You can't say such things. He won't do that. He's not a—"

"Yeah, he is! And you know it!"

Karl was silent because he knew very well.

He rose slowly.

"Karl?" She panicked and turned her head back and forth. "Karl, where are you? What are you doing?"

"I gotta go now."

"No! Please! Stay with me!"

"I … I'm sorry … I have to wait until Toni gets home. I need his permission to untie you and take care of you. There's nothing else I can do. He'd notice that immediately."

"But you gotta help me!" she screamed. Her voice broke at the last word, and she sobbed helplessly.

Karl couldn't take it any longer.

He packed the things he'd brought with him and left the cellar in a hurry.

Laura remained alone. Again.

***

When Toni came home, Karl was sitting in the living room. Without TV or radio. He sat there and waited. He'd done that all day. Ever since he'd left the cellar in such a hurry. He'd eaten nothing and drunk nothing, had only sat there waiting in the meantime, trying not to think that she might be dying. He'd had no idea how bad things were for her, but after all he'd seen today, he didn't think it would take much more for her to die.

So he sat here and waited for his brother.

Toni wore his orange uniform and an old brown jacket. He stank of garbage. He left his boots on when he came

into the living room. He took off his jacket and threw it on the couch next to Karl.

Karl twitched.

Their gazes met.

"What's up?" Toni didn't necessarily sound like someone who started the evening in a good mood. On the contrary.

"Can we talk?"

Toni raised his eyebrows. "Now?"

Karl nodded. "Yes. Please." He didn't want to beg but did anyway.

"I just got home from work and I've had an absolute shit day! The last thing I want right now is a conversation with my fat, stupid asshole of a brother! Is that clear?"

"Please!" Karl didn't want to cry, but he did.

Toni took off his shoes and threw them into Karl's lap. He caught them awkwardly and put them on the floor. His hands trembled.

"Please, Toni. What am I supposed to do? Get on my knees?"

Toni laughed. "That wouldn't be bad for a start."

But what Karl did next even he wouldn't have expected.

He rose from the couch, made some steps toward Toni … and then went down on his knees.

Toni looked at his brother, perplexed. "Are you totally crazy now? What the fuck are you doing? Haven't I been punching you in the face for too long? What do you want?"

Karl looked up at him. Tears ran down his fat cheeks. "May I please take care of Laura?"

Toni shook his head. "What does that mean? Take care of Laura? What do you want?"

"She's very ill. I'm afraid she might die if we leave her

to her own devices for much longer."

"You were with her?"

Karl nodded. The tears ran, but he made no effort to wipe them away. "This morning. But I didn't touch her. I wanted to ask you first. I … I can take care of her wounds and give her some medicine. Wrap her up warm so that … she can recover."

Toni shook his head. He looked pitilessly down on his desperate brother. "You know why I left her behind like that, right?"

This time it was Karl's turn to shake his head.

"I want that bitch to die down there. Her cunt and her asshole are destroyed. I can't fuck her anymore. And she can't take anything in her mouth anymore. She's useless, Karl. It would take days or weeks for her to get better again. That's not worth the effort to me."

He shrugged. "I had a good time with her, but you should always stop when it's at its best, right?" He laughed. "Maybe I'll get another one soon. Or I'll go back to town to fuck. Change of scenery. You understand? Probably not, but fuck it! This cunt is finished. Nobody needs her anymore. What am I supposed to do with her if I can't fuck her?"

Karl stretched out his arms and tried to grab one of Toni's hands. But he withdrew from the touch and kicked him in the stomach instead. That didn't hurt much because he didn't have any shoes on. Still, Karl had to fight for air. He collapsed.

"Please, Toni, let me do that. I'll take care of everything. And when she's fit again, you'll have a cunt that's just like new. It would be stupid to throw everything away now after it worked out so well. Another kidnapping would be far too risky. You shouldn't press your luck. Keep Laura. It's only to your advantage. You fuck her,

and I continue the dirty work. Okay? Please, say yes. Don't let her die!"

Toni thoughtfully lifted his brows and squatted next to him. "Tell me, why is this so important to you, dude? Are you in love with the cunt or what?"

Karl vehemently shook his head. "That's not what it's about. She's a human being. I feel sorry for her. I don't want her to die. Also because of you, Toni. I don't want you to become a murderer."

"Oh, that's nice of you to worry so much about me." Toni laughed scornfully.

"Toni, think about it. There's no disadvantage for you if I take care of everything."

Toni really seemed to be thinking. Thank God! Finally!

"It mustn't cost me a cent, man."

"No, it won't. I swear!"

"And she stays in the cellar! I don't want you to take her upstairs!"

"I won't."

Toni sighed and straightened up. "All right. Let's try it. But if I can't fuck her again in a week, she's dead. Do you understand?"

Karl nodded, relieved.

"And if you spend my money on anything, I'll bust your ass even worse than hers!"

"I'll do like you say. You have my word."

"Not that your word is worth even the dirt under my fingernails! But okay. You have this one chance."

Now it was tears of relief that ran down Karl's cheeks. "Thank you, Toni. I promise I won't disappoint you."

"I very much hope so, my friend."

He wasn't the only one.

***

Laura's at home in bed. It's still early, but it's getting light. She hears the birds chirping outside the window. It's summer now.

Summer!

That means: holidays!

She smiles and turns over to the other side with relief. Summer and holidays, that means she can stay in bed and sleep late. It means that a wonderful sunny day at the lake awaits her. Just chilling, bathing, reading, drinking cool beverages, and eating ice cream. And going to the beer garden in the evening with her best friend.

Life is beautiful. Everything is good. Summer and holidays. She lies at home in her cozy bed, feels the cool sheet on her naked skin …

Why naked? Actually, she never sleeps naked, but with at least panties and a top. Oh, doesn't matter! Summer and holidays! Sleep late! At home! In safety!

Why safety?

She's always safe here. Always. Mama and Papa are here. They're downstairs in the kitchen and probably have already prepared breakfast because they both have to go to work. Maybe Mama bought fresh strawberries. So delicious! And Papa will hopefully leave her an egg. Laura loves eggs for breakfast. She also loves strawberries and cool summer mornings in a cozy bed when she knows she can sleep in because there's no school. Because there won't be school for a long time! Because the summer holidays taste a bit like eternity.

She's fine. She's looking forward to sleeping longer and to the day that will bring nothing but joy and relaxation.

But not yet. Now we'll sleep one more round.

Laura takes a deep breath … until a piercing pain in her abdomen stops her.

Her period maybe? Is it time again? Hopefully she won't ruin the fresh sheet. She's not wearing panties.

While she's still thinking … again this pain. Stinging. Demanding.

Maybe she'd better get up and go to the bathroom?

Great idea, but …

What's the matter with her hands?

They're somewhere behind her back, and she can hardly move them.

Laura opens her eyes. At the same moment, the pain becomes almost unbearable.

And what she sees has nothing to do with her bright, friendly bedroom …

What she hears and smells and feels, and what she suddenly remembers, is so terrible that she opens her mouth to scream, but …

***

… there was no sound coming over her brittle lips. Her tongue stuck to her palate, and Laura couldn't move it.

Horrified, she gasped for air while she still had the pleasant peace of this beautiful summer morning in her mind's eye. But the pain quickly covered everything else. It was everywhere! Worst of all in her abdomen and breasts.

Laura whimpered because screaming didn't work.

She felt a movement behind her but was too weak to turn around. Someone was fumbling around with her hands behind her back.

Laura moaned because it hurt so much.

The handcuffs were removed, but she still couldn't move her arms. They had been in the same painful position too long. Now they just fell and hung there like two

useless sticks of skin and bone.

The life that now returned into them with the blood was burning and merciless.

Laura sobbed.

Now she noticed that someone was standing next to her.

A stocky man in sweatpants and slippers.

Karl.

Laura looked at him and wanted to say something, but instead she fell to the side like a sack of potatoes, and if Karl hadn't caught her, she might have hit her skull on the hard concrete floor.

Maybe that wouldn't have been the worst thing.

***

After loosening the handcuffs and the rope that had been holding her on the chair, Laura immediately tilted over, and he was (fortunately) alert enough to catch her.

Karl was shocked at how light she'd become. Like a bag of feathers. She weighed almost nothing. He picked her up effortlessly and carried her to the mattress.

There he gently laid her on her back and carefully pulled her arms forward to place them next to her body.

Laura whimpered like a wounded animal.

Her body was hot from fever. Nevertheless, he covered her with the blanket he'd brought from above.

Maybe she'd die. Karl didn't know much, but he knew that for sure. She looked and smelled terrible, and the light in her eyes had almost gone out.

For the first time in weeks he felt nothing but compassion at her sight. All lust had vanished.

But should he be proud of it?

Even Toni didn't fancy her in this state anymore.

That wasn't a trait to be proud of.

"Laura?" He touched her forehead which was covered with cold sweat. "Laura, can you hear me?"

Her eyelids fluttered.

"Laura?"

She nodded weakly.

"I wanna help you. I have medicine."

He'd actually scraped together all the medicine he'd been able to find. Everything was opened and partially expired, but that would have to suffice. He didn't have more and wouldn't buy anything. Toni's words were clear. There was even an antibiotic that was prescribed to him a few years ago because of tonsillitis. He'd gotten stomach pains from it and therefore stopped the treatment prematurely and got a different kind. Laura would hopefully tolerate it better.

Of course Karl didn't know whether this was a sensible medication in her condition. But he thought it couldn't get much worse, so why not try it?

Just like the ibuprofen, "For fever and pain," it said. It couldn't be that wrong.

Karl had a glass of water with a straw with him, but Laura was no longer able to swallow any pills. At the hospital she'd probably now be treated intravenously. But this wasn't a hospital.

Far from it, baby!

So Karl went up to the kitchen where he crushed the tablets with a meat hammer and then stirred them into water.

He forced Laura to drink it all and ignored her weak protests.

After this was done and she (thank God) hadn't puked, Karl started to take care of her wounds.

He disinfected the open spots with antibacterial spray

and used the entire supply of gauze in the house to bandage them.

It made him feel like a little boy playing doctor.

He wasn't much more than that either. His knowledge of wound care and first aid was almost nonexistent, but Karl did his best and managed to do it without a single erection.

A kind of best performance for him.

***

Karl now came every day to make her drink this disgustingly bitter liquid with the straw and to dab her wounds.

Laura wasn't sure if he knew what he was doing. But she understood that he really wanted to help her and that this was the only help she could expect.

So she cooperated and swallowed everything he brought her. That included lukewarm soup. Three times a day. She drank it through the straw, because she still couldn't swallow properly, let alone chew.

The stuff he sprayed on her wounds probably didn't help much, but at least it didn't hurt either, and it cooled down a bit, so she let it happen without complaining. Once per day he washed her face and intimate areas with a hard washcloth that smelled disgusting and then dried her with a very dirty towel.

He put plastic bags and several towels under the center of her body and changed them regularly, because Laura still couldn't sufficiently control her sphincter.

Karl didn't seem to mind, despite the smell. And Laura also lost the last bit of shame she might have had.

She was still naked, but she was allowed to keep the blanket, for which she was very grateful.

Toni didn't show up at all, which triggered more than

mere gratitude in her. Laura couldn't have expressed this relief in words or thoughts. It was one of the strongest emotions she'd ever experienced.

On the third day the fever slowly dropped.

The pain decreased.

Laura's self-healing powers did their job, and she felt a little better every day.

***

On the seventh day, Karl sat with her after he'd taken care of her—she could now eat the soup alone and with a spoon.

He looked at her but didn't say anything.

"What's wrong?" Laura asked insecurely.

He took her hand and put it in his lap. A loving gesture, without ulterior motives.

"I'm so happy that you're doing better," he finally said.

Laura nodded. "And I owe that only to you."

Karl lowered his eyes. He couldn't look at her now.

"I saved myself with that too," he said tonelessly. "If that's the right word at all."

"What do you mean?"

"Toni wanted you to die. He … he wanted to throw you away like a broken toy. And I … I begged him to help you."

"And he agreed?" Laura felt her lips and fingers go numb.

Toni wanted her to die? If that was true, why hadn't he killed her right away? Then why was she still here? None of that made any sense!

"Yes, he did, after all. But as always with Toni, there's also the other side of the coin."

"And that would be?"

"He gave me an ultimatum. Within a week you should be healthy enough to … that he …"

"Can continue as before." She finished his sentence. Her voice sounded as dull as she felt. Sure, she could have imagined that. He wouldn't stop. Guys like Toni never stopped!

Only when I'm dead, Laura thought and felt a desolate emptiness.

Karl nodded. "Today the week is over. He's still at work, but when he comes home …" He swallowed. "I'm afraid he'll visit you then."

"And make me what I was a week ago?" Laura whispered.

Karl raised his head and looked at her. He was still holding her hand, which was as small and delicate as that of a child.

"It won't be that bad. He's now seen that he mustn't go too far."

"What if he doesn't care? What if he wants to kill me anyway?"

"He'll think twice about that, Laura. He won't want to do without you so easily."

She stared at him. *And if he does?* her eyes asked. *What if he does?*

But Karl said nothing else. He had no answer.

***

Toni actually came to her that evening.

He didn't say a word while he looked at her.

Laura's heart beat in her throat. But her fear was relatively unfounded. She only had to give him a blowjob to get her "dinner."

She made every effort to do it exactly the way he liked

it best. She played the good girl and thanked him nicely after she'd swallowed everything.

Toni punched her in the face because she'd spoken without being asked, but otherwise he actually left her alone. Laura almost died of joy when he finally left without even touching her body.

He even left her the blanket.

When she lay alone on her mattress, still tasting his sperm in her mouth, she tried to sleep, but doubted whether her joy was even justified. Perhaps his disinterest only suggested that he was tired of her?

And what did bad guys do with a toy they no longer wanted?

***

Some simply left it lying so that someone else could take it ...

***

Toni didn't show up for the next two weeks. The only one who came to her daily was Karl.

That meant Laura didn't have to wear any shackles except for the ones on her ankles. She was also allowed to keep the blanket during the day. She had to eat dog food, but at least like a human and not on all fours like an animal, and she wasn't humiliated or beaten.

Karl wanted sex, but that was okay.

It didn't hurt. Sometimes he was even tender.

Laura felt almost like she was in seventh heaven and thanked God for each day without Toni. She asked Karl why his brother didn't show up, but he claimed not to know.

Toni had hardly been home for the last two weeks. And if he was home, they didn't talk to each other. Toni didn't make any effort to go to the cellar, and Karl accepted that without asking. He was just happy about it and suppressed the fact that it was strange.

On a hot June evening they lay next to each other on the mattress after sex and held hands while the sweat dried on their bodies. Laura had gained a little weight again, which wasn't solely due to her recovery and regular feeding (although Karl was still only allowed to give her dog food).

Laura knew that.

And Karl knew it too.

Nobody had said it yet.

Until now.

"You're pregnant, right?" Karl suddenly asked.

Laura flinched and instinctively put her hand on the small, now clearly visible bulge of her belly.

She didn't answer.

"And it could be mine. Or his," he added tonelessly.

Laura was silent. She knew whose baby it was. There was only one who had ejaculated into her vagina.

She sighed. "It's yours."

Karl let go of her hand and straightened up jerkily. He stared at her. "How do you know that?"

"Toni always came in my mouth and sometimes in my ass. You don't get pregnant from that." She looked at him. "But from what we do!"

At least she'd said "we."

Karl ran his fingers through his sweaty hair. "I'm sorry! I didn't think that …" He fell silent. What could he say without making things worse?

"Laura, what … I …"

She also sat up and put one hand on his fleshy shoul-

der. "You don't have to say anything, Karl. All you have to do is act. How do you think Toni will react? He'll also know that you're responsible for it."

Karl bit his lower lip. He was white as a sheet. "He will kill us both," he said soberly.

"All three of us," Laura added. "And you know what that means."

He shrugged. "Not really."

Laura stroked his wobbly men breasts. Her fingers continued to wander over his protruding belly and then disappeared underneath to clasp his sticky penis. Then she squeezed, very gently. And pulled. Somewhat firmer. And squeezed again. Gently.

Karl exhaled and groaned. A shiver went through his body while his penis quickly became stiff.

She'd never done that before. Not by herself.

"We gotta get out of here," she whispered.

Squeezed and pulled. Pulled and squeezed.

Karl leaned his back against the wall and closed his eyes.

Laura had trouble grabbing his cock properly under the belly fat, but what she did was enormous.

Karl shivered.

Laura instructed him with a gentle push to lie on his back. Then she sat down astride him and leaned forward until her breasts dangled right in front of his eyes as she sat down on his cock and let it penetrate her.

She moved her pelvis rhythmically and very powerfully. Up and down.

Karl threw his head back and made lustful sounds.

She closed his mouth with a kiss and rode him like no one had ever done before.

***

After she'd forced herself to seduce him like a little hooker, Laura lay her head on Karl's chest and stroked the wet inside of his thigh.

"That was wonderful," she lied.

"Do you really mean that?" Karl asked, still a little out of breath.

"Sure."

He was silent.

"Karl?"

"Yes?"

"I'm very grateful to you. For everything you've done for me so far. I know that you're also afraid of him. You've known him all your life and I can imagine how much you had to suffer. That's why you have to put an end to it now. Do you understand that? You're the only one who can do that."

Karl sighed. "And what then?"

"When?"

"When all this is over. When I get you out of here and you're back with your people … what are you gonna tell them? I'm just as guilty as Toni. Probably even more if the baby is mine."

"I'm gonna tell them the truth," Laura explained.

"And what kind of truth is that?"

"Well, I'll tell them that Toni kidnapped me, tortured me, and almost killed me. While you always wanted the best for me and finally saved me."

"Sounds good. But what about the sex?"

"I'll say it was consensual."

"But it wasn't, Laura. Not from the beginning. And probably not now."

She shook her head. "I voluntarily slept with you. Because I like you, Karl."

"What are you planning to do with the child? You're only sixteen. You certainly don't want to be a mother now."

"I don't know. I haven't thought about that yet. Maybe you can take care of it."

Karl laughed scornfully. "I'm sure no one will trust me with a child."

"Well, then … I have no idea. I can't promise anything, you gotta understand that. Maybe I'll give it up for adoption. I don't want to fool you: I don't want to raise it. But it will live. Maybe one day you'll get to know it. And I won't testify against you. You won't go to prison. In the worst case, you'd get a suspended sentence."

"Toni would go to jail."

"Yeah, sure, and he deserves it, right?"

"Yeah."

"Then you'll be finally free, Karl."

He shook his head. "I don't know what to do with such freedom."

"You'll finally live."

"I'm all alone then."

"You still have me."

He gave a resigned laugh. "Spare us both this nonsense, Laura. You know as well as I do that we'll be separate people as soon as you're no longer here. You won't give a damn about me. And that's fine. I don't deserve it any other way."

She shook her head. "You're wrong. We're both victims. I wouldn't let you down. If you help me out of here, I'll owe you for the rest of my life."

Karl snorted contemptuously. "Big words for such a little girl."

"So you don't believe me?"

"Not a word."

"Then you won't help me?"

"I didn't say that."

"And that means?"

Karl pushed her head aside and rose with a sigh. He moved away from the mattress and picked up his clothes from the floor. As he dressed, he turned his back to Laura.

"That means?" she asked again.

Karl dressed silently. When he was finished, he turned to her. "That means that I have to think about it. Okay?"

Of course it wasn't okay! But Laura had no choice but to accept it. She nodded. "Okay. Just promise me one thing."

"What?"

"Don't think too long."

***

The reason why Toni didn't come back to the cellar was Nathalie, and she was a really extreme hottie.

He'd met her at a party a colleague had organized in his apartment. Toni had already gotten into a conversation with her during the evening, and he'd been quite drunk. And since she was as drunk as he was, they ended up in bed pretty quickly.

Toni had fucked her properly. From the front and from behind, and at the end in her mouth, just the way he liked it. He'd also beaten her. On the cunt, until it was all red and swollen, and on her thick, wobbly ass. She seemed to like it because she didn't complain once. She had damn thick tits with big bright pink nipples, which he bit until they bled. That was apparently no problem for her either. What a gorgeous woman she was—with curves everywhere where they belonged. Toni enjoyed it

all very much after all those months with the skinny little cunt in his basement.

Of course, he could have fed the girl better so that she'd gain weight, but for that he'd have to invest first, which he didn't want. She wasn't worth his hard-earned money. The biggest thing he was willing to give her was a life at the limit. The thrill she'd given him in the early days was long gone. It wasn't so much fun anymore, and it took him longer and longer to get hard, which of course was her fault. When he rammed the iron bar into all her orifices, it was kind of awesome, but the last time nothing had happened, which had been boring again.

To cut a long story short, he needed fresh meat. And Nathalie wasn't the worst choice. She was twenty-seven and unemployed. She was a pretty tough drinker and occasionally took drugs, but she wasn't really addicted as far as Toni could tell. Toni didn't notice that he was an alcoholic himself.

Even though he'd put her through the wringer (and left some bloodstains on the bed linen of his work colleague), she gave him her phone number. She didn't want it any other way. Toni visited her in her shabby one-room apartment after work. He stank worse than a polecat because he hadn't showered yet, but she had to endure it now.

Right behind the door Toni threw her on the floor and tore her clothes off. He scratched her several times, which always made her moan with lust. When she was completely naked, he struck her for a while, then turned her around and brutally rammed his fist into her anus. She was dripping wet with lust.

After Toni had fucked her properly, he made himself comfortable on her couch in front of the television and let her serve him. Naked, strewn with bruises and weals,

she had to cook for him. She brought him beer and massaged his feet. Later she asked if she could sit with him, but Toni let her scrub the floor for a while. After she'd given him another blowjob, she was allowed to sit on the floor at his feet. She obeyed.

That submissive bitch was really the bomb.

If he'd met her earlier, he could have really spared himself the whole thing with the little cunt. All the effort had been basically in vain.

Nathalie would most likely voluntarily move into his basement, damn it!

But there was no point in regretting the past. At that time it had seemed extremely desirable to him to take the girl into his cellar. It had been great.

In the beginning.

The feeling of power had robbed him of all his senses.

In the beginning.

The mere thought of the little helpless cunt had given him a hard-on.

In the beginning.

Then it had all become routine. Always the same. Every evening. As if they were married or something. Totally boring. To get a kick out of it, he'd have had to do completely different things with her. Things she wouldn't have endured for too long.

The only thing Toni didn't regret was that he'd remodeled the cellar and bought the bondage and torture equipment. After all, he could always use that. For all the cunts in the world.

He'd have loved to take Nathalie there. To tie this plump curvy body so that the fat is squeezed out at all corners and ends … yes, that was exactly what he imagined to be a cozy evening for two.

Nathalie would almost certainly agree. She let him do

almost everything with her. He still had to find out whether there was anything she didn't do voluntarily.

He grabbed Nathalie's hair with one hand and pulled it pretty hard.

She moaned softly.

Toni tore her head back so far that she had to look at him.

"Say, you little bitch, would you drink my piss and eat my shit?"

The question wasn't rhetorical. He really wanted to know.

"If you need to pee or shit, you can find out right now," Nathalie promptly replied.

Toni stared at her. That woman was really great. It was a miracle that there was one like her in real life. He still couldn't believe it.

It was almost a pity that he generally only had to shit once a day, usually in the morning after his first coffee. Pissing could be arranged, though.

Toni took another sip of his beer and grinned as he kept Nathalie's thin hair tightly in his grip, forcing her to look him in the face. She breathed faster and her eyes bulged out of the sockets. Toni knew she was in pain, for this position couldn't be comfortable in the long run. He had already pulled out several tufts of hair, but that was all right.

She liked it.

And he liked it even more.

***

Toni Singer was in a good mood when he came home on a sunny Sunday evening at the end of June. He had spent the weekend with Nathalie and really liked his new role as

the owner of a very willing and tough slave girl.

He'd left her pretty damaged that evening, streaked with weals and bruises, her nipples bitten bloody, one earlobe lacerated—and her mouth odor came from the shit she'd actually eaten. His shit, to be precise.

At the moment when she voluntarily began to eat parts of the stinking turd that he'd shit on her stomach, Toni had come to the conclusion that it wasn't his cup of tea after all. The bitch swallowed the stuff without a complaint, even though she occasionally had to fight a gag. He already got sick watching. And then the stench! The fact that it came from himself didn't really make it more appetizing.

When she finally tried to rub it on her skin, he hit her so hard on the nose that it began to bleed. She immediately understood the hint.

Toni told her to clean herself and rinse out her mouth.

She did.

She brushed her teeth.

The stench remained.

So Toni scrubbed her teeth and tongue until it bled.

The stench remained.

It was amazing.

So she had to eat peppermint candies or chew gum for the rest of the day.

Toni only fucked her from behind to stay as far away from her mouth as possible.

At least the whole thing was a lesson to him.

Never again *caviar*. No, sir! Not for him.

When he finally said goodbye to her by pinching her tits again, the stench remained.

Anyway, he'd planned to stay at home for the next two days and to take care of his other bitch again.

He wasn't really in the mood, but somehow it seemed

to him to be his duty to stop by down there and remind her who was the master of the house.

Probably Karl (this wimp) had banged her during the last weeks, but not in the way she deserved. His fuck-toy was probably spoiled by now. But he'd correct that.

That would be a nice pastime until Nathalie finally got rid of the stench in her mouth. It couldn't last forever. At least he hoped.

In spite of the shit eating, he'd had a good time the last days and was in a good mood when he entered the house.

Karl squatted on the couch and watched TV.

Typical for the fat lazy bastard!

He wore a too tight T-shirt and dirty shorts. Between his wobbly thighs he held a big bottle of Pepsi.

Some things never changed.

"Hey!" Toni shouted.

Karl turned around and stared stupidly at him. His mouth was wide open, and for a short moment Toni imagined what it would be like to stuff some shit in there. That would surely get the little bum on his toes.

If it wasn't so disgusting, he'd have tried it.

"You seem so happy I'm back," Toni stated with a grin.

Karl shrugged and kept staring stupidly.

"How's my fuck-toy doing?"

Karl shrugged again. "How's she supposed to be doing? Everything okay."

"I hope you kept her on the dog food diet. I can tell when you're lying to me!"

"She didn't get anything else. Only the food every three days. You can see that on her."

"I hope so for you."

"And where have you been?"

"None of your fucking business, man!"

Karl flinched. "Okay, sorry."

"I'm going to get some sleep now and then go down to the basement. You'll make sure the cunt is clean and smells good."

I already had enough stench today, he thought.

Karl nodded. "I'll take care of it."

***

Laura cried softly as she washed herself. Karl would have liked to say something to make her feel better, but what should that have been?

They both knew what was in store for her, and there were no words or gestures to gloss it over.

"Do you think he'll notice it?" Laura asked suddenly. She wiped over her clearly rounded belly with a rag.

"Yes, he will," Karl said.

Of course he would!

"What do you think he'll do?"

"I don't know," Karl replied truthfully. "I have no idea."

A loud sob came from Laura's throat. "He might as well kill me right away, right?"

Karl was silent. He just didn't know! It was possible.

"Will you promise me something, Karl? Only one thing?"

Karl nodded without thinking about it.

"If I should die, will you write a letter to my parents? Anonymously, of course. Just so they know what happened to me. You don't have to tell anything else. Not even where to find my body. Please just tell them what happened so that they can find their peace and no longer have to search for me."

Karl took her in his arms. Her small fragile body trem-

bled so terribly. Her tears moistened his T-shirt. She smelled so good!

"You promise?"

Karl embraced her as tightly as he dared. "I promise."

"Will ... will you stay here later?"

"He won't allow that."

"I'm so scared, Karl."

Me too, Laura. Me too.

***

When Toni entered the cellar, she was sitting on the mattress with her face to the wall. She'd turned her back to him, as if to hide something from him. Her spine was clearly visible under the thin pale skin.

Toni grinned. He was really in the mood for her now, like he hadn't been for a long time.

He stepped up to about three feet from her.

Then he let the belt, which he held in his hand, slam on the floor like a whip.

She flinched noticeably but didn't move.

Then he hit the belt over her back. An ugly red weal appeared.

Laura screamed softly but still didn't move.

"Look at me, you cunt!"

She turned a little bit to the side and twisted her head toward him.

Toni struck again. A second weal became visible.

"What's the matter with you, you bitch? Turn around!"

Reluctantly she did. She kept her upper body bent far forward so that her tits hung up to her thighs. She had her arms crossed in front of her stomach.

Toni struck the leather belt over her breasts.

Laura screamed again but kept her strange posture. As

if she hid something from him.

Her belly?

"Look at me!"

She raised her head and looked at him through tangled blonde strands. Her lips trembled.

"What's up? What do you have there?"

She shook her head. "I dunno what you mean …"

The belt hit her breasts again. "You think I'm stupid? What are you hiding?"

She shook her head again. Tears ran down her cheeks. "Nothing."

"Nothing? That's nothing? Get your hands off your belly! And get up!"

Laura didn't react.

Toni whipped her right in the face. Her head flew back. A bleeding weal appeared across the bridge of her nose.

"Come on!"

She howled but finally did what he demanded of her.

It took a moment before Toni understood exactly what he had in front of him.

This girl was totally emaciated, nothing more than skin and bones. The skinny arms hung down like twigs. Only the tits seemed to have grown somehow despite everything. Plumper. Rounder. The nipples wider and darker.

But the biggest change was visible on her belly. It arched clearly over her pubic mound, the navel standing out. Her narrow waist had almost completely disappeared.

Shit!

This damn cunt had a bun in the oven!

Toni stared at her.

Of course, he should have expected something like this. He'd always been careful not to ejaculate into her

pussy, but his stupid brother had surely done exactly that. Probably this genius didn't even know that there were other ways to fuck such a slut. He'd played the good old game of *in and out*, very simple and straightforward. Unfortunately, it could turn girls into mothers. It was quite obvious. At least if he thought about it now. Unfortunately, he hadn't done that earlier. (And Karl, this damn idiot!) Maybe because he hadn't thought she'd live long enough to carry a child. Maybe because he hadn't really believed it would work for her. She was half-starved! Didn't they always say that women in poor physical condition and with constant malnutrition lost their fertility?

Wasn't that also the reason why anorectics usually had trouble getting pregnant?

Then why did it work right here?

Shit!

"So my lobotomized brother actually knocked you up," he said, shaking his head. "That's really gross. And how long exactly did you want to hide that from me?"

"Please!" she whimpered.

"*Please* what?"

Suddenly she dropped to her knees, just like Karl had done, and crawled to him. Then she held on to his legs. "Please don't hurt me, Toni! I'll do anything you want! Just don't hurt me!"

He kicked her against the chin and she flew back onto the mattress.

"Stop babbling, you bloated cow! You'll do what I want, understand?"

Laura rolled to her side and held her fat belly.

Disgusting!

"So let's unite this family now," Toni mocked and turned around to get his idiot brother.

***

In the living room, he lay the iron rod in Karl's sweaty hand.

"You can do it with the bar … or you kick it out of her! I don't give a fuck! The main thing is that she loses it. I want to see blood, dear brother! You understand?"

Karl stared spellbound at the rod in his hand and remembered that Toni had abused and raped the girl several times with it.

In his mind's eye he tried to imagine how he'd beat her belly with it until what he'd planted inside her came out.

A numbing nausea filled his throat. He wanted to swallow it, but that only made it worse.

The bar lay hot and greasy in his hand. One end almost touched the ground. Karl raised his eyes and looked at his brother, looking for something like pity in his face. In vain.

"Please, Toni, don't make me do that."

"That's funny," Toni replied with a big grin. "Your cunt down there whined just like you. You're really a cute couple. I'd almost like to let you have the little rascal, but something tells me that this damn brat has to die before I have to see his stupid face and recognize my stupid brother in it. Sorry, Karl, but everything has its limits."

He laughed out loud. "Don't be angry with me, but even you have to admit that your genes shouldn't necessarily be passed on. You really don't expect anyone to do that. Just look at yourself, man, you're so damn pathetic!"

Karl's lips trembled. He remained silent while he held the bar in his hand. Toni patted his shoulder.

"Come on! Let's go!" He stepped behind Karl and pressed his fist against his back. "After you, fat boy!"

***

When the two brothers entered the basement one after the other, Laura pressed herself hard against the wall, as if trying to disappear into it.

Karl was the first to reach her. In his hand he held the iron bar, which she knew all too well, since there was hardly a spot on her that hadn't already become acquainted with it.

She could only imagine too well what the plan was now. Karl was sweating like a pig. Or were tears running down his unshaven cheeks?

Laura turned away from him. She could no longer bear to look at him. Basically, she didn't even know what was worse: the helplessness in Karl's eyes or the wickedness in Toni's.

In a way, it was the combination of both that made up the true horror of this situation. With her face to the wall, she waited for what would happen next. Her fate was inevitable.

For a while (impossible to tell if it was seconds or hours) nothing happened. Then Laura flinched when Toni raised his voice: "Come on!"

And again Laura waited, with her eyes closed tightly.

Nothing happened.

Toni: "You damn loser! Hit her now!"

Karl: "Please! I can't do that, Toni! Don't make me!"

A rattling.

The iron bar.

Karl had dropped it.

Toni yelled, but he was so angry that his words were not understandable.

Karl howled and whimpered and could no longer be understood either.

Toni kept yelling.

Suddenly Laura was grabbed by her hair and thrown to the ground. Now she screamed too. She opened her eyes just in time to see Toni's foot floating just above her body. He was wearing the heavy work boots she had so often licked clean.

Laura wanted to gasp for air to scream, but at that moment Toni's boot crashed into her belly with full force, and all the air was squeezed out of her in a single, pain-filled blast. No sound came out of her throat. The pain numbed everything and lay like a white mass on her senses. It felt like something had broken inside her—which was probably true. It was so bad that Laura didn't even try to move, turn around, roll up, or hold her stomach. It didn't work. She couldn't do anything. She could just lie there staring into this white emptiness, which wasn't actually empty at all, because it pulsated red at the edges and hurt worse than bloody hell. So Laura lay still, almost as if she was already waiting for the next kick.

Of course, the kick came. And many more, but she didn't feel them anymore, because the white mass had already swallowed her up.

So she was spared the moment when the little bit of life sloshed red, dead, and slippery out of her and poured over the dirty concrete floor as if it was nothing.

But it had been a lot.

Only Karl recognized the small destroyed being in all the blood and slime. He saw the tiny shattered head and a foot with microscopically small toes.

An embryo, a dead embryo that had actually been his son.

Karl started to scream and didn't stop until Toni rammed the iron bar into his stomach and then dragged him upstairs by his hair.

***

Toni dragged him into the kitchen and threw him on the floor. Karl slowly straightened up and turned to his brother, who held a tuft of his hair in one hand and the iron rod in the other. He dropped the hair to grab the bar with both hands.

"So you dare to defy me!"

Defensively, Karl raised a hand. "Please, Toni!!"

"*Please* what?" Toni shouted and hit Karl's back with the bar.

Karl fell on his stomach and groaned. He lay flat on the rough wooden planks. Toni stood with his legs apart above him and hit him with the bar again.

Karl's legs twitched, and he whimpered incomprehensible stuff.

Toni struck again. A twitch and a whimper. Karl had stretched out his arms forward and tried desperately to cling to something.

Toni gasped, sat on Karl's butt, and pressed the iron bar into his neck.

Karl howled and whimpered. He didn't offer the slightest resistance.

"I should kill you, you damn motherfucker," Toni hissed. However, the fact that he could have easily done that made the whole thing somehow uninteresting.

He took the bar away and stood up, breathing heavily. Karl remained lying and didn't even whimper anymore. Only his hands twitched uncontrollably.

"Get up!"

Karl lifted his ass a little.

"Come on! Or I'll hit you again!"

Karl lifted his butt a bit more. His legs twitched. He

began to crawl. Slowly he pushed himself forward.

"I told you to get up, you fat bastard!" Toni yelled.

Karl moaned and got on all fours. He crawled on.

"*Get up*!"

Karl tried to lift himself up but didn't get far. He kept falling back to his knees. "I can't! Please stop it!"

Toni didn't even think about it. He grabbed his brother by the hair again and tore him violently to his feet. Karl screamed his head off, but it worked.

Toni threw him with full force toward a pile of dirty dishes next to the sink.

In his desperate attempt to find any hold, Karl pulled several pots and plates with him that landed on him when he fell a second time.

Again he remained lying—howling and begging.

Food scraps and shards covered the floor around him. Karl laboriously scrambled into a half-sitting, half-lying position and leaned his back against a cupboard. He didn't seem to care that he was sitting in a heap of garbage and broken glass. He breathed heavily and held his stomach. As if Toni had just given *him* an abortion. In a way, it was like that. Crazy.

Karl could hardly keep his eyes open. His chest went up and down in hectic breaths. When his brother took a step toward him, he jerked in shock, but Toni had obviously lost all interest in beating him.

He walked past him to the fridge, took out a beer, and sat at the kitchen table. He breathed heavily. He carelessly put the iron bar aside. He knew Karl wouldn't dare try anything. Years of experience had shown him that. Karl could take it quite well, and most of the time he actually kept his mouth shut when he was told to, but he wasn't the guy for resistance.

Good for him.

Instead, he'd actually knocked up the cunt. That fucking loser! Toni successfully suppressed the fact that he himself had made a mistake in this matter by letting Karl do it.

He watched his brother huddle in the corner, completely screwed, while he sipped his beer. "You're such a fucking asshole, I can't believe it!"

Karl didn't answer, didn't even look at him.

Which made Toni angrier. "Look at me when I'm talking to you!"

Karl blinked in his direction. His eyes were bloodshot. Greasy wet strands of hair hung in his face, but Karl made no effort to move them.

Toni suddenly felt provoked like he hadn't in a long time. He emptied his bottle in one go and slammed it noisily on the table.

"Did you hear what I said?" He stood up and walked toward Karl. "Look at me, dammit!"

Karl raised his head and looked into his eyes. He even pushed away the strands of hair.

That was better.

Toni squatted in front of him. "You know I had to do that, right? You left me no choice. How could you be so stupid to knock up that little cunt? I don't get it, man! Really!"

Karl, who unfortunately didn't understand it either, was silent.

"Will I finally get an answer now, motherfucker?" Toni slapped him in the face.

Although it was quite fierce, Karl hardly felt it. Everything had become numb since he'd had to see that little bloody something that had poured out like disgusting jelly between Laura's legs.

"I can't give you an answer. I don't know myself. I just

didn't think."

"You can say that again!" Toni shook his head. "Well, you can certainly imagine what comes next."

Karl, who had no idea, frowned.

"You'll now go back down there and clean up the mess. You can bury it outside next to Lupo. Or flush it down the toilet. I don't care. As long as it's gone."

"You can't expect me to do that," Karl stammered.

Yes, he could.

***

The pain was far away.

Laura only felt that something very wet and warm was seeping out of her. She'd pushed the cramps that accompanied it into the furthest corner of her mind. She'd learned how to do this by now.

She kept her eyes closed and didn't move.

At some point she was alone again, but she only realized it at the edge of her perception.

She didn't intend to open her eyes.

She didn't intend to move or get up.

She didn't intend to go on living either.

The dull blackness that grabbed her didn't feel bad at all. It smelled of salvation and oblivion.

There would be no pain there.

And no fear.

And no Toni.

She'd just lie there and wait until she slowly drifted to the other side.

There was no doubt that this would happen.

The only question was *when*.

Laura hoped it would happen before one of the brothers came back.

So she waited.

The stuff between her legs and under her bottom was getting cold. Laura began to freeze. She tried not to concentrate on it. Only the blackness mattered now. She had to hold on to the blackness so that it would finally take her far away. It had already taken far too long. She was so tired of this place and this miserable excuse for a life she had to live here.

But then the blackness slowly began to recede and made room for feelings Laura didn't want. Feelings like pain (hellish abdominal cramps, to be precise) or cold (she trembled like aspen leaves and her teeth chattered).

Her ears still worked quite well (unfortunately): she heard the cellar door open and footsteps that slowly approached. Quiet footsteps, because the person who made them probably was barefoot or wore slippers.

Without really wanting it, Laura blinked tears out of her eyes. The world took shape again. The pain in her stomach made her moan loudly. She pressed both hands on it.

A pair of dirty white socks with big holes at the toes appeared in her field of vision.

Karl.

She recognized him even without looking.

With a loud clattering, he put something on the floor.

It was a bucket.

So Karl had come to clean up the mess.

Laura forced herself with all her strength not to think about what this "filth" really was. The idea that it was *their* child was simply too absurd. Any halfway-normal person would go mad at a thought like that. It was better not to let it happen in the first place.

The art of repression was once again in demand. Fortunately, Laura had become an expert in it. So was Karl.

He'd been practicing for decades.

Now he knelt next to her and held something in his hand that looked like a big dirty rag. With only one look into Karl's face Laura noticed that it was in no better condition than that rag.

He seemed to be completely exhausted.

Laura could only guess what Toni had done with him up there, but sometimes a surmise was enough. Sometimes it was even more than you could bear.

"Can you get up?" Karl asked.

Laura shook her head.

He shrugged as if to say, "It's okay, I didn't expect it any other way."

He put the rag away and gently took her by the arms.

Laura screamed in pain.

Karl's face was also distorted with pain.

Groaning and moaning, he dragged her onto the mattress. He didn't seem to care that Laura was now staining the mattress with blood and slime.

As soon as she lay there wheezing, he turned to the cleaning rag, took it in his hand, and stared as if hypnotized at the mess on the floor. Then he suddenly threw the rag at what lay in the middle of this mess, looking like a little doll. A broken doll.

And while Laura was still thinking about whether that had really been what she was afraid of, he fell on his knees next to it and started sobbing loudly.

GAME OVER

Karl was just outside behind the house, burying the little something he'd planted in that bitch.

Toni, who actually had little sense of justice, considered this quite appropriate. This bum should clean up his own mess and hopefully learn something from it.

The question was whether what had been learned would ever be used. Toni doubted that the cunt would live long enough to get pregnant a second time. And even if she did, an "abortion" would probably be superfluous. He'd thought a lot about it lately, had considered the pros and cons, had tormented his damn brain. The result had always been the same: he had to get rid of the girl!

It had been a good idea to kidnap her. It had been fun to make the little bitch submissive and break her in properly. In the beginning. But he hadn't expected the tiring routine that this gimmick had taken on with time. It hadn't really been fun for a long time. In the meantime, she did whatever he wanted, without any resistance. A while ago the mere thought of it had been enough to make him horny, but all that had lost its allure. Especially since he knew Nathalie, but it had started before. So he'd come to the conclusion that the torture chamber in the basement had been a damn cool idea, and he didn't want to miss it anymore, but it wasn't really exciting to always have the same bitch sitting down there, whose holes he knew inside and out.

There were surely guys who were happy with it, and there were people who had been married for years without getting sick of it. And then there were guys like him. Guys who needed action and variety and didn't want to put their dick in the same hole every day.

That's the way it was.

Now, the cunt down there wasn't just some girlfriend he got tired of and wanted to send away. No, she was his victim, his prisoner, his fucking slave. There didn't seem to be much left of the person she'd once been; he'd taken care of that. So he couldn't just let her run back to her life as if nothing had happened. That would have bad consequences for him (and Karl). And it wouldn't do that little bitch much good because her life was fucked anyway.

There was only one logical consequence.

He didn't feel like it (although one could certainly make the whole thing quite interesting, not to say exciting), but the girl had to disappear. He had no choice but to end her life. The only important thing was that he had as much fun as possible for himself. If she was useless anyway, he wanted to make at least her death as sexy as possible.

Maybe Nathalie would like to join in, he thought. This woman was the most abnormal and ruined person he'd ever met. Sometimes she even seemed to outdo him in her perversion. She was perfect for some sick shit like this.

Toni liked the new idea so much that he smiled. He sat on the couch with his laptop and searched the Internet for torture videos that were as perverted as possible. Of course he soon found what he was looking for. And every tortured cunt he saw had Laura Hermann's face in his fantasy.

Toni rubbed his cock like a psycho, and by the time he finally squirted, Laura had long since been food for the worms in his fantasy.

***

After Karl buried the remains of the fetus in a small hole next to Lupo's final resting place, he went into the house to take a shower. But he trembled so much that he was unable to do so. Not now. So he sneaked back down and checked to see if Toni was there.

No Toni.

Very good.

Karl opened the small cupboard in the living room in which Toni kept the alcohol supplies that didn't need refrigeration. He decided on an almost-full bottle of cheap brandy. He sat on the couch and turned on the television without really noticing anything of the program. He didn't know when Toni would come back and how he'd react if he saw Karl drinking his booze, but to be honest, Karl didn't care. There wasn't much that was of interest to him at the time. He'd just buried his own dead child in the dirt and had left the girl he loved alone with her pain and despair. What if Toni wanted to finish him off? It didn't matter. There wasn't much more to finish anyway. Karl smiled sadly. How true. And if Toni should decide to kill him, he was allowed to do so. The main thing was that it was over. He just wanted to stop feeling and stop thinking. He wanted to stop seeing.

Karl unscrewed the bottle (his hands trembled so much that he needed several attempts) and put it to his lips, which were chapped and aching.

But not for long.

Something in his chest hurt. Maybe his heart.

Not for long.

Karl closed his eyes and drank. A comforting warmth shot into his stomach and then spread in his body. He continued to drink until the bottle was almost empty. The world had lost all its colors and contours. It was still turning, but by no means around him.

Karl leaned back and stared at the ceiling. A thread of saliva ran out of the corner of his mouth and over his chin. He didn't notice it. The empty brandy bottle slipped from his hand and fell to the floor. He didn't notice that either.

His heart didn't hurt anymore, and no evil thoughts haunted his mind. It was good, and it could stay that way.

The rough hands of fainting reached for Karl, and he gratefully allowed it to happen.

***

The girl in the cellar wasn't so lucky, and of course she didn't have such alcoholic aids.

At least Karl had given her the blanket.

She lay underneath it trembling and cramping for half the night until she was finally granted a short trip into the comforting blackness of fainting.

***

Something was wrong.

That didn't feel right at all.

Karl struggled his way back into consciousness.

He wanted to move, but somehow it didn't work as it should.

That was mainly due to his arms—they were behind his back, and he couldn't pull them forward.

Karl moaned and opened his eyes.

Bright sunlight drilled its way through his eyes into his brain. He had a terrible headache, and his mouth was as dry as sandpaper.

Carefully he turned his head to find his orientation. He was still lying on the worn-out couch in the living room.

Exactly where he'd fallen asleep the night before. Even the TV was still on. Commercials.

So much for that.

What was wrong with his arms?

Again Karl tried to move them.

No chance.

His shoulders and wrists ached the more awake he became.

Something else wasn't right.

Karl realized that he was stark naked.

He froze terribly. Besides, he'd apparently pissed himself. He had a disgustingly clammy feeling between his thighs, under his bottom and back.

With a jerk, he tried to sit up.

Not so easy without arms.

And his legs wouldn't do what they were supposed to.

Of course not! Karl saw that his ankles were tied with duct tape. Someone had wrapped it around his feet several times and probably also around his wrists.

But who?

And why?

Toni?

There wasn't any other option.

But why would Toni do that?

For what purpose?

Karl no longer understood anything.

Again he tried to sit up and finally managed to do it with enormous effort and raging pain in his head and arms. His stomach overturned several times. He closed his eyes and breathed deeply a few times. He didn't want to puke all over himself. The situation was already bad enough. Don't puke now, dear God!

The urge passed.

His head, however, was about to burst, and the sharp

stench of his own piss didn't necessarily make the nausea any better.

Shit, what's this all about?

Karl carefully turned his head in all directions—hoping to see something (or someone) to give him an answer to that question. But there was nothing except for the old filthy living room, which he knew inside and out. So he had no choice but to sit on the couch and stare at the TV screen with an empty gaze and a throbbing skull. He kept moving his hands back and forth, hoping to free them somehow.

No chance.

The tape was absolutely tight.

And while he sat there pondering his dilemma, Karl realized his bladder was full again. It wouldn't be long before he pissed himself again.

***

Karl was just thinking about whether he should finally give in to the overwhelming urge to urinate or endure the pain in his full bladder a little longer when he suddenly heard footsteps.

He turned his head and saw his brother with a woman he didn't know.

Toni wore jeans and a beige T-shirt. He seemed to be in a very good mood. The woman beside him was quite small and stocky, but that didn't stop her from wearing a skintight top and a miniskirt. In addition, she wore high-heeled shoes in which her short, sturdy legs weren't stretched much. She wore her blonde hair in a shaggy up-do. Her makeup was striking and cheap and made her look like a hooker. A nasty grin was on her face.

"Well, well, Sleeping Beauty is awake!" Toni laughed

scornfully.

The woman's grin became even wider. "And it pissed itself! Not chic at all!" Her sharp laughter pierced Karl's marrow and bone.

Where did Toni find such a disgusting woman so quickly?

Of course! She was the reason his brother had been home so rarely lately and had increasingly lost interest in Laura.

Could you believe that?

This woman seemed to be his brother's female counterpart!

Where had he found her?

And (which was even more important) what would this infernal duo do with him now?

The woman came closer and put a finger under his chin. The tip of her nail drilled painfully into Karl's flesh.

"Did the fat little boy wet himself?" She slapped him in the face, which hurt quite a lot, and then she screamed with laughter.

"Looks like Mami has to punish the little boy!"

She hit him in the face again and then lifted one foot and drilled the pointed heel into Karl's crotch.

He screamed and tried to press himself even deeper into the couch, which of course didn't work and only made the pain in his arms worse.

The bitch didn't let go. "Well, I don't hear anything!"

"I'm sorry," Karl gasped.

"I'm sorry, *Mami*! That's what you call me! Understand?"

Karl nodded. He would have done anything to make her finally take her foot away. "I'm sorry, Mami!"

She laughed.

And took the foot away.

Karl breathed in and out, trembling. The relief brought tears to his eyes.

"Thank you, Mami," she instructed him.

"Thank you, Mami," he repeated.

His bladder throbbed more than ever after this attack, and Karl knew that he'd soon be peeing his nonexistent pants.

Looking for help, he turned to his brother. "Toni, what's this all about? What do you want from me? Please tell her to stop! And please untie me so that I can go to the toilet! I can't hold it any longer …"

He fell abruptly silent when the woman's shoe squeezed his balls again.

"You gotta negotiate with her if you want anything," Toni said with a grin. "She's your boss!"

Karl stared at him without understanding, but Toni's face was like stone and without pity.

So Karl turned to the woman again. "May I please go to the bathroom? I can't stand it any longer."

"You forgot the 'Mami,'" she explained calmly and hit him again.

"May I please go to the bathroom, Mami?" he repeated, but she just shook her head.

"No, you can't, kiddo. But better hold it back, otherwise Mami will have to punish you again."

Karl endured it for half an hour. Then he let it flow and waited silently for his punishment.

The last game had begun.

***

Toni hadn't had to explain much to her about stupid little Karl and the damn fuck-toy in the basement. Nathalie had enthusiastically agreed to take part in this little game.

She loved games!

She'd already done it when she was a little girl.

Her father had never laid a hand on her, but when she was nine, he'd sent her fourteen-year-old brother Mark to her for the first time.

Papa stayed in the background, operated the camera, and gave instructions. That was all.

Never would he have done anything to her. His little princess. Quite the opposite, because very often it was Mark who was punished by their father, because he'd done something wrong or because he hadn't treated her precious little princess body properly.

Nathalie learned a lot from her father.

Papa was a terrific director.

Sometimes other men came along, but most of the time they stayed among themselves.

Nathalie didn't like being intimate with Mark and the other men at first, but she enjoyed every smile she put on her father's face, so she always tried her best.

One day, when Papa brought home "toys" and wanted to try them with his two children in the basement, Nathalie didn't like it very much either. It hurt, and she always had the feeling that it wasn't right to do these things. Not at her age. Not with her brother. And not with a father who eagerly filmed the whole thing to put it on the Internet and who often rubbed his penis with one hand while holding the camera with the other.

It was all pretty far from a normal family life. Especially because a mother who might have had an opinion about it no longer existed. She'd died of a heroin overdose at age twenty-nine when Nathalie was just three years old. There were no other family members or acquaintances who could have intervened.

There were only the three of them.

And the camera.

Most of the time.

When other men played along, it was always the worst thing for Nathalie, because their penises were much bigger and thicker than her brother's. They also smelled worse and their sperm tasted old and rancid, not as delicious as Mark's.

Nathalie went to school and had no friends, just like Mark.

Everyone knew there was something wrong with them, but no one ever tried to figure out what it was.

When she was thirteen and Mark was eighteen, Papa showed them how to use heroin. It was an interesting addition to the coke and pills they'd been taking for years.

The fucking was less unpleasant with it. The men's cocks just slipped in and there were no more disgusting smells and tastes.

At age fifteen, Nathalie left school without a degree, just as her brother had done three years before. One night, shortly thereafter, Mark lay down in the bathtub with his T-shirt and jeans and cut his wrists with Papa's pocket knife. Lengthwise, not crosswise. He wanted to play it safe.

Nathalie and Papa continued nonetheless. But now almost always other men had to come. That didn't matter much to Nathalie, because Papa increased the dose.

So it went on until her father died of an overdose. Nathalie was in her early twenties and was on her own for the first time.

Everything she knew about life had to do with drugs and sex. So she decided to go on without Mark and Dad. She found a pimp who was also her dealer.

Daddy number two.

He also introduced her to the S&M scene.

Nathalie felt very comfortable there.

She sometimes worked as a slave for dominant men, spending several days or even weeks in their hands. Mostly the whole thing was filmed and put online.

From time to time she turned the tables and made a submissive guy her own. But she only did so as long as there was at least one other dominant guy pulling the strings in the background.

That's the way it was; that's how she grew up.

Nathalie always needed a director to keep the film of her life going. For some weeks now this director was Toni.

And this time it was perhaps even love.

There was nothing between heaven and hell that Nathalie wouldn't have done for him. No matter whether she herself or others would be harmed.

The main thing was that her film continued.

When Toni told her about the kidnapped girl in his basement, Nathalie had been immediately enthusiastic. However, she was also a little bit jealous when she heard about the girl.

So she liked Toni's idea to get rid of the girl and have some fun at the same time all the better. Afterward, the cellar would belong to them alone, and Nathalie could hardly wait to submit to him with body and soul.

There was basically only one problem left, as Toni explained to her: his little brother. An absolute wimp, who, however, was perfect for the role of the male victim.

But Toni didn't intend to kill him. He made that clear to Nathalie from the beginning. He just wanted to make the boy understand where his place was.

That was okay with Nathalie. So she could easily reconcile all her inclinations. So little Karl should belong to her and she could basically do everything with him except

kill him.

A tingling idea.

It became all the more tingling when she finally entered the house with Toni and found the boy half-unconscious on the couch in the living room.

Toni allowed her to undress him. She really wanted to see his cock to decide if he was worth a fuck.

Karl didn't smell particularly good when he finally lay there stark naked, and he didn't look as good as Toni either, but he was helpless and sufficiently equipped to cause a dull tingling sensation between Nathalie's thighs.

After Toni helped her tie him up, she immediately played with Karl's penis to find out whether he was too spaced out to get a hard-on. His erection answered the question. Nathalie was about to take off her panties and sit on Karl's cock when Toni tore her away from him. He'd seen enough.

Nathalie had to go to his bedroom with him, where he fucked her properly and also spanked her ass with his belt—as a punishment for almost cheating on him with Karl.

Nathalie enjoyed the punishment to the full.

When they later came down again and Nathalie felt pleasantly sore and worn out, the little shit was actually awake and had wet himself.

The fun could begin.

***

Karl's punishment was that he had to lie on his stomach so that Mami could spank his ass properly. She used a cooking spoon Toni had brought from the kitchen.

Fifty blows would be appropriate, she explained in a chatty tone.

Karl let it happen in silence.

It seemed like an eternity before she finally gave him fifty blows. His ass felt hot and burned like crazy.

When she was finished, she stepped in front of him and shoved the cooking spoon under his chin. Karl saw some blood sticking to it, which didn't surprise him very much.

"What do you say, kiddo?" she asked with a smile.

Amazingly, Karl knew immediately what she was talking about. "Thank you, Mami," he whispered.

She nodded contentedly and took the cooking spoon away again.

"Now turn around. Mami wants to see if you're good for fucking, too."

Karl laboriously rolled on his back. Everything was wet and stank of piss—the couch as well as himself.

That didn't seem to bother Mami. She fumbled with both hands under her skirt and finally took off a blotchy slip. She threw it carelessly aside, lifted the skirt, and climbed on Karl.

Her considerable weight on his stomach made him moan. For a moment she squatted directly on his cock, but (thank God!) there wasn't much to do with it. So she moved forward until she finally sat in the middle of his face with her pussy that smelled like fish. Karl gasped for air. The stench and weight were overwhelming.

She jerked around a little, and he got some air again. He sucked in greedily, despite the terrible stench.

"Mami wants to feel your tongue, kid!" Again she jerked, moaning on him, flattened his nose, and robbed him of air. She grabbed him by the hair and pressed his face even harder into her hot hairy crotch.

Karl opened his mouth and slid his tongue over her slippery labia. What he tasted made him choke, but

somehow he continued, breathing convulsively through his nose, and licked the fleshy, stinking pussy the best he could. He felt wiry pubic hair between his teeth and tried to ignore it.

Mami moaned loudly and moved rhythmically up and down.

Soon she fell into real ecstasy.

Karl tried even harder to let his tongue circle around her fat clitoris just to finish it faster. She reached orgasm with the speed and power of an express train. Even more of her stinking juice ran into Karl's mouth and over his face. He swallowed it spasmodically.

She'd finally had enough and slipped down on him until she sat on his cock again.

Karl sucked in the fresh air, relieved —if you could call it "fresh air" in a room smelling of piss and alcohol. With relief, he opened his eyes and saw a grinning Toni standing beside him. He seemed to enjoy the show to the fullest, which the enormous boner in his pants also spoke for.

Karl, on the other hand, still couldn't get an erection, which Mami had just noticed to her great disappointment.

She slipped a little further down to his thighs, leaving a trace of slime that could easily compete with that of a slug. ****

"Mami wants to get fucked now, kid! So you better try harder!"

Karl had no idea how he should do that, even if he wanted to. But Mami seemed to have quite concrete ideas. She took his limp penis in her hand and worked on it with the speed and routine of a professional.

Even disgust, pain, and fear didn't stand a chance. Karl got hard faster than he could count to three.

Grinning and sweating, Mami crawled upward again and sat on his hard penis. Only two seconds later Karl was stuck up to the shaft in her disgusting pussy, and there was nothing he could do about it.

Mami rotated her hips, and Karl couldn't keep himself from getting hornier and hornier. Shortly before he could cum, she climbed off and continued with her hand. So she caught most of his sperm. The rest landed on his belly. She rubbed the sticky liquid into her hands and then smeared it into his hair and face.

"Well done, kid." Smiling, she patted his wet cheek. "Keep it up."

She stood up and went over to Toni, kissed him passionately on the mouth, and stroked his erection through the fabric of his pants.

"That was really hot, baby," he praised and grabbed with both hands under her skirt. "Now let's take a short break and have a drink before we go down to the basement." He gave Karl a pitying look. "And you can also prepare yourself for a lot, dear brother. We're not finished with you yet!"

The woman turned to Karl and grinned broadly. "Have you thanked me already, kiddo?"

"Thank you, Mami," Karl whispered.

"You're very welcome, kid. We'll be back soon, and then we'll take care of your little girlfriend down in the basement. And if you're a good boy, maybe you'll only have to watch."

"Please don't hurt her!" Karl swallowed. "Take me, but leave her alone! She's already been through enough."

Mami winked at him mockingly. "You'd like that, sweetie." Before she left the room with Toni, she threw him a kiss.

***

After they left, Karl tried not to concentrate too much on his pounding skull and the pain in his limbs. Instead, he tried to follow the TV program that was playing. Some ridiculous episode of a series called *Cases of Fraud*—with horribly bad amateur actors. A woman had her possibly unfaithful husband under surveillance.

Although this crap didn't interest him at all, Karl watched it in order not to think of anything else and not to have to perceive anything else. What had just happened (that he'd been raped and mistreated by a completely crazy chick while his brother had watched with pleasure) was simply too absurd. But his aching cock, his squashed testicles, and the disgustingly sticky consistency of the drying sperm on his face told a different story. Not to mention the disgusting taste in his mouth. He'd actually licked this nasty bitch's stinking cunt as if there was no tomorrow, and had more than a pubic hair between his teeth. He would have loved to wipe his mouth, but his hands were still tied.

He felt so helpless. A feeling that wasn't new for him. But now it was different. More intense! He had no choice. Once again he had no choice! Just like Laura.

Laura would have understood.

Yes, Laura …

The fact that Toni had brought this crazy woman with him didn't bode well. Karl didn't believe that he'd have done so if the matter with Laura was to continue. It was more likely that it would end today.

Game over.

For Laura.

And for him?

Karl didn't know. Despite everything that had hap-

pened, he still didn't believe Toni would kill him. But what were the alternatives? A life as a slave for the sadistic version of Bonnie and Clyde? Or was he supposed to escape into a life all alone on the fringes of society?

But for that he'd have to escape first.

His chances were rather bad at the moment.

So what should he do?

At the moment, he could only wait and ponder as little as possible.

Karl finally succeeded quite well by giving in to the shock and exhaustion and falling asleep.

***

Laura woke when the cellar door opened. A limping, naked Karl came in, his arms seemingly tied to his back and some indefinable mass stuck in his face. He was flanked by Toni and an unknown woman who was small and quite pudgy. She wore a top and a short miniskirt, both at least two sizes too small. A mean smile played around her lips. Toni also seemed to be in a very good mood.

They stopped about five feet from Laura's mattress. Karl was forced to his knees, right next to the dried-up pool of blood in which the "thing" from her tummy had previously been lying.

Laura tried to make eye contact with him, but Karl stubbornly looked down.

Toni had the iron bar in his hand. He looked at the woman and handed her the bar. She played around with it a bit and put on an almost loving smile. She winked at Laura.

"This will be the last hour of your life, girl. And we're all here to share it with you." She laughed scornfully. Toni joined in. Then they fell silent almost at the same time.

The woman held one end of the bar to her mouth and licked it with a long, whitish tongue. While she did this, she grabbed Karl's hair with the other hand.

"Bend over, kid! Head to the floor, ass up! Mami wants to fuck you a little!"

From Karl's throat came a choppy, miserable sound, but he did what he was told and tilted his upper body forward until his forehead touched the concrete floor.

The woman stepped behind him and started massaging his ass.

"You like that, don't you? Tell Mami you like it, kid."

"I like it, Mami," Karl whispered.

"Tell Mami to spank you."

"Spank me, Mami!"

He didn't have to tell her twice. The crazy woman took a big swing and let the bar bang on Karl's ass.

Laura flinched when she heard the clapping.

Karl screamed.

"Ask for more!" the woman gasped.

"More," Karl cried. "I want more!"

She struck again.

So it went on for a while.

When she finally stopped, Karl's screaming had turned into a faint whimper. The woman looked satisfied. She patted his butt and then lifted a finger in the air. Toni came to lick it before she drove it between Karl's buttocks and finally stuck it in his anus.

He whined quietly.

The woman fingerfucked him a little while, then pulled her finger out again and licked it off. She grimaced in amusement. "Mami will fuck you now properly, my little chocolate boy!"

She grabbed the iron bar with both hands and rammed it into his ass.

Karl's screams went through Laura's bones.

She knew exactly how he felt.

She understood.

***

At some point the woman stopped penetrating Karl with the bar.

Time no longer mattered.

The cool air in the cellar had become hot and sticky.

Stale.

When Nathalie finally pulled the bar out of Karl, he fell to the side and collapsed.

Toni felt a little sting in his heart and wondered just what it was (pity?) when Nathalie marched past him with the bar and over to Laura.

Toni's imagination was sufficient enough (and above all dirty enough) to envision what came next.

"There! Lick it clean!" Nathalie ordered the girl and held the end of the bar (covered with blood and excrement) in front of her face.

Laura closed her eyes and opened her mouth.

Toni had been a good teacher.

He smiled and the emotion he now felt was easier to define: pride.

As he watched Laura lick the bar without even distorting her face, he got a boner. He rubbed his cock through the fabric of his jeans, then opened the zipper and took them off. Then his shorts.

Without looking at his brother (who'd had enough anyway), he went to the two women—with his naked lower body.

"That's enough!" he shouted harshly.

Laura immediately stopped licking, and Nathalie took

the bar away.

They were well trained. His girls.

Toni smiled contentedly.

He grabbed Laura by her hair and pulled her off the mattress until she squatted in front of him.

He turned to Nathalie. "Take your clothes off."

She obeyed immediately.

Toni stared greedily at her big pale tits.

"Sit down there and spread your legs."

Nathalie went into position and presented her plump sex with a lustful look.

Toni gave Laura's head a knock with his knuckles.

"That's your pussy, girl. Lick it."

Laura crawled between Nathalie's legs and began. She didn't hesitate a second. Toni was almost surprised at how well she obeyed. What more could he ask for? She was really a first-class sex slave! Too bad he'd kill her soon.

He rubbed his cock while watching the women and his excitement grew.

Then he couldn't stand it any longer.

He kneeled behind Laura, pulled her ass cheeks apart, and spat a few times on her asshole.

The fact that she was still full of blood and fluids from the "abortion" she'd had a few hours before didn't interest him much.

Her pussy was pretty messed up, but his favorite fuck-hole still looked really good—despite the countless encounters with the pole. The self-healing powers of the human body were really remarkable!

Toni shoved his cock inside her and groaned loudly as a delightful shiver went through his body.

One last time he wanted to fuck her.

And he fucked her hard.

***

Karl was on the verge of losing consciousness. His eyelids fluttered, and he licked his dry lips several times. The pain robbed him of his mind and almost his breath.

He wanted to be unconscious.

He was just drifting away when something pulled him back to reality. He forced himself to open his eyes and raise his head.

It was Nathalie screaming with pleasure as Laura crouched between her fat thighs. Toni knelt behind Laura and raped her from behind. It was a scene for some cheap hardcore porn—if there hadn't been all that dried blood on Laura's emaciated body. So in the end it seemed more like a horror movie.

And he was like an extra. Whereby it would have been enough for a supporting role.

Karl was about to lie down again and give in to his well-deserved fainting when a thought shot through his brain like lightning: *Now they're all busy. Nobody is watching me!*

Indeed.

They had forgotten him.

For the moment.

Even Laura didn't really seem to be aware of him anymore.

What did that mean?

It was his chance, right?

But … a chance for what?

What did he want to do?

Run away?

Call the cops?

Save Laura?

Or just himself?

In a matter of seconds all sorts of scenarios shot through Karl's head. Scenarios that would or could happen if he acted one way or the other.

He saw himself in handcuffs in the back of a police car.

He saw himself running through the forest. Away. Only away.

He saw himself running through the forest with Laura.

He saw himself at a trial. Laura on the witness stand. He, Toni, and Nathalie in the witness box.

He saw himself standing in front of a gravestone with the names of his brother and mother.

If time hadn't been so short, he'd surely have found another finale for this horror movie that was his life.

But which finale would he like best?

Karl decided to focus on the element of surprise.

The game was almost over, and he wanted to hold out bravely until the end.

Karl straightened up, which wasn't easy. His face distorted with pain. His hands were still tied behind his back. Fortunately, they had at least taken off his ankle tape.

No part of his body didn't ache, but his ass and abdomen hurt the most.

As he slowly got on his knees and finally his feet, Karl felt something damp and warm running down his legs. He didn't even want to know what it was. He kept an eye on Laura, "Mami", and Toni, but they were still too busy to look in his direction.

That was okay for Karl.

He crept to the cellar door, which was ajar, so he could open it with his foot. Silently and unobserved, he sounded the bell for the last round.

***

Next to the living room couch lay his clothes, but they had to wait.

Karl walked to the kitchen.

He stood with his back in front of the drawer in which they kept the knives—even during Frieda's lifetime and his time of suffering, the kitchen had been furnished exactly as it was today, but it had been much cleaner and tidier.

Opening the drawer blindly and taking out a knife proved to be relatively easy. Cutting the tape with this knife proved to be much more difficult.

It took several minutes, and he was sweating blood in the truest sense of the word, because just like the sweat on his back, blood (and who knows what else) ran down his legs.

Karl moaned and cursed between clenched teeth. But he finally managed to place the blade of the knife so that it cut into the tape. He wedged it between the kitchen counter and his body and carefully moved up and down.

He managed to loosen the tape far enough that he could rip it open with his hands. After this he felt so exhausted that he'd have preferred to run out the door and into the woods. No matter where to.

But he couldn't do that to her.

Not after everything they'd been through together and everything she expected of him.

He had to help this girl and do the first (and probably last) good deed of his life.

There was no choice.

He'd started this shit, and now he had to finish it.

There was no turning back, because the punishment for his disobedience would be the end of his life anyway.

Karl believed it was possible that Toni would kill him for it. After everything that Toni had made this monster of a woman do to him today, anything was possible.

Yes, everything.

So let's go!

Karl returned to the living room and quickly slipped into shorts and a T-shirt.

Dressed, he felt somehow less helpless and vulnerable, even if that was a fallacy. In addition, the liquid from his butt didn't run down his legs anymore but was absorbed by the fabric of the shorts.

Karl would have liked to know what was dripping out of him, but he'd find out later.

Karl walked past his sneakers but didn't bother to put them on.

No time. No time.

He went back to the kitchen and took a look at the open drawer. He saw the remains of the tape and the knife he'd used, a relatively small knife for cutting fruits and vegetables.

He needed a different one.

A big knife.

The biggest one they had.

His mother had used it to cut meat. The blade even went through tendons and bones if necessary. She'd explained that to him once.

A long time ago. Since then it had only been used once. But not for cooking. Cooking was no longer done very often in the Singer house.

No, Toni had used it to attack the unsuspecting Laura while she was jogging and he'd forced her to come along.

That seemed ages ago.

But Karl couldn't think about it now. There was only one thought in his mind: *I hope the knife is still sharp.*

It was heavy and lay well in his hand.

Karl grasped the smooth black handle.

That felt good.

He was ready.

But for what?

He didn't want to think about that.

He just wanted to do it now.

It was good to finally do something.

For too long he'd left it to others.

As he left the kitchen to go to the basement again, sweat dripped from his forehead into his eyes. He wiped it away with the back of his hand.

The bottom of his pants felt wet, as if he'd pissed or shit himself. Perhaps both.

Never mind.

He felt better.

The pain had slipped to the edge of his perception. He only focused on the knife in his hand now.

Fuck the shitted pants! Fuck the sweat on your face! And fuck the fucking fear!

His heart had just spoken, and he'd finally listened.

There was only one person who could turn all this crap to good, and that was him. From the beginning. Laura had known it and really tried often enough to convince him, in one way or another, but always emphatically.

He hadn't listened, but that didn't matter anymore, because in the end he'd heard and he'd understood and above all, he was doing something.

Nothing else mattered!

Now you just have to do it well!

Oh yes, that was his intention.

***

After Toni had shot a good load into the little bitch's asshole, he let go of her and looked reflexively over at Karl while he wiped his cock clean on Laura's bony ass.

He froze when he realized Karl was no longer here. "Shit!"

He brutally hit Laura on the back. "Stop it, you whore!"

Laura paused and raised her head. Her lips were red and heavily swollen. Her eyes had no expression at all.

Nathalie also raised her head. "What the fuck's going on? Why did the bitch stop? I haven't cum yet!"

"I don't give a shit!" Toni yelled. "My brother's gone. Go upstairs and find him! He can't get far with his hands tied!"

Nathalie got up in a hurry. She made an effort to grab her clothes, but Toni stopped her with a slap in the face.

"We don't have time for that now! Stay naked!"

Nathalie nodded. "Yes, you're right! I'm sorry! What am I supposed to do when I get him?"

"You spank his ass and bring him back here!"

"Okay! I'm on my way!"

"That's better, woman! And woe he screws up! Then I'll make you pay for it! Understand?"

"Yes, of course!"

"Then fuck off now!"

***

In the middle of the stairs, he almost collided with the naked woman. For a moment both of them looked at each other in confusion and froze.

Nathalie opened her mouth as Karl rammed the knife into her stomach, directly underneath one of her pale breasts, which were streaked with ugly blue veins.

The blade disappeared all the way to the shaft in her soft flesh.

Everything was quiet for a moment. They both watched dark blood run in fine trickles from the wound.

Then Nathalie screamed, and they reached for the knife almost at the same time.

Karl was a little faster. He grabbed the handle with both hands. Nathalie laid her hands on his and tried to push them away. But she was too weak. In addition, her fingers slipped in her own blood.

Karl pulled as hard as he could.

The knife slipped from Nathalie's belly, causing the wound to open more.

Now the blood no longer ran but splashed.

Nathalie pressed one hand on the wound and tried to support herself on the banister with the other. She screamed her head off. Screamed for help. Screamed Toni's name.

That had to stop! Immediately!

Karl kicked a bare foot into Nathalie's soft abdomen.

She screamed even louder when she lost her balance.

She fell backward down the few steps she'd already climbed.

She lay on her back, pressed both hands on her stomach, and screamed even louder.

That had to stop!

Her blood was everywhere.

The cut Karl had inflicted on her gaped like an obscene smiley.

Her enormous breasts trembled with every wheezing breath.

Karl took a look at the cellar door.

It was closed.

The room was soundproof.

That was probably the only reason Toni hadn't shown up yet.

He should have heard that screaming nonetheless, Karl thought. Unless …

Yeah, unless he was doing something in there that made a similar noise.

Karl prayed it wasn't too late when he stood with his legs apart above Nathalie and rammed the knife down her throat.

***

His anger at Karl's disobedience made Toni tremble.

He grabbed Laura. Actually, he wanted to fuck her again, but he couldn't get a hard-on anymore, and that made him twice as angry.

So he ordered her to kneel in front of him and look at him.

As soon as their eyes met, he hit her in the face with the iron bar.

Laura's jawbone broke with a crunch. She collapsed and fell to the side. She hadn't even screamed.

But Toni wasn't through with her yet.

He grabbed her by her hair and wanted to force her to look him in the face again.

Her face looked strangely distorted. She seemed to be unconscious and just hung silently in his grip, that stupid bitch.

But she wouldn't spoil his fun. Not now!

He tugged at her hair, pulled her further up until her scrawny upper body was upright again. She was literally like a puppet in his hand.

That was boring.

He rammed his knee onto her lower jaw and reposi-

tioned it.

And there she was again. His girl!

She coughed and spat out a gush of blood, followed by several teeth.

Now, finally, she returned Toni's gaze as he wanted it.

His girl!

He lowered the bar, put it next to himself so that it would give him support as he raised his knee one more time, and rammed it under Laura's nose.

Again she lost consciousness. And again he forced her to her knees.

"Look at me, girl, while you still can! I'm the last thing you'll ever see!" He laughed. "Don't forget me, darling!" He rammed the end of the bar into her left eye.

Laura slumped down, whimpering, hanging from strings of her hair like a deformed doll. Toni had her firmly under control and straightened her up again. He shook her until her remaining eye opened. He ordered her to look at him, and Laura obeyed.

She looked at him—one eye filled with tears while the other was behind a swollen, bloody lump of skin.

Toni waited for her to beg him. But Laura was no longer able to speak or scream. With her last remaining strength, she folded her hands as if to pray and looked up at him silently with her one crying eye.

Accusing.

Toni didn't like it at all. He just took a big swing with the iron bar to not have to endure that look any longer when the cellar door slammed against the wall behind him.

***

Karl stood the.

In boxers and a T-shirt. Barefoot.

His sweaty hair hung in thick strands before his eyes.

There was blood.

Everywhere.

It looked as if he'd bathed in it.

Shorts and T-shirt were soaked with it.

Face, arms, and legs were speckled red.

His bare feet looked like he wore scarlet-red slippers.

He breathed heavily and held something in his hand that was also red.

A knife.

As he stood there, he wiped his forehead with the back of his hand and smeared more blood.

Toni stared at his brother and was—perhaps for the first time in his life—speechless.

The blood wasn't Karl's.

And there was only one other person …

Nathalie.

Toni shook his head in disbelief.

The iron bar almost fell out of his hand, but he held it firmly when he realized it was the only weapon he had.

Karl had a goddamn bloodstained knife in his hand and had apparently just wounded someone (Nathalie?).

Killed?

Toni felt torn between respect and horror. He looked firmly at Karl. "What the fuck, man?"

Karl didn't answer. But he didn't hold the knife as if he wanted to cut cucumbers with it.

"Get that knife away now!" Toni tried to appear cool and steady, even though his heart just slipped into his pants.

The expression in Karl's eyes didn't show the usual humility and fear. That was pure bloodlust! No more and no less. He'd probably lost his mind. He'd probably ex-

pected too much of him.

But that didn't matter anymore.

The only thing that mattered now was to take away the fucking knife from the fat little shithead and then give him the beating of his life!

Toni's grip loosened. He didn't notice that "his girl" fell to the concrete floor like a wet sack. He shook his hand to get rid of the torn hair and slowly walked toward his brother.

"Put it down, Karl, before anyone gets seriously injured!"

He preferred to ignore the fact that someone had definitely been seriously injured already, even if wasn't easy to ignore all the blood.

"Karl, be reasonable! You don't really want to hurt me. You're my little—"

"Freeze!" Karl suddenly screamed. His hot saliva sprayed Toni in his face.

Toni flinched but still came closer. "No, man, you're gonna stop this shit right now and give me that knife."

"I said *freeze*!" The blade shot forward in a flash and gave Toni a deep cut in his outstretched forearm.

He screamed and pulled his arm back. "Shit! Are you crazy?" His stupid little brother had actually dared hurt him.

Confused, he pressed his arm to his stomach, trying to stop the bleeding and became only now aware of his nudity. With a throbbing heart he remained in this position, barely daring to breathe.

"Karl, we can talk about anything! We're a family! What do you think? We gotta stick together after all!"

Karl gave a bitter laugh. "A family, of course. Stick together …" He shook his head. "You're a fucking dirty swine, and I've never been more than your damn slave!"

"Yes, Karl, I understand you. That must have felt like that to you sometimes, but believe me, I never wanted anything bad for you. All I ever wanted was for the two of us to stick together and make it somehow. We're so different and that's why each one of us had to take the place that was right for him. I admit that it was often worse for you. But I love you, Karl! You … we're the same flesh and blood! I'd never do anything bad to you!"

Karl snorted contemptuously. He pointed with the tip of his knife at Laura, who was lying on the floor covered in blood, half-starved, almost dead, her face a ruin.

Karl saw her shifted jaw, her smashed nose, her destroyed eye. If he hadn't known who she was, he wouldn't have recognized her.

"My God, what have you done?"

It was only a split second of Karl not paying attention to his brother, because his attention was on poor maltreated Laura, who wouldn't look like that now if he'd only shown he has balls.

This tiny moment of inattentiveness was enough for Toni. He pulled up the bar and hit it with full force on Karl's wrist.

The knife fell to the floor.

The pain was overwhelming.

Karl was so perplexed that he couldn't even scream. With widened eyes he staggered backward and held his broken wrist.

He retreated until he stood with his back against the wall.

Toni picked up the knife.

He came to him and held it to his throat.

"So you wanted to kill me with this thing, huh?"

Karl said nothing.

Toni replaced the knife with the bloody iron rod,

pressed it against his brother's throat while he pushed the knife blade under Karl's T-shirt, and drilled it deep enough into his stomach to make him bleed.

Karl expected a stabbing pain, but compared to the painful pain in his wrist, the cut wasn't worth mentioning.

"Why don't you just finish it, Toni? Come on, put an end to it! I wish you a lot of fun with the removal of the corpses." His laughter quickly turned into a cough as the bar pressed on his windpipe.

"Wait, I have to count … one … two … three … wow! Toni, you have to bury three bodies today! Actually, four. I forgot Mama. You should start as soon as possible, brother!"

Toni pressed himself close to Karl, as if he wanted to kiss or embrace him, but instead he spat in his face.

Karl didn't even twitch an eyelash. He suddenly felt strong. As strong as never before!

"I won't do you that favor, you fucking asshole! *You* will live and be a good boy and help me with the corpses!"

"I ain't gonna do shit."

"Dude, you stay here until all this shit's done and you do the dirty work. Just like always, little brother!"

Toni took the bar from Karl's throat and held the knife in front of his face instead. "Here's the plan: I'll take you upstairs and finish what I started down here. Later, I'll get you so you can dispose of the bodies."

Karl's lips trembled. "Please, Toni, don't do it. Don't kill her. I beg you!"

"Oh, suddenly you appeal to my compassion again! But that won't work, Karl, so don't bother! The bitch is as good as dead. And you can be glad if I forgive you for your disobedience!"

Karl looked over at Laura, who was just moving, and

suddenly returned his gaze with her one bloodshot eye.

She wasn't the same girl Toni brought here half a year ago.

She wasn't even a shadow of that girl anymore.

Everything about her was dead by now. Mutilated. Extinguished.

At that moment Karl wished for nothing more than to go to her and take her in his arms, to tell her that everything would be all right, even if that wasn't true.

But Toni wouldn't allow that.

For Toni, she was already dead.

In a few minutes, he'd beat the last spark of life out of her body. If she was lucky, he'd use the knife.

It was a miracle anyway that she was conscious and looked at him.

With this one eye.

"Laura, I'm so sorry!"

Toni grabbed him by the collar of his T-shirt. "Stop whining! Move your ass!"

He pushed him rudely to the door.

"We're going up together now. And remember, I'm right behind you with the knife!"

Karl felt the blade against his back as he walked through the door. Toni's hand lay on his shoulder.

He left the iron bar behind. Laura wouldn't be able to reach it (if she was able to move at all) because her chains were too short.

***

They had to climb over Nathalie's dead body to get to the stairs.

Karl and Toni left bloody footprints.

Karl didn't even look.

Toni whistled through his teeth. "You did a great job!"

Karl was silent. He slowly climbed the stairs.

Toni was very close behind.

Close enough for Karl to smell his sweat and hear him breathe.

Karl felt his brother's breath on his neck.

He felt the throbbing pain in his broken wrist, which he pressed firmly against his chest with the help of his intact hand.

He felt the blood (and whatever else) still seeping out of his sore anus.

He felt the cut on his belly.

He felt the hard concrete under his bare feet.

He felt his heart beating wildly, threatening to blow his chest.

He felt tears, hot as lava, running down his cheeks.

He felt all this very clearly and without any doubt.

He knew just as clearly and unequivocally that this was now his last chance to save Laura.

The risk of getting killed himself was high.

But it was a chance. In spite of everything.

He could die, and Laura would do the same.

But he could also survive and Toni would die, and then Laura would be saved.

He'd get her out of that goddamn basement!

He'd make sure this game was finally over!

The risk wasn't calculable, but he had no choice but to take it.

No choice!

So Karl Singer staked everything on one card.

The last card in this game.

It required courage.

Courage he didn't have.

But this fucking madness finally had to stop!

Yes, he had no choice.

***

Karl had now reached the second-to-last step.

It was a steep staircase.

A long staircase.

And he was out of breath.

Just like Toni, who was panting behind him.

Again, Karl became aware of the knife in his back.

It was easily possible that it would stick deep in his body in a few seconds.

That was the risk.

One of many.

Fuck it!

Karl closed his eyes. Seconds became minutes.

He let go of the injured hand, which would have hurt under other circumstances, but now he didn't feel it.

There was only him and this one chance.

With his healthy hand he reached for the banister. Paused. He supported himself.

And threw himself backward against his brother with full force.

Toni lost his balance when his younger brother's almost two hundred pounds hit him unchecked.

That crazy motherfucker just threw himself into the knife! he thought, completely perplexed as he fell, followed by Karl, who now actually had the knife in his back.

Toni was the first one to hit the floor.

Moaning, he remained lying next to Nathalie's body and in her blood, which now mixed with his.

It ran in streams from a laceration on the back of his head.

It wasn't the only injury.

When Karl fell on him with the force of a truck, Toni's legs broke.

Then his jaw.

And several ribs, which now drilled into his lungs.

Toni roared until he ran out of breath and only a loud rattling could be heard.

"Move … from … me … down …" Toni wheezed. He coughed and spat blood and teeth.

Karl rolled off him.

He seemed unharmed after the fall.

Except for the knife in his back.

And the broken wrist.

But in comparison to Toni, he'd indeed been lucky, which was probably also due to the fact that Toni's body had slowed down his fall.

"You … son of a bitch … you … did … this … on purpose …" Toni choked noisily. Even more blood and teeth gushed out of his mouth.

His left foot was twisted at an unnatural angle, and a white bone protruded from his right knee, not to mention all the blood seeping from the back of his head and from his mouth.

***

He was fucked. Definitely. He wasn't dangerous to anyone anymore.

Karl slowly got to his feet. He tried to pull the knife out of his back with his uninjured hand and finally made it. It hurt, and some blood ran down into his briefs. But the injury didn't seem too bad.

Nothing but a trifle compared to the pain in his wrist.

A real blessing compared to his brother's condition.

Karl held the bloody knife in his hand and looked piti-

lessly down on Toni, whose eyelids fluttered.

The dirty bastard was dying.

Karl felt nothing.

Toni opened his eyes. "W—why …?"

Karl shook his head. "I don't owe you anything, dude. Not even an answer!"

Toni coughed again. There was a lot of blood.

His body twitched.

Now he didn't look at Karl anymore.

His eyes were open, but his gaze was broken.

Game over!

***

"Everything's gonna be all right now. I'm almost there. Everything will be fine," Karl muttered when he entered the basement.

But all his newfound courage collapsed like the Twin Towers on 9/11 when he saw Laura. Her lifeless body with the remaining eye closed.

He'd taken too much time, wasted it on his fear and his self-pity.

Had everything been in vain?

No!

Groaning, he bent over the pile of cloth lying on the floor next to Laura. The furious pain in his wrist was there again. Karl ignored it. He rummaged through his (dead) brother's clothes and finally found what he was looking for.

The key fit, and Karl opened the lock on Laura's ankle cuffs.

She couldn't be dead.

Not now!

Not after all that!

He slipped the iron cuffs from her ankles and lifted her blood-drenched body.

It felt warm.

Warm and fragile.

He held her in his arms. He managed to look her in the face. Or what was left of it.

"...oni?"

Karl didn't understand. Not immediately.

What he understood, however, was the fact that it wasn't too late.

Laura was alive.

Still!

"Dead," he finally said. "Both of them."

Laura nodded.

She wasn't able to do more.

But more wasn't necessary anyway.

***

He put her on the couch in the living room.

He wrapped her in a blanket.

Gently stroked her.

Did he cry?

Laura could only guess. The lid of her remaining eye weighed tons. She was too weak. Only felt the pain raging in her body. And the warmth that now penetrated her skin. Karl's warmth.

For the first time Laura thought she might have liked him.

Somehow.

At first she'd never have thought that possible.

Later she'd hoped to use him for her own purposes. In the end, that must have worked.

Even if differently than expected. But wasn't that al-

ways the case?

She thought he was too fat and sometimes smelled really bad, but his face was really pretty and he had lovely eyes.

He was warm and soft.

And indeed, he'd been icy cold and tough when it mattered.

It could have been said that he'd done his job well, without chickening out and without complaining.

Laura felt proud of him.

There was so much left in her.

Maybe she'd have told him that if she hadn't been in such pain. And maybe it would have changed everything.

Maybe not.

She felt Karl getting up.

Where was he going?

She laboriously opened her eye. It seemed to take forever.

When she could finally see something, she recognized Karl coming back with a cell phone in his hand, which he now put on her stomach.

It was an older model, full of scratches and cracks.

Just like its owner.

Laura looked at the cell phone without touching it.

"The battery is charged," said Karl. "We have a network signal here."

Instinctively, her hand grabbed the phone and finally held it.

"The emergency call is stored," Karl explained calmly. "I only have one request left."

Now she looked up at him. One last time.

"Wait another twenty minutes before you call, okay?"

"W—why?"

"Please! Okay?"

She nodded slowly.

Karl sat to her on the couch and put an arm around her. “I’m so sorry for all this, Laura. Don’t forget that!”

He stood up.

Then he went away.

Just like that.

***

There was only one place he wanted to be now.

Very close to her.

Mama.

***

After he’d left Laura in the sun-drenched living room and could rely on nothing but her promise, he went up to the first floor.

There he stood in front of his mother’s locked bedroom door.

He bowed his head until his forehead touched the cracked wood.

That was good. He didn’t have to go inside because he couldn’t bear what he’d see in there.

It was good just to stand out here and touch the door.

He felt close to her here.

Like he always had.

“I’ll be right there, Mama,” he whispered hoarsely.

He sat with his back to the door and ignored the pain.

Soon he’d no longer feel it.

He only hoped Laura would keep her promise and give him enough time.

He knew he’d lost a lot of blood. The weakness spread noticeably, and black dots danced before his eyes.

It probably wouldn't take much longer.

That was good.

Karl stretched out his legs.

His right hand hurt too much to move it even one inch. He couldn't reach out his arm to cut his wrists.

But there were other important arteries. For example, in the thighs. All you had to do was cut deep enough.

With the left hand it was a bit more difficult, but Karl did quite well.

He hit the right femoral artery, and that was all it took …

***

Karl Singer died five minutes before the police stormed the house.

Laura had waited exactly twenty minutes before she called 911.

She'd done him this last favor.

EPILOGUE

Thursday, September 3, 2015

The first leaves had already changed color.

It had been an unusually hot and dry summer, so the colors of autumn came a little earlier this year.

Laura could see it from her window.

She'd got the bed by the window, as she had to stay longer than most patients.

Almost one and a half months had passed since the horror in the Singers' basement, but her wounds were still open.

She'd undergone the first two facial surgeries and a uterine procedure, which ended with its removal.

Many more surgeries would follow to restore her face to some extent.

Never to be herself again, because that was over.

Laura Hermann no longer existed.

She'd been replaced by this strange, disfigured, scarred person with only one eye and no heart.

She sometimes felt like a doll that an evil child had first broken and then thrown into the garbage. Then, some other stupid kid came by and took her along to patch her up again.

A stupid idea.

She'd never have children. Neither good nor evil ones.

The only one she'd had was dug up behind the Singers' house and buried anonymously in some cemetery.

Laura didn't want to know.

But she thought about it nonetheless. Very often.

And she dreamed.

In her dreams, the child was alive and about three years

old.

It was a little girl with blonde hair.

She was sitting on a bloodstained basement staircase waiting for her.

But every time Laura reached it, she turned around and stared into empty black eye sockets and a bloody, wide open mouth screaming silently.

Then Laura woke, trembling and bathed in sweat, wondering each damn time whether it was even possible to shout silently with such a mouth.

How could that work?

Maybe only children who were already dead before they were born could do that.

Because fate had condemned them to eternal silence.

And Laura screamed every time. On behalf of her dead child. For all dead children.

Until a nurse came and gave her an injection so she could sleep.

Dreamless.

It worked with the syringe.

The syringe also helped against the pain. At least the physical ones, which was why she really longed for the thing at some point.

Yes, the dreams, the pain, her broken body, the whole damn trauma of her captivity—that was one thing.

Her dead father was the other.

She couldn't believe he'd given up, that he'd simply fucked off without knowing what had happened to her. At least he could have waited until they found her body or something. But no, the motherfucker had run away quietly and secretly, while she went through hell only a few miles away.

Only the thoughts about her family had kept her alive at all.

She'd fought and held out.

She'd come home just to find out that she no longer had a home.

She'd wanted nothing more than to be Laura Hermann again, who had parents and friends. Who went to school and talked about boys. Who liked to giggle and was still a virgin and wanted to know what it was like to have sex with a boy.

Yes, she'd wanted to know and now she knew. And God alone could perhaps help her forget all that again.

Annika had not visited her yet. She was probably afraid of what she'd see in her face. Laura couldn't blame her. She herself was afraid of what she saw in her face.

And that wasn't because of the injuries.

It was because of what was behind them.

What had happened to her soul.

The only one who might have understood a little was as dead as the one who did it to her.

The good thing about it was that there would never be a trial in which she'd have to relive everything.

Karl had judged himself and his brother as well as that terrible woman. In the end they had found another body, as Laura later learned. Behind the door where Karl had bled to death were still traces of the deceased Mrs. Singer and her cats. Just like Karl had told her.

Whether Toni had killed his mother, which Laura had assumed, or whether she'd died a natural death, as Karl had assured her, could no longer be determined beyond doubt. The fact was that Mrs. Singer had been forgotten by her sons and eaten by her own cats.

And it was also a fact that there was no one left who could have been held accountable. Not for that and not for what would accompany Laura until her death.

Some distant relative made sure the three Singers were

buried in a grave as nameless as Karl and Laura's unborn child.

They didn't want to attract much attention.

That was pure wishful thinking, of course.

The Singer house was now empty and barricaded, but this didn't stop onlookers from regularly snooping around.

Sometimes they broke into the house and took photos, which they published on Facebook under the title "Bavarian House of Horrors." They had even filmed the traces of blood on the stairs and in the basement, which gave the whole thing the necessary "spice."

Laura's mother had advised her not to deal with all this, but Laura noticed that it helped her somehow, so she regularly Googled the Bavarian House of Horrors and always found something new.

Sometimes it scared her, often it was just some bullshit, but most of the time it made her feel better, and that was all that mattered.

Because forgetting wasn't the solution.

AUTHOR S NOTE

Dear readers:

I hope most of you who started reading this book stayed with it to the end. I can imagine that it wasn't easy for some of you.

I felt the same way when I wrote it.

Nevertheless, it was a story that was inside me and had to be told exactly as I told it.

We often hear in the media about terrible things that people do to other people. We can hardly believe it and just shake our heads, and we want to forget it as soon as possible. Most of the time we prefer to look away and don't want to deal with these things.

But it happens.

Every day.

Everywhere in the world.

These perpetrators really exist.

Just like the victims.

And looking away isn't a solution.

I wanted to know what it's like to look at it.

All the time. To the bitter end.

It makes you angry and speechless, but maybe (hopefully) it also makes us think and helps us to become a little more sensitive about the things happening around us.

Thanks to everyone who accompanied Laura and me through this story.

Forgetting is not a solution.

Until the next time …

Simone Trojahn, August 30, 2015

Addendum of March 25, 2018

Dear readers:

More than two years have passed since I released KELLERSPIELE (translator's comment: the German original of *Basement Games)* as my first hardcore thriller. A lot has happened since then. There have been a lot of positive but also some negative comments. A book that divides minds and has changed my life forever. Because it brought me the success I needed to turn my hobby into my profession.

Therefore, I'm very happy that Michael Merhi of REDRUM BOOKS has made this new edition possible, which makes the book shine in new splendor, both from the inside and outside. Thank you very much for that, dear Michael.

Special thanks to my editor, Marion Mergen, who once again managed to get the most out of my story. Thank you very much, dear Marion, that was great fun!

I would also like to thank you, dear readers, because without you, none of this would make sense. You have a place in my heart, and I'm only really satisfied when you are. Thank you so much for your loyalty and support.

If you would like to contact me personally, you can do so via my author page on Facebook or by e-mail.

You are also welcome to join my group, Simone Trojahn Fans, on Facebook.

Contact:
facebook.com/simonetrojahn
t.simone80@googlemail.com

HAPPY BIRTHDAY SHORT-STORY

by Simone Trojahn

Frustrated, Doug slammed the paper on the side table. This screaming! Simply unbearable! He'd been looking forward to a relaxed early spring afternoon in his garden, which meant the world to him—and now? One could neither read nor think a clear thought in this noise. And it wasn't the first time.

Cursing, Doug struggled to get out of his garden chair. The jerky movement sent a violent wave of pain through his spine. His kneecaps creaked as he stomped toward the house in rage.

At sixty-nine, Doug was no longer young. After decades in the factory, he had truly earned his retirement. But Doug hadn't reckoned with his new neighbors, from whom he was separated only by a hedge—which he had planted as a privacy screen around his property years ago. There was nothing like privacy. Doug Keller didn't like people, and his misanthropic inclination had worsened since he'd retired.

Now the annoying work colleagues he'd had to deal with for so long were finally history. For five years now, Doug had the peace and quiet he thought he deserved. It had been wonderful for a while. He'd even been able to teach the mailman to simply place the mail on the small bench in front of the front

door, where it was protected from snow and rain.

Doug was always at home, but he hated to open the door for anyone. Instead, he liked to stand behind the curtain in the kitchen and peer out the window until the mailman—or whoever wanted to bother him—disappeared. Occasionally, salesmen or Jehovah's Witnesses came, but Doug would bet they'd give up soon. He appreciated nothing more than the loneliness and tranquility—but that was over at that moment.

Angrily, Doug slammed the front door behind him. Because of the warm weather, he had tilted open all the windows in the basement. Now he slammed them shut to turn off the noise from the neighbor's garden. But he could still hear the damn brats. Like a dervish, Doug hurried into the living room, switched on the TV, and turned up the volume until his ears hurt. At least he couldn't hear the children anymore. Thank God!

Exhausted, Doug dropped into his TV chair. He'd left the newspaper outside, which he actually wanted to read. Now he had to watch some boring cooking show he didn't want to see at all. And who was to blame? Doug would have preferred to cry. He was so angry.

Four weeks ago, the fat cow next door showed up at his door for the first time. She had a gift basket with her filled with wine, cheese, salami, and chocolates. Plus a greeting card in which she introduced herself and her family as the new neighbors.

Doug, of course, hadn't opened the door but had secretly watched through the kitchen window as the platinum-blonde woman with the fat bottom waited in front of his door, wringing her hands. She rang the

bell two more times before turning to leave. She kindly left the basket on the bench.

With a pounding heart, Doug waited about ten minutes before he went to the door and took it in. A welcome from the new neighbors, Ellie and Martin Miller with the children Sarah, Max, and Leila. Three children! Good God! They all had signed the card, the front of which was decorated with a basket filled with flowers.

With a disgusted expression, Doug shredded the card and threw it in the trash. Then he devoted himself to the contents of the basket. He hated cheese, and the sausage was too hard for him. But the wine looked promising; at least it wasn't a cheap brand. He emptied the bottle while watching TV that night.

That was the end of his interest in the new neighbors. He had no intention to thank them or make any other kind of contact. He simply didn't care about the people.

That changed abruptly when two weeks later Doug was being lured into the garden by the first warm rays of spring sunshine.

Unfortunately, Doug wasn't the only one. The screaming from the neighboring garden immediately got on his nerves. And it didn't stop! Two nerve-racking hours passed before Doug finally escaped while muttering a curse.

Since then it went like this every afternoon, weather permitting. Doug tried to enjoy the mornings when the kids were at school, but at that time his terrace was shaded and it was too cool to sit outside. This would get better in summer, but it was April now. Doug had thought about visiting the neighbors to thank them for the shitty basket and to take this op-

portunity to point out that the noise had to stop. They could do whatever they wanted, as long as they were quiet. He hadn't done it yet. Since he was a retiree, he had hardly spoken five sentences in a row with another person, and he wanted it to stay that way.

He'd been single since his youth and only had a few distant relatives who lived far enough away to not get on his nerves. Doug's only social contacts had been his colleagues at work. He'd had to pull himself together quite a bit to deal with them properly. Of course, it had always remained a superficial working relationship. Doug didn't want it any other way.

He'd already been a loner at school—and proud of it. The only girlfriend he'd ever had, at the age of twenty, had given him a bad feeling in the pit of his stomach. Doug was relieved when she finally turned to another guy. They'd slept together two or three times, which hadn't satisfied and somehow frightened him. Sex wasn't Doug Keller's cup of tea.

He once read in an article that there were people who had no need for physical closeness. They were called asexual. Doug didn't give a shit about terms. With the help of this article, however, he understood what was wrong with him. It calmed him down. He found life with himself to be perfect. He had his job, his cottage, and his garden. In fact, Doug Keller loved this garden and every single plant in it more than he had ever loved a human being. Even his parents had been quite unimportant to him, and at their funerals he had only squeezed out a few tears of decency.

The only thing that really meant anything to Doug was his plants and his peace. Now in his old age, relaxation and peace were the be-all and end-all. He

loved to do the gardening in the warm sunshine, and no matter how much his bones hurt and creaked, Doug would never hire a gardener to botch his work and perhaps end up wanting to chat with Doug as well. He also loved to sit in his garden chair, slurp a cold beer, and read. None of this was possible since the new neighbors had moved in with their dirty brats!

Now Doug spent most of his time in his armchair and let himself get lulled by the television. The garden grew wild, and the beer no longer tasted good. And all this just because of those damn neighbors!

At night in bed, Doug whispered their names, which burned themselves into his brain like a mantra, wishing them death and the devil on their backs. He hadn't seen any of them except the woman, but hearing them was enough. Doug suspected the man was at work most of the time. When he got home, the kids would be in bed. Lucky man! And the wife? In Doug's fantasy, she squatted her ass in front of the TV all day, neglecting the household and not giving a shit about what her kids were doing. She surely dreamed of fucking the mailman—or some craftsman. Doug knew women like that. With their fat asses and hanging tits, they were useless for nothing but squeezing out one ugly brat after another from their worn-out pussies. Long live America! How could it have come to this? Doug had once heard that families in China were only allowed to have one child. That was perfect! The world's population grew too fast. It was time to pull the ripcord.

Unfortunately, it wasn't in Doug's hands. He had to come to terms with the facts—and the noise. But should he really put up with it?

Why don't you just go over there and give the cow your opinion?

Unfortunately, Doug wasn't very good at 'giving an opinion'.

Does that mean you just let them get on your nerves?

The thought drove Doug crazy! He couldn't make it that easy for them! He suffered like a dog, damn it! This penetrating screaming of the children made him sick and robbed him of the last good years of his life! He needed a plan. Something he could do to put an end to it.

And then came that mild pre-summer evening when fate finally gave Doug a chance.

***

Since the neighboring children had been unbearably loud again during the day, Doug didn't sit on the terrace before the evening of this warm day in May. He took a six-pack with him and wrapped himself in a blanket as a precaution. He was too old to risk pneumonia. He couldn't read in the dark, but he enjoyed the silence. Finally he dozed off.

When Doug woke up, it was chilly. He wrapped the blanket tighter around him and stayed seated for a moment. There were voices from the neighboring garden—this time no children, but Mom and Dad, who probably also ended the evening on the terrace. In the silence of the evening, their voices could be clearly heard.

Doug held his breath and made himself very small, which was nonsense, of course, as he was protected by the hedge. They couldn't see him, and he couldn't see them.

"You're really late," the woman said. Doug noticed the reproachful tone in her voice.

The man sighed. "I told you we have a lotta work until the new project is done."

"And what comes then? The next project?" The woman sounded angry and provocative. Maybe she'd been drinking.

The man sighed again. Did he have an affair? Doug wouldn't have been surprised.

"What's the point, Ellie?"

"I'm tired of having to do everything on my own! In case you forgot, it's your daughter's birthday on Monday! Didn't you want to take care of it and order a clown?"

"Of course I haven't forgotten! What do you think of me?" Now he sounded really angry. "I'll help you with the preparations at the weekend. But we have to postpone the clown thing until next time …"

"Why?" she interrupted him. "That should be the highlight!"

"I've checked on that. Most of them are booked for months in advance, and the prices are a joke. I'd prefer to put the money into gifts. She gets more out of that."

"But Sarah's counting on his show."

"Because once again you couldn't keep your mouth shut. Sarah's only eight. She can still have many clowns."

"Oh yes? With a father like you, I tend to doubt that."

"What does that mean? I bust my ass here so that everyone is well and that's the gratitude I get, or what?"

Doug took a big sip from his Budweiser. His pulse

raced. The view behind the façade of the picture-book family! That was more exciting than any television program.

"You know, sometimes I hate you," the woman growled.

"Not as much as I hate you," the man replied.

The woman sobbed. Shortly afterward a door slammed, and Doug could only hear the man cursing quietly. "*Fuck*! Damn bitch! That stupid cow!"

Wasn't that lovely? Doug grinned. No surprise that the nerves of this family were raw. If it was his family, Doug would have decided long ago on an extended suicide. Not that he'd ever made the mistake of starting a family.

When he was sure there was nothing else to hear from over there, he fought his way out of his chair and stretched his stiff limbs. The farce on the other side of the hedge was worth the pain. Then he remembered what they'd said about the birthday party scheduled for Monday. Even without the clown, this party would be hell. Not only three, but a whole horde of children would party loudly in the neighboring garden. The idea alone drove sweat of stress to Doug's forehead. And the only thing he could do was hope for bad weather.

Or?

***

Being eternally single, Doug knew how to take care of himself. He always cooked fresh food because he didn't trust the industrial crap. But he'd never baked before. He didn't have a sweet tooth, and there had never been an occasion to bake. He wasn't necessarily

the type of person that anyone invited to a party. While reading a brand-new baking book, in his arthritic hands he turned the muffin molds, which he'd just bought in the supermarket. Doug had grabbed the book there and bought the necessary ingredients for chocolate muffins on the spot. Children love them! After buying the ingredients he'd been to a costume shop, because the supermarket only had Halloween costumes. Doug Keller had no idea about children and only knew they had fucking loud voices, but he'd once heard that they liked clowns. For whatever reason. He found clowns horrible. The colorful rubber mask lying in the box on his kitchen table stank pathetically and would make him sweat, but it was for a good cause.

The end justifies the means. That's the saying, right?

Yeah, that's what people said. Doug turned away from the ugly rubber mask with the colorful synthetic hair, put on his reading glasses dangling on a string around his neck, and read the recipe that promised "the tastiest chocolate muffins for any party."

Little Sarah should have something to celebrate, after all. And if her father didn't want to organize a clown for her, then Doug from next door would do the job. It was finally time for a little neighborly help.

***

Monday morning started with a lot of excitement and more screaming. Sarah wanted to unpack the gifts before school. The night before, Ellie had explained to her daughter that this was not a good idea. Time was too short. She could pick a gift to unwrap immediately. The rest was for later. Yesterday, Sarah had

agreed, but today she burst into tears when she had to choose one.

"Take this one," ten-year-old Max suggested and grabbed the biggest package.

"Hey, don't—that's mine!" Sarah snatched it from her brother's hand.

The paper tore in one spot and gave enough view to ruin the surprise. It was a Barbie house. Sarah screamed and slapped Max in the face, which of course he didn't leave unanswered. And so the next round was on.

While Ellie intervened and tried to settle the dispute between her two elders, six-year-old Leila grabbed another parcel and ripped it open. What was wrong with these children? And where was the guy who had knocked her up with these kids?

Ellie was on the brink of a nervous breakdown—the presents had all been torn open, and the kids were still quarreling—when Martin finally showed up. Freshly showered and smelling like a mountain meadow. It was nice that he was dressed up while she had to play the predator tamer.

Ellie snorted as he came into the kitchen and took Sarah in his arms. "Happy birthday, my big one."

Sarah grinned and suddenly seemed blissful. She kissed her father on the mouth and clapped her hands. "Look, Dad, I already unwrapped them."

"Wow! What's all this?"

Max and Leila were silent now and watched with big eyes as Sarah showed the gifts to her father.

Martin finally turned to Ellie. "I'll drive the kids to school. Then you can prepare everything in peace."

Ellie nodded. There was nothing wrong with this suggestion. "When are you coming home today?"

"I'm trying to hurry, honey. If all goes well, I'll be here at six."

The party was supposed to start at three in the afternoon and would last about two hours. Ellie was anything but enthusiastic, but there was probably no other option. She nodded weakly. At least she wouldn't be alone cleaning up. If everything went well.

***

Doug was a passionate gardener. In order to keep away unwanted vermin, he did not shy from using the chemical mace. A few years ago he had acquired a good supply of pesticides, which were now piled up in his cellar. You never knew. If the dosage of the stuff was high enough, it wouldn't just kill snails and cockchafer grubs. Sometimes Doug laid out baits in his garden for the annoying cats that shit all over the neighborhood. One had once eaten so much that she'd died right on the terrace. A fat cat with reddish-brown fur that had stared at Doug in agony with her eyes bulging out. The cramps had lasted almost an hour. Doug had made himself comfortable with a beer in his garden chair to watch. First the animal twitched, and then bloody vomit came out of its mouth. It shat blood and whined so terribly that Doug had to cover his ears.

At the sight, a feeling spread in his abdomen that he wasn't supposed to have. Maybe he wasn't asexual after all. Maybe he liked dying cats. When the animal was dead and Doug was a little disappointed because the spectacle was over, he stowed the carcass in a garbage bag and sprayed the terrace with the hose. He

was very happy that he'd thought about planting this hedge in time.

From then on, Doug mixed even more pesticides into the raw meatballs he laid out on his porch. From time to time he was lucky and could watch an animal die—mostly cats, once also a badger. Normally, however, the mucky animals made it through the bushes to die somewhere else. The frequent animal deaths were of course discussed in the neighborhood, but nobody had ever suspected Doug Keller, who lived so quietly and secluded behind his hedge. He couldn't be accused of anything. After all, everyone could do what they liked on their property. Kill burglars, poison cats …

Today, Doug baked muffins for the birthday party of a kid. After all, you were never too old to learn something new. He even enjoyed it. He put the empty green bottles in a garbage bag while the smell of baked goods filled his kitchen.

A beautiful day for a party.

***

Together with her own, eight children cavorted in Ellie's garden this afternoon. She had prepared some games to keep the crowd happy. After the gifts had been unpacked and the first sweets eaten, there were sack race and can knockdown competitions, a few dance games, and a little treasure hunt that Ellie had prepared with Martin the day before.

However, after more than two hours, the children got bored, and Martin was still not to be seen. Ellie decided to let the kids romp a bit and prayed to God that none of them would get hurt on the big trampo-

line or fall off the swing. She already had enough bustle today anyway. She loved her children but had to admit that they drove her mad. Perhaps it would have been easier if Martin had been home more often. Maybe she was a bad mother. The fact was, she would make the sign of the cross several times when this day was finally over. She let the children play in the garden, went through the open patio door into the living room, sat on the couch, closed her eyes, and tried to block out the noise for a moment …

***

Did I fall asleep?

As if bitten by a tarantula, Ellie jumped up and looked into the garden, where the screaming of the children had just reached a new level. At first she wasn't sure what she saw. Was that a clown? Ellie rubbed her eyes.

Martin said it wouldn't work …

Well, apparently her husband had only wanted to surprise her—and the children, of course—and he had definitely succeeded.

Ellie stepped into the garden, but nobody noticed her. The birthday party had gathered around the clown, who was distributing something. Cake? No, it was muffins with chocolate, which all children liked the most. But who was that? The guy looked pretty strange. The rubber mask that hid his face reminded Ellie more of a horror clown. The hairs protruding in all colors of the rainbow didn't make it any better.

What is he wearing? Ellie asked herself as she slowly approached. *Is that pajamas?*

The kids didn't seem to mind. They jumped around

happily. A few had already started to stuff the muffins in their mouths. Among them was Ellie's youngest daughter, Leila, who waved chocolate-smeared hands at her. The lower half of her face was brown. Ellie's heart was beating like crazy when she finally arrived at the strange clown surrounded by munching children. She noticed that the garden gate was open.

So that's how he got into the garden.

Shouldn't he have rung the doorbell?

"Excuse me," Ellie said to the clown.

The eyes that stared at her from the rubber mask made Ellie think of a wild animal. "Did my husband send you?" She wished Martin was here now, but he had invented unpunctuality, so to speak.

The clown hesitated for a moment, then he nodded and offered her the last muffin on the tray.

Ellie shook her head. "No, thank you, I—"

There was a scream. Ellie turned around. A black-haired girl had thrown up on the trampoline. Damn, she'd expected something like that! The other children had quickly run away from the trampoline.

"Excuse me," Ellie said with a shrug. "I gotta take care of that." She turned away from the silent clown and ran to the sobbing girl on the trampoline, who held her stomach and threw up again.

Oh, shit! What now? I need to get something to mop up!

But why did the girl scream like that? It sounded almost inhuman.

At that moment, someone tugged at Ellie's skirt. She looked down and saw her daughter Leila. Was that blood? The red stuff sullied Leila's dress and mouth. The little girl also held her belly and vomited over Ellie's sandals. Then she fell over and lay on her back, twitching.

"Leila? What's wrong?" Ellie dropped to her knees and bent over the cramping child.

"Mom?" She turned around and saw her son holding half a muffin in his hand. He was as pale as a ghost and held his belly. The rest of the birthday party, including the birthday girl, was now lying in the grass, twitching and puking.

The muffins! Ellie thought. She slapped the candy out of Max's hand. "The clown," she screamed. "Where's the clown?"

The clown was gone. Meanwhile, Max collapsed next to his sister. He also cramped. Ellie pulled both children closer to her, touched them, talked reassuringly to them. Then she let her eyes wander over the battlefield of her garden. Everywhere was twitching bodies, blood and vomit. She saw her daughter Sarah, who lay motionless under the swing.

At that moment, Leila stopped breathing. Ellie grabbed the girl and hit her on the back with all her might. She had to wake up! Now! Now!

But Leila didn't wake up.

Then Ellie pulled her dying son into her arms, put her head back so that the warm sun hit her face. She screamed into the blue sky until she had no voice left.

***

The woman had had problems for a long time. Her husband and acquaintances described her as unstable and mentally stricken ill. The husband blamed himself for the terrible event because he'd left her alone on the day of the birthday party. After all, she'd expressed her concerns beforehand. That morning, she had yelled at her children and had been completely

stressed because of a harmless argument.

Now they were dead. Poisoned with muffins into which the woman had apparently mixed a pesticide that had been banned for years. It would probably not be possible to find out where she'd gotten it from and where she had disposed the empty bottles. She'd carefully washed off the baking utensils and put them back in the cupboards. No residues could be found on them.

The five girls who had come that afternoon to celebrate her daughter's birthday had not survived. When the horrified husband arrived at home, two of them had still been alive but died shortly afterward in hospital without regaining consciousness. The suspected culprit was sedated and transferred to a psychiatric facility. She made no understandable statements, only talked again and again about a clown with colored hair who had come into the garden to hand out muffins. Her husband had initially wanted to engage a clown for the party but eventually didn't. That seemed to be very hard on her. She kept talking about this clown and could only be brought to her senses with the help of medical restraints and strong medication.

The police asked around the neighborhood. No one had seen a clown. There was only this crazy woman who had poisoned eight children and now wanted to blame the crime on an illusion of her sick mind. She was declared insane and would probably spend the rest of her life in psychiatric care. The husband stayed in the house for a while until he sold it and moved in with his girlfriend. The new owners were a childless, middle-aged couple who loved peace and quiet as much as Doug Keller.

They had a cat, though.

PUBLISHING PROGRAM

www.redrum-verlag.de

1. Bad Family: *Simone Trojahn*
2. Selina´s Way: *Simone Trojahn*
3. Basement Games: Simone Trojahn

REDRUM CUTS

1. Witch Juice: *Simone Trojahn*

SIMONE
TROJAHN
WITCH JUICE
REDRUM
HORROR - CUTS

SELINA'S
Psycho
WAY
Thriller
SIMONE TROJAHN
REDRUM

SIMONE
TROJAHN
BAD FAMILY
THRILLER
REDRUM

REDRUM loves you!

REDRUM liebt dich!

Printed in Dunstable, United Kingdom

82576837R00204